They stood toe to t̶o̶e̶ ✓ **W9-DCB-018** for a fight, two pairs of eyes flashing danger signals. Hannah's nostrils flared as she inhaled the heady essence of Penn's male scent. Fists knotted at her sides, she tried desperately to control the trembling of her limbs.

"Hannah," Penn said hoarsely. "Do you do it to me deliberately? Does it pleasure you to see just how far you can shove a man without running aground?"

Her mouth felt dry. Her palms were damp. She couldn't have spoken if her life depended on it.

"I'm warning you, woman, we're already in shoal waters. Don't push me too far."

They were so close she could feel his warm breath. The heated scent of his body rose around her, enclosing her like a silent, irresistible invitation. Unconsciously, Hannah tilted her face, her lips parting as her eyelids began to sink under their own unbearable weight. She could almost taste him. Drowning in sensation she had never before dreamed of, much less experienced, she swayed forward as his hand touched her back.

A woman and a man, both fighting their feelings, and both losing their hearts. . . .

The Warfield Bride

THE
WARFIELD
BRIDE

by

Bronwyn Williams

A TOPAZ BOOK

TOPAZ
Published by the Penguin Group
Penguin Books USA Inc., 375 Hudson Street,
New York, New York 10014, U.S.A.
Penguin Books Ltd, 27 Wrights Lane,
London W8 5TZ, England
Penguin Books Australia Ltd, Ringwood,
Victoria, Australia
Penguin Books Canada Ltd, 10 Alcorn Avenue,
Toronto, Ontario, Canada M4V 3B2
Penguin Books (N.Z.) Ltd, 182-190 Wairau Road,
Auckland 10, New Zealand

Penguin Books Ltd, Registered Offices:
Harmondsworth, Middlesex, England

First published by Topaz, an imprint of Dutton Signet,
a division of Penguin Books USA Inc.

First Printing, June, 1994
10 9 8 7 6 5 4 3 2 1

 Topaz is a trademark of Dutton Signet,
a division of Penguin Books USA Inc.

Printed in the United States of America

On October 8, 1880, the schooner *Cox* was lost off Hatteras bar, along with her captain, Dick Burrus, and her crew, William A. Ballance, Litchfield Styron, George L. Styron, Russell Austin, and Walter Gaskins. Our grandfather, Dozier Burrus, also a member of his uncle Dick's crew, did not make that particular journey. Had he done so, this book would never have been written.

To the memory of those men, and to the men of the U.S. Lifesaving Service and their successors, the U.S. Coast Guard, this book is dedicated.

Dixie Burrus Browning

Mary Burrus Williams

(writing as Bronwyn Williams)

Chapter 1

IT was too late for second thoughts. Even if he'd had the option, Penn told himself, he would not have done any differently. Adam needed a wife before he got in any deeper with the Drucker girl, and as there were no suitable females in any of the villages on the island, Penn had done what had to be done. He had sent off for a woman for his brother to marry.

Oleeta Drucker, bedamned! Warfields didn't marry Druckers. Never had, never would. If Adam didn't know that, it was damned well time he learned.

Dirty gray clouds scudded across the sky, spitting rain, as the three eldest Warfield brothers set out to meet the boat. It would've been better, perhaps, if the woman could have seen the island for the first time under gentler conditions. Seeing it now, she might not believe there were days when the sun shone clean through the water to dance like emeralds off the sandy bottom. Or nights when the thrashers and the mockingbirds sang to the moon for hours without once repeating a verse. Hannah Ballinger hadn't sounded skittish in her letters, but it was hard to tell about women. Penn could read the sky and the water and know to the hour when the wind would shift or fall off, or how long before a storm would hit. But reading a woman was like trying to see the far side of the moon. Women weren't made for men to understand.

A raw wind whipped sand halfway up the legs of Penn's shaggy roan gelding as he led him out of the lea of the boathouse. James was to drive the cart. James hated driving the cart, but then, so did Adam, and right now Penn couldn't afford to get Adam any more riled than he already was.

It never occurred to Penn to drive the thing himself. Captain Pennington Carstairs Warfield, named for his father, who'd been named for a three-master out of Boston, was keeper of the station. It was hard enough to maintain proper authority, with a crew consisting solely of his four younger brothers, without having to poke along in the utility cart while they rode on ahead.

The village of Paragon Shoals, presently consisting of the landing, a variety of livestock, and five empty houses in varying stages of disrepair, lay three-quarters of a mile west-sou'west of Paragon Shoals Lifesaving Station. Penn knuckled the gelding's nose with a gentle fist and slipped the bridle over his head. He didn't always use one, but the occasion called for a degree of ceremony. "Wind'll likely lay before morning," he observed.

"Damned boiled bacon's give me a bellyache," muttered James, hitching old Aristotle to the crudely built cart.

Adam said nothing. He'd been sulking ever since Penn had first announced his plan to kill two birds with one stone, the first bird, in a manner of speaking, being Adam.

Watching his handsome twenty-seven-year-old brother sling a long leg over the back of the mount he had recently cut out of the herd of wild horses that roamed the Outer Banks, Penn wondered if he should have talked it over with them before he'd sent off for the woman. He wasn't in the habit of talking things over. A man was either a leader or a follower. Penn had never been given a choice.

Besides, dammit, Adam had to be steered away from the Drucker girl. The village needed rebuilding. This marriage would accomplish both ends. As the man in charge, Penn had to think of the common good. Adam would come around, he told himself. He was a good boy, but sometimes he was inclined to shy at the bit.

The reins lay slack against Pegasus's thick neck. A slight pressure from Penn's muscular thighs turned the big ugly roan toward the deserted village. By the time the *Hamlet* warped alongside the ancient five-plank wharf some thirty minutes later, the three eldest Warfields, their transportation moored to an abandoned net-drying rack, were standing by to inspect the bride Penn had ordered for the reluctant Adam.

Step one in his master plan, Penn thought with satisfaction. The rest would follow in due course.

Wishing she had a looking glass, Hannah squinted into the pitted and salt-stained porthole in an effort to see her reflection as she adjusted her bonnet. The yellow scarf was a mistake. It hadn't seemed so awfully bright when she'd seen it in the shop window. It had been a cold, rainy day, and the scrap of silk had been the exact color of buttercups under a summer sun. Impulsively, she had entered the shop, telling herself that a bride should have something new, even for a second wedding. Even when she was in mourning. Even when she had scarcely enough money to feed a mouse, let alone trick herself out in fancy silk trimmings.

At least, she told herself now, it should divert attention. Suddenly overwhelmed with guilt, apprehension, and weariness—but mostly with guilt—she tucked the scrap of silk into the neck of her cape and adjusted her black felt hat with the three drooping feathers. Taking a deep breath, she turned toward the narrow companionway ladder, her awkwardness due only in part to her advanced state of pregnancy. She had been traveling for fourteen hours on this miserable, rolling, stinking tub, and that after a long train ride during which she'd shared a seat with a garrulous woman and two squabbling, train-sick children.

The yellow silk scarf was for courage. God alone knew she needed that! What she'd done was wicked and downright deceitful, and she'd been flat-out terrified ever since she'd mailed off the letter, three days after burying her husband, agreeing to marry a man she had never met. At that point she would have wed the devil himself so long as he would have helped her get away.

By the time she gained the deck, the two-man crew of the *Hamlet* had already commenced unloading freight. She saw her single trunk set ashore alongside a sack of beans, two of cornmeal, several sides of bacon, and a keg of nails. Over the rattle of flapping canvas and the screeching of gulls, she heard someone say, "Beggin' yer pardon, ma'am, if ye'll step this way, Oi'll set ye ashore."

Forcing her stiff lips into a smile, she thanked him. The young mate had done his best to make her voyage comfortable, but the *Hamlet*, which plied the several villages along the Outer Banks hauling mail and whatever supplies were needed out from the mainland, had no passenger accommodations. Hannah had been forced to share space with an assortment of freight, tools, and spare rigging.

Clutching her gray melton cape around her, she carefully made her way down the shaky plank onto the wharf. Thanking the shy young mate, she murmured a silent prayer and braced herself to face her new future.

Oh, my mercy, this was *it*?

Panic clutched her throat as she searched the desolate landscape for some sign of life—let alone some sign of welcome. Cold rain slashed her face. Overhead, dark clouds sagged low enough to snag the mast of the creaking old schooner. The air reeked of strange and vaguely frightening things, while an endless stretch of brown marsh, punctuated only by wind-stunted trees and a few unpainted buildings, faded off into the misty distance. The scene resembled nothing so much as a handful of building blocks tossed down by a willful child.

Hannah was still despairing when the sound of a cleared throat made her start. Turning anxiously toward the far end of the wharf, she saw three men standing rigidly at attention. They'd been hidden from view by the canvas jib that had billowed out over the narrow wharf.

Knees trembling, she searched the face of the man nearest her. Was he the one?

He was big. Not plump—just *big*! Wind plastered his black suit to a body that seemed almost violently masculine. He'd obviously been bred for just such a raw, wild place.

She swallowed hard, unable to tear her gaze away from the compelling figure in black serge and salt-stained boots. Thinking of her dear, frail Edward, so recently laid to rest, she wondered again, is this the one?

There was a leathery leanness about the man, as if he'd been honed by the elements right down to the heartwood, all softness worn away. Yet he wasn't old. Somewhere in his late thirties, she judged.

Stealing another look at his face, she forced her attention beyond the small scar that sliced diagonally across his angular jaw and collided head-on with a pair of eyes that were all the more startling for being set in a face that might have been rough-hewn from a chunk of dark, splintery wood. Beautiful eyes. Vivid blue eyes. Eyes that were more a source of light than a reflection of it.

The three men stood solidly against the wind, oblivious to the slashing rain. They stared at Hannah. She stared right back until the stiff wind that whipped her voluminous garment against her back caught the ends of her scarf and tore it from her throat.

Too late, she grabbed for it, then watched in horror as it caught the blue-eyed man across the face, molding to his features in the instant before he snatched it away. Seeing his blunt, tanned fingers against the buttercup silk, Hannah felt a strange release of tension.

He was the one. He had chosen her, and with the help of a gust of wind and a silk scarf, she had chosen him.

Just as her pale lips trembled in a tentative smile, the man turned toward his companions. Hannah, mesmerized by the spell of those intensely blue eyes, had barely noticed them.

As the silence stretched into a brittle void, Hannah's nerve wavered. Almost too exhausted to stand, she was held erect solely by pride, for at the moment, pride was all she had, and it was fading fast.

Peering sidelong at the two other men, she judged them to be younger than her intended. Like her intended, they were dressed in black. The letter had said the man she was to marry was a member of the U.S. Lifesaving Service. All three men were dressed alike, except for minor decorative details such as the greenish stripes on their sleeves, and the numbers sewn there. The tallest of the trio was strikingly handsome, with green eyes and wind-blown yellow curls, though his good looks were rather spoiled by a sullen expression. He looked angry. Perhaps he'd had something better to do with his time than greet his friend's bride-to-be.

The man on the far end, slender and brown-haired with a narrow, clever face, looked . . . intense. Cool, but not necessarily unkind.

Three men. Yet, once again, Hannah's gaze was drawn to the hard-looking man with the bright blue eyes. Every instinct she possessed told her that this was the one. This was the man who would give her shelter. The man who would lend her his protection. The man who would promise to cleave only unto her for the rest of their days on earth.

Unconsciously she released her pent-up breath. An older man might have been more understanding, more tolerant. Even so, there was a certain steadiness about this Captain Warfield. Goodness knows she needed a strong, steady man.

But what she needed most of all at that moment was a bed that would stay still long enough for her to crawl under the covers and sleep for a solid week.

For a year!

First things first. Hannah was nothing if not a realist. Which made it all the more strange that something inside her that had been frozen for a long, long time suddenly seemed to be thawing.

It was then that a tiny foot thrust against the side of her belly. Her heart gave a funny little thud, and she clutched her cape tightly around her body. Oh, my mercy, what was she thinking of? There was still *this* to be dealt with. She could still be sent packing before she'd even had the chance to take off her bonnet.

"Mrs. Ballinger?" The voice matched the man. Deep, rough, with an odd, lilting brogue that fell strangely on her ears. "I'm Cap'n Penn Warfield, keeper of Paragon Shoals Station." He held out her scarf.

Ignoring the scrap of yellow silk, Hannah fanned her hands over her bulk in an instinctively protective gesture. Dear Lord, he *couldn't* send her back! Where would she go?

Through stiff lips, she murmured a response, holding her cape together with both hands against the tug of the wind.

Penn Warfield rammed the scarf into his uniform pocket. He cleared his throat and spoke again. "These here are my brothers, ma'am, Adam and James. There's two more, but they're on patrol."

The baby shifted suddenly, and Hannah's heart executed a quick double-step as her hopes began to dim. Only now did she realize how much she had counted on his being a kindly older man, a man who would be tolerant of a woman in her condition once he got over his initial shock. She had half managed to convince herself that such a man might even welcome a baby to light up his twilight years.

For days, ever since she had committed herself to this desperate act, guilt and fear had warred inside her. Fear had brought her this far, but guilt was now the victor. She should have told him in her letter. Lying by omission was still lying. Yet if she had, he might not have wanted her. Under the circumstances, she hadn't dared take the risk.

"I'm very pleased to meet you all." It took her three attempts to get the words out. Her voice refused to work properly.

As the cold rain soaked through the shoulders of his serge coat, Penn felt as if he'd blundered into a quicksand bog. *This* was Hannah Ballinger? *This* was the bride he had ordered for Adam, the woman who was supposed to take the boy's mind off old

Drucker's daughter, and in due time, commence the repopulating of the community of Paragon Shoals?

A widow, she'd said. Twenty-four, which was only three years younger than Adam's age—seven years younger than his own thirty-one. Old enough to be settled, young enough to be manageable. She'd listed as accomplishments reading and ciphering, plus all the usual housewifely arts, including tending the sick, and said she was not put off by isolation, hard work, nor rigorous climate. He had warned her specifically against those.

According to her letter, she was neither dark nor light.

Penn considered her hair. Brown, she'd called it, yet under a bonnet that was flat-out ugly, it seemed to capture and hold the light of an unseen sun, glinting back red and gold.

Eyes plain gray, she'd said.

There was nothing plain about them. They were large for her small face, the changeable color of the Pamlico on a cloudy day, reflecting light and shadow, hinting at depths an unwary man could drown in.

Neither plain nor pretty? Penn couldn't decide. All he knew was that there was something purely spellbinding in her pale, translucent skin, her high cheekbones, and the shallow dimple that centered her small, firm chin. Not pretty in the way Margaret had been pretty, but far from plain. As for her mouth . . .

He swallowed hard as sweat filmed his body. Taking a deep breath, he smelled again the faint hint of violets that had clung to the scrap of yellow silk that had blown across his face. It had fair knocked him off his feet! Soft, silky, smelling of flowers and a woman's skin, it had triggered a crazy response in him that had scattered his thoughts like a shoal of mullet.

Penn told himself that he was overdue a trip to Rosabelle's. That was all it was, all it could possibly be. If he could harden at no more than the touch of yellow silk cloth, he was in worse shape than he'd thought.

Scowling, he continued his inventory. Neither thin nor stout, she'd said. Hard to tell about her construction, for she was carrying more rag than a five-masted schooner, but it appeared to him that she was somewhat more stout than otherwise.

Fine. Scrawny women weren't to his taste—that is, to Adam's.

Hannah waited. The *Hamlet* was preparing to depart. Would he send her back? Should she tell him now, before it was too late, or had he already guessed?

Staring at the toe of her best black shoes, she braced herself to face what had to be faced. True, she had deceived him. If he sent her back, it would be no more than she deserved. But if he thought for one minute she was going to climb meekly back aboard that wallowing old bathtub and put out to sea again before she'd had a hot soak and a good night's sleep, he was very much mistaken. If Captain Warfield didn't want her, then she would find someone who did. Surely someone in one of those gaunt, unpainted houses stood in need of a capable companion.

"Fetch her gear and set it aboard," he ordered, and Hannah's last hope plummeted.

"Oh, wait—sir, please," she began. But then the two younger men began carrying her things to the cart, not the freighter, and her hopes lifted again. "The tan hatbox," she said hurriedly. "Mind it, if you will. The strings aren't strong."

"Yes'm." The clever-faced one with brown hair carefully set her three hatboxes on the seat and then hefted her large trunk as if it were no heavier than her reticule, and while the golden Adonis still wore a sullen look, he obediently collected her valise and assorted parcels and dumped them into the cart on top of her trunk. Hannah prayed the rain would let up before everything she owned in the world was soaked clean through.

The brawny warrior with eyes like pieces of summer sky stood between her and the cart, and Hannah waited, holding her breath. Surely he wouldn't allow her luggage to be loaded on the cart if he meant to send her back? Was he playing with her? Had he guessed her secret, and was punishing her for deceiving him?

"Mount up, then. Ma'am, you might's well ride in the cart with James," he said, and Hannah nearly fainted from relief. He was keeping her, then.

Penn and Adam rode out ahead of the small, cumbersome cart. Adam was first to break the silence. "I'll not marry her, you know."

Penn glanced over his shoulder at the cart that was already falling behind. "Lower your voice. It'll take a week to fetch out a preacher," he said calmly. "Time enough to get acquainted."

"Penn, I told you—"

"And I told you. You'll obey me in this, Adam." It was a direct order, and Adam knew it. They all obeyed Penn. Always had. He'd been left in charge of the family at the age of fifteen when their mother died, their father having been lost at sea the year before. Gentle by nature, but hard by necessity, Penn had always done what he considered best for his brothers, including getting them into the service as each of them came of age.

"Listen, Penn, Oleeta, she's not what—"

"She's a Drucker. Warfields don't marry Druckers."

"Why not? God's sake, man, just tell me why not?"

Fortunately, at that moment, Peg, sensing his master's tension, shifted into a bone-rattling trot, precluding an answer.

Hell, Penn didn't know why not! Whatever had happened between the Druckers and the Warfields had happened years ago, before his time. He was only carrying on the tradition passed on to him by his father, a seaman whose memory grew dimmer with each passing year. "Warfields and Druckers don't mix," the old man had told him. "Family traditions is important, boy. Don't you never forget that."

And Penn never had.

That had been his father's first visit home after James had been born. By then, James had been going on two years old. The visit, as Penn recalled, had not been a pleasant one.

Paragon Shoals station stood like a solitary outpost at the edge of the world. Wind had piled sand around the huddle of buildings that included a tall, unpainted station house, a privy, a boathouse, a shed, and a lookout platform that laddered up a distance of some fifteen feet above the beach. The resulting dunes, built up slowly over the years, had parted the seas of many a storm that had flooded across the narrow stretch of barrier island.

The two men were still outside when the cart arrived, the widow Ballinger clutching her cape together with one hand and clinging to the side with the other.

Hannah pried her fingers from the splintery wood. Her heart plummeted. *This* was to be her new home? This bleak, barren outpost? Dear Lord, it was about to be swallowed up by the sea!

Standing stiffly between boathouse and shed, Penn surveyed his domain, assuring himself that all was shipshape and Bristol fashion. He knew himself to be a good keeper, firm, but fair. There was no slack on his watch, despite the fact that the station was presently short three hands, the remaining crew consisting solely of his four younger brothers.

"Welcome," he said, gruffness disguising his modest pride. He stood back to allow Adam to assist his bride-to-be down from the cart, and without looking directly at the woman, tried to discover what she thought of it all. He was proud of his station, having served here since he was twenty-one years old, working his way up from number seven to keeper.

When she continued to stare, doubts began to arise. He should've left a lamp lit. Place would have looked more welcoming. And the fire—they'd let it burn down after dinner. It would be cold inside. They never used the small fireplace, for the wind blew down the chimney, creating more of a hazard than a comfort.

Knowing the boys, they would have left their things scattered in the common room when they'd gone out on patrol. He didn't always bear down on them as hard as he should. Since they'd recently lost three hands, all those left worked long hours with little time off for enjoyment.

What if the woman thought he had brought her here to be housekeeper for the slew of them?

Staring down at the rime of brine that stained his thick boots, Penn admitted silently that he'd been guilty of thinking she might help out a bit around the station. But that wasn't the main reason he had sent for her. He had done it for Adam's sake, because he didn't want Adam bringing shame to the Warfield family. He had done it for the sake of the deserted village of Paragon Shoals, where three generations of Warfields had lived and died.

Funny—for a few minutes there, he'd nearly forgot all that.

She was still perched up there on the cart, looking pale as a fish belly, and Adam, blast his stubborn hide, hadn't made a move to help her down. Biting off an oath, Penn reached up and scooped the woman into his arms, lowering her to the ground. He sniffed, trying hard to ignore the faint fragrance of violets that seemed to cling to her skin. His mother had smelled of lye soap and fried sowbelly. Margaret had smelled sort of sweet, like dried fig leaves. The women at Rosabelle's—

Blast the women at Rosabelle's! He didn't want to think about them now. He knew for a fact, however, that not a one of them smelled like a violet.

Fighting down the unsettling beginning of arousal, Penn wondered what was wrong with him. He'd never been this quick on the trigger before, not even with Margaret, and she'd been his wife. And certainly not with any of the girls at Rosabelle's.

Leastwise, not after the first few hours.

A conscientious man, Penn saved up his hell-raising for the times when his younger brothers would not be influenced by his example. Several times a year he visited Norfolk, where he proceeded to consume a modest amount of whiskey before spending as many days as he could afford at Rosabelle's Sporting Club for Gentlemen.

Only recently had he learned that his brothers had dutifully followed his example and saved up their own hell-raising for the times when they visited the mainland.

All except for Adam.

With Penn leading the way, they had nearly reached the station house door when two young men came racing over the dunes, flattened on the backs of a pair of shaggy, wild-eyed ponies.

"Josiah, Malachi, meet Adam's woman," Penn announced when they slid off their lathered mounts practically at her feet.

Adam's woman?

Confused, Hannah looked from Penn to the scowling Adonis with the golden hair. *Adam's* woman?

Not *his* woman then, she thought with a sudden sense of loss. Of course, the one called Adam was far handsomer. Younger, too, if that mattered. With his battered nose, his scarred jaw, and his powerful build, Captain Warfield was as different from her late husband, Edward, as night was from day, and yet . . .

And yet, there was something about him. Something steady, reliable. Something that had drawn her to him from the very first.

The brown-haired one, James, stepped forward and said, "This here's Josiah—other one's Malachi. They're twins. Don't let 'em rag you too much, ma'am. They're good boys, but inclined to be wild."

Warily, Hannah responded to the angelic, nearly identical, smiles. "How do you do? Have you been racing on the beach?"

"Oh, no, ma'am. Beach patrol," panted the one called Malachi.

"Mal had the south run, me the north," put in Josiah. "I won."

"You did not!"

"Did so!"

By the time she was shown inside the spartan quarters, Hannah was damp right down to her garters. The rain had mizzled all day, dampening what it didn't outright soak. She would have given all she possessed for a hot bath, a pot of chocolate, and a clean, warm bed, but none seemed immediately forthcoming.

The three older men had disappeared, leaving the twins to show her around. Reeling from exhaustion, she examined what she supposed would be her new home. Did women actually live at a lifesaving station? There was certainly no sign of a woman's touch so far as she could see. Both the walls and floors were bare wood, the walls darkened with age, the floors sanded by constant use.

There was a vast iron range in one corner, and a wooden table with eight spindle-backed oak chairs. Off to one side in a long, narrow room that ran the length of the building, four canvas cots, neatly spread, were ranged along the walls, with at least a dozen more stacked at one end. An assortment of masculine garments hung from nails on the wall.

It was obviously a very male establishment, and Hannah peered in briefly and then backed out.

"We sleep in there and eat in here, ma'am," Malachi told her. "Next year we're fixing to build us another cook house. Had one, but it burned down."

"That there's the ladder," Josiah remarked, pointing to a set of wooden rungs that mounted the wall to end at a trapdoor, "that went up to the topside watch tower. Second floor was near 'bout finished when lightning hit the tower and come close to burnin' the whole place down. Me and Mal, we're rebuildin' it."

Hannah smiled uncertainly and continued to study her bleak surroundings. A single door opened off the far end of the large common room. Dare she hope it hid a feather bed, a fireplace, and a bathtub? The only fireplace she saw was cold, unfortunately, and there was no sign that indoor plumbing had found its way out to the village of Paragon Shoals on Hatteras Island.

"Where did you put my things?" she asked, tactfully indicating that she would prefer to cut short the grand tour.

"Still in the cart, but it's in the shed, ma'am. Penn says I'm to set you up a cot and hang a curtain over it, and then we'll tote your gear inside. Josiah's gone to fetch canvas and a hammer. Pick your corner," Malachi offered cheerfully.

An hour later, the other three members of the family had still not appeared. Hannah was seriously considering the possibility that she had wandered into a madhouse. True, the inmates were a cheerful and obliging bunch, but quite, quite mad.

"A bath, ma'am? It ain't raining hard enough to get much of a runoff, but if you'd like to have a go at it, I'll fetch soap and a towel. Wind's a mite cold, though."

"Ladies don't do it thataway, peabrain," growled the smaller of the twins by half an inch. Both sported a crop of bright red hair and a plethora of freckles, but Malachi's nose, like Penn's, had obviously been broken at some time.

"James and Adam's on patrol. Penn's in the shed. Who'd see?"

"It just ain't right, that's all. Ladies washes in hot water, in tubs, not under gutters."

"How would you know? You ain't never even met a lady."

"You know Perdita at Rosabelle's? She was a lady before she took up the profession, and she told me that la—"

"Josiah, go split wood! Malachi, man the beach tower!"

Three sets of eyes turned toward the door. Two pairs of legs hurried outside. The remaining pair threatened to collapse under their extremely tired, extremely disoriented owner.

Penn, shirtsleeves turned back and collar unbuttoned despite the raw January weather, looked even larger inside the station house than he had outside as he strode across the gritty floor to frown at the scrap of canvas that had been nailed over one corner of the barren room. He lifted it, peered behind it and nodded. "We've got plenty of pillows. I'll fetch you another blanket. Supper's at four. Mal's cooking."

A dozen questions logjammed in Hannah's throat. "What are all the spare cots for?" she asked finally.

"Crew. Survivors." And when she continued to look perplexed, he added, "Shipwreck. Folks stay here until they're fetched."

Privately, Hannah thought it rather a shame for anyone to have survived a shipwreck only to succumb to the cold, damp hospitality of Paragon Shoal Lifesaving Station. But then, who was she to judge? She was only a new inmate. She shivered.

"You're cold. Wet clothes. Cook fire'll have the place warmed up directly."

She nodded again. Not only was she cold and wet, she was still rocking from fourteen hours of being tossed about like a cork in a whirlpool.

Penn shifted his weight to the other foot, and she stared, mesmerized by the subtle flexing of all those barely concealed muscles. He was a stranger. He could break her in two with one hand if he was of a mind to, yet she wasn't afraid of him, which was rather remarkable, under the circumstances.

"Ma'am—that is, Mrs. Ballinger—"

"It's Hannah," she said softly, unaware of the silent plea in her eyes.

"Yes, ma'am, your letter said so. What I mean to

say is, if you'll take off your wet things, I'll hang 'em on a nail by the stove."

Hang 'em on a nail by the stove, Hannah thought with a slightly hysterical urge to giggle. The cape had been a part of her first trousseau, and had cost her dearly. For five years, knowing she would likely never own anything so fine again, she had carefully brushed, aired, and mended it. She had removed the worn gray coney trim when it had begun to look more like cat than rabbit, and sewn on new braid just last fall, adding the buttercup yellow scarf the day before she had left home.

"Ma'am?" Penn reached out a hand that was darkly tanned and callused, but surprisingly well kept for all that, and Hannah knew that the time had come. With a sigh, she stood and unfastened the frogged closing at her throat, her hands shaking as the moment of truth drew near.

"Did I happen to mention in my letter that I'm in the family way?" she murmured as she allowed the garment to slip from her shoulders.

Chapter 2

A tree stump would have been more expressive. Penn stood there, arms crossed over his massive chest, and stared at Hannah's protuberant belly under a shapeless black gown that, even to his inexperienced eyes, showed signs of having been let out far beyond its original design. Slowly he lifted his eyes to hers. In a slightly strangled voice, he asked simply, "Why?"

Hannah let out her breath. She had unconsciously braced herself against—against what? His anger? His rejection? With bitter humor, she told herself he could hardly send her back when the only means of transportation was already miles away by now. She doubted he would spare one of those ugly creatures paddocked out behind the shed, even if she could ride it. "I was afraid," she said.

"Afraid that I—that is, Adam wouldn't want you?"

She shrugged, and Penn closed his eyes. God help him, he did want her. Against all reason—against all that was decent, he wanted this woman he had brought out here as a wife for Adam. Had wanted her for himself the moment he'd first gazed into those damnably clear eyes. The moment he'd felt a wisp of yellow silk brush over his face and inhaled the unlikely fragrance of violets.

And to his eternal shame, he wanted her still.

He was depraved. Or deprived, he thought with his own brand of bitter amusement. For a man who'd been without a woman for more than half a year to be aroused by a comely young widow was hardly to be wondered at. But to want her when she was ripe with another man's seed was plain crazy! Penn had always considered himself to be a sensible man.

More shaken than he cared to admit, he reached for her heavy cape and carefully hung it on a nail behind the stove, smoothing out the folds. "Galvanized," he mumbled. "Won't stain it with rust."

"Galvanized? That's *all you have to say*?" she marveled.

His hands gripped the thick fabric, wondering what the skin of her neck would feel like between his two hands. Damn her wicked, deceitful soul! Why had he even bothered to try his luck with women again? He'd have done better to let Adam find his own bride!

Only he didn't care for the direction the boy's interest was taking.

The woman was obviously waiting for him to reach some decision, but for once in his life, he couldn't. Torn by anger, disappointment, and something he couldn't put a name to, Penn didn't know what to say.

It had been his experience that women couldn't be held to the same standards as men. His mother had dropped one and quite possibly three bastards while his father had still been alive. Penn bore his father's features, Adam his coloring, while the other three resembled no one on either side of the family so far as Penn could tell.

Then there was his wife. Penn had been barely twenty, Margaret only seventeen when they'd married. She'd been a beautiful, laughing girl who, for a little while, had almost succeeded in making him forget his responsibilities. He'd wanted to give her the world, but all he'd had to offer at first was a fisherman's wages, an unpainted house that had since washed out to sea, and four younger brothers to care for. In the end, not even his surfman's pay had been enough to hold her. She'd left him and run off to Norfolk with a patent medicine peddler. Later he heard she'd died in childbirth.

James and Adam insisted she'd left him only because she resented being burdened by his family, but Penn had always secretly wondered if he was lacking in some essential quality that a woman needed. Certainly he'd had no complaints from the women at Rosabelle's, but that was different. They were paid to comply, not to complain.

Penn stood rigidly at attention, seething inside, although none of it showed on his weathered face. The woman had lied to him! She had misrepresented herself, which was the same as lying. For Adam's sake, he should send her on her way.

Trouble was, the Drucker girl would still be here.

Dammit, it had all sounded so simple when he'd worked it out in his head! First, marry Adam off before he got in too deep with the Drucker girl, next find a wife for James, and a year or so later, do the same for the twins. They could build a church, and in the off-season, once the babies started coming, they could build a school. Pretty soon, people would be flocking to move back to Paragon Shoals. It had all seemed so simple, re-building the village one logical step at a time, the way the wind built a dune around a single blade of grass, one grain of sand at a time.

Reluctantly, Penn admitted that for once in his life, he might have miscalculated. That shook him rather badly. Unaccustomed to having his plans go awry, he didn't quite know how to deal with it.

But dammit, *she* needn't know that!

Not until he was confident that his feelings were under control did he turn to face the woman. "You asked if that was all I had to say. No, madam, that's not all I have to say, but since I'm not a man given to making hasty decisions, I'll study on the matter and give you my verdict when I've thought it through."

And with that, Hannah told herself wonderingly as she watched the tall, powerfully built man stalk across the empty room, she would have to be con-tent. She sighed, absently shoving her windblown hair back up under her bedraggled black hat. Hav-ing lived on the edge of despair for five years, she should be accustomed to it by now.

Left to herself, she poured water from a bucket into a battered kettle and sat it on the stove to heat. Except for a few remaining butterflies, her stom-ach was hollow, having emptied itself several times in the course of her journey across the sound. She wasn't at all certain she could keep anything down, but she had a feeling she was going to need all the strength she could summon before this day was over.

Once the kettle began to steam, she found a tin basin, dented and pitted, but scoured to a high polish, and filled it. This she carried to her alcove and set it on a stool. Given her lamentable lack of privacy, she washed as much as she dared and then removed the pins from her hair and brushed it vigorously, taking pleasure in the mindless, familiar task.

Her baby had been unduly active of late. With a tired smile, Hannah sat on the edge of her cot and placed her hands lightly on her swollen belly. Closing her eyes, she allowed her mind to drift out of focus, the way she had done so often in the past when she'd been too weary to run, even had it been possible, and too troubled to rest. Stretching out on the cot, she reached back in her memory box at random and drew forth . . . the acrid smell of a coal fire burning on the grate, the taste of hot, milky chocolate laced with cinnamon, the way her mother used to make it. The gentle touch of Edward's soft hand on her shoulder and the sound of his fine tenor voice singing "Flow Gently Sweet Afton" to the wheezing tones of the mirror-top organ in her father's parlor.

Supper was indeed served at the unseemly hour of four o'clock. When a bell clamored in her troubled dreams, Hannah struggled awake, confused by the alien sounds—not only the echo of the bell, but the omnipresent roar of the surf and the muted murmur of masculine voices. Forcing herself to rise, she became painfully aware of every stiff, aching muscle in her body.

Someone—one of the twins, she assumed—had covered her with a scratchy woolen blanket. Like everything else in this desolate, forsaken place, it smelled of salt, dampness, and mildew.

Josiah was laying the table with tin plates and thick white mugs when Hannah emerged from her alcove, having put on a fresh, if wrinkled, gown—this one the brown serge she had remade, using one of Edward's old coats for added material. She had twisted her hair and pinned it into its usual coil. With no looking glass, it was impossible to do much in the way of grooming, but then, vanity had never been one of her besetting sins.

Reluctantly joining the others, Hannah silently admitted that at the moment, she'd have been hard-pressed to name one sin, besetting or otherwise, that didn't have to do with the man standing at the bare window, staring out into the gloomy gray evening. Irrationally, she wanted to strike out at him, to wipe that stony, superior expression off his face. She wanted to force him to acknowledge her presence, which so far, he had not done. She wanted to—

"It's beans, bacon, and biscuits, ma'am," said Malachi. "I picked all the weevils out of the flour, but they're a mite burnt on the bottom."

"Crunchy biscuits are nice." She managed a smile for the sake of the anxious boy. "Is that truly coffee I smell?"

Josiah practically tripped over his own large feet scrambling to pour her a mug full. "Here ye go, ma'am. You don't take milk or sugar, do ye?"

Hannah did, but tactfully denied it.

"We got molasses, but the sugar got wet, so Adam boiled the last of it up with some leftover biscuits for pudding day before yesterday."

Hannah carefully replaced her mug on the scrubbed table, no longer quite so hungry. She glanced across the room at the tall solitary man who had yet to acknowledge her presence. Following her glance, Malachi said, "Don't mind Penn, ma'am. He don't mean to be disobliging. He's just broody when the weather turns thisaway. We're shorthanded, and it's weather like this that sets ship against shoal. It ain't a kindly time of the year."

Hannah couldn't have agreed more. At least near the vast iron range, it was comfortably warm. "Where are the others?"

"Still out on patrol, ma'am. Adam's always late when he takes the no'th'ard run." He cut a sly glance at Penn, who had finally deigned to join them at the table. As the unsmiling man walked into the glow of the Aladdin lamp, Hannah was struck by a phrase she had once read.

Lone wolf. If ever she had met a man who fit the description, it was Pennington Warfield. Despite the fact that he was surrounded by his brothers, who obviously worshiped him as some sort of minor deity, there was something terribly alone about him. A certain distance in his eyes. A certain reserve in the way he held himself.

Was he really as aloof as he appeared? Had someone once told him that a smile would break his face right wide open?

You're being entirely too fanciful, Hannah

Ballinger. The man is duty-driven, tough as oak-tanned leather, and surly as a bear with a festering sore!

The bacon was underdone, and the biscuits were indeed burned black, for which Malachi apologized again. Before she could respond, Penn asked terse blessings on the lot and commenced to eat.

It could have been manna from heaven and Hannah would have choked on it. Was he or wasn't he going to send her back? And what was wrong with Adam? And if she stayed, would she be expected to share what was essentially a single room with five men, all strangers to her?

If she left, where could she hide? What could she live on? How could she support a son when she couldn't even support herself?

Folding her napkin beside her untouched plate, Hannah clasped her hands tightly in her lap and asked herself the most worrisome question of all. Had she inadvertently left a trail? She had been so careful, but making her arrangements so hastily, she might have overlooked something. If Thomas—

Penn cleared his throat. Hannah's heart plunged. "If you're done with supper, ma'am, I'd like a word with you," he said.

Here it came. He had made up his mind to send her away. Rising abruptly from the table, she was acutely aware of several sets of eyes focused on her belly. Neither twin had spoken a word to her directly about her condition, but they had goggled, and then made such a point of not staring she'd been hard put not to laugh. Even now she could feel their curiosity nibbling at her like squirrels at a corncrib.

"If everyone's done, I'll wash the dishes," she offered.

Malachi's broad grin rearranged a few hundred freckles. "That'd be right fine, ma'am! I'll fetch the dishpan for you."

"The duty is yours, Malachi," Penn said sternly. Turning to Hannah, he said, "I thank you for your kind intentions, ma'am, but my crew knows their responsibility."

What was it her old Sunday School teacher used to say? The road to perdition was paved with good intentions? The Lord alone knew what the road to Paragon Shoals was paved with.

Penn led her to the mysterious door at the far end of the room and ushered her inside what appeared to be a mixture of office and bedroom. As she brushed past him in the narrow doorway, Hannah couldn't help but notice that he, at least, didn't smell of salt, damp, and mildew—nor of burned biscuits, either. For so long, she had been used to the smell of a sickroom—that and the strong pomade her wretched brother-in-law, Thomas, used on his thinning hair—that she had forgotten what a real man smelled like, if indeed she'd ever known.

Woolens and soap. Rain and cold air. Horses. Something dark, smoky, musky—something that made her nerves crackle alarmingly.

"Be seated, madam."

Obeying the curt command, Hannah lowered herself awkwardly onto one of the two oak straight chairs in the room. All her movements were awkward now, a fact that made her unduly self-conscious. There on the desk between them lay her yellow scarf, folded into a precise square and looking as out of place in this spare, masculine domain as a pig in a parlor.

Curiously, she looked around her at the gleaming, wall-mounted lamp, at the wooden, rope-handled trunk, at the three shelves filled to overflowing with books. And the single bed. Not a cot, but a real bed with a real mattress.

Swallowing hard, she glanced away. He had brought her into his holy of holies to give her the bad news, and all she could think of was how wonderful it would be to curl up on his bed, with a pillow between her knees and a soft quilt over her, and sleep until hunger woke her again.

"Your scarf, madam," he said, handing it across the desk. Their fingers touched, and Hannah felt her face grow warm. Felt her whole body glow with heat.

Oh, my mercy, I've clean lost my wits!

"Yes. Thank you." She clenched her jaw, determined not to allow her feelings to show, no matter what the verdict.

Penn began toying with his pocketknife. Then, abruptly, he laid it down again. "I'll be making arrangements for you to leave on the next boat out, Mrs. Ballinger."

Hannah's vision blurred, and she opened her eyes wider to accommodate the sudden moisture. "Thank you, Captain Warfield. I'm sorry I didn't suit."

"It's not that, ma'am. Well, it is, but the thing is, this is no place for a woman in your condition." He hadn't meant to soften, but dammit, why did she have to sit there looking like—

He cleared his throat. "Meanwhile, you'll use this room. I'll move my things out directly."

Tension spun out into a brittle thread, linking two pairs of eyes, one deep, gold-flecked blue, the other clear, pain-filled gray. Don't send me back, for I've nowhere to go, Hannah wanted to plead. She had sold her wedding band for the train fare from Raleigh to Elizabeth City to catch the boat.

Once more, pride rose to the occasion. "That won't be necessary," she informed him. "I'll be perfectly comfortable in the place the boys made for me." One of the twins had even gone so far as to pick a bouquet of some red-berried shrub and set it in a blue glass bottle on her trunk. She had been so touched by the small kindness she'd almost wept.

"Your pardon, madam, but you'll do as I say."

"*Your* pardon, sir, but I'll do as I please." The excessive politeness was as brittle as broken glass. They glared at one another, mouths clamped tight, jaws stubbornly set.

Penn broke first. "Dammit, woman!" he cried. Shooting to his feet, he began pacing the cramped room, his energy beating at her in waves until she was stung to retaliate.

"Don't swear at me, Mr. Warfield! And don't tell me what I can or cannot do! You brought me here. I didn't seek you out. And if you think I'll jump to your command, then you're sadly mistaken. *And*, I might add," she said, surging to her feet just as he made a starboard tack around the desk, "the sooner you arrange my passage back to civilization, the better it will suit me!" She waited, trembling, for God to strike her down for the lie.

The woman was so close Penn could feel the heat

of her body. Close up, he could see the faint shadow of blue veins at her temples. She was so pale—so damned vulnerable—how the devil was a man supposed to deal with a woman in her circumstances?

Reaching out, he took her by the upper arms to move her aside and prayed for patience. "Madam, there's one law at my station, and one law only," he informed her stiffly. His prayers were obviously not being answered. In frustration, he gripped her arms harder. "That law, madam, is whatever I damn well say it is! So *sit* down and *pipe* down until I think my way clear of this confounded mess you've got us in!"

Her belly was pressed against him. It was rock hard, not at all soft, the way a woman should be soft. Yet all he had to do was look at the blasted female, much less touch her, and he would become aroused!

My sweet soul, he didn't need this!

"Listen here, ma'am, it's your own good I'm thinking of," he said, making a conscious effort to soften his tone. "The nearest village is more'n an hour's cart ride in either direction, and so far's I know, there's not a midwife between the Cape and Chic'macomico, anyways. It's just not sensible to keep you here. You'll be far better off back home on the mainland where help'll be close to hand when your time comes."

With a funny little sound that was half sob, half laughter, Hannah stared down at the hands on her arms, at the long, square-tipped fingers with their neatly pared nails. They were the hands of a working man, unlike those of her father, who had been a preacher—unlike those of her husband, who had been an invalid for the last five years of his life.

Good hands. The thought came unbidden, even as those hands eased their grip and he began to pat her clumsily on the shoulders.

And then he swore under his breath and jerked his hands away, and Hannah swayed on her feet. The day had been a long one. Three days long, to be exact. Her train had pulled into the depot in Elizabeth City at eleven-ten yesterday morning, and she'd had a wait of several hours before the boat sailed. Once they had left the protected waters of the Pasquotank River, there'd been little enough opportunity for rest, and none at all for sleep. Suddenly, even a narrow canvas cot seemed like heaven!

"If you'll excuse me, Mr. Warfield—" She turned away, and Penn, his eyes bleak in his stony face, watched her walk across the bare room, the soles of her small shoes gritting on the floor that was never quite free of sand. Even ballasted as she was, there was a womanly grace to her movements.

Aye, and that was the hell of it, he thought, staring down at the yellow silk scarf that had fallen to the floor when he'd grabbed her. Against the scarred and water-stained surface, it looked as out of place as the fragile wildflowers that bloomed on the windswept beaches.

Somehow, they survived. Could she?

Penn picked up the scarf and held it against his face for a moment, inhaling deeply. Why did he have to be the one to say yea or nay? Why couldn't he, for once in his life, do something stupid and impractical for the sheer joy of it?

He had been drawn right off to her face—to that firm little chin with its contrary dimple. To something he saw in her eyes. Even knowing she had deliberately misled him, knowing she was meant for Adam, he was still drawn to the blasted female! Which was surely stupid enough, only there was damned little joy in it! How the devil could a man lust after a woman who was carrying another man's babe in her belly? It wasn't seemly!

But there was no denying the fact that he saw her first as a desirable woman, next as another man's widow, and last of all as Adam's intended.

Carefully, Penn folded the scarf away and placed it on the shelf above his bed. Then, dragging out his chair, he reached for his glasses and settled down to post his journals, which had been neglected for far too long. The moon was just rising when he closed the last book, capped his ink well, and stepped outside to test the weather.

James was just riding in off patrol. "Seen Adam?" the number two surfman asked.

Penn shook his head. "His bridle's not on the wall yet."

The temperature had risen after dark. The rain had stopped sometime during the last watch, and as Penn had predicted earlier that day, the wind had fallen off considerably. It wouldn't last. The glass had risen briefly, but it was already falling again.

"Mal's been coughing right bad," Penn said quietly. "Let him sleep, I'll take his run for him. I've some pondering to do, and I'd as lief do it outside."

James unsaddled his horse and let him into the paddock without a word, leaving Penn with the uncomfortable feeling that his brother knew precisely why he was going out on patrol. As senior officer, Penn had his own duties, which didn't include riding the beach patrol that linked station to station along the entire chain of barrier islands. But Paragon was three men short, one having recently retired, one having married the daughter of an Elizabeth City merchant at Christmas, and one having left the service just two weeks before for the ministry.

Besides, he told himself, summoning Pegasus with a low, distinctive whistle—tonight he damn well needed a head-clearing run along the beach.

"Report?" he said quietly.

"No sails in sight at last light," James told him, and Penn nodded. He wasn't expecting trouble, but it was his duty to be prepared for it at all times.

Only sometimes trouble could come from an unexpected source and catch a man off guard. When that happened, God help them all.

Chapter 3

THE ride did him little good. By the time Penn met the Chicamacomico patrol halfway between the two stations to swap tokens and report all clear, he was cursing the impulse that had made him think he could direct the lives of his four brothers the way he had done since he was fifteen, much less rebuild an entire community. The only life that showed any sign of being affected was his own.

Cursed woman! Those damnable eyes of hers had haunted him every step of the way. One minute they seemed to be accusing him, making him feel guilty when he'd done nothing to feel guilty about, the next minute they were pleading with him so eloquently that against his better judgment, he felt like allowing her to stay.

But when they smiled at him, that was the worst of all. He would find himself hardening like a randy young stallion scenting a fresh mare.

And, dammit, it didn't make sense! A woman in her condition—!

Over the next two days, Hannah learned something of the duties of a lifesaving station and the men who served there. She learned that they were required to live in during storm season, to patrol the shore during the storm season, and to attend shipwrecks at any time of the year. The Warfields, their soundside home having been destroyed in the storm of '94, lived at the station year-round. Their five-mile section of beach was patrolled whenever Penn deemed conditions warranted, regardless of the season, with watch kept from the tower on days when the visibility extended at least three miles in all directions.

About Penn himself she learned little more than that he ran what Malachi called a devilish taut ship. That although he tried to hide the fact, he wore spectacles, which made him look oddly vulnerable, to write up his endless reports.

And that he read adventure stories. According to James, Penn had never been more than two hundred miles from home in any direction, yet the man who lived adventure daily read stories written by men who only dreamed of doing the kinds of heroic deeds Penn took as a matter of course.

Having recovered somewhat from her journey, Hannah offered to help out with the cooking. It was either that or starve, for not one of the Warfields, so far as she could determine, could cook anything fit to eat.

Not that there was much to choose from, she mused as she sorted through the supplies in the pantry off the kitchen corner. Flour, cornmeal, and sugar borrowed from another station. Salt fish— fresh fish when they caught it. Wildfowl and occasionally venison when anyone took the time to go hunting. "Used to be wild boar in the village. Mean as homemade lye, but good eatin'," said Josiah.

"Hmm," murmured Hannah, surveying the supply of bacon, lard, beans, onions, and—"Well, wonder of wonders, a sack of dried apples!"

Malachi promptly snitched one. Munching, he told her that Adam usually boiled them with molasses, James fried them with bacon, and Josiah tended to serve them as is.

Hannah made a pie.

"What the devil is that?" Penn demanded a few hours later, letting in a gust of wet, cold wind before he could slam the door shut behind him. Five minutes until four. Hannah had learned already that Penn did everything by the book, according to a schedule that was chiseled in granite somewhere in the brass-bound recesses of his hard head.

He sniffed and sniffed again, glaring accusingly at Hannah. With a wary smile, she brushed a wisp of hair off her heat-flushed face and told him, hoping there wasn't some obscure rule against apple pie in his confounded book of regulations.

James, fresh off patrol, and for once without his usual poker face, sniffed and then followed his nose to the warming shelf over the kitchen range. "Apple pie? Thought I must be dreaming. I could smell it a mile down from the station." His smile was all the more welcome for its rarity, and Hannah began to relax.

And then Penn stalked across the room and slammed himself into the keeper's room, where he remained until four o'clock had come and gone.

The pie was demolished in one sitting. The twins, slated to take the next patrol, gobbled down twice their share and then finished up the platterful of baked beans and crisp bacon. Josiah belched loudly. Malachi jabbed him in the ribs with an elbow, and Josiah poked him back with a fist.

"You don't belch around a lady, peabrain!"

"How would you know, fartface?"

"What them two hellions mean, ma'am, is they enjoyed the supper right smart," Adam said, and Hannah nodded, hiding her smile. He was strikingly handsome when he wasn't sulking—and even when he was—yet her gaze kept straying back to the closed door at the far end of the room.

Malachi's cough was no better. Hannah made a mental note to mix up an elixir for him, and wondered if he'd take it amiss if she offered him her woolen muffler before he went on patrol.

"Overwash by the stump bed's getting quick," James warned with his mouth full. "Better take to the dunes just south of the wreck and ride 'em all the way to the other side of the burnt tree, else you'll likely bog down."

"Isaac said Durants reported a three-master headed north abreast Trent Hills. She'll be off the Inner Diamonds 'fore dark." That from Adam, who had eaten politely, thanked her politely, and gone so far as to offer her a tentative smile for her efforts.

While they were finishing their coffee, Hannah learned about the areas where ancient tree stumps showed up in the surf at low tide, and about the quicksand patches that shifted from place to place along the beach depending on conditions, and about that most treacherous quicksand of all, Diamond Shoals, a few miles offshore and directly in the major shipping lanes.

While the boys were preparing to leave, Hannah fetched a rose-colored muffler from her wardrobe trunk and, grimacing, Malachi grudgingly allowed her to wrap it around his neck. She could have kissed his flaming red cheek, but contented herself with patting it, instead. "There, now—that should help," she murmured. "Malachi, don't you have a hat? It's raining out there."

"Wouldn't stay on noway, ma'am. Wind's blowing a gale."

"I could lend you—"

With a look of sheer panic, he said, "Gotta go, Miz Hannah."

They were on their way out the door, Mal still coughing, when Penn emerged from his office and pinned her in his sights. He looked thunderous. Hannah's brief feeling of warmth drained away. She didn't even ask herself what she had done to displease him this time. She managed to do that simply by existing.

Biting back a sharp rebuke, she swallowed sudden tears. Her emotions were wildly unreliable these days, up one moment, down the next. Carrying her son had turned her into a different woman, one she hardly even knew, and the backache she'd woken up with from sleeping on that dratted canvas cot didn't help matters one whit.

Turning back to the range, she said, "I saved back a plate of—"

"I'm not hungry. Adam, those wheels still need greasing. James, there's a rung loose on the beach tower ladder. We're three men down as it is—last

thing I need is to lose some damned fool to a broken neck!"

Adam took one look and fled, but James was
made of sterner stuff. "There's no call to be swearing in the presence of a lady, Penn. Miz Ballinger
don't deserve the raw side of your tongue."

"I'll decide what Mrs. Ballinger deserves and
what she don't. Now get about your duties. I want
that ladder back in service now! Some harebrained
idiot's trying to make it past the Inner Diamonds in
a hard nor'easter. We'll need all hands on watch tonight in case he sets 'er onto a shoal."

At that moment, Malachi's barking cough came
clearly through the door, and Penn's scowl deepened. When James touched her lightly on the arm
in passing, Hannah sent him a grateful look. Seeing it, Penn turned away and shouted, "Malachi!
Get on back in here!"

Was it always this way in an all-male stronghold,
Hannah wondered helplessly, or was it because of
her unwanted presence? If she were one of his
crew members, God forbid, she would have
crowned the wretched creature with a skillet long
ago. No wonder his expression reminded her of
one of those wicked wild boars the boys had told
her about. He had the disposition of one.

The door opened, letting in a blast of rain.
James, garbed in oilskins, eased out as Malachi,
still hacking, stepped inside. "I'm already on my
way, Penn, honest," the boy said apologetically.

Penn eyed the rose-colored cashmere scarf with
lifted eyebrows, but when he spoke again it was
only to say, "I've a need to blow some of the cob-
webs out of my brain, son. I'm going to take your

run tonight. While I'm out, check the shot line in case we need it by morning."

Thus it was that Malachi, still coughing but warm and dry at least, spent the next few hours in the boathouse inspecting rescue gear while Penn battled a cold, driving rain in darkness so thick no man could have seen a flare had it gone off ten yards in front of his face.

Hannah managed to locate ingredients for a simple cough syrup. A lemon would have helped, and honey would have tasted better than molasses, and Penn might be angry at her for raiding his medical supplies for brandy, but the boy needed something, and this was the best she could do. If he didn't get any better, she'd poultice him. Nursing was one thing she did know.

Long after Malachi had gone to sleep, she bundled up in her cape and took James a mug of black coffee fresh off the boil.

"Don't you dare set foot on this ladder, ma'am," he called down. "I'll come down and fetch it, and I thank you kindly."

It was a wild night. Even exhilarating. Only yards away from where they stood, the surf lashed against the shore, flinging spume high above the dunes. "How long before the patrol comes in?" she shouted against the wind.

Meaning Penn. He had set out wearing only a canvas coat, the largest set of oilskins, according to Malachi, having been damaged beyond repair the night lightning had struck the cupola and blown the shingles off one side of the station house.

She could barely see a foot in front of her. Hair whipped out from under her scarf and blew across her face as James stepped down from the bottom rung to take the hot drink she'd brought him. He brushed it away, and for an instant, his hand seemed to linger on her cheek.

Or had she only imagined that? On such a wild night, one's imagination was likely to get out of hand.

"Go on back," James yelled. "Get back inside before you get drenched, Hannah."

"I will, but do you think—I mean, how can anyone see in all this? You said there was quicksand."

"He'll be all right. Don't fret none over Penn. He's not inclined to set a foot wrong."

Except when he'd sent off for a mail-order bride that no one wanted, Hannah told herself. That had been a misstep of major proportions.

She must have fallen asleep. It was the sudden shriek of the wind, shut off by the slam of a door, that awakened her. Hannah sat up stiffly, still in the clothes she'd worn all day. Below and above her canvas curtain, the dim light of a single lamp cast strange shadows. For a moment she was back in the house on Elm Street, and she clutched her belly protectively. Then hazy memories began to return. The train trip, the boat . . . the station.

Not Elm Street, then. Rising awkwardly, she parted the curtain and peered out. Oh, my mercy, Penn was soaked to the skin and the house was cold as a tomb. Grabbing up her wrap, Hannah hurried across the room to poke up the fire she had banked earlier. The kettle and three pots were all filled with water that was still hot, and she dragged out the washtub and began filling it.

"Come, sit here and take off your boots," she ordered. "I'll warm you a blanket and you can get out of those wet clothes."

"Go to bed," Penn growled, but he was shaking almost too hard to make himself understood.

Hannah had spent too many years dealing with a bedridden and irritable invalid to be offended. Men, even the meekest and kindest of them, made terrible patients. "Do as you're told, and do it quickly, or I'll pour this kettleful of scalding water over your ungrateful head."

"Lady, you're just begging for trouble, aren't you?"

"Don't be childish," she retorted. That particular tactic had usually worked on Edward when nothing else would do. "You said you were shorthanded. I took it to mean you couldn't spare anyone, not even yourself, but perhaps I was mistaken."

"Pour the damned water in the tub, then!"

But before she could even lift the kettle off the stove, he was beside her, taking it from her hands. "Got no business lifting anything this heavy." He grumbled something about her condition, and then ordered her to bed again. "Don't know what you're doing up at this hour, anyhow."

"I couldn't sleep." Wretched crosspatch! She would have sooner bitten off her tongue than tell him she'd been waiting up for him.

He eyed her bulk until she turned her back and pretended to busy herself with the blanket she had unfolded and hung from the row of nails on the wall behind the range.

"Hannah—Mrs. Ballinger— That is, thank you. Now, will you please just go back to bed?"

"I made some soup. You need something hot inside you."

Once again Penn was struck by the unlikely mixture of emotions this woman aroused in him. Guilt, anger, lust—and something beyond the physical that scared the devil out of him because he didn't understand it.

Hoping she would mistake his flushed face for windburn, he said, "There's no call for you to cook, Mrs. Ballinger."

"There is if I want to eat."

He was silent for a moment, and then Hannah was astonished to hear him chuckle. The sound went through her like a hot summer wind through a field of tall grass. Arms crossed over her rounded belly, she watched him tug off one heavy boot and then the other. His woolen socks were soaked. He was wet clean through, but, until she was safely behind her curtain, she could hardly ask him to strip down.

"Put your feet in that tub," she ordered, and after rolling up the legs of his pants, he obeyed. Reluctantly. Obviously, the man was unaccustomed to taking orders, especially from a woman.

The thought pleased her enormously, and she continued to watch, helpless to turn away, as he settled onto the stool, steam rising up around him. From the look on his face, one would have thought she had scalded him, but she'd tested the water herself.

"Well?" he grumbled. "Is this what you wanted?

If you're planning on standing guard over me all night, madam, you may as well stand at ease."

At ease! Around him?

Not for the first time, it occurred to Hannah that her life had lately taken a most peculiar direction. Else why was she standing here in the middle of the night, quite literally at the ends of the earth, watching a big, overbearing stranger with the most captivating eyes in the world soak his feet in hot water?

Absently rubbing her aching back, she wondered if she could have fallen asleep in her own familiar bedroom and woken up in the middle of someone else's nightmare.

No . . . if this was anyone's nightmare, it was her own.

Avoiding Penn's quizzical look, she waddled over to the stove and dipped a bowl of the bean, bacon, and onion soup she had made earlier, then poured a mug of coffee and laced it with a liberal dose of brandy. The daughter of a Methodist preacher, she'd spent the first eighteen years of her sheltered existence in one parsonage or another, helping her sainted mother tend the sick, comfort the grief-stricken, care for the bedridden, and pray for the downtrodden among her father's flock.

Oh, yes, Hannah had learned her lessons well. And look where it had landed her.

Handing him the blanket, now toasty warm, she clasped her arms over her full breasts and said, "Then if you don't need anything more, Mr. Warfield, I'll—"

"It's Captain Warfield," Penn corrected. He distinctly remembered signing both his letters to her

Captain Pennington Warfield, USLSS, Paragon Shoals Lifesaving Station. In times like these, a man needed all the authority he could muster.

She had signed her letters to him Hannah Ballinger, relict of the late Edward Ballinger. In only the few days she had been there, he had come to think of her as Hannah. Somehow, that surprised him. "Thank you for your kindness, ma'am," he said gruffly, indicating with his free hand the hot water, blanket, soup bowl, and mug.

"You're most welcome." Hannah stepped back, needing to put distance between them. There was something unsettling about seeing a large, bad-tempered man shawled by a blanket, naked halfway up to the knees. The last thing she needed now was to be unsettled, not when she was so desperately trying to hold the remnants of her shattered life together.

"Yes, well . . . good night, then," she murmured, and turning, she waddled quickly toward her small safe corner of Paragon Shoals Lifesaving Station, leaving Penn to stare after her.

The next morning Penn seemed none the worse for his experience. No sign of fever or cough. No sign of a smile, either, Hannah thought ruefully, watching him check his weather instruments and make notations in a ledger. Like clockwork. Do this, do that, document it all, and if you've a spare moment, drill, drill, drill!

Malachi was getting ready to go out on patrol, and she listened for his cough, which seemed to be improved. Evidently the molasses, balsam, and brandy had done almost as well as her honey, whiskey, and lemon elixir.

"I could make you a poultice to wear under your shirt," she offered.

Lacing up his thick-soled boots, he glanced up, an engaging grin on his freckled countenance. "If it's anything like that cough medicine you made for me, I'll take it."

Suspecting that the brandy had been the main attraction, she said, "Oh, it's even better. Onions, ground mustard seed, and lard. And turpentine if you have it."

His face sagged comically. "Don't trouble yourself, ma'am."

"It's no trouble," Hannah said, enjoying the novelty of teasing repartee. It had been so long since anyone had teased her, she'd almost forgotten how to respond.

"Yes'm, but if it's all the same to you, I think I'd rather eat raw possum."

Hannah nodded sagely. "An old island remedy, I take it? Before you come back off patrol, I'll see if I can locate a possum willing to make the sacrifice."

Malachi laughed, and Hannah did, too, and then he was gone. She turned to find Penn staring at her. For a long moment their eyes held. Hannah could have sworn words passed between them, but for the life of her, she couldn't have said just what words.

Who are you that you can care for my brothers as if you were their mother? Who are you that you tease them as if you were the sister they never had? Who are you that you burst into my life just as if you be-

*long here and make a nest for yourself before I can
send you away?*

"You're not sleeping well," Penn said curtly.
When she would have protested, he held up a stay-
ing hand. "I've removed my things from the office.
I'll see to having your trunk moved in directly.
You'll follow my orders on this, madam."

The baby jabbed hard under her breast, and
Hannah caught her breath, gripping the edge of the
table. "Captain, I told you—"

"For God's sake, Hannah, sit before you fall! Last
thing I need around here is a—"

"Fallen woman?" The words escaped before she
could bite them back, causing Penn to glower at
her. The man had absolutely no sense of humor,
she thought sourly.

However, she sat. In the presence of such an in-
timidating figure, she wasn't sure she could have
remained standing much longer. Hannah had been
intimidated by experts, using both subtlety and
outright physical force. With Penn, it was something else entirely. For the life of her, she didn't
know why the man affected her this way.

"Malachi's cough is better this morning," she
said breathlessly, and then cursed the breathless-
ness lest he think it was due to his presence. Lately,
she'd had trouble breathing, walking, sitting, and
even lying down. And now her back was aching because there was no way she could get comfortable
on a bed so narrow she couldn't even roll over
without getting up first.

But wider or not, she knew she could never sleep
in *his* bed.

Silently, Penn continued to study the woman before him. She bothered him. She was nothing at all to him, and yet she bothered him, and blest if he knew why! Granted, women were scarce on this stretch of the island. And a man had certain needs. But he was no young stallion, feeling his oats. It weren't as if she was beautiful, or even available. She was wearing something loose and shapeless in a shade of brown that put him in mind of the swales after a hard winter. Not what he'd have called a pretty color, nor even much of a color at all . . . yet it suited her.

Dammit, he was a by-the-book man! And Hannah Ballinger wasn't in any book he had ever read! "Cap'n Dozier'll be back in the *Hamlet* in a few days. Be ready," he muttered as he stalked past her and slammed out the door.

"Be ready!" Hannah mimicked. It was a wonder someone hadn't long since wrung the man's neck like a Sunday chicken on Saturday afternoon!

As a girl, Hannah had been impatient and impulsive by nature. Self-pity had never been among her failings, not even after her bridegroom of one week had climbed a tree to pick an apple from the topmost branch and fallen out, injuring himself so gravely that he had never recovered. Over the course of the next five years there had been no room in her life for either impatience or impulsiveness.

Answering Captain Warfield's advertisement had been more an act of desperation than of impulse. As for patience, there came a time in a woman's life when patience alone would no longer serve.

The twins, who were as full of chatter as a flock of finches, had told her all about the deserted village, and the people who had all gradually died or moved away. Malachi had offered to show her around, but when she'd inquired about the possibility of removing to one of the empty houses to await the freight boat, he had insisted they were all quite impossible.

"Leaky roofs, leanin' walls, some of 'em's been washed clean off'n the foundations. What furnishings weren't hauled off's likely not fit for more'n stove wood by now."

"But surely I could clear out a single room to sleep in until the boat comes," she had countered.

"Stoves'd be all rusted up. You'd still have to come back to the station to cook—I mean to eat," Josiah had put in.

She knew what he meant, and assured him that she had no intention of shirking her self-imposed chores.

The twins had just come in off patrol. Normally, they would have slept until James and Adams returned from the second patrol and then gone out again. Malachi had explained that with the crew reduced to a bare minimum, there was little time to do more than sleep, drill, and stand watch, which they took in turnabout fashion.

"Clear days, when the sea's calm and visibility's good, we stand a watch on the tower instead of patrolling. Them's the worst days of all, on account of Penn, he makes all hands that ain't standing watch either drill or scrub down ever'thing in sight."

"And you'd rather race along the shore, I take it?" Hannah teased.

"Yes'm. That is, we don't exactly race, but I'd rather do most anything than scrub down a floor."

Malachi yawned prodigiously, and Josiah jabbed him in the ribs. " 'Scuse yourself, peabrain!"

The youthful lifesaver begged Hannah's pardon and then offered to drive her to the village in the pony cart. "I could leave you there, and then one of us can fetch you before we go out again."

As Penn was conveniently away checking the lines between Paragon and the next station to the south, Hannah didn't wait to be urged. Had he been there, he would never have allowed her to go. Since learning of her impending confinement, all five brothers had treated her like a piece of fine porcelain. "Just let me get a broom and a pail, and—do you suppose I could borrow a piece of soap?"

"Ma'am, you don't need to be doin' no work," Josiah protested.

"Maybe you'd better wait a spell, Miz Hannah. Penn'll show you around soon's he finds the time," Malachi said.

But time was the one thing Hannah lacked. Between her cumbersome body and her erratic emotions, the sooner she removed herself from this place, the safer she would feel. Nor did she dare wait for the captain to show her around, because as much as she instinctively trusted the man, Penn Warfield made her uneasy. Five minutes in his presence and her pulse began to misbehave, her breathing got all out of kilter and she began thinking things no self-respecting woman, much less one in her eighth month of pregnancy, should be thinking.

"I'll not overwork, I assure you, but if I want to catch my breath, I'd as lief be able to clean off a patch to sit on."

* * *

It was Josiah who drove her through the deserted village and then pulled up between two of the soundest of the few remaining houses. He named the former owner of one, now buried in the front yard, his children scattered across the mainland, and then reluctantly helped her down from the cart. "This ain't no place to go sightseeing."

But Hannah wasn't sightseeing. There was no telling just when the *Hamlet* was going to return, but when it did she had no intention of being hauled meekly back across the sound and dumped out on the dock at Elizabeth City like a sack of cornmeal.

"What about that one?" The house was gaunt and innocent of paint, yet oddly inviting for all that, probably because of the rosebush. A rambling, weatherbeaten thing without a single leaf, it stubbornly persisted in climbing over a leaning, snaggle-toothed picket fence, a wash house, and the bleached skeleton of a fallen cedar, as if hanging on for dear life against the elements.

"This here was Miss Marthenia's old place. Raised a passel o' young'un's here, but they're all gone now. Ma'am, you want to watch where you put your feet. If you go getting yourself all mommicked up, Penn'll use my lights and liver for turkle bait."

Hannah had already learned that a turkle was any variety of shell-bearing reptile rather than some exotic mixture of turtle and turkey.

As the cart trundled off across the island, leaving her alone, she pictured the place in the springtime with hundreds of small, ruffled blossoms lifting toward the sun. If a rosebush would thrive in this inhospitable climate, she mused, then there was hope for anything.

Hope? Heavenly days! Here she stood, newly widowed, pregnant by a man not her husband, a man who had vowed to keep both her and the child she carried. To escape a life of shame, she had leapt at the chance to marry a man she had never met, only to be rejected after two miserable days of traveling. Her baby was due in three weeks, she hadn't enough to pay her fare back to the mainland, even if she'd had a place to go and a means of surviving once she got there.

And she felt *hopeful?*

Against all reason, she did indeed. For five endless years, little in her harshly circumscribed life had made sense. Why should she expect it to begin now?

Three hours later, Hannah was sprawled across a bright blue bench in a kitchen that was freshly scrubbed and really quite habitable, if one didn't take into account the mouse holes in the baseboard, the missing windowpanes, and the rusty hulk that had once been a cookstove.

She had located a serviceable bed in the cozy attic bedroom, plainly but neatly built of unfinished pine. She would like to think that some man had built it a long time ago for the bride he had brought to this house. A powerful man, perhaps, with eyes as blue as an October sky, with shoulders broad enough to bear the world's woes, with strong, capable hands and a heart full of . . .

Oh, my mercy! She was so tired she was

giddy—so tired she was happy, which, under the circumstances, was nothing short of ridiculous.

Scowling, she reminded herself of all the things she would need. Dishes. Utensils. Food. Linens. Everything!

But the small room just off the stairs would have made a lovely nursery. If she were going to be here long enough. Facing east, it would catch the morning sun, and on a summer day, the scent of roses would drift in through the window, and the sound of the surf would carry quite clearly, like a constant lullaby.

Sighing, she absently massaged her aching back with a grimy hand. She would have to ask Malachi and Josiah to move the bed down for her. Even in her present state of euphoria, she knew better than to attempt those stairs one more time. And that mattress, unless she was very much mistaken, had recently harbored a family of mice. Possibly still did.

But for a few days, it could be made to serve. After that . . . well, who could tell? She would think of something. She would have to, because it simply wasn't in her to give up.

Shadows sloped across the floor. It was growing late, past time for the twins to have come for her. Surely they couldn't both have forgotten her. She might even have set out walking back if it weren't for this dratted aching back of hers! If she hadn't taken such care not to bend or lift or strain, she could have understood it, but she'd been careful. All she'd done was sweep and scrub. If anything ached, it should have been her knees!

Gazing proudly around at her new kitchen, Han-

nah felt a surge of pride not untinged with possessiveness.

*Pride and possessiveness? Oh, my mercy, Papa
would have had me on my knees repenting for
hours!*

Perhaps it was a good thing she would soon be
leaving it all behind. But at the thought of leaving,
her chin wobbled in a surge of self-pity that was totally out of character. Drat it, where was that cart,
anyway? Had those scamps forgot all about her?

"You start weeping now, Hannah Matthews
Ballinger, and I'll disown you," she muttered, gathering her strength to start the long walk back to the
station.

Already today she had wept over a faded ging-
ham bonnet, forgotten on a nail behind the attic
door, over a bedraggled rag doll with the sawdust
leaking from her body, and one lonely jar of pre-
served melon rind in a dark corner of a kitchen
cabinet.

"No more tears today, madam," she said firmly.
Feet braced apart, she reached for the windowsill
and finally managed to pull herself up to a standing position. But before she could take a single
step, she felt a slow, wet warmth began to spread
down her legs.

Chapter 4

INSIDE the station house, Penn was coldly furious and making no effort to disguise it. "You mean to tell me you allowed that woman to spend the day alone in the village? God knows, I never thought you were overburdened with brains, but that's going too far, even for you two numbskulls!"

The twins, still foggy-headed from oversleeping, cut identical guilty looks at the glowering man before them. "We didn't mean no harm," Malachi mumbled. "She wanted to go."

"She'd have walked if we hadn't took her," said Josiah.

Penn suspected they were right, which did nothing to improve his temper. "She could've broke her leg. And snakes don't sleep real sound, even in winter, dammit!"

"Or one of them ol' boar hogs could've come sniffin' around," Josiah put in, and Malachi poked him hard on the shoulder.

"You didn't have to go sayin' that, peabrain! 'Sides, there ain't none left."

Outside, James was just riding in off patrol. He slid to the ground, rubbed down his mare, and after pitching a meager forkful of dried grass into the trough, slung his bridle at a nail on the wall. Mal and Josie's bridles hung beside it, which meant they were still here. Adam's nail was still empty, which meant he was still out.

But then, Adam was always late on the northern run. As a rule, James tolerated his brother's tardiness well enough, but being three hands short was beginning to take its toll on dispositions. All in the world he wanted at the moment was a hot supper, accompanied by a pint of strong black coffee, and followed by a good six hours of sleep before he had to set out again. Better yet, a few clear days during which a tower watch would suffice, only then they'd be drilled until they dropped.

Just as he left the shelter of the shed, Adam crested the dunes, in no noticeable hurry so far as James could see. "Reckon you lingered to watch the sun go down," James said sarcastically.

"Oleeta baked raisin cakes," Adam replied, a broad grin on his handsome face. It was an open secret that Adam's girlfriend rode south to meet him whenever she could elude her father. The single thing Penn and Noah Drucker had in common was a powerful dislike of the match, not that either man seemed able to prevent it.

James's thin lips flattened as he turned toward the station house. If the poor fool wanted the Drucker girl enough to run crosswise of Penn just to steal a few minutes with her every day or so, it was no skin off his nose. Still, he'd have thought that a man with Adam's looks could have done better than a drab little mite with no more to say for herself than a lizard on a knothole.

"Come on, time's a-wasting," he muttered. Both

men trudged through the deep drifts of sand. James shoved open the door and halted. Behind him, Adam paused, a frown slowly replacing the grin he habitually wore after being with Oleeta.

The room was cold. There was no smell of food, nor even of coffee. On the far side of the room, three men faced each other in a silent confrontation, two against one.

James and Adam traded mystified looks and waited until Penn waved them impatiently into the room. Then, wheeling away from the two red-faced surfmen standing stiffly at attention, their wrinkled garments and unshod feet indicating they'd been rousted from their beds only moments before, he barked out a command.

"Report!"

"Aye, sir! Wind nor' nor'east, twenty to thirty knots, freighter hull down to the south'ard, three-master beatin' north, ridin' light," James stated. "No sign of trouble."

In turn, Adam reported a barkentine standing to the east under full sail. Less sensitive to the tension than James, he asked about the lines between Paragon and points south.

"Back in service for now, anyhow," Penn said shortly. He'd been out since first light, tracking down and jury-rigging the broken telephone line that had been discovered when he'd tried to speak to Captain Hooper at Little Kinnakeet station just before dark the night before. He was tired, filthy, and hungry after having spent the day on a job that wasn't going to last much beyond the next high tide. "God knows when the linesman'll show up."

"Where's Miz Hannah?" Adam ventured. His

gaze shifted hopefully to the range in the corner of the high-ceilinged room. It was past four and there wasn't a pot on the stove.

"Soundside," Penn snapped. "These two gourd-heads here drove her over and dumped her out to explore!"

"Josie took 'er, I'm fixin' to fetch her back right now," Malachi said earnestly. He was almost in tears.

"You'll ride patrol. Gear up, the both of you! Josiah, take the southern run, Malachi, you head north. Keep a close lookout. I don't like the sound of that surf."

As the boys wheeled away to finish dressing, with only one wistful look toward the bare kitchen table, James crossed to the range and laid his hand on its glossy black side. Stone cold. He nodded to the wood basket, and Adam began gathering up an armful of split pine.

"Forget it. We'll not have time," Penn said tiredly. "I'm worried about the woman. She's just fool enough to set out walking, and the way my luck's been running lately, she'll likely end up halfway to Chic'macomico before we catch up with her."

"She don't strike me as stupid," James said mildly. But he was already donning the foul-weather gear he had just shed, glancing regretfully at the empty coffeepot.

"She's a woman, isn't she?"

James and Adam shared a speaking look. Both knew the eldest Warfield had never held women in particularly high esteem since his wife had run off with another man some nine years before. Penn never talked about her, but it was too much to hope he'd forgotten. One more reason why they'd all been stunned when he'd sent for a mail-order bride for Adam—none more so than Adam.

Which was nothing to the way they'd felt when the woman had showed up ripe as a peapod. In the few days she'd been there, however, the widow Ballinger had fit in surprisingly well. Of course, Adam still refused point-blank to marry her. Short of holding a gun on him, there wasn't a whole lot Penn could do about it. Still, James, for one, would be sorry to see her go. She was comfortable company, besides which, she was a right fine cook.

With the setting of the sun, the temperature had dropped precipitously. Penn took a blanket from the locker and added it to the emergency supplies he'd stacked beside the door, which included splints in case of a broken bone, brandy in case of shock, and a clean, sharp knife in case of snakebite.

"Hitch up," he ordered curtly. "James, you'll drive. Adam, fire up the stove, refill the wood box, fill all pots with water and set 'em to boil. She'll likely be chilled when we fetch her back." Under his breath, he muttered something about hoping that was the least they had to worry about.

"You think she might've fallen through a rotten plank and broke something?" James asked as they set off across the island.

"What I'd like to think is that by now she's halfway across the sound aboard the *Hamlet*, but the boat's not due in, and her gear's still here. Being a woman, she's not likely to go off and leave all her fribbles and furbelows behind."

James, hunched over the plank seat, slapped the

reins against Aristotle's shaggy hide. "Somehow, Miz Hannah don't strike me as that kind of a woman," he said quietly.

"Women is women. Not a cent's worth of difference betwixt 'em."

"Where you planning on looking first?"

Penn had been constantly raking the horizon for any sign of life. Under a bleak late January sky, nothing moved, not so much as a crow on the wing. "God knows. Josiah said he off-loaded her betwixt Miss Marthenia's and Isaiah's place. She could be anywheres by now. Might've took some wild start and set off walking back to the station when Mal never showed up."

"If she'd took it in her head to cross over and walk back along the shore, we'd have seen her, coming in from patrol. Reckon why she wanted to go to the village anyhow? Nothing there to see."

"Why? Because neither she nor them twins has the brains God give a conch shell, that's why!" Penn covered his increasing anxiety with anger. "Can't that damned animal go any faster? I'm going to ride on ahead and check Miss Marthenia's place. Josiah said she seemed to take a shine to that old rosebush that's pulling the fence down."

Hannah had done her best once she realized what was happening to her. Above all a sensible woman, she refused to give in to fear. Whatever happened next, it could hardly be worse than what had happened the night it had all begun.

"Never you fret, we're safe now, love," she whispered, stroking her writhing belly protectively. "The Lord willing, he'll never find us here."

For a while, she had almost lost the habit of praying, but it was about all she could do at the moment. She had no real notion of how she would look after her newborn son. She would simply have to contrive somehow. The important thing was that Thomas could have no way of knowing her whereabouts. If he decided to search for her so as to get his hands on the son he coveted above all, since his own wife was unable to conceive, he would think first of her cousin who lived up in the mountains near the Tennessee border.

Knowing that, Hannah had run in the opposite direction, first clipping Captain Warfield's advertisement from the evening paper and hiding it carefully in her sewing basket. Waiting for a reply to her letter, she'd been in constant fear lest Jarnelle or Thomas should get to the mail before she did.

She'd been lucky. No one knew about the advertisement. No one knew about the letters exchanged. No one could possibly know that she had sold her wedding ring to purchase a train ticket, using the name of Miss Jane Smith, and all at a time when most women would still be incapacitated with grief. Even now she was shocked, herself, at how devious she'd been forced to become, but at least her baby would be safe. There was no possible way Thomas could ever trace her to this farflung outpost of civilization.

Between pains, Hannah managed to dip another pail of water from the half-rotted rain barrel outside. Next she made a pallet from her cape and slipped off one of her petticoats, tearing it into squares. Having watched the parsonage mouser take care of a newborn litter more than once, she had a rudimentary notion of what to expect. Lacking a sharp instrument to cut the cord, she managed to break one of the few remaining windowpanes and then washed the sliver of glass, placing it carefully on the bench beside her.

"Please, God, don't let me do this all wrong," she prayed, gasping as a fresh seizure locked the air in her lungs. Her cotton drawers and shift were soaked clean through, she was drenched in sweat, and it was growing colder by the minute with wind whistling down the chimney and through the broken windows.

The pains came, as nearly as she could gauge, about five minutes apart. After the very first one that had hit her—at least, once she had recognized it as something other than a simple backache—she had set out to walk back to the station. The twins had obviously raced back out on beach patrol, clean forgetting their promise to come and collect her. As sweet as they were, they were inclined to be a mite heedless.

Bundled up against a howling wind that whipped her hair about her face and forced sand into the very pores of her skin, she had made it as far as the vine-covered fence before another clawing pain had brought her to her knees. When it ended, she had turned and made her way back into the house, resigned to the fact that, in all likelihood, she would have to manage this business by herself.

So be it. She bolstered her courage with the thought that women had given birth on battlefields, during blizzards, in covered wagons, and in the bowels of crowded, storm-tossed ships at sea.

At least she had a roof over her head and four walls to provide her with privacy.

Aside from the mouser, Hannah had also tended several women when their time came. As a minister's daughter, she'd been expected to lend a hand wherever it was needed. Unfortunately, as an unmarried woman, she had always been shunted out of the room before the actual birthing process commenced. She knew how to boil water, how to sew baby clothes, and how to brew all manner of soothing herbal teas, but when it came to the actual process of guiding a new life into the world, she was only now beginning to realize how much she didn't know.

A fresh surge of pain drew her knees up against the hard knot of her belly, and she gripped the edge of the bench that was the only piece of furniture the room contained. Dear God, she was being torn asunder! Panting to catch her breath a moment later, she prayed that the twins wouldn't belatedly remember her and burst in on her now. Her modesty and dignity aside, they'd be terrified if they saw her in this condition!

Mindlessly counting down from five hundred in an effort to keep from thinking of all the things that could go wrong, she had reached four hundred and twenty-seven when she heard the sound of voices. Torn between relief and embarrassment, she struggled awkwardly to a seated position on the floor and tugged her skirts down over her ankles. A smile was quite beyond her, but at least she could try to look composed. Teaching the facts of life to young gentlemen wasn't what she'd set out to do, but at this point, she feared there was no help for it.

Penn slammed to a halt in the kitchen doorway, looking as if he'd been poleaxed. James, racing inside two steps behind him, collided with his broad back. "What's wrong?" the younger man asked. "What's going on? Is she here? Is she all right?" The first thing Penn had seen when he'd stepped inside the front room was the station's heavy-duty broom. Then came the sound of movement from the back of the house, and something that sounded like a groan.

Ignoring his brother's question, Penn glared down at the woman on the floor. "Would you mind telling me," he asked, each word standing alone, "just what the bloody blue blazes you think you're doing?"

Hannah gazed up at both men, her spirits sagging even lower. It needed only this. "I'm afraid my son has a rather dreadful sense of timing," she said with a parody of a smile.

Every vestige of color drained from Penn's face. Moving quickly, James shoved him aside and knelt before her. "Hannah, are you sure?"

"Well, I've never done this sort of thing before, but I can't think why else I'd be . . . ah-h-hh," she broke off with a groan. Here it came again. Giant hands squeezing her belly, breaking her back, tearing her apart inside. "Oh, please," she whispered, sweat pouring off her waxen face.

"Jesus," Penn muttered. Shoving the younger Warfield aside, he knelt and placed one hand on her forehead while he peered suspiciously into her eyes.

"I *don't* have a fever," Hannah ground out. "It's a stomachache. Or a backache. Or maybe it's only—ah, dear God in heaven—!" She bit her lower lip until the blood came. "Maybe it's only—gas pains!"

"We've got to get you home." Penn went to lift her, and Hannah protested feebly.

"There's not time!" she wailed.

"You can't do it here. There's no way to heat this place short of burning it down."

"Then burn it down, I don't care!" Her voice dwindled off into a moan. When the pain released her, she fell limp, eyes closed, face as colorless as the strips of petticoat she had laid out on the freshly scrubbed bench.

Kneeling beside her, both men scowled. James looked at Penn for guidance, and Penn, catching sight of the shard of broken glass positioned so carefully beside the torn strips of cloths and the pail of cold water, swore softly. Never in all his thirty-one years had he felt quite so helpless.

"Fetch the cart up to the door," he said tersely. "Tear down the damned fence if you have to, but don't waste time. I don't know how long we've got, but I do know we've got to get her home before things go much further."

Penn had helped more than one mare drop her foal. Leastwise, he'd stood by, ready to bear a hand if need be. Invariably, the process took under an hour, and the mare usually managed quite well without him. There'd been that one time when he'd had to reach in and—

But this, he sensed, was a different matter altogether.

As James hurried out the front door, Penn called after him, "Tie Peg behind the cart! I'll ride with you and carry her—we don't want her all shook up."

The trip to the station was an endless purgatory. Hannah, bundled up in a blanket and her own cape, clung to the man who held her on his lap, his black woolen coat open to shield her face from the worst of the wind. Her sodden skirts were probably soaking right through to his limbs, but she was too miserable to care and too scared to be embarrassed.

Between pains, Hannah pressed her face against Penn's hard, warm chest and thought of what would have happened if he hadn't found her in time. Whatever the future held, the present at least was in his capable hands. It was a surprisingly comforting thought.

How was it possible, she wondered distractedly, to feel so totally alone and so completely safe at the same time? The absurdity of it struck her, but before she could give way to hysterical laughter, the pain came again to snatch her breath away. By the time she was free of its clutches, the back of Penn's hand was bleeding where her nails had dug in. His shirt was torn where she'd caught the coarse cotton fabric and hung on, too distraught to know or care what she was doing.

She tried to apologize. "There, hush now, girl, you'll do all right," Penn rumbled, his voice somehow reaching her through the fog of pain.

After what seemed an eternity, Hannah sensed that they were no longer moving. Penn handed her down into Adam's waiting arms, then leapt to the ground and took her back. How strange, she thought absently, filling her lungs with the comforting, masculine scent of Penn's body as he bore her into the warm station, that even with her eyes closed and her body one enormous bundle of pain, she could tell whose arms held her.

"It's taking too damned long," James whispered hours later. He had just ridden in off patrol.

"Well, what the devil do you want me to do, run her up and down the shoreside until she broaches?" Penn whispered back, his voice every bit as fierce as his expression.

It was nearing morning and still nothing had happened. Hannah's pains were no closer together, yet each one seemed to leave her weaker, paler— less able to withstand the next surge. The watch had changed and changed again. In the next room, the twins were sleeping soundly.

Penn had not slept at all.

"Sky's clearing," Adam reported cheerfully, coming in a quarter of an hour after James. Both men turned on him and signaled quiet.

Chastised, the tall surfman completed his report in an exaggerated whisper. "No running lights, no flares. Sea's running strong, but the wind's falling off some."

Which was more or less a duplicate of James's most recent report. Standing at the tall, salt-hazed window overlooking the surf, Penn studied conditions as the first streak of dawn brightened the eastern sky. He crossed to the glass, rapped it lightly and nodded. "Rising," he said. "Let Mal sleep awhile longer. His cough's still not cleared up.

Josiah can man the tower. Adam, fetch me that book on animal husbandry. It's on the shelf with the canned goods." He had removed his journals, his clothes, and most of his books to the main room when he'd bedded Hannah down in his office.

"How do you spell ani—"

"It's the green one, about so thick!" Penn held up two fingers, and Adam nodded. The boy had his good qualities, but book learning didn't happen to be one of his particular strengths.

"Coffee's made," James said quietly. "I'll fry up a pan of bread. Don't reckon it'll help none to go hungry."

But before he could do more than lift the lid on the floor bin, an anguished cry arose from the keeper's room, where Hannah had been dozing between labor pains.

"Something's happening," Penn whispered. He was already on the move, covering the distance at a run.

"Something's changed," said James, right behind him.

"Reckon it's time?" called Adam, still searching the shelf for a green book about so thick.

Before he was even through the door, Penn was barking out orders. "James, fetch the brandy and a mug of hot water. Adam, rouse Josiah and set him on watch. Set Mal to cooking up something. Anything! And then bring me that damned book and stand by!"

But no amount of taking command and spitting out orders could speed up the process. "My son," Hannah panted some forty-five minutes later, "will be born when he's blessed well ready to be born, and not a moment sooner."

"Stubborn little cuss," Penn murmured admiringly. Holding her hand, he was unobtrusively counting her pulse between seizures. "What makes you so sure he's a boy?" he asked to distract her.

James leaned over and wiped her face with a cold cloth, and Hannah smiled her thanks, but it was a weak effort. She felt about as limp as the washcloth, after what seemed weeks of agony. Punishment for her sins, she told herself. Although surely a merciful God wouldn't count it against her that she had been physically too weak to fight off a monster who had caught her by surprise and used his superior strength against her, threatening to turn her and Edward, his own brother, out into the street if she said a word to anyone about what had happened.

Her eyelids drifted down. *Please, Lord . . .*

"I heard an old woman down Trent Hills way say once that boy babies was carried different from girls. Is that how you know?" Penn asked. He wanted to keep her talking, to keep her eyes open, her mind alert. In his ten-year career in the service, he'd been called on to perform all manner of offices for female survivors, but this was a new experience. It purely scared the stuffing out of him.

"Madame Zilda—fortune-teller—county fair," Hannah whispered. "Never should've gone—Papa was so angry. Madame saw many—sons. Said my whole life would be—changed by my sons."

Biting her lip, she braced herself against the tightening agony that threatened to rend her apart. When eventually the pain released her, drenched in sweat and noticeably weaker, she drew in a shuddering breath and gripped Penn's hand. "Please, God, let him be all right!" she whispered. "Don't let me do this all wrong!"

Penn managed to get some watered brandy down her throat. He set James to boiling a slab of corned mullet. It would be strong and probably taste like the very devil—of the five of them, James was the worst hand at cooking—but Hannah needed nourishment. He could see her strength ebbing, minute by minute.

He continued to hold her hand long after he'd stopped counting her pulse. Held it tightly, as if he might impart some of his own strength to her fragile body.

Had it been like this for Margaret? His wife hadn't wanted a child—not Penn's child, at any rate. She'd complained almost from the first at having to care for his four younger brothers, and Penn had done his best to make it up to her, buying her small gifts he could ill afford whenever a drummer came by, sparing her the heaviest chores. But fishing was long, hard work and not always productive. He was often too tired to do more than fall into bed and sleep for the few hours before time to go out and fish his nets once more. They had never gone hungry. He had prided himself on that much, at least, but providing for a family of six didn't allow much in the way of luxuries.

Margaret had been seventeen when they had married. An only child, indulged by her widowed father and spoiled by three elder brothers, she had wanted Penn to take her to Norfolk to see all the shops and buy her pretty frocks and bonnets. But a fisherman who was forced to squeeze every minute from every hour of daylight could ill afford either the time or the money.

When he had lost both boat and nets in a hard, three-day nor'easter, with no quick means of replacing them, he had left home to join the lifesaving service. He'd been scared, proud, discouraged, and hopeful, but most of all, he'd been determined to make something of his life. For Margaret's sake. The day he had received his first pay packet, he had proudly set out for home, stopping only to gather a bouquet of beach flowers along the way. He'd planned to hand over his entire pay to his wife, but the house had been empty, the stove cold, and the hooks where her gowns hung, empty.

It had been eighteen-year-old Adam who had reluctantly broken the news. Margaret had left two days before with a drummer who peddled notions and patent medicines up and down the banks.

Penn had not gone after her, nor had he spoken her name from that day to this. Adam, with James as second in command, was put in charge of the twins when Penn left to go back to the station. He still had a family to keep, and running after a wife who didn't want him wasn't going to help matters.

Nearly two years later, he had heard that Margaret had died in childbirth somewhere up in Virginia. If he had mourned her, none of his brothers had known about it.

Suddenly, Hannah's fingers gripped his hand fit to break the bones. Her breathing had changed. She was gasping, and there was a panicky look in her eyes.

"Hannah? What's happening?" Ignoring modesty,

Penn folded back the blankets that covered her writhing form. "Adam, get James in here!"

From the stool in the corner, where he'd been poring over the green book, Adam looked up, his wide green eyes puzzled. "Penn, what does p-a-r-t-u-r-i-t-i-o-n spell?"

"James!" Penn shouted, never taking his eyes from his patient. "Front and center! *Now!*"

James appeared in the doorway, his hands wet, a towel tucked into the waist of his uniform pants. "What's going on?"

"I think we're getting somewhere! Hand me one of those sheets, we'll need something to wrap him in. Easy, Hannah, easy, baby—I know it hurts, sweetheart, but—whoa! Something's coming. James, grab that book and read what it says about what part's supposed to come down first!"

Penn's movements remained reassuringly steady as he folded Hannah's nightgown back over her belly. She'd managed to get into it with his help between pains the night before, but he'd insisted on staying with her. Seeing her slender back, he'd been shocked at how very fragile she was, her skin so pale it was almost translucent. She'd been terribly embarrassed by his presence, but there was no help for it. He would have pleaded blindness if he'd thought it would help, but he could no more have left her alone than he could have walked to Diamond Shoals.

At the moment, modesty was the last thing on anyone's mind. Alternately groaning and cursing, Hannah bore down with all her strength, helpless against the forces that beset her.

"Here we go," James said quietly, frowning at the

text. "First indication is rupture of—uh-huh—lots of water. Reckon that part's already took place. It says normal presentation takes fifteen to twenty minutes." He raised a stricken face and said, "God, Penn, this has been going on since yesterday! That can't be right!"

"I know, I know, dammit, but what am I supposed to do about it? If that telephone line hadn't broke again, I'd have raised every female between Hatteras and Oregon Inlet and had 'em all standing by! Read some more—what happens next? Maybe women and mares is different."

"I think maybe you'd better roll her over, Penn. It says here she's supposed to be lying on her side with all four legs—yeah, well . . ."

Penn dropped to his knees, swearing. "Oh, Jesus, sweet Jesus, here he comes!"

"In normal presentation, it says, the front feet come first, heels down, followed by the nose and then the shoulders, and—" James broke off and frowned. "That don't sound right, does it?"

"She ain't a horse, James," said Adam in a mild and reasonable tone of voice. "Maybe women is more like cats, and it don't make no difference which end comes out first, 'cause they're all done up in a skin bag, anyway. You reck'n?"

Penn, hands outstretched, ignored them both. And then Hannah gave a low, wavering groan, which was followed by a thin, mewling sound.

Penn continued to sweat and swear.

James dropped the book.

Adam picked it up and held it reverently against his chest.

Then Penn said softly, "Hand me that sheet, will you, Jay? Miz Hannah's little girl don't seem to think much of our hospitality, do you, sweet-pea?"

Chapter 5

THE presence of one small, pregnant woman had made a difference in the lives of the keeper and crew of Paragon Shoals Lifesaving Station, but somewhat to their surprise, they had quickly become adjusted.

The presence of Mistress Sara Mirella Matthews Ballinger was another matter altogether.

"Don't she do nothing but squall?" Malachi grumbled after having been kept from his sleep for an entire watch.

"Damn right. She wets," his twin muttered sourly. Josiah had drawn laundry duty. The wind-whipped lines between shed and boathouse were constantly filled with flapping napkins and other small, indescribable articles. After securing the last white square to the sagging line, he turned the tub down over a stump and adjusted the support pole.

James, setting out on patrol, hooked a hand around the necks of both his brothers and butted their heads together. "Quit complaining. Your gizzards enjoyed a week of good cooking before Miz Hannah took to her bed. Them that dances has to pay the piper."

Adam hurried past, his golden curls glistening in

the bright sunshine. Mal sniffed and uttered a sound of disgust. "Bay rum! I can always tell when he's meetin' you-know-who. Reeks like one o' Rosabelle's sportin' ladies."

Adam grinned good-naturedly and led out his walleyed bay. "Smells better than what you been washin' in, little brother."

Mal threw a broken clamshell at Adam's big-booted foot and James laughed, slipping the reins over his own mount's head. "Little tyke's got a grip onto her, though. Grabbed my finger this morning and I liked to never got it back."

"Got a pair o' lungs onto her, too."

The baby had been named in honor of Hannah's mother and the late Mrs. Warfield, Sr., and given Hannah's maiden name as a bonus. They'd all had a hand in the task, the twins first offering the names of several ships that had gone down nearby within the past few years.

"Penn, he was named after a three-master," Josiah had explained.

"No he weren't, peabrain, he was named after Pa!"

"Well, Pa was named after a three-master out o' Boston. Same thing."

Under consideration had been *Strathairly*, after a schooner-rigged screw steamer that had met her doom only a little ways north of the station back in '91, only no one had been too clear on how to pronounce it, much less spell it. *John Shay*, after the schooner that had piled up farther south in '89, had been dismissed as the wrong gender, but the *Annie E. Pierce* had been a close contender.

It had been Penn who had cast the deciding vote.

"She's just been launched, boys. She'll have her own name, not one that's already come to grief." His eyes had met and held Hannah's over the head of the infant, and the others had waited respectfully for the moment to pass. Then they'd all taken a hand in arranging the names selected in the proper order.

For the first few days after the birth of Sara Mirella Matthews Ballinger, Penn had guarded mother and child with a single-mindedness that, even for him, was remarkable. He had scheduled visits and allowed each man to hold the tiny infant for precisely one minute under his careful supervision.

As February progressed and the weather held fine, with excellent visibility, patrols often gave way to tower watches, thus freeing one man for other duties. Hannah suspected that she and her daughter comprised the major part of those other duties, but there was little she could do about it for the moment.

"How'd you come to be such an expert on young'uns?" James asked once when Penn found fault with the way he supported Sara Mirella's head.

"I was thirteen years old when the twins was born, remember? Seemed to me I drew more'n my share of the duty."

One evening, Malachi and Josiah drew forth a pair of rust-speckled harmonicas and serenaded mother and child until Penn came charging into the room to chastise them for a total lack of respect.

"I don't understand," Hannah said, after the boys

had been sent to inventory the number of Coston flares on hand and check something called a shot line. "I thought it sounded rather nice."

"Them songs are unfit for a lady's ears," Penn muttered, his own ears suspiciously pink.

Hannah had to laugh. "Penn, I assure you, I didn't take any harm, nor did Sara Mirella."

"All the same, it don't show proper respect."

"If you say so. However, unless a piece of music appears in a hymnal, or one of Edward's songbooks, I probably wouldn't recognize it, no matter who played it. I'm afraid I'm remarkably uneducated in matters of secular entertainment." She saw no reason to explain that having been raised in a parsonage, the only child of elderly parents, and confined to nursing an invalid husband for the past five years of her life, there had been scant time to cultivate frivolous pursuits.

As there was no question of Hannah's moving back to her curtained-off corner with Sara Mirella, the life of the station quickly settled down around the new circumstances. When the office door was closed, Penn remained outside. If he desperately needed something from within, he rapped softly and waited for permission to enter. As Hannah grew stronger, they drifted into a tentative sharing, with Penn sitting quietly at his desk of an evening, reading a dog-eared copy of *Robinson Crusoe* or *Moby Dick* while Hannah stitched on some small garment or another.

The watches and patrols went on. Drills, housekeeping, and sleep was fitted in and around the primary duty of the service. Penn was as diligent as ever, but except when his duties took him farther afield, he usually managed to remain within call of mother and child. In his absence, the duty evolved to Adam, who more often than not, turned it over to James.

Hannah had come to enjoy the company of the dark-eyed, quiet James, who managed to stay handy without being obtrusive. There was always gear that needed looking after—it seemed that what didn't need oiling needed polishing, and what didn't need polishing was in need of calking or sanding or whitewashing.

Or splicing. All five men were adept at that fascinating bit of nautical handiwork. Hannah determined to learn how to weave the end—the *standing* end, as James informed her, of a rope—or rather a line or a hawser—into that intricate knot called a monkey's fist.

The freight boat came and went, leaving mail and a stock of supplies that included such delicacies as canned milk, canned peaches and canned tomatoes, and a twenty-five-pound sack of sugar that was already rock-hard. Nothing more was said of Hannah's leaving.

Not that she had forgotten her new home in the village, but it would have to wait. Mal and Josie promised to patch the roof and board up the windows until glass could be measured for and ordered. And something would have to be done about a stove if she planned to remain for any length of time.

The days passed in lazy succession, with tiny, bald-domed Sara Mirella thriving on the attention of five stalwart champions. They all doted on her, some more openly than others. The twins were obviously her slaves.

As for Hannah, who was soon chaffing under her enforced idleness, she enjoyed the twins' antics—the face-making and gay music designed to entertain their new heroine. She counted it a distinct triumph when she got a laugh from James, or more than three successive words out of Adam.

But it was Penn whose presence affected her in a way that none of the others did. Somehow, he managed to spend more time with Hannah and her daughter than any of the others, without neglecting his responsibilities as keeper. Not that he particularly coveted the chore, but as he was quick to point out when James offered to relieve him, he *was* the man in charge, after all. Responsibility for all hands was his and his alone.

When his charges napped, Penn caught a few hours of sleep, but he was awake again at the first hint of sound from behind the closed door of the keeper's room. Gradually, he began to assume even more responsibility, closed door or not.

"Wet again, poor little mite," he whispered one evening after Hannah and her daughter had retired for the night. Carefully, he lifted the tiny infant from her makeshift cradle, part of the station's rescue equipment that had been converted into temporary use. "Damned if you ain't leakier than a rusty bucket," he whispered, careful not to rouse the sleeping woman nearby.

Deftly, he changed Sara Mirella's clothing from the skin out, marveling that so much sound and fury could have as its source such a minuscule scrap of humanity. "Shhh, don't wake your mam, sweetpea. She needs her rest." Lifting the babe, he cradled her in his arms, two finger supporting her small head, and rumbled what was obviously meant to be a soothing lullaby under his breath.

His efforts evidently satisfied Sara Mirella's untrained ear, for she was asleep again within minutes.

From the narrow bed in the corner, Hannah watched drowsily, vaguely aware of an ache somewhere deep inside her that had nothing to do with the healing process.

He was so stern, so rigid. A real by-the-book martinet where his precious rules and regulations were concerned, as if it mattered one whit, Hannah told herself, whether or not a journal was posted during the first watch or the fourth, or the floor was swept once a day or even once a week. It weren't as if this barren shoal of an island constituted the hub of civilization. Here, day followed night, sun followed rain, the wind blew incessantly and the seas pounded unceasingly.

And each day, rain or shine, Captain Warfield, USLSS, set the duty roster, saw that his orders were carried out to the letter, scowled over his endless journals and his endless reports and wrote endless letters in an effort to secure additional hands. In slack times he policed every square inch of his barren domain and then drilled his small crew in setting up various rescue apparatus and launching the heavy surfboat with the few hands available. That was the official Penn Warfield.

Yet behind the black serge uniform and the stern visage, Hannah had come to know another Penn

Warfield, a man who had once carried her in his arms as tenderly as she now carried her own child. A man who had cause to know her body more intimately than her own husband ever had—more intimately than she herself ever had—yet who had never once embarrassed her by an untoward look or word.

A gentle man who now held her little daughter as if she were the most precious thing in all the world.

"Sorry we woke you, Hannah," he murmured. Turning, he placed Sara Mirella in her arms. "Here, you'd best take her. I thought she was asleep, but she's commencing to fret."

It was past time to nurse her, but Hannah could hardly do that in Penn's presence. "I could have changed her," she said, brushing her lips against the tiny smooth scalp. Born three weeks early, Sara Mirella—the daughter who was to have been a son—was still nearly bald except for a few wisps of tawny pink down.

"You need your rest."

"You need your rest, too. I'm keeping you from your bed, and she's keeping you all from your sleep. It's a good thing we'll be leaving soon." If not, perhaps, going quite so far away as he had hoped.

Penn's expression altered subtly, his eyes avoiding her own. "Leave matters to me, if you please, madam. When it's time for you to go, I'll make the arrangements."

And with that she had to be content. She could hardly do otherwise at the moment. All the same, she needed to make her own plans for the future, and the less Penn knew about them beforehand, the more peaceful her life would be.

At least she was earning her keep again, having had all she could stomach of boiled bacon and fried cornmeal mush, varied now and then by a briny chunk of corned fish or a stringy, musky-tasting wildfowl one of the men shot down over the soundside. Penn had pitched a royal fit the day he'd come in and found her in the kitchen beating up a batter for corn bread five days after Sara Mirella's birth. James had ventured the opinion that she might be rushing things a bit, but Adam and the twins had been openly delighted.

Short of tying her to the iron bedstead, there had been little Penn could do without losing his formidable dignity. She was not, as she reminded him, a member of his crew. Neither was she one of his brothers. In other words, she was not his to command.

Long after Penn had left her that evening, after Hannah had fed her daughter and replaced her in the makeshift cradle, she thought about Penn Warfield and the odd effect he had on her. She was no inexperienced schoolgirl, to be smitten by a handsome face and a pleasing manner. Not that Penn possessed either. Edward, a schoolteacher who had attended her father's church, had been her first love, and loved him she had. It had nearly destroyed her when they had learned after his accident that he would never again walk—never again dance, never make love, nor father the family they had both wanted.

Yet this aching pull she felt whenever Penn was nearby was something altogether different. Not love. She hardly knew the man, and he was completely outside her experience.

But even she could see that Captain Warfield was a strikingly attractive man. Not sweet, the way Edward had been sweet. Not handsome, the way Adam was handsome. Some women might not find his rough-hewn features pleasing at all, but from the very first, Hannah had been drawn to something about him. Something she couldn't begin to understand. Even before the baby had come, when such feelings should have been the last thing on her mind, whenever they'd found themselves in the same room together her nerves would commence to tingle. Neither one of them had been able to sit quietly for long, but must stalk around, touching first one thing and then another, like two strange cats confined in one small space.

No, it wasn't his looks, although those were well enough. He was much younger than she'd first thought. At times he seemed even younger than his thirty-one years. His eyes were truly beautiful, and the lines of maturity in his weathered face only added to his attractiveness rather than diminishing it.

But it was something else. And whatever it was, Hannah suspected that if she ever wanted to take control of her life, she'd best make plans to move out of the station and find some way to look after her daughter. Rescuing shipwreck victims was the business of the men of Paragon Shoals Lifesaving Station. Taking in stray females to raise most definitely was not.

As Adam approached the halfway house, he kicked his mount into a gallop once more. She was waiting. He hadn't been sure she could get away. They were never sure, but they managed to meet at least two or three times a week.

"Been waitin' long?" he asked. His sea-green eyes spoke words he was too shy to voice, but Oleeta always seemed to understand.

She held out her arms, and he slid off his horse and walked into them as naturally as if he'd been doing it all his life instead of only the past year and a half. "Not long. I knew you'd come. Mal said Penn's so taken up with the new baby these days, he don't care which run you take."

Which was true. Sometimes Penn ordered Adam to take the southern run, knowing full well why he wanted to go north, but lately he'd had his mind on other things.

"I've not got much time. I raced the first mile so I'd have more time to spare on this end. There weren't no sails in sight."

"I know you wouldn't never shirk your duty, Adam. Not even for me," Oleeta said earnestly. They were seated in the shelter of a dune above the shack that marked the halfway point between the two stations, on high ground so as to see anyone approaching from either direction. Adam's arm was around the girl, her head on his shoulder. She had brought him a chunk of cold crackling corn bread, but that could wait.

"Ah, God, 'Leeta, I wish we was married already. I can't stand not being able to see you no more than this!"

"I'll speak to Paw real soon, I promise, if you'll speak to your brother."

He'd spoken to Penn. Not once, but a dozen times. It was about as effective as talking to a conch shell. *Warfields don't marry Druckers. Never did, never will.*

Sighing in frustration, he found her mouth even as his hands homed in on their twin targets with practiced ease. The daylight patrols were doubly dangerous. Both knew what could happen if they were discovered, yet they couldn't stay apart, even knowing that nothing more than a few kisses would be possible.

Adam spread his coat on the sand and lowered her to the ground, bracing his weight on his arms to lean over her. With one finger, he traced the line of her cheek, flushed with the glow of the love that pulsed between them. She was so beautiful, all tan and brown and ivory. Not fancy and colorful, like Rosabelle's women, but quiet and good and true. She made him feel ten feet tall.

"Let me talk to your paw, 'Leeta," he pleaded. "If I tell him how we feel, he's got to allow us to get married. I can make him see reason."

"No! You don't know Paw like I do. He's—well, he's got his ways, is all. He don't say much, but—"

"He don't beat you no more, does he? I couldn't stand that. If he ever lays a finger on you again, I swear I'll—"

Gazing up at the handsome face of her lover, Oleeta placed a finger over his lips. "I know you would, Adam. You're the bravest, smartest, beautifulest man in the whole world, but Paw don't know you like I do. He ain't beat me in a long time, but he has his good days and his bad days. I'll set it before him next time I get the chance, I promise.

But right now ain't a good time. Chester snuck off duck huntin' day before yesterday and dropped Paw's shotgun overboard, and Paw was fit to be tied. He shut Chester up in the attic and hooked the door and wouldn't even let me take him no food, so I got to get back real soon so I can sneak him something before Paw gets home." Noah Drucker worked sporadically as mate on a freighter out of Englehard, his schedule maddeningly irregular.

Over the next several minutes, the muted roar of the nearby surf and the occasional whuffle of the banker pony standing patiently at the mooring post behind the halfway house covered a variety of whisperings, murmurings, and a few soft groans. It was painful, being so much in love and so helpless to do anything about it.

Reluctantly, Adam rose and held out his hand. Then, standing downwind of Oleeta, he brushed the sand off his clothes and tucked his shirttail back inside his trousers. "It'll be dark next time," he promised, his virile young body achingly aroused at the thought of what their next brief meeting would hold.

"I'll try my best to sneak out. Paw said he might have a run up to Baltimore City in a week or so. Lately, he just sets around the house and drinks till time to go to bed."

At the thought of his lover living under the thumb of a brute who beat her, starved his own son, and periodically deserted them both for weeks on end, Adam knotted his fists in frustration. "I'm going to talk to him, 'Leeta. It can't be no worse than this."

"Adam, I'll do it real soon, honest I will, only I got to wait for the right time. He'll be in a good mood when he gets back from the Baltimore run. Workin' always sets him up for a spell, 'cause he don't never drink when he's working."

The right time had better come soon, Oleeta Drucker told herself silently as she watched her beloved mount up and ride out to swap tokens with the patrol from the north. Else, she'd commence to show, and then Paw would do more than beat her. He'd likely kill her and then take out after Adam with his shotgun. Paw didn't hold with loose behavior. He was a real God-fearin' man when he was sober. Drunk, he'd as soon tackle the devil himself.

Hailing the mounted rider from the station just north of her own village of Salvo, who happened to be a cousin on her mother's side, Oleeta began the long trek back home.

Chapter 6

PENN frowned over his journal. He resisted wearing his spectacles, telling himself it had nothing at all to do with Hannah's presence. He didn't really need the things, but only wore them occasionally when his eyes were unduly tired.

Damned lamp chimney wanted cleaning! No wonder he couldn't see. Besides which, when a man didn't get more than a few hours sleep at a stretch, his eyes were bound to give out on him now and again. It didn't mean he was no longer young, it meant only that the government required too blessed much in the way of scribbling.

"Document this, enter that, log this, list that," he grumbled.

From his own desk chair, the only truly comfortable chair in the station, came a soft sigh. Hannah sat quietly, cradle on one side and mending basket on the floor. She'd been turning a collar on one of Josiah's shirts. "I'd be glad to help if you'd show me what needs doing. I write a fair hand."

"No need." Penn rubbed his eyes and turned a tired smile on her. He recognized one of his wool stockings in the basket beside her chair and felt his gut give a peculiar lurch. "You don't have to take on our mending along with everything else you do around here," he said gruffly. All the same, he had to admit that there was a surprising degree of pleasure to be found in watching a woman's hands set to such a homely task.

Hannah's small, shapely hands were both capable and graceful. It came to him that he'd never thought much about a woman's hands. Margaret's had been soft and pretty, but not particularly capable of handling a needle.

He cleared his throat. "Truth is, I'm a right fair hand with a needle, myself. Comes from mending sail and tying net, I reckon."

"I don't mind," Hannah said quickly. "I much prefer to keep busy. I'm afraid I've been a dreadful burden, and truly, I never set out to be."

Their eyes turned toward the cradle, where Sara Mirella was trying unsuccessfully to force a tiny fist into a birdlike mouth. "She's hungry," Hannah murmured, tactfully refraining from saying that the sooner he left, the sooner she could nurse her daughter. Lately, they had developed a certain ease between them, but just beneath the surface was a wariness that came from the intimacy they had shared when Sara Mirella was born.

Evidently, Penn got the unspoken message. Raking back his chair, he stood and carefully wiped the nib of his pen. Placing it precisely two inches to the left of his journal, he stoppered his inkwell and aligned it precisely one inch from the southwest corner of the wooden box that held his official papers.

"You don't have to— I didn't mean—"

"I'd best see about this lamp, anyways," he said.

"Chimney needs cleaning. Wick could stand trimming, too."

Their eyes suddenly met, hers as clear and gray as a summer rain, his the fathomless blue of the Gulf Stream a few miles off the Cape. Just as suddenly, they both looked away, uncomfortable with the quick awareness that could spring up between them so unexpectedly.

Hannah began poking a thread at the needle she held at arm's length, and watching her efforts, Penn frowned. "You should've spoke up sooner about the lack of light. Ought not to try to sew when you can't even see to thread a needle."

"I can see perfectly well. Well enough, at any rate. I had a pair of spectacles, but they were—um, broken a while back, and I never got around to having them mended."

Penn sent her a skeptical look. "You're not old enough to need spectacles."

"Age has nothing to do with it," she said calmly. "My father wore spectacles from the time he was seven years old."

Penn, holding the still smoking lamp, appeared to reflect on that information. "Is that a fact?" he said, a slow smile creasing his tanned cheeks.

"That's a fact." As much as she appreciated his rare smiles, Hannah did wish he would leave before the front of her dress became any wetter. No matter how she padded herself with towels, it took only the sound of a fretful cry to make her bosoms spring forth like a pair of fountains.

The moment the door closed behind him, Hannah lifted the baby from the cradle, holding her with one arm while she unfastened the buttons at the front of her old gray serge. "There, dumpling, mind those little fists of yours, or we'll never get this task accomplished," she murmured, marveling all over again that such perfection could come from such a shockingly violent act.

The Lord moved in mysterious ways, her father used to say. Hannah couldn't agree more. If in His infinite wisdom, He had devised some scheme dependent on her marrying, only to have her husband suffer a tragic accident that left him a helpless invalid, dependent on the charity of a wicked older brother until the day of his death some five years later—a plan dependent on her conceiving a child after a single, terrible act of violence, being forced to run away to escape a life of utter degradation and ending up in, of all places, a lifesaving station—why then, no doubt He would reveal it all to her in His own good time.

During the following week, just when Hannah was convinced that nothing ever changed but the weather on this barren strand of land that elbowed out into the Atlantic some thirty-odd miles off the mainland, several things occurred to change her opinion.

The first was when James, riding north just before dark during a fierce nor'easter, had come across wreckage in the surf. He had fired off a Coston flare, summoning help from the station, but it had been obvious that the three men hanging onto the tangle of rigging just beyond the breakers could well be swept away before help could arrive.

The sloop, which he recognized as belonging to a fisherman from Scarborotown, just north of

Kinnakeet, had obviously run into trouble offshore and its captain had been hoping to beach the vessel before she sunk. Had the wind and the tide cooperated, he might have made it.

Moving quickly, James dismounted and grabbed the coil of line attached to his saddle, securing it to his belt. Swiftly, he shed his coat and boots and plunged into the breakers. The sea was rough, dirty, but the tide was slack. In another half hour, however, the tide would have turned and the current would be hard to overcome.

Keeping his eyes on the three men clinging to the broken mast, he waded out as far as possible and began to swim, his lean body plowing forcefully through the churning seas, diving under the biggest ones. By the time he came as close as he dared, one of the survivors had managed to toss him a lead line, to which he attached one end of the line he carried, the other having been made fast to the saddle horn. He had trained the mare himself, and had no doubt that she would know her duty.

"One at a time!" he shouted. "Swing overboard and hang on tight until I get to you!"

As darkness slowly descended, James caught each man and managed to swim him to shore, guided by the single light line. He dragged the first one up onto the beach and covered him with his own canvas coat before plunging back for the next.

By the time Penn and Adam arrived with the beach cart, all three survivors were on shore, huddled against the biting wind with James's coat and a saddle blanket shared among them.

"'Bout time," James panted. He was bent over at the waist, hands braced on his knees, head hanging, as he struggled to catch his breath. The last man had been a dead weight, one hand badly gashed and a shoulder dislocated when the mast had fallen on him.

Without bothering to reply, Penn examined the injured man, then strapped both arms so that they wouldn't suffer more damage. He loaded them carefully into the beach cart, covering them with a tarpaulin and several blankets. Adam galloped off to alert the station, and for once, Penn didn't quibble over having to drive the cart.

"I'll ride the wash as far as I can," he said quietly referring to the hard-packed sand nearest the water's edge. "Tide's piling in fast, though. It's going to be rough once we hit the high ground. Hold him as best you can, Jay. I laced his brandy with laudanum." All three men had been given restorative spirits.

James tied the docile Mollie behind the cart and eased aboard, and the other two men made room for him to kneel beside their injured shipmate. "Times like this, I wish horses had wings," he muttered. "Easy now—" He moved to steady the injured man as the cart lurched on a patch of gravel. "The hard part's over. Never guess what we've got at the station," he went on, intent only on distracting the man until the laudanum could take effect. "A woman. A real, live city woman with a genu-ine baby. Reckon you'll take one look at Miz Hannah and thank your Maker you had the good luck to come ashore where you did so she can take care of you."

By the time the tedious journey ended, Adam had reached the station and spoke to Little

Kinnakeet Station by phone, requesting transportation and any medical assistance at hand.

Hannah had soup, heated blankets, and gallons
of hot coffee. She quickly saw to the two uninjured
men, then turned to help Penn deal with their
mate.

"You don't need to be here, Hannah," Penn declared.

"Nonsense. I'll hold, you pull, then we'd better
deal with that hand." She drew the poor half-
drowned man against her and held him tightly
while Penn manipulated the dislocated collarbone.
The laudanum and brandy helped the miserable
seaman bear the necessary pain, but nothing could
keep Hannah from turning green and breaking into
a cold sweat at the soft sound of success.

Penn eyed her intently, then ordered her to her
bed. "I'll deal with the rest," he said gruffly. "Go
on, now—last thing I need is a fainting female on
my hands!"

If Hannah had been tempted, one glance at
James, leaning against the far wall, changed her
mind. Marching across the room, she confronted
him, hands on her hips. "You look dreadful!"

He managed a smile, but his normal olive com-
plexion was a pasty shade of gray. Muttering under
her breath, Hannah ordered him out of his wet
clothes and then hurried to drag the tub from the
stoop to a corner behind the stove and fill it with
hot water. The other men had been given dry
clothes and hot sandbags to warm their feet while
they sipped brandy-laced coffee, and generally
fussed over. Meanwhile James had been quite forgotten.

"You get in that tub and soak!" she ordered.

"Yes'm," James said meekly. He had managed to peel down to his long underwear, with a blanket draped over his shoulders for modesty, but he was still shivering.

"Do you want me to peel you down and shove you in right up to your ears?"

The color came back in a rush, and hanging his head, James mumbled something rude and shambled off.

Hannah watched him go, fully determined to keep her word if he so much as hesitated. She had nursed one man for five years, doing the most intimate things a body could do for another. If James Warfield thought she was about to let him come down with an inflammation of the lungs just to spare both their sensibilities, he would soon learn otherwise.

Once he disappeared behind the vast range, she surveyed the situation. Cots had been brought in and set up along the far wall. All three men were now resting quietly and warmly.

Which left Penn and Adam to be seen to. They hadn't been half drowned, the way James had, but all the same, they needed to rest. A militant gleam in her eye, she turned toward Penn, who was laying out his journal and preparing to document the rescue while he waited for someone to come for the survivors.

"Penn, I do believe that can wait until morning, What you need is—"

"Hannah," Penn said quietly. "Go to bed."

Such was the look he gave her that she turned and went without a squawk.

* * *

It was well into the third watch, yet Hannah was unable to sleep. She knew when the twins left on patrol. She knew that Penn had set Adam to manning the beach tower as an added measure, and that James was still sound asleep.

Draping a shawl about her shoulders, she tiptoed across the common room and peered through the door to be sure he hadn't grown restless and kicked his covers off. He hadn't, but she pulled the coarse woolen blanket up to cover his ears. Years of tending an immobile man had taught her that when the ears were warm, the rest of the body felt less chilled.

Turning away, she nearly collided with Penn, who had come to stand in the doorway. "You do too much," he observed softly.

"Little enough. Leastways, I didn't have to risk my life tonight. I never knew . . . I never dreamed . . ."

Penn looked from Hannah to James and back again. *James? James and Hannah instead of Adam and Hannah?*

She lingered beside him, and Penn wondered just what she would have done had he not interrupted. Unconsciously, he came to attention. His eyes narrowed and his nostrils flared as he inhaled the warm womanly scent of her body. Violets and soap and an essence that was purely personal, purely Hannah.

Then, abruptly, he stepped back, bidding her a clipped good night. If there was a look of hurt in her large gray eyes as she hurried past him, he pretended not to notice.

God, what next? Why couldn't things go along in an orderly fashion the way they were supposed to go? It would be a damned sight easier all around if people would only listen to reason and follow the rules!

Massaging his temples a few hours later, Penn resignedly put on his spectacles. In deference to the infant who had slept through the entire drama, he had brought his journals out to the kitchen table, but somehow, he'd not been able to concentrate.

A few feet away, Hannah cleared the breakfast dishes from the table, banked the fire, and began to make preparations for the next meal. That done, she looked in on James, who had slept soundly for the past six hours, then made a cup of strong tea for Penn, who'd had more than enough coffee, sweetened it liberally, and placed it beside him.

"You're worn to a frazzle," she said, and he looked up at her. In the yellow light of the oil lamp, his eyes were almost black. "Penn, don't you ever sleep?"

"Now'n again, when I've nothing better to do. Don't you?"

"Enough."

He flexed the tired muscles of his shoulders, and Hannah barely restrained herself from touching him. "I should have ordered you to stay abed this morning," he said gruffly.

"I'd not have paid a bit of attention. I'm not one of your surfmen, Captain Warfield, in case it escaped your notice."

His smile was bleak and tired, and Hannah appreciated the effort it must have required. She wondered what he would say if she were to press her thumbs on either side of his neck and commence to knead the tension from his knotted muscles.

"I noticed," Penn said, reaching out to place his callused hand over hers for one brief moment. "Believe me, madam, I noticed."

The very next day, one of the station's herd of banker ponies, some of them only recently captured and barely broken, unaccountably sickened and died. Mal was heartbroken, for he had single-handedly captured the stocky, mahogany-colored stallion that had eluded the men of three stations, and had counted on racing him against Chicamacomico during the summer months, when there was time for such activities.

"I do hope it wasn't a contagious disease," Hannah murmured, and Penn sent her a thoughtful look and ordered a watch to be placed on the herd for the next few days.

Thankfully, none of the others ever sickened.

"Never took to captivity," James said.

"Stallions seldom do," said Penn. "Lot to be said for freedom."

"Proud devil. Would've been a damned shame to geld him. You see the way he took after that young stallion Josie brought in last month? Weren't no question who was in charge."

"Don't make it any easier to be penned up, man nor beast. Mal should've known better than to try and keep two stallions in the same herd. It never works."

Hannah, pegging the wash out behind the boathouse, pondered the exchange. She didn't know much about horses, but she did know about captivity. And she was learning that even freedom could be a two-edged sword. She resolved to double her efforts to ready her new home, despite the difficulties of going back and forth carrying Sara Mirella, hammer and nails, and various cleaning equipment, without Penn's knowledge. It was her intention to move before he had time to line up his arguments. Under her own roof—even if it was only a borrowed one, and leaky at that—she would better be able to stand firm against intimidation.

Two days later, when the weather held out a promise of spring, four of the station's five men were summoned to help Little Kinnakeet rescue the survivors of a packet that had caught fire and come ashore a mile north of the village of Kinnakeet. Hannah was torn between using the opportunity to work on her house and remaining at the station to serve in whatever capacity she could.

She stayed. Six hours later the exhausted men trooped back to the station, disheartened at having been unable to save the captain and one of the enginemen, both of whom had perished when fire had spread to the forward hold, causing an explosion.

Once more in awe of their quiet heroism, Hannah ached to offer comfort. Instead, she offered coffee, a thick, tasty stew, and warmed blankets.

Such rough men they were, living alone without the civilizing effect of a community. Yet they cared so very deeply—Penn perhaps more than any, because of his nature and because his was the responsibility. James was quieter than usual, and even the twins seemed subdued. Hannah had been both surprised and touched the first time she had watched the wild, lovable scamps shed their roles as clowns to step into another, far more serious role. She was coming to understand why Penn insisted on drilling them all so persistently in the little time they had between chores and patrols.

According to his schedule, Mondays were devoted to putting the premises and all equipment in order. Even the privy had to be rendered slick as a pig's whistle, according to Josiah. Tuesdays, if more than three hands were available, they practiced launching the heavy vessel in the surf, never an easy task at the best of times. On Wednesdays they drilled with the signal flags. Hannah had coveted the colorful flags for quilt covers the first time she'd seen them displayed. Especially the diagonally striped one of red and yellow wool bunting, which she'd been informed represented the letter Y in the International Code.

Thursdays they hauled out the rescue gear and practiced firing the Lyle gun, erecting the sand anchor, and setting up the breeches buoy, all with Penn's big patrol watch timing them at every stage of the procedure.

On Fridays they practiced first aid and artificial respiration, with the "victim" usually complaining loudly of bruised and broken ribs. Which left Saturdays for personal chores and Sundays, which were free, save for patrols and the brief service Penn conducted. Extremely brief. Usually no more than three or four mumbled lines, hats off and heads bowed.

Oddly enough, those few muttered words invariably brought tears to Hannah's eyes, and for the life of her, she couldn't say why.

Now fully recovered from her confinement, Hannah was more determined than ever to remove to the house in the village. She was considering asking the twins to get on with patching her new roof one day when Penn rapped on the door and politely requested a moment of her time.

He never came in uninvited these days, not since the time he had barged in while she was nursing Sara Mirella. With a shawl barely covering her breast, she'd been so startled she hadn't had time to react before he had backed out with a flaming face and a mumbled apology. It had taken longer than usual for her milk to come down, her nerves were that tight. The next few times she had seen him, his face had looked suspiciously red.

"Come in," she invited now. She rearranged the bodice of her dress, six years old, remade twice, and now uncomfortably tight across the bosom. She waited for him to enter, then waited for him to speak his piece, after which she fully intended to make a request of her own. It was time.

When he continued to play with Sara, holding his finger out for her to grasp and chuckling when she succeeded, Hannah decided she may as well get it over with.

"Penn, I've been thinking—the *Hamlet*'s come and gone several times. I can't very well stay on here at the station much longer. We've disrupted your lives too long as it is, and I can't tell you how much I appreciate your hospitality, but it just won't do."

"I agree," he said, and her heart sank. A polite protest wouldn't have broken his back, would it? He didn't have to be so blessed agreeable!

"Well, fine," she said with determined brightness. "Then you'll not take it amiss if I ask the boys to help out?"

"Ask away, not that I think they'll be of much use. The preacher's all that's needed so far as I know, and I've already sent for him. We've not been a part of his regular circuit lately, but he sent word through the Signal Office at Hatteras that he'll likely be able to get up this way sometimes before the first of March."

Hannah felt as if the wind had been knocked right out of her sails. "The *preacher*?"

He nodded, his attention still focused on the baby. "I never met the man, but I reckon he can read the words well enough."

"Th-the words?"

"Well, she needs christening, don't she?"

Hannah closed her eyes and prayed for composure. Christening! For a moment she'd thought he meant— "Yes, of course she does. I've even made her a gown from one of my—that is, from some things I had in my trunk. It should do nicely for a christening gown." What would he say if she asked him and his brothers to stand as godfathers? Was five an overabundance?

Penn bent over and lifted the infant up, holding her with practiced ease in his large, work-hardened hands. "Aye, little lady, he'll have his work cut out for him, won't he? Mistress Sara Mirella Matthews

Ballinger, of Paragon Shoals on the Outer Banks of North Carolina. Now, don't that sound impressive for a little lady no bigger'n a pin fish?"

Hannah had to laugh. Her heart swelled at the warmth and kindness she had come to expect from these remarkable men of Paragon Shoals Lifesaving Station.

But all thought of godfathers and christening, much less asking for help in moving to her new home, fled when he said, "Aye, and while the parson's here, we might's well get the wedding behind us. Adam, he's had time enough to get used to the notion. I don't see no point in waiting any longer."

Chapter 7

ONLY by dint of long practice did Hannah hold her peace. Once over the shock of learning that Penn still planned to marry her off to a man who didn't want her any more than she wanted him, she quietly reaffirmed her decision to leave. Time enough to tell him when she was putting on her bonnet to walk out the door.

Her new home was already as clean as soap, water, and willing hands could make it, the bed moved downstairs, the mattress aired and mended. Her biggest remaining problem was the lack of a stove, both for cooking and for heating. There was a small fireplace, but the twins had warned her that as the chimney was cracked in several places, she'd do better not to risk using it.

For herself, she wouldn't have minded the lack of heat so much, but for Sara Mirella's sake she couldn't afford to take chances. The days were still brisk, the nights downright cold. Still, spring couldn't be all that far off.

Hannah had been at the station nearly six weeks. After the baby was born, the men—even Penn, in his rigid, regimented way—had treated her as if she were a rare and delicate flower, and she had taken shameful advantage of it for a little while. The temptation had been too great, for she couldn't recall the last time she had been coddled. Or even the last time she had felt secure.

Hearing their self-conscious whispers when they thought she was asleep and were trying not to wake her, it had been all she could do not to laugh. Or to cry. She's always heard that childbirth had a lingering effect on the emotions, and goodness knows, she was living proof of that!

The day after Sara had been born, she'd overheard Malachi declare that there must be something wrong, for he'd had to cook his own breakfast at four that morning.

Josiah had agreed. According to the green book, he'd said, both mother and foal should be on their feet shortly after the event.

Penn had informed them both that women were different from animals. "They're even different from one another." He'd sounded puzzled, and she'd wondered at it at the time. Captain Pennington Carstairs Warfield—puzzled? Confused?

Not in a million years.

Adam had joined them then. "Reck'n you ought to know, seeing how you're the only man here who's ever been married to one."

Which had set Hannah to wondering about Penn's wife. Mal had mentioned her only once, saying she'd died a long time ago. What had happened to her? What had she been like? What was it about her that had made Penn love her enough to remain single all these years?

It hardly took a genius to figure out what *she* had loved about *him*.

Penn was having problems of his own. It had been a mild winter, with few storms and fewer wrecks, but March was a treacherous month. A man couldn't afford to let down his guard. The greatest threat facing him at the moment, however, was not a natural disaster, but a personal one. Once again, Adam had flat-out refused to marry Hannah and her daughter.

"You've had time enough to come to know her," Penn argued. "She's a fine woman. A man would be proud to claim both females."

"Stow it, Penn. There ain't nothing in the regulations that says a keeper can force a man to marry."

"Well, she can't stay on here thisaway, dammit!" Penn roared. "A single female living with five single men? It ain't decent!"

"There's two females. Hannah and Sara Mirella."

"A baby don't count! If word was to get out, there'd be talk, and trouble always rides the wake of gossip. I got no intention of running afoul of regulations on account of you're too jackass-stubborn to follow orders!"

"Then *you* marry her if you're so all-fired set on keeping her here," Adam shot back.

Even in his shirtsleeves, without a smidge of gold braid in evidence, Penn reeked of authority. Shoulders squared, he allowed his number-one surfman a single moment to dwell on the possible consequences of being hauled up before a review board for insubordination. Then, in a deadly soft voice, he said, "I don't need to remind you, Surfman

Warfield, that Miz Ballinger's reputation is in grave danger here. It's your sworn duty to protect all them that's in danger, so we'll not discuss the matter further. You'll take the third patrol."

"Patrol! But the sky's clear as glass! There ain't no surf to speak of, and James is on the beach tower."

Penn ignored the protest. "Until time to ride out, you can commence picking oakum to calk the number-two boat. When you get done with that, tighten the bolts on the sand anchor. Hereafter, when I issue a direct order, number one, the only thing I want to hear from you is, Aye, sir, and the only thing I want to see is your ass in full retreat. Is that clear?"

Penn's shoulders sagged as his younger brother stalked off, stiff as a six-foot oar. He'll come about, he told himself, wondering just when he had lost control of his station, his crew, and his own well-ordered life.

Dammit, his plan was a sound one! He'd tested it from all angles without finding a single flaw. First settle Adam with a wife—and now a baby. Next, find a woman for James. Someone steady, with a fair amount of keel to her, because James was inclined to be moody. By the end of summer if they all pitched in, they could have the two soundest houses in the village in good repair. Then, in a year or so, he would look for a pair of likely girls for Mal and Josie.

But the marrying couldn't wait much longer. Keeping a woman of any sort in a station house was irregular, but keeping an unmarried woman unchaperoned among five unmarried men would never be tolerated. Regulations were clear regarding morality and propriety, and Penn had always lived by the book.

He stood scowling out through the salt-hazed window until the mewling sound of a hungry baby distracted his attention. The scowl melted from his face like salt in a hard rain.

Once Adam and Hannah married, he reminded himself, they would all be uncles. He'd never been an uncle before. Damned if he weren't liking this plan of his better all the time!

The next day, Adam rode in off patrol with Oleeta perched on the rump of his walleyed bay. They had met the night before, and made love with a fierce kind of desperation. Afterward, lying entwined on an old scrap of canvas, they had talked.

"Penn says she can't stay there alone, but he don't much seem inclined to send her back where he found her. He's bound and determined I'm going to marry her so's she can stay on at the station and cook for us and darn stockings and all, and I ain't been able to get him in a good enough mood to tell him about us."

Some things couldn't wait on a good mood, Oleeta thought despairingly. She knew Adam was brave enough to tackle her paw, yet he lacked the courage to go against his own brother. She, on the other hand, would have far rather risked her luck with Penn than with Paw, who was going to holler the house down and most likely take his belt to her if she didn't move out of the way fast enough.

Sighing, she pressed her face against Adam's naked chest, salty from her tears and his own sweat.

She loved the scent of him, the feel of him—the goodness that was so much a part of him. "Why don't Penn marry her hisself?"

Adam's smooth forehead creased. After a while, he said thoughtfully, "That's what I asked him. Seems reasonable enough, don't it?"

"For a reasonable man, I reck'n it is."

"Maybe it's something to do with Margaret. Penn, he changed considerable after she run off. He weren't sorrowful nor nothing like that, exactly— more like he just pokered up. Sort of closed in on himself. James said it takes something out of a man to have a woman run off on him like that." He shook his head, perplexed. "Whatever she took out of him, I don't reck'n it ever got put back."

Absently, Oleeta stroked the small, flat nipple on Adam's smooth chest until it was no longer flat. It always amazed her, the effect she had on this man who could surely have had any woman he wanted.

But he wanted *her*—plain, ordinary Oleeta Drucker. And she wanted him. And someway, God willing, they were going to be together if they had to run off and marry against both their families. For the sake of the baby they'd made together, they had to.

"Couldn't James marry her?" she ventured.

"Don't see why not. Likes 'er well enough. But first we got to get around Penn. See, he's got this thing about doing everything in order, accordin' to the book. I'm the number one, since I'm older and joined up before Jay did. He's only number two, even though he's smarter'n me and—"

"Don't *say* that! Don't you *never* say bad things about yourself, Adam Warfield! You're as smart as any of 'em! You're the finest man I know, and you're the prettiest man in the world, and that's the Lord's honest truth, so don't you never set yourself back behind James or Penn or no man, y'hear me?"

Adam melted inside like a tallow candle. He wondered how he had ever been lucky enough to latch onto this woman before someone else discovered her. "If you say so, 'Leeta, I reck'n I'll have to believe you. You ain't never lied to me yet."

No, she thought, but there's something I haven't found a way to tell you yet. Something real special. "You're going to have to tell Penn," she whispered, fear clutching her heart like a cold hand. "Real soon, Adam. Promise? I'll talk to Paw as soon as he gets back from Baltimore City if you'll talk to Penn."

Adam shifted uncomfortably on their sandy canvas bed. " 'Leeta ... what if I was to ask you to come stay to the station for a spell to keep Hannah company? It'd give Penn a chance to get to know you."

"He'd never stand for it. He'd send me packing right off."

Adam toyed with a wisp of her silky hair. It was the color of a marsh hen, sort of dark, mingly brown, like her eyes. "No, he wouldn't, neither. Penn said he don't think it's proper for Hannah to stay there without another woman to give her countenance. That's why he's wantin' me to marry her so fast. You could help with the baby and all, too. She's noisy and she wets a lot, and when she was first borned she looked like a baby bird that'd just been hatched out, before it gets its feathers, but she's lookin' better. In a good light, she's even showin' some hair on her head."

"I don't know, Adam, if Paw was to find out—"

"He won't find out if he's off to Baltimore City. By the time he gets back, we might even be married. Penn, he's already sent for the preacher."

In the end, the thought of living under the roof with her lover, even with Hannah and the baby and all his brothers present, won out over Oleeta's doubts. "I'll try to meet you here tomorrow evening. Paw's likely to be gone for at least another week. Maybe more. Chester can stay up to Chic'macomico with Aunt Zenobia for a few days. She don't fuss at him like Paw does."

"Then you'll come home with me?"

"I reckon." She laughed, pressing his hand more tightly against her breast, which in turn set off all sorts of tickly feelings in her private parts. "Meet me here tomorrow, then. I'll bring my comb and my other dress."

Adam hugged her fiercely. "If you ain't here, I'll ride over and fetch you right out o' your house. Ol' Noah, he wouldn't much like that, I reck'n."

When Adam rode up the next day with Oleeta astride the mare's rump, her skimpy bundle rolled up in a scrap of canvas, the tremors that rocked through the station began out by the boathouse, where James and Malachi were greasing the wheels on the beach cart.

"Have you lost your *mind*?" James demanded, smearing a streak of grease across his forehead as he shoved his dark hair off his face.

"Nope. Penn said it weren't respectable for Han-

nah to live here without no other woman, so I
brung one."

"Hey, Oleeta, did your paw let you come?" Malachi was grinning from ear to ear. The beach cart
could wait. He wouldn't miss the look on Penn's
face for anything! All hell was fixing to break loose
in about two minutes, and Josie was still out on the
south patrol.

But the hell that broke loose was of another
kind. When Adam opened the door, the noise
stopped him in his tracks.

"I've done everything I know *how* to keep her
quiet," Hannah shouted over the sound of the baby's howls. "If it upsets you so, then I'm sorry! I'll
remove to the village this very day, stove or no
stove!" She stomped up and down the floor, sand
gritting under the soles of her neat black high-tops,
murmuring distracted there-theres to the wailing,
red-faced infant.

"What stove? What the devil does stoves have to
do with anything? And you're not removing nowhere, madam! Now hand over that baby before
she breaks ever' window light in my station!" Penn
was planted foursquare in the doorway of the keeper's room, his hair standing on end, spectacles riding low on his twice-broken nose, and a spatter of
ink across the front of his white shirt. "Wouldn't
surprise me none if you'd gone and left a pin
a-sticking into her stern!"

James murmured from behind the pair of new
arrivals, "They've been going at it thataway for the
past two hours. Sara didn't do nothing but cry all
night. Hannah's wore to a frazzle trying to keep her
quiet, and Penn's wore to a frazzle trying to figure

out how to get out of this mess he's landed us all in. Welcome, Miss Oleeta. Don't reckon you know nothing about muzzling babies, do you?"

Adam's arm tightened protectively around his woman. God, if he'd tried to pick a worse time, he couldn't have done it in a hundred years. "Don't the green book say nothing about—"

"Adam, don't be an ass. You ever heard a foal carry on the way that young'uns carrying on?"

Oleeta quietly detached herself from Adam's side and met Hannah midway of her course. She held out her arms. "Here, let me have her, ma'am. You look mommicked up something awful."

Hannah stared at the other woman—hardly more than a girl, really. She looked familiar, but at the moment, Hannah wouldn't have cared if she'd had two heads and a ring through her nose. "I don't know what you can do. I've never seen her like this before. It's really not a pin. I looked." Her voice trembled as she fought tears. She had not slept for two nights now. The first night had been bad enough, but by holding her and bouncing her and singing until she near about lost her voice, Hannah had managed to keep from waking the others.

But all day long the poor little mite had been going at it this way, stiff as a board, red as a beet, kicking and howling fit to wake the dead. Even Penn, usually the most tolerant of men where Sara Mirella was concerned, had finally lost patience.

At which time Hannah, exhausted and at her wit's end, had got her back up and vowed to leave that very minute if she had to walk every step of the way, her trunk on her back.

Penn had rudely reminded her that in that case,

she'd be walking on water, which only served to remind her that she had yet to tell him of her plans. Heaven help her when she did that! "I'd as lief try to walk on water as to put up with a brass-bound bully who thinks the world revolves around his precious rules and regulations!"

After that, things had rapidly gone downhill.

"Likely it ain't no more'n wind," Oleeta said now. "She's got a bubble stuck in her craw, and it's a-hurtin' her. Come to 'Leeta, little sugar, we'll bust that wicked ol' thing loose, won't we?"

While the others watched in varying degrees of astonishment, the small, plain girl in the faded calico frock with the patched shawl around her shoulders perched herself on a chair, plopped Sara Mirella across her knees facedown, and commenced to bounce her, whacking her on the back with every jounce.

"She's hitting her, Penn," James whispered fiercely. "Do something!"

The girl ignored him. "Go ahead, little sugar, spit up, 'Leeta don't mind none if you wet her skirts. You just cut loose, y'hear?"

And Sara Mirella did. Before any of the onlookers could react to the rough treatment their beloved Sara Mirella was receiving, the baby broke wind loudly and then fetched up a noisy belch. In the sudden silence, Hannah, Penn, Adam, and Malachi stared, thunderstruck, as a tiny fist gathered up a handful of skirt and stuffed it into a small pink maw.

After that, of course, there was no question of Oleeta's being asked to leave. For the time being, she was given the curtained-off corner that Hannah had occupied before the baby had come, and although Penn glowered even more than usual and didn't address a single word to the newcomer, neither was he openly rude.

Two days later, life at the station was as calm as a saucer of tea, at least on the surface. Hannah welcomed the company of the younger girl, finding her surprisingly mature for her age. The two women divided the tasks, making short work of keeping the men fed and in clean clothing, keeping the ever-present sand that was tracked in every time a door was opened swept out, and keeping Sara Mirella dry, well fed, and content.

The first thing Hannah insisted on was that Oleeta show her how to bring up gas bubbles before they could create too much chaos.

"How'd you know so much about babies?" she asked. They were folding diapers, sheets, and uniform shirts. If the station boasted a flat iron, Hannah had not been able to locate it, but with the wind whipping the wrinkles from every garment pegged to the clothesline, only a stickler would find cause to complain.

"I got a brother. I was five when Chester was born. Maw didn't thrive, so I mostly had the carin' of him."

Hannah murmured something sympathetic about that being a dreadfully young age to be burdened with the care of an infant.

Oleeta shrugged. "I didn't have me no doll. Miz Herbert next door showed me what to do when he was took bad with the colic." She touched her belly, not for the first time, and Hannah wondered absently if she suffered from monthly miseries. Some women did. Hannah never had.

The twins spent a good deal of their spare time on the roof, noisily affecting repairs to the cupola that had been destroyed by lightning shortly before Hannah had arrived. As the weather continued to hold fine, a watch was maintained from the beach tower during the daylight hours, with the beach patrolled only after dark. Several sails were sighted, but no distress signals. Well fed, their housekeeping duties cut to the minimum, the men were able to drill for hours on end, setting up the rescue apparatus with the beach tower serving as a ship's crow's nest and the boathouse ramp as the shore. Hannah and Oleeta watched from the window as full-grown men were hauled a good eight feet off the ground along a slender line, their long legs dangling from holes in what appeered to be a big canvas bucket.

Signal flags were run up rapidly in varying combinations while Penn kept time with his big patrol watch. Once or twice, he even professed himself to be satisfied with the results, at which times the twins would turn a few cartwheels in the sand and call each other extremely crude names.

Occasionally, Hannah and Oleeta helped fold away the signal flags. Hannah still coveted the Y for a quilt cover, for all the good it was ever likely to do her. Except for a solitary crate left behind in a freight office in Raleigh, she had brought all her worldly possessions with her, which hadn't been all that much. Most of her wedding linens had long since been worn out, with an invalid husband to care for. Her sister-in-law, Jarnelle, had begrudged her the use of a single table napkin, and the small sum Hannah had been able to put away had gone to buy cloth to be made into baby clothes.

One way or another, Hannah found herself spending far more time than she should in watching the men drill. They were a striking lot, James with his dark coloring and his narrow, clever face, Adam with his golden good looks, and the irrepressible twins. But one man stood apart from all the rest. Not as handsome, nor even quite as tall as Adam, Penn had a quality that Hannah had never found in any other man. If asked to put a name to it, she would've been stricken dumb, yet even when he was scowling, or squinting, trying to write in his journal without benefit of his spectacles, or lost in the adventures of Captain Ahab or Robinson Crusoe, it was there.

Perhaps she should petition Congress to erect a new lighthouse, warning unwary women away from the keeper of Paragon Shoals Lifesaving Station.

Hannah knew she should be spending every spare minute in the village, putting the finishing touches on her house. Instead, here she was, wasting still another day watching the man standing on the beach, his powerful limbs braced apart, arms crossed over his massive chest. He'd left off his black uniform hat rather than risk having it swept from his head by the frisky March wind, and now sun glinted down on his dark, windblown hair.

She felt a quickening in her loins and turned away. *For shame, Hannah Ballinger! Have you lost*

*all sense of decency? Stove or no stove, the sooner
you get away from this place, the better!*

On the surface, life at the station remained calm
and peaceful. The twins often played music for
them at night, setting several sets of feet to tap-
ping. They never missed an opportunity to play
with Sara Mirella, while James, without making an
issue of it, found numerous ways to be helpful.

But there were undercurrents. Hannah wondered
if she only imagined the constraint between Penn
and Oleeta. Adam had finally lost his sullen look.
He smiled often, and his smiles were downright
breathtaking—at least Oleeta seemed to think so.

Still, something was definitely amiss. The sooner
Hannah could leave, so that life could settle into its
natural pattern at the station, the better it would be
for all concerned.

It occurred to her that she had made that same
resolution more than a few times lately, yet here
she stuck, like a cat at a mousehole. But with work
on the cupola and Penn's constant drilling, not to
mention the watches and patrols, the twins had
found little time to spare for removing a workable
stove from another house into her own.

At least, Hannah thought of it as her own. *Her*
rosebush. *Her* picket fence. *Her* blue bench and
pine bed and cedar trees in the front yard. *Her* basket of wild grasses setting in the ruined fireplace,
making the whole room look more cheerful for all
its lack of furniture.

"I reckon it's like the laws of salvage," Malachi
said when she'd voiced her doubts about moving
in. "First man to get a line onto a deserted vessel

owns salvage rights. Them houses has been deserted for years. If you want to salvage that old place of Miss Marthenia's, I don't reckon nobody's going to try and stop you."

Josiah's offering was somewhat more practical. "Need you a stove, though. Weather'll warm up some come May. You can go on cookin' and eatin' here to the station, but you don't want Sara Mirella to catch a chill."

"Who's going to catch a chill?" Penn demanded, having walked in on the tail end of their conversation. "Dammit, Josie, you're supposed to keep that blasted wood bin filled!"

"But me'n Mal, we split near 'bout a cord just yesterday. There's half a stack right here in the . . ." His freckled face flamed as he slowly came to attention. "Yessir. Sorry, sir. I'll see to it right away."

In his rugged, weathered face, Penn's arctic blue eyes never wavered. Coatless, hatless, his shirt open at the throat, he was totally without a badge of office, yet no one could possibly doubt his authority.

It occurred to Hannah, not for the first time, that strip, stark, jaybird naked, Pennington Warfield could stand under a gutter in a downpour and command the rain to stop and start at his convenience, and it probably would.

Chapter 8

NO one spoke for a moment. Josiah made for the back door with Malachi right on his heels. Mal, with an apologetic glance over his shoulder, snatched two cold biscuits left over from breakfast and then hurried out the door after his twin.

Oleeta went on folding diapers, her dark eyes wary and watchful.

Hannah tapped her foot rapidly on the bare wooden floor. One of these days, she told herself, someone was going to take that bull by the horns and shake him up good and proper. And as no one else seemed inclined to try it, she just might have a go at it, herself!

However, she would just as lief have the bull in a sweeter frame of mind first.

"No one's caught a chill," she said repressively. "If it happens to be a mite cool in here, it's because I damped down the fire to bake that drumfish James caught yesterday, along with two molasses cakes. They do better in a slow oven." Her foot continued to tap. "Now—would you prefer a lemon sauce made without lemons, or a hard sauce made with a dollop of your medicinal brandy?"

It was the most she'd had to say to him since

their shouting match the day Oleeta had arrived.
Guilt vied with the crazy feeling of exhilaration
that invariably afflicted her whenever he was near,
but no hint of either emotion showed on her face.
If there was one thing Hannah had learned to do
well these past five years, it was to hide her feelings.

Penn looked from one woman to the other, his
narrowed eyes mistrustful. Her spine as stiff as a
poker, Hannah stood her ground, arms wrapped
tightly around her body in an effort to contain her
rising temper. She'd never even realized she *had* a
temper. Evidently, it had been quietly growing over
all those years she'd been forced, for poor Edward's
sake, to swallow her temper at Jarnelle's hurtful re-
marks about indigent relatives and the high cost of
charity.

According to her father, temper was one of the
many paving stones on the pathway to hell. Pride
was another, and debt still another.

Hannah conceded that she was as good as lost,
for she had to confess to all three. As reluctant as
she was to admit it, she was indebted to Penn
Warfield, for if it hadn't been for him, she would
now be established, according to Thomas's expressed plans, in the rooms over the carriage house
as a convenience for him and an unpaid servant for
his wife.

The Lord alone knew what would have happened
to Sara Mirella. Thomas had eyed the increasing
bulge under Hannah's skirts with ill-concealed satisfaction, but Hannah knew he'd been thinking of a
son to carry on the Ballinger name, not a mere
daughter.

Jarnelle had known, of course, but rather than throw them all out on the street—Edward, Hannah, and the straying Thomas—it had suited her far better to have one more tool to use in manipulating those around her. Just as it had suited Thomas to endure his wife's meanness in order to remain married to her fortune.

Thanks to Penn Warfield, Hannah had escaped them both. She might have lied by omission—twice. The first time by not mentioning her pregnancy and the second time by allowing the Warfields to believe the baby was her husband's. She had fully planned to confess the truth before she remarried, but as she no longer planned to remarry, she couldn't see what good purpose it would serve.

The thing that continued to puzzle her, however, was why, when Adam had obviously already found a bride to his liking, Penn had gone ahead and placed the advertisement in the Raleigh papers.

Strange man. She would give a pretty penny to know what went on behind that tough, enigmatic face. She knew for a fact that he was an honorable man and a capable one. He was also a very private man. She was coming to suspect that he was also a very lonely one.

"Hard sauce, I reckon."

Startled back to the present, Hannah blinked. "Hard sauce? Oh. For the cake. I promise you, then, I won't use more than a tablespoonful, for I'm sure you have better uses for your brandy."

Penn moved over to where the baby lay on a blanket, kicking and waving her fists while she experimented with various sounds. Her small features were becoming more distinct by the day, her tiny dimpled chin a miniature replica of Hannah's own, and her few wisps of hair more red than brown, although that, as well as the blue of her eyes, could change.

"Reckon most anything's better than lemon sauce made with vinegar," Penn conceded. "What do you think, sweetpea?"

Oleeta went on folding, and Hannah swept her a sidelong glance. The girl had regained some of the color that seemed to leach from her face every morning. This morning again, Hannah had heard the retching from behind the curtained corner. It had been the same for the past three days. Oleeta hadn't mentioned it, and Hannah hadn't wanted to intrude, for she knew firsthand what it was like to have no more privacy than three snails in a single shell.

It might just be the bacon, which was getting a mite rancid. Or perhaps the change in water, although rainwater was rainwater, and the station's water storage was scrupulously maintained.

Still, Hannah suspected it was something quite different. Which meant that the sooner this marriage business could be settled to the satisfaction of all concerned, the better off they all would be.

Except, perhaps, for Penn. She'd heard a fanciful description from the twins of Penn's famous proposal to repopulate and revive an entire village, including schools, churches, and—according to the irrepressible Mal—perhaps even a modest bordello.

Josiah had blushed, poked him hard on the shoulder and told him to batten his hatch, and dismissing the matter as wishful thinking on Malachi's part, Hannah had laughed. The whole thing had sounded so monumentally arrogant. But then, Penn Warfield was a monumentally arrogant man, not that he would ever admit it. No doubt he considered he was merely doing his duty to the best of his ability. Doing it by the book, following every one of his beloved rules and regulations, which seemingly covered everything from the way in which a cork jacket must be folded before it could be stored away, to the right way to sweep a floor. *With* the grain of the wood rather than against it, if you please.

God save them all from such stubborn arrogance!

Then again, when that arrogance was tempered, as it was on rare occasions, with such incredible gentleness—when the rock-ribbed stubbornness slipped now and then to reveal a hint of vulnerability—Hannah sometimes found herself wondering how his Margaret could ever have left him.

At least she did when she wasn't wondering how the woman had stood to live under the same roof for more than a single day.

As the hands on the patrol clock neared the time for the watch to change, Oleeta hastily finished her chore and slipped out the door. Penn, suspicion darkening his face, moved to follow, and Hannah stepped forward to bar his way. Privacy was in short supply at Paragon Shoals Lifesaving Station. Those two sweethearts deserved to be together whenever they could steal a few moments, and if she had anything to say about it—and she intended to say plenty!—their baby was going to be born under far happier circumstances than her own.

Penn gazed down at her, one slashing eyebrow lifted quizzically. "Did you need me for something, Hannah?"

"I just wanted to thank you for inviting Oleeta to stay. She's a dear girl, isn't she? I don't know what I would have done without her these past few days, with the baby so colicky and all." And when he continued to stare at her without saying a word, nervousness unhinged her tongue still further. "Mercy, she can turn a hand to most anything at all! That big fish James caught? It was Oleeta who dressed it. The twins were up on the roof sawing and hammering on the cupola, and I hated to call them down, even though Mal had offered to dress whatever James caught. I declare, that fish had scales as big as a saucer!"

He hadn't moved an inch. "Well, say something, for heaven's sake," she exclaimed. "Don't just stand there like a stump!"

"You did a right fair job of it. I didn't pick out more'n a dozen or so bones."

Hannah closed her eyes and prayed for the grace not to strangle the man on the spot. How could any man be so thoroughly maddening? "Yes, well . . . I'm sorry about the bones," she said tightly. Sorry you didn't choke on one, she added silently.

"Was there something else you wanted to tell me?"

Any person who didn't know him might have mistaken the sparkle in his eyes for amusement. Hannah, however, knew better. He was furious because she'd stopped him from following Oleeta and

keeping her away from Adam. "No. That is, I . . ."
Here's your chance. Go ahead, tell him, you goose!
Tell him you're moving into the rosebush house, and
Adam and Oleeta need to marry as soon as possible.
Tell him he's stubborn, arrogant, and insensitive, and
you've had quite all you can stand of living under his
thumb!

On her blanket, Sara Mirella began to fret. Without a word, Penn crossed to where she lay and
lifted her up in his arms, making soft little sounds
in his throat as if he hadn't another thing on his
mind.

Maddening creature, he wouldn't even give her
the satisfaction of a good fight!

Impatiently, Hannah stalked over to the counter
and began to dump sugar into a bowl for the sauce.
Pounding out the lumps, she screwed up her courage. Someone had to settle this business of Adam
and Oleeta, and if neither of those two had the
gumption to do it, why then, she would do it herself! And then she would tell him she was moving
into the village, and there wasn't a blooming thing
he could do about it, because he didn't own her
and he didn't own the rosebush house, and contrary to what he obviously believed, no one had yet
crowned him king of all creation.

Muttering under her breath, Hannah blew a wisp
of hair off her face and continued to pound away,
too caught up in her own exasperation to hear
Penn's approach.

"If you think I don't know what's going on
around here, madam, you're mistaken," Penn said
softly from three feet behind her.

Startled, Hannah nearly dropped her pestle.

"You do? Oh, well—I mean, that's just fine! Um . . . everything?"

"It's my business to know what goes on."

He was practically breathing down the back of her neck. How could a body be expected to conduct a civil discussion with a great, hulking tyrant hanging over her shoulder so close she could smell the mixture of horse, sweat, and lye soap?

Whomping the pestle against the rock-hard lumps, Hannah declared, "Well, all I can say is, it's about time! A blind man could see they're smitten with one another, and it's not as though she's in any way unsuitable. Oh, she's young, but that'll change soon enough. In fact, I find her remarkably mature for her age."

She didn't once pause in her pounding. Penn, leaning against the wall-mounted locker beside her, continued to watch her small, erect back and the skirts that swished with every stroke of her right fist. So far as he'd been able to tell, she had seven gowns, one for each day of the week and none outstandingly pretty. The best of the lot had been the white one she'd hung on the line to air.

Idly, he wondered how she would look in one of those low-cut frocks like the women at Rosabelle's wore, with her bosom all puffed up and a tantalizing glimpse of garter when her skirts swirled just so.

No. Not Hannah. She didn't need tight corsets and red silk ruffles. What she needed was something gentle, something ladylike—something that would set off her creamy skin and those clear gray eyes with the tantalizing flashes of gold. Like that white gown with the bunched-up fullness at the stern and all those tiny little tucks in the bow ...

Meanwhile, Sara Mirella, blithely unaware of his consequence as a uniformed officer of the U.S. Lifesaving Service, contentedly gummed a black serge lapel.

When no comment was forthcoming, Hannah rested her pestle and sighed, wondering if she'd done more harm than good. Now that he'd broached the matter of Adam and Oleeta, however, she was determined to see it settled before moving on to her own case. Bracing herself, she said, "Penn, they love each other so much, it almost hurts to be near them. There's no reason in the world why they can't marry." When he made a sound like a rusty windlass, she rushed on, knowing that once she lost her momentum, she might never regain it. "If you're thinking of my feelings in the matter—that is, if you're embarrassed about bringing me all the way out here to marry the poor boy, and him changing his mind, then please don't give it another thought. Truth to tell, I needed to get away far more than I needed a husband. Certainly no woman needs a husband who doesn't want her. I—I'll pay you back the fare, I promise."

Just how, she didn't know, but she silently vowed to repay every penny he had spent on her behalf.

"Madam, you haven't a notion of what you're talking about."

Hannah made the mistake of looking directly at him then, only to wish she hadn't. His eyes had turned glacial again, and her heart sank. Those poor children! No wonder they were so miserable, if this was what they'd been up against.

Not that Adam was a child. He was three years older than her own twenty-four, but there was a childlike quality about him that Hannah found alternately endearing and exasperating.

"Penn, she loves him, and it's obvious that he's dotty over her. If you ask me, I think they bring out the best in each other."

"No one asked you, madam, and I'll thank you to quit meddling in matters that don't concern you. Kindly remember that you're here on sufferance."

Her jaw dropped. *"Sufferance?"*

It was the wrong word to use on a woman who had truly lived on the sufferance of someone else for five indescribably miserable years. Hannah, still holding the mixing bowl, slammed it down hard, scattering grains of sugar across the lye-scrubbed surface of the countertop. "Allow me to remind you, sir," she said through clenched jaws, "that I am here by your invitation!"

"May I remind *you*, madam, that that invitation was issued to one Hannah Ballinger, childless widow?"

"You didn't say one blooming thing about childless, and besides I *was* a childless widow, at the time."

"Don't split hairs. You deliberately set out to deceive me!"

"What I'd *like* to split is *your* hair! *And* your skull, and everything else, right down to that insufferably smug look you wear like it was part of your blasted uniform!"

Penn launched himself away from the locker, temper blazing up to meet her own. Step by step, he forced her against the counter's edge. "There! I knew you'd show your true colors sooner or later! Widowed preacher's daughter, my eye! More likely you're nothing but a lightskirt who got herself into a fix she couldn't get out of!"

"Oh, and you'd know all about lightskirts, wouldn't you? Don't think I haven't heard about Rosabelle's! I believe you're said to hold some kind of a record there for—"

Ears flaming, Penn shouted her down. "Stow that bilge, madam! I'll keelhaul those two tattletales! I'll tie 'em to the tower by their blasted ears! That's no way for a lady to be talking!"

"A lady?" she drawled with exaggerated innocence. "Then you do admit there's a lady present?"

By now, Penn's face matched his ears. "I was referring to your daughter, madam. Leastwise, she's innocent in all this."

"And stop calling me madam!" Hannah yelled. "You make it sound like an insult!"

"If I were of a mind to insult you, *madam*, you'd damned well know it!"

They stood toe-to-toe, two rigid bodies braced for a fight, two pairs of eyes flashing danger signals. Hannah's nostrils flared as she inhaled the heady essence of male sweat and freshly washed woolens. Desperately, she tried to recall her father's words about loving one's enemy, turning one's other cheek, forgiving assorted trespasses, and the promised inheritance of the meek.

Unfortunately, her brain could not get past the business of loving one's enemy and refused to budge. Fists knotted at her sides, she tried desperately to control the trembling of her limbs. Thank goodness for all her layers of petticoats. If the wretch ever discovered the effect he had on her, she would die of shame!

And he would die laughing.

"Hannah," Penn said hoarsely. "Do you do it to me deliberately? Does it pleasure you to see just how far you can shove a man without running aground?"

Her mouth felt dry. Her palms were damp. She couldn't have spoken if her life depended on it.

"I'm warning you, woman, we're already in shoaly waters. Don't push me too far."

If a bolt of white-hot lightning had sizzled all the way down to the gritty soles of her shoes, she probably wouldn't have noticed a thing. But if Penn had dared to lay a finger on her at that moment, she would have gone up in a shower of sparks.

Or worse, melted all over him like candle wax.

And heaven help her, she wished he would!

They were so close she could feel his warm breath. The heated scent of his body rose around her, enclosing her like a silent, irresistible invitation. Unconsciously, Hannah tilted her face, her lips parting as her eyelids began to sink under their own unbearable weight. She could almost taste him. Drowning in sensations she had never before dreamed of, much less experienced, she swayed forward. His hand touched her back just as her left breast encountered something warm and soft and—

Soft?

The instant before Penn accepted her unspoken invitation, Sara Mirella let out a howl. He jumped back, clutching the baby to his chest. Hannah, stricken with embarrassment and guilt, managed to bury both under a guise of maternal solicitude. Dear Lord, she'd nearly squashed her own child in her rush to throw herself into the arms of a man, with poor Edward barely cold in his grave!

Snatching the infant from him, she whirled away, trying desperately to hide something that felt suspiciously like disappointment.

Face the color of copper paint, Penn spun on his heel and stalked across the room. Every pot and pan on the wall rattled as he slammed out the door.

Moments later Hannah sank down onto the nearest chair, clutching her squirming baby against her bosom as if for protection. Oh, my mercy, what had come over her? What did it all mean?

More to the point, how did one make it stop?

That evening after supper, James offered to rock the baby to sleep for her. As a surprise, he had retrieved a broken rocking chair from one of the houses and patched it up, crudely but effectively. James was not the station's finest carpenter.

What he was, Hannah told herself as she took her plate and fork to the sink, was a very dear friend who, in his own quiet way, saw far more than was comfortable. She had a feeling he hadn't missed the excessive politeness she and Penn had exhibited toward one another for the remainder of the day. No doubt he had drawn his own conclusions, and Hannah didn't even want to guess what those might be.

"Let me give her her supper and change her into her nightclothes, and then you can take her while I wash up the supper things," she said.

"Oleeta can do the dishes," James offered.

"Oh, but 'Leeta and me, we was fixin' to mend that section of fence where that new sorrel broke through," said Adam.

"In the dark?"

"It ain't dark yet. 'Sides, it don't take much light to bend on a section of bobwire," Adam said defensively. It was obvious to Hannah, at least, that mending the fence wasn't all he had in mind.

Oleeta opened her mouth and then shut it again. She didn't have a whole lot to say when Penn was nearby, but Hannah suspected that if it ever came down to a fight for her Adam, she would be a real tiger.

Penn gave no indication of having heard a word spoken. Face as hard as a knot on an oak tree, he shoved back his chair, slammed his dishes down onto the counter beside the galvanized sink, and stalked out the back door.

For a long time, no one spoke. Then James said mildly, "Reckon he wants to take a lookout from the tower before dark. Evening patrol's overdue."

Adam stood and drew out Oleeta's chair, and Hannah, watching the tender way he managed to touch her in the process, felt an uncomfortable thickness in her throat. Their love was so vivid it almost hurt to watch. As the couple left, she met James's eyes.

He nodded. "Trouble. Don't know as there's much to do about it, though."

"Why?" Hannah began covering the food. The twins would ride in starved any minute now. They could never wait until she reheated anything. "For the life of me, I can't understand why Penn's so set against the match."

"Old grudge. Pa warned him off the Druckers last time he come home before his ship went down off Jamaica. Penn never said why, nor I don't guess Pa did much explaining. Pa weren't big on explaining."

"A grudge! You mean a family feud? Mercy, there's hardly enough people here on the Banks for a real feud, is there?"

"Not in Paragon—leastways, not anymore. Plenty to the no'th'ard, more to the so'th'ard, most of 'em kin to Warfields or Druckers or both. Reck'n maybe a hundred years ago, some Drucker set his fence a foot or two over onto Warfield land, accidental like—or maybe some Warfield took up oysters from a Drucker's bed, all unintentional. Whatever started it, seems like we're bound to hang onto the grudge, even if none of us knows why no more. Family tradition."

"Oh, for heaven's sake, as if we poor mortals didn't have troubles enough." Hannah snorted her impatience. "I'll go give Sara Mirella her supper if you'll cover the bread and set that ham back on the warming shelf. The boys'll be in any minute now, hungry enough to eat their boots right down to the soles and then gnaw the nails."

James grinned. "You're commencing to sound just like you was Banks borned, you know that?"

Hannah shook her head, laughing. He was right.

She was halfway across the room to the keeper's office when the outside door burst open. Adam, his face looking remarkably like Penn's in the fast fading light slanting through the tall windows, gasped out, "Flare to the so'th'ard, 'bout a mile, mile 'n' a half down. I'll raise Little Kinnakeet, tell 'em we're on the way."

James was on his feet before Hannah could even draw in a breath. "Better let Chic'macomico know we won't be patrolling to the no'thard for a spell."

"Done. You go help Penn roll out and hitch up, I'll be out directly!"

The change that came over these rough men in times of emergency was electric. Hannah didn't even pause. Sara Mirella's supper could wait. Hannah had been at the station long enough to know that all hands, even inexperienced ones, were needed in an emergency. "I'll ready the first-aid box and get out the big coffeepot. Shall I start setting up cots, or wait?"

"Wait," said James. He was already ringing up the stations to the north and south. A few terse words were barked into the receiver before he slammed it onto the hook on the wall-mounted, golden oak box and strode toward the keeper's room.

"James, can I get something for you?" Hannah asked anxiously.

He shook his head, and then Penn came in with Adam on his heels, and both men made directly for the keeper's room. Hannah followed and stood hesitantly outside the door, feeling helpless. Surely they didn't have to write up a rescue *before* the fact!

While she was still dithering, the three men emerged, brushing past her without a word, their official business, whatever it had been, evidently completed.

And then they were gone.

The baby, upset by all the commotion, began to

cry in earnest, and Hannah decided she may as well feed her now and be done with it, for she would no doubt be far busier later.

Wishing she could watch the activity outside, if not actually participate, she proceeded to nurse her greedy daughter, emptying first one breast and then the other. Sara Mirella seemed determined to make up for her meager birth weight in the shortest time possible.

By the time she was done, Hannah found herself somewhat calmer. Nursing usually had that effect on her. It was as she was buttoning up her dress that her gaze was drawn to the letter box on Penn's desk, which for once was slightly askew. A slip of paper projected from under the lid, as if it had been caught when the box was hastily shut. The inkwell had been left open, and one of the pens had fallen to the floor.

Absently, she picked it up and replaced it. Penn was usually so meticulous, adhering strictly to the old adage of a place for everything and everything in its place. Under the circumstances, she supposed, it was no wonder he had left his desk in something of a mess. By the time he finished documenting the night's events, it would no doubt be in an even greater mess.

Meanwhile, outside, Oleeta helped roll the heavy beach cart down the ramp, working shoulder to shoulder with Penn while James and Adam raced for the paddock. In an emergency, old enmities were evidently forgotten. Adam got a line on Aristotle, led him out and backed him up to the beach cart, and James completed hitching him up while Adam hurried back for the boat carriage team. Some stations used manpower to pull carts, but being perennially shorthanded, the Warfields had been forced to adopt other means.

They moved like clockwork, choreographed by years of practice.

Hannah finished buttoning her gown and, holding a drowsy Sara Mirella in her arms, hurried to watch from the door. Grimly she ignored the small voice that whispered softly of danger, of lives risked, lives saved—and lives lost.

Adam led out two of the calmer geldings and Oleeta held them steady while the men wheeled the lifeboat carriage into position. The years of constant drilling made the task look deceptively easy, but Hannah wasn't fooled. It was backbreaking work at the best of times. At the worst . . .

But she refused to think about the worst.

James drove the beach cart, Adam the boat carriage, while Penn mounted Pegasus and galloped on ahead. Silently, Oleeta came and stood in the doorway with Hannah. Just as the last rays of coppery light faded from the western sky, the men disappeared over the dunes.

"How did you know what to do?" Hannah asked, almost jealous because the younger girl had been able to help.

"Older brother in the service. Drowned two year ago. Two cousins there to Chic'macomico station. Reck'n I growed up with it."

"They need more men."

"Most men comes from the villages closest the stations. Paragon ain't got no more men."

Hannah sighed. There was that, of course. Suddenly, Penn's determination to rebuild an entire community didn't seem quite so absurd.

"Tide's out. That's a blessing," Oleeta observed after a while.

Hannah looked at her questioningly.

"Long's they can ride the wash, they'll not likely get bogged down too bad. There's gravel patches to the north, but Adam says the beach betwixt here'n Little Kinnakeet's been real good ever since that last nor'easter."

"By good, you mean hard enough to drive on, I take it?"

Oleeta nodded, still staring at the thick gray dusk that had swallowed up the crew of lifesavers. "Leastwise, on the trip south. Storm's fixin' to cut loose 'fore long, though. Them breakers is all churnin' up ever' whichaway."

The night was endless. Hannah fed Sara Mirella again and put her down to sleep. Before turning down the lamp, she cleaned the pens and stoppered the inkwell, then lifted the lid of Penn's box of official papers to slip the loose pages inside. There were three scraps, each torn from a single sheet of paper. No more than two lines were written on each—two lines easily, if unintentionally, read at a glance.

"I, Pennington Warfield, bequeath all my worldly possessions to Sara Mirella Matthews Ballinger, daughter of Hannah Ballinger."

"Oh, no. Oh, God, no!" Hannah whispered. Pain stabbed her so fiercely she closed her eyes, but not before she had seen that James had made a similar bequest, leaving his possessions to both her and her daughter, to be shared equally.

She closed her eyes without attempting to make heads nor tails of Adam's scrawl, but not before she saw the large letter O.

Dear God, keep them safe, for I love them all so dearly!

Hannah made coffee while Oleeta started a pot of soup. Both women chopped onions, which was a perfect excuse to shed a few tears. Hannah cut the bone from the ham and added it to the pot.

"Saw two more flares while you was in settlin' the baby," Oleeta said. "Looked to be more'n half-way down to Little Kinnakeet."

"Josiah should have been in off patrol before now."

"Prob'ly saw the flares when he was headed back and kept right on a-goin'. South patrol from Chic'macomico'll know to cover for him."

"Couldn't we call somewhere and find out what's happened?"

"Penn'd tie my innards in a hard knot if I was to use his lines. We ain't official."

"We're the only ones at the station. Surely that gives us some official standing?"

"You want to tackle it, you go right on ahead. Me, I got trouble aplenty heaped on my plate."

Hannah dug out a basket of mending. She couldn't halfway see without her glasses at night, but anything was better than sitting around fretting about what might be happening outside.

Waiting. Sometimes it seemed as if she'd spent half her life waiting. Waiting to grow up, waiting for Edward to notice her, waiting until her wedding day, and then . . .

She sighed, slipped the darning gourd inside one of James's woolen stockings and stared at the dark window again. They'd been gone for hours. The sea was sounding rougher by the minute, even though a bank of fog had moved in over the water and a light rain had commenced to fall.

"By trouble," she said, forcing her thoughts back inside the security of the station house, "I suppose you mean Penn's not wanting you and Adam to marry. Perhaps you should tell him about the baby. May as well bring it out into the open. Soonest tended, soonest mended."

There followed a long silence, and then, "I 'spected you knew," the younger woman said quietly. It was a trait she had, one that Hannah had come to admire—that quality of calmness. "Adam, he don't even know yet. It'd only worry him, and I'm a sight better at worryin' than he is."

A gust of wind blew something against the side of the house. At the clattering sound, Hannah's eyes widened.

"Lid blowed off'n the slop jar I set out on the porch."

"Oh. If it's any comfort to you, the sickness probably won't last much longer."

Oleeta smiled, her thin, olive-skinned face almost pretty in the lamplight. "I'll take most any comfort I can get, thank ye, ma'am."

Searching for something more to say to fill the uneasy silence, Hannah asked whether she wanted a boy or a girl.

"It don't make me a speck o' difference. Reck'n a

boy'd be less trouble, though. If I was to have a
girl, and she was to look like Adam, we'd have ever'
boy from Currituck to Core Sound a-snortin'
around, kickin' up sand a few years down the road.
Adam, he's some pretty, ain't he?"

Laughing, Hannah agreed that Adam was indeed
"some pretty." They fell silent again, Hannah
squinting over James's stocking, Oleeta sitting quietly with her hands folded in her lap. After what
seemed hours, the wind dropped off, but the rain
continued to fall and the pounding surf was like
constant thunder. Even without the rain or the
drifting patches of fog, the darkness was impene-
trable.

Now and then Hannah rose and crossed to the
doorway, gazing toward the south. "They'll come
when they come," Oleeta said calmly. "Worryin'
don't help none. Prayin' might."

And so they prayed, each in her own way, each
for all the lives at risk, and more particularly for
one special man.

The fog was a problem. The vessel, a small
schooner-rigged screw-steamer, had run aground a
mile and a half south of Paragon Shoals. Malachi
had spotted her just before dark and set off a flare,
summoning aid from both Paragon and Little
Kinnakeet, and letting the steamer know she'd
been sighted.

He'd stayed on position, knowing that help
would soon be on the way and he would be needed
to direct the men to where the ship had last been
sighted. The combination of increasing darkness,
fog, and drizzle had swiftly cut visibility to no more

than a few yards, and that only intermittent. Fifteen minutes later, he fired off another flare. And
then one more after another quarter hour had
passed. Still no sign of the wagons, but he never
doubted that help was on the way.

The ship had answered his first flare with a blast
from her steam whistle, but that had been nearly
three-quarters of an hour ago. For all he knew, she
could be broken apart by now.

"God help the poor devils," Malachi muttered,
straining in vain to see through the darkness. He
had thrown off his coat and was untying his boots,
ready to attempt to swim out and try to locate the
wreck in the darkness and bring a line back to
shore, when he spotted the lanterns bobbing down
the beach.

Almost before the wheels had stopped rolling,
Penn had the Lyle gun set up. He barely had
enough crew to man his boat, much less launch it.
"Here comes Hooper's crew now! Adam, James, get
the sand anchor set up!"

"Light offshore!" James yelled, and sure enough,
flickering through the thick darkness, there was a
feeble glow.

"Throw me that quoin!" He jacked the gun into
position, knowing that every minute saved could
mean a life spared.

The men worked with quiet efficiency. The crew
from Little Kinnakeet Station arrived, and while
James and Adam set up the sand anchor, Penn and
Mal helped launch Kinnakeet's lifeboat in the angry
surf.

"Sand anchor all secure!" Adam shouted.

The crew from Paragon readied the rescue gear

for the breeches buoy as Penn took aim and fired at the flickering target. The ship's lantern could be doused at any moment, and once they lost sight of it, they might fire off lines for a year without striking a target.

Line whistled off the faking box, and Penn prayed without even being aware of it. The lantern from Kinnakeet's lifeboat bobbed in the heaving waters. They'd made it out past the breakers, but they still had a ways to go.

And then the boat's lantern was doused. "Boat over!" someone yelled, just as Mal shouted, "Limp line!"

The Lyle gun's shot line had fallen short.

"Wind's gusting! Wait for a lull!"

"Fetch me another box!" Penn shouted, and another faking box was hastily set into place, the spindles removed and the gun readied to fire again.

Offshore, the ship's lantern flickered off, but was quickly relighted. Someone cried out that the lifeboat was righted again.

Penn fired once more, and this time the projectile found its mark. Someone aboard the stricken steamer located the weight and made the line fast to the rigging. Whether or not they'd heard the firing of the gun over the roar of the seas, they had seen the torches and known to keep alert for the line.

After that, all three crews worked steadily, two from the shore and one aboard the ship. Just as the lifeboat headed back with the first load of survivors, Penn's shot line was secured. Once the tail block and whip were in operation, a hawser was bent on and hauled out to the wreck.

Five men were brought ashore by breeches buoy. The lifeboat went out again, but capsized twice in the rough seas before it could get near enough to effect a rescue.

The score, when the ship finally began to break up in the pounding seas just before daylight, was eleven rescued, four lost. The four had been lost when they'd run aground, crushed beneath a falling stack.

Silently, the two crews headed back to their respective stations. Kinnakeet took the survivors, as it had brought an additional wagon.

Malachi, by now numb with exhaustion, whistled up his mount and with the help of Josiah, who had joined them sometime during the night, climbed aboard and immediately flopped forward, his face buried in the shaggy mane. The two youngest members of the crew rode on ahead, leaving James to bring the cart and Adam the boat carriage.

Penn was the last to leave the scene, but finally there was no more to be done. Wearily, he slung a long leg over the gelding's back, allowing the reins to fall slack. Pegasus knew the drill by heart. To the north would be fresh water, a dry stall, and a rack of sweet, dried grass.

Gradually the silhouette of the station house, with its nearly completed and only slightly crooked cupola, emerged against the brightening eastern sky. Another day was dawning. Eleven lives had been saved. Penn offered up a tired prayer for the four lives lost and a word of thanks for the safety of his crew and Captain Hooper's.

And then his thoughts turned to Hannah. He was headed back in after a night spent doing what he'd done so many times over the course of his career. Nothing out of the ordinary. It was only what he got paid to do.

But somehow, this time it felt different. For the first time in a long time, he felt as if he were going home.

Chapter 9

THE lines of strain were clear on Hannah's pale face by the time the men began to arrive. First the twins, both sound of limb, but half asleep. Thank God, she thought fervently, even as her gaze flew beyond their two drooping red heads to the dark figure on the big roan gelding.

He was safe. He was back where he belonged. Hannah breathed another silent, heartfelt prayer of thanks. Wordlessly, she stepped back inside the door, beckoning them all in to the hot meal and dry beds that were waiting. If the cart was bringing survivors, she was ready for them, as well. Being a country preacher's daughter was not so very different from being a part of a lifesaving station, after all.

The twins slid off their mounts, their movements and gestures mirror images, and began leading the tired beach ponies toward the paddock. Before they reached the gate, Penn rode in. Dismounting, he gathered up their reins along with his own and nodded toward the station house. "Run along inside, boys, you've done a good night's work a'ready."

High praise from a man not given to such,

thought Hannah as she welcomed the two youngest Warfields. They were both pale with exhaustion, their freckles standing out like rust specks on white linen.

"Are you all right?" she asked anxiously once they were inside, but she lingered at the door, her gaze drawn back to where Penn was looking after the three tired horses.

At that moment, James and Adam crested the dunes with the cart and boat carriage. Hannah's hand flew to cover her mouth. No survivors, then. Dear Lord—!

"What is it? Is it Adam?" Oleeta cried. Rather than linger at the door, her heart in her eyes, she sadly feared, Hannah nodded and crossed to the stove, where she began dipping up large bowls of steaming soup. "He's fine, Oleeta," she said, but the girl was gone.

"Kinnakeet took the survivors," said Mal. "We didn't lose none, but four was lost when she run aground." He sighed, and the sound was oddly heart wrenching from a boy she had come to look on as a clown, a merry scamp.

"Oh." Forcing a smile, she said, "Well . . . we've gallons of soup made. You'll grow tired of it before it's gone, I'm afraid. I, ah—I don't suppose anyone's hungry now?" It was all she could do not to gather the pair of them onto her lap and comfort them the same way she comforted Sara Mirella. They were little more than children, entirely too young to lead such dangerous lives.

"Ain't tired of it yet, though," Josiah said with an echo of his usual impishness. "Ma'am, I'm plumb starved!"

"Nearly 'bout wore out, too," said Malachi. He kicked off his wet sandy boots and peeled off stockings in a similar condition, then leaned back against the wall and closed his eyes. His skinny legs were sprawled out halfway across the narrow space between table and wall, his toes all puckery and pale.

Poor babies, Hannah thought as she placed two steaming bowls of the thick bean and ham-bone soup on the table. If they were my sons—

Sons! The fortune-teller had said on that June afternoon nearly a decade ago that her whole life would be changed by sons. She hadn't said *whose* sons.

"Don't know whether to eat it or bathe in it," Josie quipped, making them all laugh. Oleeta came back inside, her face flushed, and began serving up corn bread while Hannah refilled the molasses pitcher, both their eyes straying again and again to the door.

"They'll be in directly," said Malachi, the words muffled by the thick chunk of bread he'd just bit off.

"Don't talk wi' yer mouth full, peabrain." Josiah had revived enough to come to the table.

"Better'n talkin' wi' yer brainbox empty, fartface."

One twin grabbed the basket of bread, dragging it closer, and the other snatched away the molasses pitcher. Hannah glanced at Oleeta and shook her head ruefully, and then a gust of warm, damp air blew inside as the door opened to admit the three elder Warfields.

With her heart tripping crazily, Hannah sought

out Penn. Their eyes collided. Dimly, she was aware of the others, aware that Adam had walked directly into Oleeta's outstretched arms, neither of them uttering a word. It was as if the rest of the world was suddenly lost in a fog bank, and she was drowning in the blue depths of Penn's very soul.

Dear Lord, she thought, what had he been through? He was soaking wet, and pale as a ghost. His hair hung in thick, wet clumps, yet the rain had ceased hours before. Which meant that he'd had to—

She didn't want to think about what it meant. She most definitely didn't want to dwell on the implications of those three telling scraps of paper they had left behind. He was home safe now, and that was all that mattered. His red-rimmed eyes were dark with exhaustion, he smelled of sweat and horse and brine, and it was all she could do not to throw herself into his arms and stay there forever.

And then, somehow, James was standing between them, his brown eyes burning intensely in his narrow face. Smiling his rare, sweet smile, he said, "Makes a right nice change to have a hot breakfast waiting, Hannah. I thank you kindly."

Tears welled in her eyes and she ruthlessly blinked them back. "Get out of those wet clothes before you catch your death, every last one of you," she scolded, her voice more than a little unsteady.

"Yes, ma'am." James's smile faded, and for an instant, he reminded her of—

Who? Someone she had once known, probably. With her emotions still seesawing all over the place, it was a wonder she wasn't seeing faces in every knothole on the wall!

Adam and Oleeta drew apart slowly, and Penn, shucking off his big boots, grunted. Hannah preferred not to take it as a comment. Oleeta dished up three more bowls of soup while Hannah refilled the pitcher, her skirts swishing in a sudden excess of energy.

"Drenched to the skin, every last one of you," she muttered. "Catch your death of cold, see if you don't! And would you look at all that sand! My knuckles will be rubbed raw before I'm done with all that washing, I can tell you right—"

"You've not been asked to do our wash, madam," Penn said tiredly. "I'll thank you to—"

"Oh, hush up!" She slammed the big stoneware pitcher down on the table hard enough to set the cutlery to dancing. What did she care for her wretched knuckles, anyway? For the sake of having them all home safe again she would cheerfully have scrubbed every wet, sandy rag they possessed until it fell apart in her hands!

After a quick, silent meal, Penn stalked off to his office, barking an order over his shoulder for the twins to hit the cots, right smartlike. "Adam, man the tower. Thank God, it's clear enough, we won't have to ride patrol today, but keep a sharp lookout for bodies coming ashore."

"Way the tide's running, they'll likely fetch up halfway to Hatteras Inlet if they weren't trapped in the rigging," James said as he pushed back his chair and placed his dishes in the sink.

"Start getting the gear back in commission, I'll be out directly."

Hannah watched him disappear into his office and close the door behind him. She thought of those three wills and took a single step to follow, and then stopped. She couldn't. If she so much as looked at him right now, she might do something that would not only rob her of every vestige of pride, but would probably jeopardize her whole future, as well.

Inside the small room, Penn stared down at the sleeping infant. His wide shoulders sagged, but the color had begun to return to his face. "Sleep safe, little sweetpea," he whispered. He closed his eyes for a moment, half in prayer, half in weariness. When he began to sway on his feet, he opened his eyes again, braced his shoulders, and went out to ready the lifeboat and beach cart for the next time of need.

Once again, Hannah was forced to put off her plans to move. There was still the stove to be dealt with, and her roof leaked rather badly, despite the twins' efforts. Soon, though, she promised herself. Once the weather warmed up, it would be easier, and surely spring was almost here. At home, the willows would be showing green, the tulips budding, and the dogwood blossoms ready to burst.

Lately, it seemed that whenever she glanced up from her work, James was nearby. He smiled often, and James was not overly given to smiling. He passed the time of day whenever they met, talking about the baby, about the weather—about the vast improvement in rations since Hannah had come to live with them—and James had never been given to small talk.

Simple friendship was an element that had long been absent from Hannah's life. After Edward's accident, when they'd been forced to move from Kernersville to Raleigh to live with Thomas and Jarnelle, she had left behind all that was dear and familiar, and in particular, her many friends. Only now was she coming to realize how much she had missed it all. For the past five years she had been too busy even to think of anything but getting through another day.

Friends. James, unlike the ebullient twins, was not gregarious by nature, which made his overtures all the more precious. Malachi and Josiah had accepted her right off, had even accepted her pregnancy without comment. Even Adam, once she'd learned to make allowances for his half-sullen, half-shy reticence, had not been openly unfriendly so long as Penn wasn't trying to push her into his arms.

An unspoken affinity had grown between Hannah and Oleeta during the brief time the younger woman had been at the station. They had worked well together once Oleeta understood that despite Penn's original plans, Hannah was no threat to her relationship with Adam.

Just the opposite, in fact. Hannah was securely in their corner, for reasons of her own. With Adam and Oleeta married and living in the village there would be all the more reason for Hannah's presence there. Two women, living as neighbors, would be company for each other while the men were at work. Not to mention the fact that Penn's ambitious plan to repopulate the community of Paragon Shoals would be that much closer to fruition.

Hannah sighed, folded the last napkin and added it to the stack on the bed. So far she had found neither the courage nor the right moment to announce her plans. She had hoped to be under her own roof by now, but the twins had suddenly discovered the urgency of finishing the cupola watchtower. Surely in a day or so they would get on with moving her stove and patching her still leaking roof. Surely in a day or so . . .

In a day or so, Hannah promised herself, she would screw up her courage to tell Penn. No more had been said about the preacher marrying her to Adam when he came to christen the baby, which was a good sign. She wished she could consider it a victory, but it was at best a stalemate.

Stubborn, maddening man! He had them all jumping to his tune!

Oh, he was gentle enough with Sara Mirella, but where Hannah was concerned, they couldn't agree on a solitary thing. If she said white, he said black. If she said hot, he said cold.

The windows were a perfect example. "We wash our glass with vinegar," he had told her one day recently when she'd spent the entire morning polishing every pane of glass in the station.

"Oh? Personally, I find that ammonia works better." He would have to catch her looking her worst! Her hair was tumbling halfway down her back and her dress was baggy enough to house a troop of jugglers.

"You've no call to be washing windows at all. They're scheduled to be washed down the last day of every month."

"What if I should want to see out in the meantime? The salt clouds them up faster than I can wash them."

"Then look out the blasted door, madam! Just don't let me see you climbing up on a chair to reach a window again, is that clear?"

"Clearer than your windows, at least."

They had glared at one another, and Hannah had wondered if anger was supposed to make a body feel all bubbly and tingly inside. Funny, she couldn't remember reacting that way before.

Then there was the matter of the blankets. "We air out blankets in May and November, madam."

"But they stink *now*."

"Wool smells like sheep, madam, and sheep don't smell like roses!"

"They might, if you sunned them occasionally," Hannah retorted sharply. She had just finished hanging out eight musty woolen blankets, pegging three to the lines that ran up the sides of the beach tower when she ran out of clothesline.

"Then hang the damned things on the other side of the house, but keep 'em off my blasted flagpole! You'll have every ship on the Eastern Seaboard piling up on the shore, trying to read your signals!"

"Your blankets are gray. Your signal flags are red, yellow, blue, and white. I assure you, any man with two eyes and half a brain can tell the difference."

"And I assure *you*, madam, that—"

"What's more," she interrupted, "if you saw fit to run another clothesline across the yard, I wouldn't have to resort to using your silly old flagpole!"

"If I strung up one more line around here, *madam*, I'd likely break my fool neck on the blasted thing! Place's already got more lines than a cat's cradle!"

"Can I help it if there's more wash than there are clotheslines?"

"You can train that young'un of yours properly! Damned britches are scuppers awash every time I go to pick her up!"

Which was so profoundly unfair that even Penn had the grace to blush.

With spring officially arrived, the weather holding fair, and the new, only slightly crooked, cupola in service, watch was kept from atop the station, with beach patrols maintained only from dusk until dawn unless visibility worsened.

Even so, it seemed to Hannah that Penn was working harder than ever, what with his constant drills, his endless record-keeping, and his persistent policing of every corner of his domain. Which made her more determined than ever to leave every square inch of the station in pristine condition when she moved to the village. It was the least she could do in return for the Warfields' hospitality.

She washed every day, for there were always linens and baby things, despite the fact that Penn refused to allow her to touch a single garment of his. He laundered his own uniforms, woolens and all. Lacking a flat iron, which Malachi had borrowed, according to Josiah, to anchor a muskrat trap in the creek, he smoothed them beneath his mattress with the creases more or less in place, and heaven help anyone who dared criticize the results.

Whenever she could steal a few hours, Hannah walked to the village, carrying Sara Mirella on her hip, to wander through her new house and gloat. Her very own roof, be it leaky or not. Her very own rosebush, even now putting out buds. Her very own bed, her own blue bench, and her very own crockery, scavenged by the enterprising Malachi from among the other houses.

Amazing progress, when she recalled the Hannah Ballinger who had warily stepped ashore only a few months before, half sick, fearful of the future and even more fearful of the past. She'd been greeted by a cold rain, a deserted village, and three stern-faced men in black, each one of whom had looked as if their face would crack wide open if they attempted a smile.

It had been almost more than she could deal with, having only just buried her husband. But she'd dealt with it. Lacking a choice, she had dealt far better than she would have dreamed possible, and gradually she had come to see the island as bleak, but not necessarily unfriendly, its inhabitants as harsh, but also strong, kind, and reliable.

Not to mention occasionally shocking.

Sometime during the night it began to rain, and due partly to the darkness, partly to the drone of rain on the roof, Hannah slept later than usual the next morning.

Oh, mercy, she thought, Penn would be wearing a rut in the floor with his pacing, waiting to get into his office to post his everlasting journals! Quickly, she threw on her old gray serge—really, she was going to have to do something about her clothes! They'd been let out and gusseted to a fare-thee-well, and now they all needed taking in again.

Sara Mirella was drenched, as usual. Recalling Penn's cross words about her scuppers—whatever they were—being awash, she scooped her up, grabbed a handful of dry clothing, and hurried out.

He wasn't pacing. He was nowhere in sight. Oleeta was standing by the east window, staring out through the newly polished glass.

"Am I terribly late? Is Penn fit to be tied?" she asked breathlessly. Evidently, he'd given up on getting to his desk and gone about his other duties, which meant he'd be crabbier than ever. Nothing set him off like a break in his precious routine.

"Late for some, not for others." Oleeta didn't take her eyes off the window.

Sitting, Hannah laid her daughter across her lap and changed her from the skin out. She carried the wet things to the rinse pail and then crossed to stand beside Oleeta, wondering what the big attraction was. Drilling, she supposed. In the rain. Running up signal flags, or racing to see how quickly they could launch the boat in the surf without capsizing, and if they capsized, how quickly they could right her and scramble back aboard.

And then her eyes grew round as marbles. "Oh . . . my . . . mercy," she whispered.

Oleeta laughed. Like James, she wasn't given to laughter, nor even to smiling. "See that there scar on Adam's stern? He says he got it scrambling over a bobwire fence tryin' to outrun Mr. Isaiah's old boar hog. Tore the seat plumb out'n his britches."

Hannah clamped her eyes shut and then opened them again, one at a time. She goggled, gasped, and cried, "For heaven's sake, Oleeta, come away from that window!"

"Them twins is so skinny-assed they could both set in the same teacup. James, now—he's narrow, but he sticks out more. Reck'n of 'em all, Adam's got 'bout the finest stern end. Them little hollers in the sides of his—"

"Oleeta! Hush! I can't believe you're doing this!"

The girl chuckled and went right on gazing out the window at the row of men bathing under the overflowing gutters. Hannah stared in dreadful fascination, unable to look away. "Oh, my word," she breathed. "Never in all my born days . . ."

"Never? 'Pears to me you done missed something real nice, then. I'd ha' thought, seein's you was married and all, you'd ha'—"

"This is—this is what the twins meant when—" Hannah stammered. "That first day, when I— Oh, my dear sweet mercy, we shouldn't be watching, Oleeta."

But she watched, and continued to watch, while four bare backsides were sluiced down under the gutters, four pairs of feet were soaped, and four heads were ruthlessly lathered and then rinsed off.

Four. Not five. Two skinny, flat-butted redheads; one tall blond, his long limbs ever so slightly bowed—and one shorter, darker-skinned figure with lean hips, a narrow waist, and broad shoulders, who, at the moment, was seriously reaming out his left ear.

"If you're a-waitin' fer Penn, he don't wash wi' the others. He likes the downspout over to the far end. Adam says it's 'cause it's hidden behind the cistern and Penn, he's bashful, but if ye ask me, he jest don't want to stand 'longside Adam thataway. Reck'n not many men could stand up to Adam. He's 'bout the—"

"Oleeta! For heaven's sake, you mustn't say such things!"

"Well, he is," the younger woman said, innocently defensive. "I ought to know."

When the men trooped inside, having dressed in the boathouse, they were in a jovial mood, even James. Their hair was still wet and they smelled of soap instead of sweat and salt water, and Hannah couldn't look at a single one of them without turning fiery red.

"James, Penn says you got the tower," said Adam. Then he turned to Oleeta. "I'll haul in the washtub," he said softly, shyly. "Sky's fixin' to clear off. I got the first watch tonight, but I'll be in by eight."

This time the color burned right down to Hannah's shoe soles. She knew very well what they were planning, as did everyone else within hearing.

Which, fortunately, did not include Penn.

While James paused to tickle Sara Mirella under the chin on his way to the tower ladder, the twins were lifting every lid on the stove to see what was available for breakfast—at least, to Hannah's way of thinking it was breakfast. It was ten in the morning. According to the station's schedule, they were about to have dinner!

By the time Penn came inside, having taken his weather readings and entered them in the proper journal, Hannah had herself more or less under control. She tried not to look at him, but she couldn't help but notice that his hair, when it was wet with rainwater instead of seawater, held all the iridescence of a crow's wing.

Had he truly stood naked under the eaves like the others? She couldn't imagine such a thing.

And then she did. All too clearly for comfort! Seeing him beside his brothers as he cut the orders for the day's duties, she studied them together. The twins were a good head and a half shorter, and far more slender, with James falling somewhere in between the two older Warfields and the two youngest. Adam, of course, was tallest of all, and except for his bowed limbs, which Hannah would never have noticed had she not seen him without his trousers, the picture of perfection.

But it was Penn on whom her gaze lingered the longest. In spite of all she could do, Hannah found herself picturing him naked, his powerful limbs braced apart, shoulders hunched slightly under the deluge from the roof as he scrubbed himself with the harsh brown soap they all used for bathing, washing, and scrubbing the floors. She knew from personal experience that his arms were enormously strong. His chest was broader than any of the others, and she happened to know that it was patterned with dark hair, because once she had seen him with his shirt unbuttoned.

Living as they all did, she told herself, cheeks burning, it was a wonder that was *all* she had seen!

But it wasn't the thought of a male chest that was making her feel all breathless and weak now. It wasn't even the thought of a row of fairly ordinary backsides. It was the thought of one particular set of taut, narrow hips, swelling into muscular thighs, that made Hannah drop Sara Mirella's clean gown and then gabble like a turkey when Penn reached down to pick it up for her.

The devil take her cursed imagination! "Th-thank you," she mumbled, cheeks burning.

"You look feverish. You're not sickening with something, are you?"

"Goodness gracious, no! I never felt better in my life!"

He gave her a peculiar look, but Hannah didn't see it, for she had already scooped up Sara and was scurrying from the room as if a battalion of wolves were snapping at her heels.

Lust! It was one of the very deadliest of the dozen or so deadly sins, according to the women who had met regularly at the parsonage when she was growing up to sew for the poor and shred the reputations of everyone else. And although Hannah had barely had time to begin exploring the realm of fleshly pleasures before that part of her marriage had ended, she knew very well what lust was. It was what Thomas had felt for her.

It was what, God forgive her, she had come to feel for Penn Warfield.

There was no help for it, she would simply have to leave here, stove or no stove, leaks or no leaks. It was either that or consign her wicked soul straight to hell!

That night for the first time in months, Hannah dreamed about the night Thomas had come to her room in his maroon silk dressing gown, reeking of whiskey and cologne. With Edward in a drug-induced sleep in the next room, she was catching up on the mending.

She frowned at the interruption, for Thomas had never before entered her room without first knocking, and never so late at night. "What is it? Does Jarnelle need me for something?" Thomas's wife was some fourteen years his senior, and pretended to poor health when it suited her purposes.

"You don't need to strain your pretty eyes that way, my dear."

Actually, the sewing she did for Jarnelle was one of the least onerous of her chores. Aside from nursing a husband whose constant pain and irreversible decline was heartbreaking to watch, Hannah was usually up before daylight, conferring with the cook on the day's menus, directing the only remaining maid, an elderly widow, and then doing most of the light housework herself to save the poor woman from a scold. For one reason or another, maids never lasted long in the Ballinger household.

But her real duties began when she cooked Edward's breakfast and spent the next few hours trying to coax him to eat a few bites.

At first, when they had thought there was hope of at least a partial recovery, Hannah had tried to cheer her husband by talking of the future they could still share, with Edward tutoring private students in Latin and the classics while Hannah taught herself beginning bookkeeping. Between them, she had assured him, they would be able to live a full and happy life.

But by the time Hannah's parents had died a year later in the big influenza epidemic, it was rapidly becoming obvious that Edward would never regain his full strength. He had already ceased to dream.

Soon he ceased even to pretend there would be a future. He had begged Hannah to leave him to die, which was absurd. She loved him. She had always loved him, and she always would, but they both hated being thrown on the dubious hospitality of Thomas and Jarnelle. Actually, it was Jarnelle's money that supported them all, her home in which they were forced to live, which rankled even more.

And then Edward had suffered a bout of pneumonia, after which his condition had quickly deteriorated. Hannah had lost more weight than she could afford to lose, trying to look after Edward, trying to satisfy Jarnelle's increasing demands, and at the same time, trying to avoid being alone with Thomas, whose unwelcome attentions were becoming more and more difficult to evade.

"Thomas, you really shouldn't be here," she had told him, more frightened than she dared to reveal. There'd been something different about him that night.

"You're too pale, my dear. I brought you a glass of wine."

"No, thank you." She had slid her glasses back up on her nose and pretended attention to the hem of the sheet she was binding, praying he would go away before she had to call for help.

Who could she call? Mrs. Audley, the cook, had gone home. The maid stayed only until the dinner dishes were done. Neither of them would have come to her aid. Mrs. Audley needed the job too much to risk losing it, and Mrs. Snopes was too arthritic to move faster than a snail's pace, even if she could have found the courage.

As for Jarnelle, she was in the other wing of the

house, her teeth in a cup, a nightcap on her griz-
zled hair, snoring loud enough to wake the dead after several postprandial brandies.

"It's champagne, my dear, you'll like it." Thomas
came closer, holding the wineglass under her nose.

It was whiskey in a champagne glass. Inexperienced she might be, but even Hannah could tell the
difference between whiskey and champagne. It
wasn't the first time Thomas had attempted to
press hard spirits on her. "Shhh! You mustn't wake
Edward, I just got him to sleep."

But they both knew there was small chance of
waking the man in the next room. The new physi-
cian believed in dosing him with laudanum, which
Hannah despised, but then, who listened to a mere
woman, especially when that woman was only an
indigent in-law?

Thomas took her hand and wrapped it around
the glass. Very pointedly, Hannah placed it on the
table beside her. "Thomas, I'm really awfully tired.
You shouldn't be here. It's not at all fitting, and you
know Jarnelle and Edward wouldn't—"

"My wife is a cold woman, Hannah. She's of no
more use to me than that poor wretch in there is to
you. Why shouldn't we take what comfort we can
from one another, m'dear? A woman like you needs
a man, and I—" Without warning, he lunged.

Hannah scrambled across the bed, scattering her
sewing. She was reaching for the scissors when
Thomas caught her hand, crushing her wrist in his
surprisingly strong grip.

"Don't play girlish games with me, Hannah. I've
seen the way your eyes follow me around. I know
what you're thinking—I've been thinking it, too."

He scowled at her eyes, half hidden behind her wire-rimmed glasses. Before she could stop him he had snatched them from her face and flung them across the room, where they struck the mantel and shattered.

"You're drunk!"

"Not too drunk to show you what you've been missing, you wicked little tease. Now come here and let Tommy show you how a real man treats a woman."

Hannah opened her mouth to scream, and all his pretense of persuasion ended. She fought him like a tigress, tearing the lapel from his robe, pulling out handsful of his thin, pomaded hair, leaving a trail of red marks down one side of his face. But the match was unequal from the start. His wiry strength inflamed by the alcohol he had consumed, he slapped her hard. While her ears were still ringing, he struck her again and then he fell upon her, carrying her down to the bed.

Later in the night, Hannah had dragged herself up to sit in the rocking chair by the window that looked out over the roof of the carriage house. Her jaw was throbbing, her eyes were swollen, and her nightgown hung in shreds. Softly, she had sobbed until daybreak. Then, with nowhere else to turn, she had quietly dressed and tiptoed to the west wing to knock on Jarnelle's bedroom door.

"So. He had you then, slut. Well, don't come crying to me. Stir up the fire while you're here, and then see to my breakfast."

Hannah gasped. "How can you—"

"Spare me your outrage. You think I don't know what goes on under my own roof? Why do you think I can't keep any decent help unless they've got one foot in the grave?" She pulled off her ruffled nightcap and gave her scalp a thorough scratching. "Lucky for you I never married the bastard for what was in his britches. I married him because I needed a way to get out from under my father's thumb, and Thomas was the only man who asked me. He wanted money. I had it. I own him, lock, stock, and barrel, and in case you forgot, my fine lady, I own you, too."

"Jarnelle, you can't mean that. You can't possibly—"

"You know nothing about anything, so kindly shut up. I'll do the talking, you'll do the listening. As well as anything else I want you to do, is that clear?"

Hannah swallowed hard, quite beyond speech.

The older woman nodded once, and her sunken lips stretched into a thin grimace. "Well enough. Then listen carefully, because one word from me and that corpse you call a husband can rot in the gutter for all I care, and you right along with him. I'll turn you both out so fast your head'll spin, don't think I won't."

"But Edward—but Thomas—your own husband's brother—"

"You think I care for that? Listen to me, little Miss Butter-Won't-Melt, a woman don't have it easy in this world. I got where I am by using my brain, and I intend to stay there. I own the biggest tobacco warehouse in three counties, but it don't do me a speck o' good without a man to do my business for me. Thomas isn't as stupid as he looks. He knows better than to try and steal from me. He minds well enough, and he knows which side his bread is buttered on, and that's all I care about. If he wants a woman now and again, better you than me, and you'll keep your prissy little mouth shut tight if you know what's good for you. How long do you think your precious Edward will last in the poorhouse?"

That had been nearly a year ago. Thomas hadn't come to her room again, but only because Hannah had taken to shoving a bureau in front of the door each night before she retired.

But not even a heavy mahogany bureau could hold back the nightmares. They had started soon after she had discovered she was increasing and continued until after Edward had passed away. Since she had come to Paragon, she had almost forgotten how very frightening they'd been.

Until now.

James and Penn met outside the door of the keeper's room, Penn in full uniform, despite the lateness of the hour, James in a pair of hastily donned trousers and a rumpled shirt.

"I thought I heard something," James whispered.

"Likely just the baby. Go back to bed."

"You might as well go, too. Hannah'll quiet her down."

A silent challenge passed between the two men. "You're on duty in little more'n an hour," Penn said. "Best get some sleep while you can."

For a few moments it seemed as if James would argue, but then he nodded once and turned away.

Penn waited until he was gone, then quietly opened the door just as a series of soft, muffled sobs emerged from the mound of covers on the bed that had once been his own.

Chapter 10

PENN laid a hand on her shoulder. Or at least, what he supposed was her shoulder. Under the twisted mass of bedding, it was hard to tell. "Hannah? Wake up now, you're dreaming."

A whuffle of sound emerged from the covers. A groan, and then something that sounded like the drone of a bee. "Nnnnn . . . nno!"

The blankets were flung aside, and a wild-eyed Hannah sat up, staring around as if she expected to see the devil taking aim with his pitchfork. The glazed look in her eyes made Penn suspect she still wasn't fully awake.

Without a single thought for the proprieties, much less rules and regulations, he gathered the trembling figure in his arms, rocking her much as he would have rocked Sara Mirella. "There, now, sweetpea, easy as she goes . . . easy, now . . ."

Nightmare. He recognized the signs, having had a few of his own, the most frequent of them being that he was crawling on his hands and knees in the rut of a cart track, with a team of oxen bearing down on him. Unable to escape the deep groove of the track, unable even to cry out, he could only watch the massive hooves and the heavy cart wheels loomed closer and closer.

A dream of being lost at sea—that he could have understood. Or being unable to reach a foundering ship in time to help. But it was never a sea dream. His worst nightmare was always of being locked onto a course, unable to veer away though his life depended on it.

"Hannah, stop shaking so hard. You're safe now. There's nothing to fret about."

Her hands were ice cold, yet they seemed to burn his skin right through his shirt. He sat on the edge of the bed and drew her onto his lap, pulling the blanket up over her. She was stiff as a board, all pokered up to fight for her life. Penn's deep voice rumbled soothingly, but he felt as if he'd suddenly been cast adrift on an uncharted sea.

Beside the bed, the baby slept soundly in her makeshift cradle. Penn offered up a distracted thanks, for he didn't know what he would've done had he been called on to deal with two distressed females at once.

Cope, he supposed. He always seemed to manage somehow, with the help of God.

But right now his attention was focused solely on Hannah. Focused, more specifically, on the parts of her body that were making contact with parts of his.

He shifted uncomfortably, hoping she was too wrapped up in her own world to notice what was happening to him. Because it was damned well happening, and there wasn't a thing he could do about it short of diving overboard and swimming a fast mile or so through the surf.

"Hannah . . . you all right now? Think you can go back to sleep?" He began easing her off his lap, but she only clutched his shirt all the tighter. "Sheer off now, we're not in danger of foundering."

From the cradle below came a soft, sleepy whimper. He froze. This was no time for Sara Mirella to tune up. If Oleeta came barging in and caught him, it would be downright embarrassing.

Not that he was doing anything to be ashamed of. Wishing didn't count. Did it?

Sara let out a full-fledged yell. Penn winced, and Hannah murmured something and started to pull away. "Hold on there," he whispered, "I'll fetch her up to you."

Which he did. Instead of using his God-given brain—instead of using the perfect excuse to leave her, he scooped up the fretful baby from her warm bed, and jiggled her once or twice in his arms, which immediately shut off her cries. In the darkness, he could sense her hazy dark blue eyes on him. For a dab of a thing, she had a way of staring at him that occasionally made him wonder if her baby's mind didn't take in more than it was given credit for.

"Got an appetite onto you, don't you, sweetpea?" he teased in a voice totally unlike his normal bark. "Gonna be bustin' out of your smalls any day now." And to Hannah he said, "She's a mite leaky. Want me to bail her out for you?"

"No—that is, if you'll just hand me a napkin . . ."

With one hand, Penn fumbled for the fish basket of baby britches. "I could light the lamp."

"No! That is, no thank you. If she sees the light, she'll want to stay awake and play, and I'd just as soon she slept the rest of the night after I—that is, after she's been fed."

Standing awkwardly beside the bed, Penn could only sense the movement nearby as Hannah held the baby on her lap, unfastened the damp garment and dropped it into the pail, and then fastened on a dry one, all by feel. It never occurred to him to wonder how she could do so much in the darkness, for many times he, too, was forced to work blind. Ships didn't always choose the most convenient time to pile up onto a shoal, nor was a lantern or a torch always handy.

"All secure now?"

"Yes, thank you. And thank you for—for your kindness, Penn," Hannah said, her voice thick with embarrassment. "Good night."

Unwilling to be dismissed quite so easily, Penn settled back onto the foot of the bed. "I'll just stand by in case you need a hand."

"Oh, no! That is, it's not at all necessary. I—we've disturbed your rest enough, as it is."

"I'll sleep better, knowing you're all squared away."

And in spite of her embarrassment, there wasn't a blessed thing Hannah could do about it, other than issue a direct order, and he was far better at that than she could ever hope to be.

All the same, knowing he was sharing the intimate darkness with her, she winced at each small sound as the greedy infant suckled her overflowing breasts. At the first whimper, her milk had risen. If Penn thought Sara Mirella was leaky, what would he have said if he could have seen the way her breasts reacted? More than once she'd had to wipe a trail of milk off his desk where she had spouted halfway across the room.

"Growing some, isn't she?" he asked after a while. Without light, the small room was surprisingly companionable. In the quiet of the night, Hannah could hear Penn's breathing, feel the occasional shift of his weight on the mattress.

"She's gained enormously, thank goodness. The little gowns I made her are already snug."

"We'll have to send off for some more next time Cap'n Dozier comes in. Make out a list."

"Penn, about that . . . I've been meaning to talk to you. You know—"

"Her christening frock—reck'n she's already outgrown that, too?"

"What? Oh. No, I made it some larger, not knowing when I'd be able to have her christened. But, Penn, about this plan of yours?"

"Malachi says you've been fixing up Miss Marthenia's old house. Is that where you want to move to?"

Hannah's shoulders drooped in relief. Finally, it was out in the open. "You don't have any objections? Mal and Josie said it wasn't likely that anyone would come to claim it, and anyway, a house is better off being lived in than standing empty. Mal even mentioned salvage rights, although I'm not sure that applies to houses."

"It don't. Don't always apply to ships, neither, but that's not a problem. Miss Marthenia was my mother's first cousin, so if it's rights you're worried about, then Adam's got about as much right as a body needs."

Adam. Dear Lord, he was still planning to marry

her off to Adam! Was the man stone blind? Was he so blessed single-minded he couldn't see what was going on right under that battered beak of his?

It was all she could do not to tell him that unless he wanted his nephew to be born out of wedlock, he'd best let Adam pick his own bride! "I've been planning to move as soon as the boys can get my stove installed. They borrowed one from the house that has the tree across the front porch, and—"

"Nate's. Spring tide last year. Nor'easter blew for six days, tide washed half the houses off their footings and cut a slough right through the graveyard."

"Oh. Well ... about my new stove. It's awfully rusty, but at least the doors open and the lids come off. I can burn the rust off and then polish it up, and—a list, did you say? I'd better add stove polish. I'll have a few more things to order when the *Hamlet* comes in, but, Penn, you might as well know right now that—"

The sounds of movement from outside the room reminded Hannah that it must be nearing four in the morning. Time for breakfast. Time for the next watch to begin. Time for Penn to slip out, unless they both wanted to answer questions that Hannah, for one, would just as soon not have asked.

She could just imagine the knowing look in Oleeta's eyes if she thought they'd spent the past hour together here in the darkness. And James's. James gave the impression of seeing everything, saying very little, but feeling far more deeply than he let on.

"We'll discuss it later," Penn said, and she could feel the mattress shift as he rose, knew to the instant when he came to stand beside her at the head of the bed. She could feel his warmth, feel his strength, and her face grew damp as she thought about the fact that she'd been calmly nursing her baby, her breasts exposed in the darkness, while he sat but a few feet away.

"Well . . . just so you know that I'll be moving as soon as someone can take my trunk over in the cart."

"We'll talk about it directly," he repeated, his deep voice as soft as sea foam, as relentless as the tide.

Which didn't mean directly at all. It meant they would talk about it whenever Penn decided they would talk about it, and not a moment before.

Hannah heard the sound of the stove lid being opened as Oleeta uncovered the banked coals and poked in a few sticks of pine to heat up the oven for the breakfast bread. They took it in turns, Oleeta cooking breakfast, Hannah dinner, and both working together on supper.

She sighed as the door opened on a sliver of light and Penn left her. "Blast and botheration," she swore softly. She'd been that close to getting the matter settled, once and for all. Why on earth did anyone think four in the morning was a suitable time for breakfast? Why couldn't lifesavers follow the same civilized customs as the rest of the world?

"In a few days, dumpling," she muttered to the small bundle of warm, squirming humanity in her arms, "we'll be taking our breakfast whenever we blessed well feel like it, and not when some ugly old clock on the wall tells us it's time!"

Sara Mirella purred contentedly and kneaded the soft flesh of her mother's breast.

"Yes, and what's more, we won't have any big old sandy boots tracking up our nice clean floors, nor any old rule book telling us when to sneeze and when to say grace! And when it's four o'clock in our house, we'll have a civilized clock that chimes four times, and not eight!"

Sara Mirella belched noisily, and Hannah went on with her plans. Tomorrow—the day after, at the very latest. And she was *not* delaying her move on account of any blue-eyed, hardheaded man who couldn't tie his own boots without consulting his blasted rule book!

The next morning, Hannah, with the baby beside her in a basket, was outside pegging up the wash when James found Penn alone in the common room. "We'll turn out the surf boat after dinner. Pass the word," said Penn. He tapped the barometer, glanced at the clock, and made a notation in his weather journal.

"I'll round 'em up directly. Adam's tending the horses, and Josie's casting a line out for drum. Mal spotted a school a few minutes ago from the roof tower. Penn, you got a minute?"

"Not much more. The March report's past due."

"Then I'll make it short. I don't need your permission, but I'd like your blessing, all the same. I'm fixing to ask Hannah to marry me."

From the sleeping room on the other side of the partition came a stifled gasp. Neither man heard it.

"You're *what*?"

"Well, it won't scuttle your plans, it only shifts

'em around a bit. Adam's dead set on having Oleeta, and there ain't much you can do about it, seeing as how he's plenty old enough and it don't have nothing to do with the service. Now, me, I'm free, I got no—"

"Forget it."

"—commitments, and I—"

"I said *forget* it! You're not marrying Hannah. When the time comes for you to marry, I'll find you a woman, and it won't be no widow with a baby."

In a voice so cold Oleeta froze where she stood, a sheet half unfurled across one of the cots, James said, "Meaning no disrespect to Ma, but damned if you ain't just about the dumbest son of a bitch I ever run across in all my born days."

"Stow it, surfman," came the warning growl.

"In all your book reading, did you ever read the one about the dog and the manger?"

"If that's all you have to say, number two, you're dismissed."

"That ain't all I have to say, but it'll do for now. Just remember this—*sir*. You might be in charge at the station, but you don't have no say over what I do on my own time!"

At the sound of the front door slamming back against the wall, Oleeta let the sheet fall. Before she could lose her nerve, she raced down the long sleeping quarters to the door at the end and burst into the common room just as Penn was about to disappear behind the door of his office.

If looks were lightning, she'd have been fried in her tracks. "Wait a minute," she panted.

"I'm busy!"

"I reck'n you better take time to hear what I got to say. It won't take long once I catch my breath."

Flaming blue eyes narrowed under dark, glowering brows, Penn stood there, looking like a picture out of one of those books of his that she'd glanced at when she'd been dusting. All he lacked, Oleeta thought with a sudden irreverent urge to giggle, was a horned helmet and a fistful of thunderbolts. "Yes, well—it's about me and Adam. We're fixin' to have us this baby, an'—"

"You're fixing to *what*?"

Oleeta stood her ground, knees quaking under her threadbare calico. Adam had told her once that the crust was all on the outside, and underneath, Penn was as soft as an oyster. But even Adam admitted that a body could get cut up right bad before he ever got to the soft part.

Sagging against the door frame, Penn closed his eyes. He wiped the sweat off his forehead and heaved a sigh big enough to flap flags. "Godamighty, what next?"

It was nearly dark when Hannah and Oleeta finished cleaning up after supper. There'd scarce been time to breathe all day, let alone talk, what with the linesman from up the beach calling in just before dinner to say that his cart had broke a wheel and he needed help hauling his gear to where a washed-out pole was threatening the lines, and then the wasps building a nest under the seat in the privy. They were just lucky Josie had spotted them before someone had been stung. Aside from burning out the nest and nearly burning down the privy, they'd had to listen to the twins' dreadful jokes about em-bare-assing situations.

"When's your father due back from Baltimore City?" Hannah asked. She knew Oleeta had been able to stay only because her father was away.

"Any day now, I reck'n. I ought to be headin' on home. Paw'll pitch a fit if he ever finds out where I been."

"You have more nerve than I have," Hannah said admiringly as she finished kneading the bread for morning, covered it, and set it on the warming shelf to rise.

"As to that, I reck'n it takes right smart nerve to come out here to marry a man you ain't never even seen, and you in the family way." Spreading the coarse cotton towel over the rack, Oleeta sent her a sidelong glance. "Leastwise I worked up my nerve this morning and told Penn about the baby. I ain't even told Adam, yet." She grinned, and Hannah was struck once again by the odd feeling that she had known her from somewhere before.

"So that's why I could hear him yelling all the way in here when they were rolling out the boat. Mercy, that man's got a set of lungs on him! Is it all right, then? About you and Adam?"

"We never got that far. He give me this look that made me feel like a flounder a-fixin' to get hisself gigged, and then slammed hisself into his office. Good thing the baby weren't asleep in there."

"Oh, we've worked out a schedule. Sara naps while Penn's drilling, and he does his desk work while she's awake. I told him, um—this morning— about moving to the village, so I suppose he's had a double dose today."

"Yes, well, he still ain't said Adam and me could get married."

"Adam's of age."

"I ain't. Paw'll have to sign me over to him, if I kin ever work up my nerve to tell him."

Oleeta, now picking over beans to soak for the next day's dinner, glanced up at Hannah and said, "I done overheard something today. I never did hold with tale bearin', but I reck'n you ought to know that James is a-fixin' to ask for your hand."

Stupidly, Hannah stared down at her hand. "James?" James. "Oh, my mercy, as if things weren't complicated enough!"

"Leastwise, he put it to Penn."

James. He was her friend. They got on well, and truly, she did need a husband, she supposed. Only . . . "And—?" Hannah prompted weakly.

"Penn, he said when the time come, he'd find James a wife, and it wouldn't be no widder-woman with a baby."

Hannah's eyes blazed with anger, and then, just as quickly, glazed over with tears. "Damn all men to hell and back," she swore softly, which, for a preacher's daughter, was as good as consigning her own soul to perdition.

So be it. One way or another, men had managed to mess up her life to the point where she didn't know if she could ever put it back together again.

"We'll just see about that," she said softly, her eyes taking on the glint of steel.

Chapter 11

A morning fog lay heavy above the shore as the twins rode out on patrol. Overhead, a hungry gull protested the interruption as he searched for his breakfast in the surf. From inside the station came the comfortable clatter of kitchen chores, and now and then, the murmur of male voices arose from the nearby shed.

Hannah, her thoughts distracted, stared absently at the half-filled wash boiler, an empty bucket in her hand.

Penn hadn't precisely said she couldn't move to the village. But he hadn't exactly said she could. Stubborn, hardheaded man, he had to know that marriage with Adam was out of the question now. Why was he so dead set on that particular course of action that he wouldn't even entertain the thought of her marrying someone else? Someone who actually wanted her?

Just being wanted, never mind being asked, was a great boon to her self-confidence, which had been badly eroded over the past few years. The thing was, did she want him?

Truthfully, she didn't. Not as a husband. Forwarned, perhaps she could avoid being asked. She wouldn't hurt James for all the world. He was a wonderful man and a good friend. He simply wasn't the man she wanted for a husband.

Even so, it hurt to know that Penn thought she wasn't good enough for him. *"It won't be no widderwoman with a baby!"*

What was so awful about a widow with a baby? Why did he dislike her so? Because she'd deceived him? She had done that, all right. Deceived him far more than he could know. But if a widow with a child was good enough for Adam, why not for James?

Because James was smarter than Adam, and therefore deserved someone special in the way of a wife?

Adam was as handsome as a picture on a Valentine card. Didn't he deserve someone just as special?

Of course, Adam had found his someone special, and it most definitely was not Hannah Ballinger.

Round and round her thoughts went, like bees on a mock orange bush, while Hannah toted buckets of water to finish filling the washtub. Inside the boathouse, Adam was working on a balky axle, expressing himself with frequent curses and grunts. Adam had a way with horses and mechanical things, for all his slowness in other areas.

From the shed, where James and Penn were working, came the quiet murmur of James's voice followed by Penn's sharp retort. What reason did Penn have to be so short? *She* was the one who had been insulted.

Men. Hannah dumped in another bucket of water from the cistern and threw in a small chunk of brown soap. For two cents she would grab Adam by his ear, march him right into the shed, and force him to demand his rights. Adam was twenty-seven years old, for pity's sake, even if he did sometimes seem younger than the twins. He had a responsibility to Oleeta and that baby of theirs, and the sooner he faced up to it, the sooner they could begin to put this whole mess to rights!

As for James . . .

Hannah sighed. Draining the water from the rinse pail, she dumped the soggy contents into the heating wash water while she considered once again the possibility of James as a husband.

The plain, unvarnished truth was, she didn't want to marry James. Granted, he was smart and kind and attractive, with his dark brown hair and his olive skin and his narrow, clever face. He had never been other than kind to her or Sara Mirella, and any sensible woman would snap him up in a minute.

But drat it, it was none of Penn's business! Let him bellow his blasted orders until he was blue in the face, it wouldn't make a particle of difference. Just because he'd been head of the family since he was fifteen years old—just because he had been anointed king and keeper of Paragon Shoals Lifesaving Station—that didn't mean he had dominion over every living soul within the sound of his roar!

Snatching up her wash stick, Hannah jabbed at the mound of napkins and tiny sheets as the water began to simmer, muttering under her breath as she rehearsed what she would like to say to the whole bloody Warfield clan, if only she could screw up her nerve.

"Adam Warfield, you grab that girl of yours and haul her off to the landing, and the minute that preacher sets foot off the boat, you tell him he'd better fetch his book and get to marrying, or he'll have me to answer to!"

To James, she would have to say, "Thank you for the honor, but I do believe we suit much better as friends than we would as husband and wife. You deserve someone young and fine, someone unburdened by a family. Someone who will love you the way you deserve to be loved."

Unfortunately, Hannah could never be that someone. Without knowing precisely why, she was as sure of that as she was of her own name, and she suspected that James was coming to care more for her than was comfortable between friends.

As for what she would say to Penn . . .

Scowling, she poked down the billow of bedding and napkins that floated up, then lifted the heavy, steaming wad on the end of her stick, waited for it to drain, and swung it over into the rinse water, her mind working furiously.

How on earth had an otherwise sensible, mature woman got herself into such a fix? Why did she even allow an autocratic despot to get under her skin this way? For two cents, she would march right up to him and tell him to his face what she thought of him and his outrageous plan for reshaping the world to his own specifications!

Sighing, she shoved her hair back off her forehead, sparing only a fleeting thought to all the luxuries she had left behind. Indoor plumbing. A gas range. A wonderful laundress who collected and delivered twice a week, and fresh vegetables, milk, and ice delivered to the door by cart every morning.

She sighed again. Four cents gone already, and not a penny's worth of satisfaction to show for it. The trouble was, no matter how she tried to ignore the wretched man, she couldn't. Her ears invariably tilted toward the sound of his voice, never mind that it was usually growling out orders. She had only to see the way his stern countenance melted when he looked at her baby—or even the way he took care of the twins without their even being aware of it—and her heart sang as if spring had just burst out after a long hard winter.

Oh, yes, do tell him all that, Mrs. Ballinger. Give him that power over you, and while you're at it, why not offer yourself for a doormat?

But before she could tell anyone anything, the opportunity was lost. First Adam came down the boat ramp, wiping greasy hands on the seat of his pants. Ever watchful, Oleeta just happened to step outside the kitchen door to throw out the potato peelings in time to meet him, and Hannah looked on as they came together. The fog was already beginning to burn off, and sunshine glinted on Oleeta's dark brown hair and Adam's windblown golden curls.

Hannah turned away, tears blurring her eyes. Love was so very vulnerable. Thank goodness that part of her own life was finished, for she didn't think she could have endured it again.

A few minutes later, Oleeta returned to the kitchen, a glow in her cheeks, and Adam swung the paddock gate open, calling through the shed door,

"Penn, I'm ridin' down to Little Kinnakeet to fetch a part for the axle."

The walleyed bay called Red trotted up, swinging her head from side to side. "Frisky, ain't you?" Adam reached for her and she danced away. He lunged. "Whoa there, you cross-eyed old sea hag, you wantin' to go swimmin'? Is that what set a sandspur under your tail?"

With one foot, he kicked the gate shut behind him as he bridled his mount and slung one long leg over her back. "Be home in time for dinner," he called out to Hannah, who only nodded as her mouth was full of clothes pegs.

With a line full of white flapping baby clothes, she had turned to go inside a few minutes later when a soft sound caught her attention. She glanced over her shoulder in time to see Penn's big roan gelding, Pegasus, trot through the open paddock gate, tossing his head as he took off at a gallop after the others.

"Penn!" she screamed. Throwing down her basket, she started running after the horses. "Penn, hurry! They're getting away!"

"Je-*ye*-zus—!" James swore as he appeared in the door of the shed.

"Get the lines!" Penn yelled. He was already on the move, sleeves rolled up over his brawny forearms, shirt unbuttoned halfway down his chest in spite of the brisk breeze.

"Who left that damned gate open?"

Their words tumbled over one another while Hannah stood helpless, watching the herd disappear in the distance. By the time the two men raced past her, each carrying a coil of line with a dangling loop in one end, the herd was halfway across the island, hooves, tails, and shaggy manes flying.

"What happened?" asked Oleeta, poking her head out the door.

"The horses got out. Penn and James went after them."

"Adam?"

"He'd already gone. I, uh—I think the gate didn't quite shut behind him."

"Lordamighty, if that ain't just what we need, somethin' else fer Penn to hold against him."

"What can we do?" Hannah asked, staring after the two men, who were running flat out across the narrow stretch of grassy plain that separated ocean from sound.

"Keep out'n the way. They'll likely fetch up over to the sound side, sweet as cane sugar. They was all borned wild, 'ceptin' for that roan o' Penn's. He come from over to Hyde County. Now'n again, they just like to run free for a spell, but they know where the sweet grass is. They know where to get fresh water, 'thout havin' to dig all the way down to the roots to find it."

There were still the beds to be made. Gradually that chore, all except for Penn's cot, had been taken over by the women. There were dishes to wash and floors to be swept, bread to be made and the beans to tend.

And, of course, Sara Mirella required attention. Lying on a blanket on the floor near the kitchen table, where sunlight from the east window slanted across her waving fists, she was impossible to ignore. Oleeta jingled a pair of spoons tied together on a string, and Hannah leaned over to tickle her belly, humming snatches of a song she remembered from her own childhood.

It was an easy, comfortable scene, with the smell of coffee and baking bread and boiling beans. And it was into the midst of that comfortable scene that a madman burst.

The door was flung back against the wall. Both women looked up to see the wiry old man, a mop of wild hair flying around a thin dark face and a pair of burning black eyes. "Daughter, you have brought shame to my house," he declared in an awful tone.

"Paw! I didn't know you were—"

"Fetch your bonnet before I take my belt to you right here!"

Oleeta, her face leached of all color, fled to her small corner and disappeared behind the curtain. Hannah lifted her baby off the blanket and held her protectively as she stared in horror at the white-haired, rag-clad stranger. *This* was Oleeta father? Dear Lord, the man looked demented!

"Sir, won't you—?" Hannah had been about to invite him to take a chair and have some refreshments, hoping to defuse the explosive situation, but he ignored her as if she weren't even present.

"I'm ready, Paw," Oleeta said breathlessly, tying the strings on her meager bundle. To Hannah's knowledge, the poor child owned three gowns and a single nightgown, each more ragged and faded than the last. Hannah had offered to remake one of her own gowns for the younger girl, only to be frostbitten by a proud refusal.

There were questions she wanted to ask, advice she wanted to give—explanations that needed to be made, but she was not even given the chance to say goodbye. With one furious glance over his shoulder, the enraged man grabbed his daughter by the wrist and jerked her through the door, her nimbleness alone saving her from a nasty fall.

Half in shock, Hannah hurried to the door in time to see Oleeta scramble up behind the old man and clutch his filthy, ragged black coat. After one expressionless look over her shoulder, the poor girl turned away, her face hidden by a sheaf of dark hair. The horse, a sorry specimen that looked as if it not only had a skin disease, but hadn't been fed in a month, laid back his ears, giving Hannah the fleeting hope that it would refuse to move until the men returned.

It was a vain hope. One hard kick in its flanks set it into a jarring gallop, and she could only pray that Oleeta wouldn't fall off. The ride alone was bad enough, in her condition. But something told her that right now, that was the least of the poor child's worries.

The men were back by noon, Penn riding Pegasus and James up on Mollie, leading all but three of the station's herd behind him. They turned the horses into the paddock, and while Penn rubbed down Peg and Mollie, James quickly examined the rest. A swelling above the hock of the chestnut filly might have to be poulticed, he was saying as the two of them walked tiredly into the common room.

"God, I could skin that boy alive," Penn muttered.

"Later on after they're cooled down I'll pitch in some dry grass and bail 'em some water. Reck'n they've had sufficient for a spell. Be damned lucky if they don't bloat." James looked tired, and for once, his dark brown hair was less than neatly arranged.

Hannah poured hot coffee, even though the day was growing uncomfortably warm now that the fog had burned off. Judging from his wet clothing, his torn shirt, and the bruise on his right cheek, Penn had got the worse of it. There was a streak of blood down one forearm that might or might not be serious.

But it was his expression that made her hesitate to speak.

"Them two mares'll likely be hanging around outside the fence come morning," said James, "if that damned devil stallion don't herd 'em up t'ward the inlet."

Penn closed his large hands around the thick white cup of coffee and said nothing. For a single moment, Hannah thought he looked weary, desolate, and heartbreakingly vulnerable.

"I'll get Adam to take a look at the filly when he gets back," James offered. "He'll know if she needs a poultice."

"He didn't know enough to shut the damned gate," Penn grumbled.

Gone was the fleeting look of vulnerability. Hannah decided it had all been an illusion, anyway. Penn Warfield was about as vulnerable as a grizzly bear.

"No, but he does know horses right well. Give the boy credit."

The boy, Hannah wanted to say, was older than James. She refilled the coffee cups and kept her mouth shut.

"I want that axle repaired first off. It don't do to have the beach cart down."

"Cart's not much good without a team to pull it," James said reasonably. "If that filly's gone lame, it'll take a right smart spell to break one of the others to harness."

Penn's only response was a grunt as he glowered down at his coffee cup. It occurred to Hannah that when he returned, poor Adam was going to have more on his mind than axles and poultices. She didn't look forward to having to tell him that his sweetheart was gone.

When the time came, it was even worse than she'd feared. Hannah had seen Adam surly before, seen him sullen and downright petulant, but never had she seen him lose his temper. It took James and Penn together to hold him back from going after Drucker. All afternoon she could hear them outside, Adam's voice angry, Penn's deeper voice firm—James sounding a calm counterpoint between the two.

Peering out the window over the sink, she saw Adam storm off, leaving Penn and James arguing, and thought, what now? Mercy, all it needed now was for the twins to have a falling out.

By suppertime, the tension had spread so that even the baby was affected by it. She fretted almost constantly while Hannah served up the drumfish and potatoes topped with chopped raw onion and fried cracklings, the way Oleeta had showed her.

"Is the cart horse going to be all right?" she asked in an effort to break the uncomfortable silence. The twins were sharing a tower watch, and now and then their bursts of laughter drifted down through the open window.

"She'll do," Adam replied curtly.

Lovely. So much for polite conversation.

"Would you care for another biscuit?" she asked Penn.

"I've had sufficient," he muttered.

She was sorely tempted to dump the bread basket over his head and be done with it.

One more day, she told herself. One more day, and old stoneface could pour crackling grease on his blasted rule book and eat it for supper because she wouldn't be here to cook for him! If any of the others cared to barter food for her services as a cook, a laundress, and a seamstress, why then, she would consider it. At least until the seeds Josie had ordered for her arrived, and she had her garden growing, and Malachi taught her how to fish and catch crabs. He had even promised to find her a nest of duck eggs to hatch and offered Adam's services to build her a pound so that she could have a supply of eggs and fowl.

James glared down at his meal. He had a small cut on his brow that she could have sworn hadn't been there when they'd got back from chasing the horses. "What happened to your forehead?" she asked.

The look he gave her would have blistered paint.

James, Hannah marveled. The man who, according to Oleeta, wanted to *marry her*?

Oleeta must have misunderstood.

Turning to Penn, she asked with determined cheerfulness, "Did you take care of that cut on your arm? I did offer, you know."

"Don't fret yourself none, madam."

Madam. So they were back to that, were they?

Somehow, they got through the rest of the miserable meal, but Hannah fully expected to dole out more than one dose of baking soda before the night was ended. For once, Penn hadn't even bothered to say grace. Not that he was an overly religious man—at least, not by the standards Hannah had grown up with. But evidently, the rules called for a service on the Sabbath and prayers before meals, and normally, Penn would have chopped off his own right thumb before he would've broken one of his blessed rules.

And so it went. Penn brooded. Adam sulked. James took the last tower watch before sunset, and warned Adam to catch some sleep because they were to ride out on patrol at dusk. Not a one of them lingered in Hannah's company, and it occurred to her that that was something she would miss after today. Sitting in the keeper's room mending while Penn read or posted his journals, now and then sharing a line from one of his books, or some new achievement of Sara Mirella's.

"I'd swear she can tell one twin from the other," she had told him just recently.

"What makes you think so?" Penn had peered at her over his spectacles, his lean hard face momentarily softened by lamplight.

"Well, Malachi lets her suck molasses off his little finger, and she always smiles at him first."

Penn had smiled at that—Penn wasn't a man who smiled freely—and Hannah had wondered at the time how she could ever have thought him hard.

Now she wondered how she could have endured living in his presence for nearly three months. No wonder he hadn't been able to keep a wife.

The twins, asleep behind the partition, were slated to go out on the midnight patrol. Adam was running late, but then, he'd taken the north run, and Penn, for once, hadn't argued.

James came in first. He took care of his horse and tack and let himself quietly into the station. Penn was waiting for him in the common room, in a chair tipped back against the wall, with his brawny arms crossed over his chest. It had eaten at him constantly, this business of James and Hannah, ever since James had told him he intended to court her and marry her if she would have him. Before he could even finish making his case, Penn had responded with a single word.

"No."

"Damn all, Penn, you can't still be planning to marry her off to Adam! Adam's already sired a baby onto Oleeta! He'll have to marry her, and that leaves Hannah free to marry the next man in line!"

"No. I've got my reasons." Arms crossed over his chest, Penn had dared his number-two surfman to defy him.

"I don't need your permission," said James, his dark eyes blazing with banked fire. "I intend to court her, and if she'll have me, I intend to marry her and take Sara Mirella as my own, and there ain't one damned thing you can do about it, because there ain't nothing in regulations against a man marrying."

Penn's eyes narrowed. He came up out of his chair. In a voice that was deceptively soft, he said, "It's *my* regulations that run this station, and my regulations say you won't."

"Do you know what's wrong with you, big brother?" A look of wonder dawned on James's face. "I just now figgered it out. You want Hannah for yourself. You want her, but you're afraid if you get her, she'll up and run off on you, same as Margaret did."

That was when Penn slugged him. At the last minute he pulled his punch, because James was at least forty pounds lighter, if somewhat quicker on his feet. All the same, James ended up on the floor, rubbing his sore jaw, while Penn leaned over him, torn between guilt and the dawning of an unwelcome truth.

"Go to bed," Penn said tiredly. He was close to the end of his rope. Twice within the past twenty-four hours they had fought over the woman. Neither of them had ever been given to violence.

"I'm not done with this yet, Penn. I figger Hannah's got a say in who she marries."

"Go to bed," Penn repeated. He was past tired. The day had begun at four that morning and gone downhill from there. His head ached, his legs burned where the damned cat-claw briars had ripped into him, and the cut on his shoulder was feeling feverish. The last thing he needed now was a mutiny on his hands.

"We'll talk tomorrow," he said grudgingly. But not about Hannah, he added silently.

Chapter 12

THE twins had ridden on off patrol a few hours before dawn and come in hungry, as usual. There was food cooked, and fresh coffee made, but Hannah was nowhere in evidence.

"I ain't gonna like it much when she's gone," remarked Josiah.

"Then you better think of some way to keep 'er here, peabrain." Malachi grabbed four big biscuits from the basket on the warming shelf. Splitting them on his plate, he poured half a pint of molasses over the lot and cut into them with knife and fork. "I done run out of excuses."

"You didn't have to go and patch her roof!"

"Well, you're the one that ordered seeds and found 'er that there stove!"

Another few biscuits disappeared from the basket. After a while, Malachi said, "Reck'n where Penn is?"

He knew where James and Adam were, for they had ridden out on the dawn patrol just as Malachi and Josiah had come in.

"If he ain't in his bed, he's prob'ly up on the roof. Lately, he stands tower watch a lot."

"Keeper ain't supposed to stand watch."

Josiah shrugged. "You want your gizzard reamed out, you tell him what he ain't s'posed to do. Me, I'd just as lief go on breathin'.'"

"If he was to marry Hannah, she could go on livin' right here at the station."

"Then she'd have to put up with you, fartface. 'Sides, Penn ain't gonna marry no woman. He ain't the marryin' kind."

"Done it once, didn't he? Gimme that molasses. Dammit, peabrain, there ain't none left in the pitcher!"

"Then get the jug. Sure he done it once. That's why he ain't never gonna do it again. He don't get on with women, else why'd Margaret run off on him?"

"Well, hell—I ain't no woman! How'd you expect me to know?"

"You know Perdita at Rosabelle's? She said all the women there light up like a Coston flare when they see him walkin' up the street from the docks. Reck'n why Hannah don't like him? He ain't all that bad."

The last of the biscuits disappeared, and the two young men fell silent, each remembering the un-smiling man who had been both father and mother to them for as long as they could remember. Remembering the strong arms that had rescued a pair of heedless adventurers from the brink of disaster more times than either of them cared to recall. Remembering how many times the seat of their britches had fair smoked from the timely application of an oak-tanned palm.

Remembering the many times those same hands had gently soothed aching heads and turbulent bellies after a bout of overindulgence—of green grapes, or Miss Marthenia's figs, or Mr. Isaiah's enriched, double distilled, homemade spirits.

They had tested his patience every day of their young lives, and knew it well. They also knew that no matter how rigid and unyielding he might seem to outsiders, Penn Warfield would lay down his own life before he would hurt a living soul.

In the open cupola high on the rooftop, leaning on the rail that was only slightly off true, Penn stared out at the eerie sight of moonlight illuminating the cloud of salt haze that drifted just above the surf line. Watching the last patrol ride out earlier, with Adam taking the no'th'ard leg, he had smiled bitterly, knowing full well what the boy intended. Instead of swapping tokens and turning back at the halfway house, he would ride on to Drucker's place. It was purely against regulations, but for once, Penn couldn't seem to generate much anger.

He only hoped the old man didn't take a shotgun to him.

God, but he was tired! Sometimes it seemed as if he'd been swimming against the tide all his life, losing more ground than he gained.

Papa, I did my best, and I failed. You told me once a long time ago that Warfields don't marry Druckers. I vowed then I'd carry out your will, but there comes a time when a man's got no leeway. If he don't take a different heading, he'll founder, and someone's bound to get hurt.

The someone, in this case, being the babe Adam had sired onto the Drucker girl.

Which led Penn's thoughts along another path.

Hannah and her baby. Penn alone had brought them here. His alone was the responsibility. And no matter how willing James was to bear the burden, Penn couldn't allow it. He damned well *wouldn't* allow it!

Absently massaging his fevered, throbbing shoulder, he rearranged things in his mind, trying in vain to force them into an acceptable pattern. Hannah and Adam?

That road was closed now.

Hannah and James?

No, dammit! She was his responsibility, not James's!

Inside his aching head a persistent voice echoed, "You want her for yourself, want her for yourself, want her for yourself . . ."

Did he?

Damned right he did! Wanted her so blessed much he couldn't sleep of a night for thinking about her soft body lying beside him in the darkness, smelling of violets and a woman's warm muskiness. Lying beside him, lying beneath him—sitting astride him with her shiny, pale brown hair flowing down over her naked breasts . . .

So where's the snag? What's holding you back, Warfield? Afraid she'll tire of you the way Margaret did? Afraid she'll run off and leave your carcass to rot in the sun like a stinking dog shark?

Bilge. He respected the woman. He respected all women, no matter what they had done, for women had more disadvantages than men. Hannah had deceived him, true, yet he no longer held it against her. A woman alone, in desperate need, evidently with no family to turn to—what choices could she have had? In her favor, she had made herself useful. The boys liked her. Adam tolerated her. James . . .

Once more Penn heard in his mind James's heated words. He scowled. Dammit, he was *not* jealous! A man had to care deeply for a woman before he could be jealous, and Penn had run plumb out of that kind of caring a long time ago.

Besides, whatever feelings he'd had for Margaret all those years ago when he'd been too young and green to know his brain from his bowsprit had been cut right out of him when she'd run off with another man without so much as a word of goodbye.

It wasn't love he was feeling. It sure as the devil wasn't jealousy! He was just tired, that was all. Tired of being short sufficient hands to launch his boats in a timely fashion, tired of being short sufficient hands to space the patrols so that every man got his fair share of sleep and free time, and the occasional trip to the mainland to trim his wick.

Come to think of it, Penn thought wryly, he could barely recall the last time his own wick had been trimmed. Maybe that was all that ailed him. When a man's mind couldn't rise above his own groin, he was in serious trouble. These days, about all it took to step his mast was a glimpse of petticoat flapping on a clothesline, or a few strands of silky brown hair against a pale, tender nape. It was getting to be downright embarrassing, the length of time he was forced to spend with a book in his lap, afraid even to walk away for fear she would see the condition he was in.

Dammit, it weren't as if he hadn't carefully charted his course! All he'd wanted to do was to keep Adam from getting in too deep with the Drucker girl. At the same time, it had seemed like the perfect opportunity to rebuild the community and restock it with Warfields. He had gone over it from every angle without finding a single leak, only to have the blasted thing founder before it was even launched!

Hannah had moved the jet buttons on her best gray gown as far as she could move them, but it was still loose in the waist and uncomfortably tight across the bosom. She had covered the reworked seams with black silk twill, and added a bit of lace ruching to the high collar and cuffs, which hardly disguised the fact that it was years out of date, and had undergone entirely too many remakings ever to recover. Clothes had never been particularly important to her, but oh, how she wished she had something more festive to wear for the grand occasion.

Her white muslin, with the pin-tucks and the box-plait folds at the back? It had been a part of her trousseau. She had worn it only once, for Edward had thought it made her look sallow. Edward had had an artist's eye for color.

Besides, it was hardly practical for moving. Her gray would serve far better, and the yellow scarf would lend a jubilant touch.

Because it was a day for celebrating, after all the delays to mend the roof, to find and install a workable stove and patch up enough furniture to get by with, and board up windows until she could afford to buy glass.

Heaven only knew when that would be. She might not starve, but unless she could hire herself out as cook and housekeeper at the station, there was no way Hannah could see clear to earn a single penny. She would have to rely on barter, and without the means to travel to the nearest village, it would have to be with the station. Which meant she was right back at the mercy of the Warfields.

But tomorrow would be soon enough to think about that. Today was purely for celebrating her new independence, no matter how precarious it seemed at the present.

Hannah had moved her belongings a few at the time until all that was left was her wardrobe trunk, which held most of her winter clothes and the remainder of a bolt of muslin she had brought to make baby clothes. Some of it could be made into sheets, seamed up the middle, which wouldn't be comfortable, but was definitely better than nothing. If the weather turned cold again, she would be sleeping in too many clothes to feel the minor discomfort of a flat-fell seam, for she refused to borrow the station's blankets. Although she had been persuaded to accept the loan of a feather bolster.

"Come along, dumpling, let's get you ready to go home. James has promised to drive us over in the cart as soon as he comes in off patrol."

Less than an hour later, Hannah was perched up on the weathered plank seat beside James, her trunk and valise behind her, the baby wrapped in a light blanket on her lap. The day had turned off sunny and warm, which she took as a good omen. Certainly far more encouraging than the bleak, stormy weather on the day she had arrived.

She tucked a flap of blanket over Sara Mirella's fuzzy crown against the bright glare of the morning sun as James clucked the sluggish beast into motion. Aristotle had been the only horse to remain in the paddock when the others had fled. Lacked the energy, Malachi had said.

Too stupid to know what an open gate was for, according to Josiah.

"I'm going to miss you all," she said, looking back over her shoulder at the huddle of buildings that constituted Paragon Shoals Lifesaving Station.

"Won't hardly have the chance. Twins'll be over to your house at the first sign of smoke from your chimney. I loaded up a sack of flour and some beans, coffee, sugar, and bacon. Make a list, I'll see to the rest of it."

"Oh, please, James, you don't have to—"

James brushed off her thanks. "You'll likely be feeding us, same as always. That is, if it's not too big a burden."

"It's no burden at all, but you mustn't think you have to support me. That's not at all necessary."

The look he gave her as they plodded through the deep sand ruts was a little too knowing to suit her fragile pride. "Reck'n it's some different, living in a city full of fancy houses, fancy people, and all. Out here on the Banks, we don't have much, but we take care of our own, Hannah. If we need you, we'll feel free to call on you. Likewise, you're going to have to rely on us for what you need. The twins, now—they'll keep you in fish. They'll set a net and show you how to salt down what you don't eat right off. I'll show you Mr. Isaiah's oyster bed before I go, but you'd best let me shuck 'em for you, leastwise until you get the hang of it."

Hannah, her eyes burning fiercely in the bright sunlight, murmured something appropriate. She was hopeless when it came to prying shells apart. Either she cut herself on the shell, or she cut herself on the knife, or she slid the whole mess off into the sand. She had learned by the time she was twelve to dress fish or fowl, and she could slice a slab of bacon as evenly as a deck of cards. A preacher's living, while adequate, seldom ran to servants. But clams and oysters were another matter.

"I'll send Mal over to dig up your garden patch. Josie's already sent to the mainland with Cap'n Dozier for enough seeds, sets, and slips to get you started. Miss Marthenia's got about the finest fig tree in the village, and there'll be more blackberries than you can eat, come July. Penn and me, we'll look in from time to time."

James swayed lazily with the lurch of the wagon, eyes facing the shaggy behind of the graceless old gelding. He might have been a casual acquaintance, passing the time of day with her, but they both knew he was throwing her a lifeline, one that she desperately needed.

Oh, my mercy, she thought, pride was a wretched companion! Two tears streaked crookedly down Hannah's cheek, and she ducked her head to brush them away on her leg-o'-mutton sleeve. "I don't know why you should be so nice to me," she squeaked.

Gazing straight ahead at the stunted woods surrounding the few houses, James said, "Don't know no reason why we shouldn't." Dark eyes enigmatic, he slanted her one of his rare, sweet smiles. "Reck'n Adam'll be spending right smart time over here in the village once he settles things with Drucker. Boys better tune up their mouth harps. Looks like they'll be playing the wedding march once the boat comes in."

"Adam and Oleeta, you mean."

He nodded, and Hannah wondered if Oleeta could have misunderstood what she'd thought she heard. James certainly didn't appear smitten, but if he was, how on earth was she going to deal with it without either losing his friendship or hurting his feelings? Mercy, what a fine line to have to walk! Sometimes it seemed as though she'd been walking a tightrope over a sea of disaster half her life.

"Then there's the christening," James went on as he pulled up in front of her new home. "Can't forget that, can we, little sweetpea?" He chucked Sara Mirella under her tiny chin, and Hannah pretended to interest herself in gathering up her belongings.

Sweetpea. That was Penn's special name for her daughter. Honestly, it was sheer foolishness to choke up over something so trivial! She should be shouting with glee. She had finally achieved her freedom. She had a home of her own and no one to fear, and for the first time in her entire life, her future was in her own hands.

But Penn hadn't even told her goodbye, she thought, surreptitiously wiping another tear on a corner of the baby's blanket. He had watched James load her things onto the cart, and then, be-

fore they could even pull away from the station, he
had whistled up that great ugly horse of his and
galloped off down the beach.

James had spared her a single look, then slapped
the reins and they'd headed off in the opposite direction. "Rides like the devil's on his heels, don't
he? Him and that horse of his, sometimes I swear
they think with one brain. Wouldn't surprise me
none if they don't swim out to the bar before they
come in. Penn does that sometimes in the summertime, when he's got worrying on his mind." James
had spoken idly, not looking at her, for which Hannah was grateful.

But he *could* have taken time to say goodbye and
wish her well. It wouldn't have killed him to be polite. After all, she'd been a guest in his home for
three months . . . in a manner of speaking.

"Better not try to use the fireplace," James
warned as he brought in the last load from the cart.

"No, I won't. The boys warned me." It was a tiny
little fireplace, crudely built and hardly large
enough for a scoop of coal, even if she'd had the
coal. "I stuffed the cracks with mud because Mal
said he thinks that's where the mice are getting in."

"There'n everywheres else." James spared her a
quick grin. "Tried your cookstove out yet?"

"Not yet," Hannah admitted. Somehow, the day
didn't seem quite so warm and sunny as it had a
few moments ago. All the boarded-up windows, no
doubt. "Josiah looked down the chimney and said
he couldn't see any obstructions."

"I'll set a fire, just to be sure she draws proper.
What about your cistern?"

"Oh, it's completely ruined with salt, at least until I can bail it out and scrub it real good. Malachi rigged me a water barrel and filled it from the station, and borrowed a section of gutter off the house with the tree on the front porch."

"If you're any good at praying, you might want to pray for rain. The way that young'un goes through britches, you'll likely end up beating her smalls out on rocks in the creek. And there ain't no rocks around these parts bigger'n a grain of sand."

"My, you're such a comfort to me," Hannah teased.

Sara Mirella began to squirm, and Hannah made a place for her by padding a fish basket with a layer of clean napkins while James shaved tinder and poked it under the split of pine he had brought in from the wagon. Hannah hadn't even thought about firewood. He scraped a match on the back of the stove and dropped it in, and then watched the stovepipe for leaks.

Hannah watched James. He didn't look as if he were harboring any deeper feelings for her than the twins, or Adam did. But then, James had always been chary with his feelings, not sharing them easily.

After a while, she got out one of the pots she had salvaged and poured in a dipperful of water, placing it on the top of the stove, which was ticking and clicking as the old metal began to heat up. "The least I can do is offer you a cup of your own coffee, if you'll take it black."

"I'll send over some tinned milk the next—"

"No. James, you mustn't spoil me, for I'll not like it, I promise you."

They argued about the roles of pride and independence versus neighborliness until the water boiled. Hannah threw in a handful of grounds and got out two of the coffee cups she had borrowed until she could find some way to send for her own.

"Your father's a minister, I understand," said James.

"He was. He and Mother died in the influenza epidemic not long after Edward and I were married. They passed away only a week apart, and as awful as it sounds, I'm almost glad—I mean, that if one went, the other followed. They were so very close, I'm not sure either would have wanted to go on alone."

"They had you. Or did you move too far away after you married?"

"No, I—that is, Edward and I— Goodness, that boiled quickly, didn't it? I seem to have got myself a very efficient stove!"

And as the afternoon wore on and the clouds blocked out the sun, they talked of sickness and neighbors, of parents and friends. If Hannah wondered why James stayed, she didn't let it worry her. He was surprisingly easy to talk with—as easy as Edward had been in the early days, before his illness, helplessness, and drugs had changed him beyond all recognition. If she'd had a brother, she would have liked him to be very much like James. Quiet, supportive, with a quick understanding and a way of meshing his thoughts with hers so that there were no hard edges, no long, uncomfortable silences.

She was completely at ease in his presence, entertained by his stories of the people who had once lived in this same village, of pranks the twins had played in times past—and times more recent.

So why on earth did her thoughts keep straying to a tall, solitary man on a big, ugly horse, riding hell-bent along the shore? Thoughts of those powerful thighs pressing against the horse's sides kept creeping into her mind, even while she was talking with James about such prosaic things as collards and storm blinds and thunder squalls.

She had a guest—she had a hundred things to do to settle into her new home, and here she sat, harboring lurid thoughts that no lady would be caught dead thinking. Thoughts about thighs. Male thighs. Long, powerful, muscular male thighs that led to—

That led to shame and disgrace! Hannah Matthews Ballinger, you're a fallen woman!

James stayed on until after dark to be certain her stovepipe would cool down safely. By the time he drove off, promising to return with a supply of tinned milk and whatever else they had in excess, Hannah was too tired to argue. It seemed the men of Paragon Shoals Lifesaving Station—at least some of the men—had taken her on as a project.

A project was different from charity . . . wasn't it?

Chapter 13

SHE was gone, damn her, and good riddance! From now on, he would have a bed to sleep in! No more rolling off onto the floor. He would have a desk to work at. No more having to plan his work around a sleeping baby. No more bits of silk left lying about, smelling of violets—no more embroidered female fripperies flapping on his clothesline right out in the broad daylight, to fill his head with all sorts of crazy notions! No more being woken up out of a sound sleep by a grizzling young'un, or the sound of a woman pacing the floor, singing foolish songs about courting frogs and gray geese!

No, and no more soft, husky laughter ringing out to catch him unaware. No more laughing gray eyes, reminding him of sunlight dancing on pewter water. No more quiet hours of reading and mending, swapping comments on this and that, through the early watches of the night.

And no more coming home, wet, weary, and discouraged, to the life-giving warmth of a woman's welcome. A welcome, Penn reminded himself, that had been more for James than himself.

Women! They made a damned fine job of complicating a man's life, but that was about all they were good for.

Penn had long since discovered that a brief plunge into the surf went a long way toward clearing his head, not to mention cooling his ardor. Now, slinging the wet hair off his forehead, he turned back toward shore, guiding Pegasus with a slight pressure of his thighs. The water had been icy at first, from the Labrador Current that flowed down to meet the Gulf Stream just off the Cape, but his body had quickly adjusted. He had swum the horse for a spell, then slipped off and swum beside him, and then climbed back onto his bare back and turned toward ashore.

So she was gone. He had watched her leave.

With no more than a subtle shift of his weight, Penn signaled a command, and the raw-boned gelding swing north and broke into a gallop. For some twenty minutes they raced along the shore, man and beast alike glorying in the momentary freedom before turning back. Then, Penn's torso swaying with the motion, they plodded homeward. The roan's tail whipped back and forth as deer flies, drawn to the scent of sweat and salt water, swarmed around them. Penn slapped a bite on his shoulder and winced at the dull ache.

She was gone. So be it.

He told himself she would come to no harm, for they would still keep a close watch over her. After a spell, if she proved hardy enough for life on the island, he might even reconsider and allow her to marry James.

Then again, he might not.

A few minutes later he arrived at the station to find that two new hands had arrived.

"These here is Luke and Silas Garner," announced Malachi, presenting a pair of strangers in ill-fitting uniforms before Penn could even finish rubbing down his horse. "They're our new hands. Luke says they was farming over to Hyde County, but it's been too wet to plow, so they went to pullin' stumps. They had to quit when the mule bogged down and it took five men half a day to haul 'im out. That's when they figgered they might's well join up fer a spell."

By the time Penn had sounded the depths of the brothers Garner, the light wind had dried his clothes on his body, leaving his hair stiff with salt. He felt as if he'd been turned wrongside out and hung on a flagpole to dry, but at least he had two more hands.

The Garners, he learned, were boatmen after a fashion, having grown up trapping in the swamps across the sound in the winter months and running a trotline in the summertime to augment their farm income. One was a passable cook, the other could read and write. Neither could swim more than a few strokes, but Penn figured that was a fault that could swiftly be overcome.

"Where's Adam?" he asked. Having finished going over the grounds and equipment with his new hands, they were still standing outside the station.

"Ridin' in now," Josiah, pointing north, called down from the tower. "Looks like he's still all in one piece. Ain't even bleedin', far's I can see. Old Drucker must not—"

"Number four!" Penn roared.

"Aye, sir!" Josiah's head disappeared inside the cupola, and on the ground below, Malachi snickered. Both knew that when Penn called them by rank instead of by name, it was time to take cover.

"Malachi, show these men where to stow their gear and then report back to me. Where the hell is James?"

"He ain't back yet ... sir. Reck'n he stayed to visit a spell with Hannah."

Penn prayed for patience. It had been hours since James had driven off with Hannah and the baby. How long did it take to off-load a trunk and a few parcels?

"And take down that canvas curtain, dammit!" he barked as the boy hurried into the station house. "Then report back to me for lifeboat drill!" Turning a pair of farmers into surfmen wasn't a job he tackled every day. For the most part, a station's men came from the nearest village, weatherwise men who had grown up with boats and the sea. Failing that, he supposed he should make the best of what he'd been sent.

Adam galloped in over the dunes, and Penn watched without comment while he saw to his mount. Thank God he had come back alone this time. And in one piece. The rest could wait until Penn had the time to deal with it.

"Report?" he snapped.

"Some dunnage come ashore just north o' the halfway house."

"You stayed on to investigate?"

Adam's smooth cheeks reddened under his brother's scathing regard, but he held his ground. "I met Oliver riding down from Chic'macomico. He said it weren't nothing but junk that washed down the beach from that sloop that went aground up near the inlet last month."

"You're late."

"There's tower watch. I weren't on patrol."

"Any time a surfman is on that shore, he's damn well on patrol!"

Sullenness slipped like a dark shadow over Adam's even features. "I weren't exactly on the shore. I rode on up to Drucker's to tell him that me an' Oleeta was going to get married soon's the boat come in. I already had the paperwork done."

Penn leveled a look at his younger brother that would have felled a lesser man. Adam was slow, but he was no coward. Penn was aware of a feeling of grudging pride in the boy, both for standing by his woman and for standing up to his superior officer when he felt circumstances warranted it.

And for that heresy alone, Penn told himself, he needed his head examined.

" 'Leeta says she told you 'bout the baby. I didn't lay off to put her in the family way, Penn, I swear. But I ain't sorry it happened. I sent her'n the boy off to their ma's folks up the beach so Drucker wouldn't take a belt to her, an' Chester wouldn't get hisself whupped a-standin' up for her. Soon's they was out o' the house, I told the old buzzard we was goin' to get married, and there weren't nothing he could do about it less'n he wanted his own grandchild to be borned in shame."

Slowly, Penn shook his head. "It's a wonder the old heathen didn't take an ax to your scrawny neck," he said, a reluctant grin creasing his tanned cheeks. "In his place, I probably would."

Relaxing visibly, Adam said, "You ain't near as mean as you make out."

"For God's sake don't let on, or I'll lose what little control I've got around here," Penn growled. "Go on inside. Make yourself known to the two new hands. Farmers!" he jeered, but with a grin on his face. "Grab something to eat if you can find anything. Twins can take the first patrol, the rest of us has got lifeboat drill. Come tomorrow, I reck'n we may as well start patching up another house over to the village."

But by sunset, when the first patrol was due to go out, James had still not returned. Penn had put the new hands through their paces, relenting only when the one who claimed to be able to cook offered to see to a long overdue supper.

The orders of the day had been cut before the additional men had arrived. After the evening meal, Penn sent the pair of them out on first patrol with the twins. At least they knew their way around horses—although he rather suspected they'd be more at home with a team of mules than with the half-wild banker ponies the station relied on for transport.

Alone in the station, for Adam had chosen to ride north again, promising to be back in time for the second patrol, Penn rummaged in the medical supplies until he found a half-empty bottle of brandy. He slapped a handful on the place on his shoulder that had been bothering him, then poured more in a coffee cup and went to stand before the window that faced out onto the village.

A light wind had sprung up just after the sun

went down. He could barely make out the roof of Miss Marthenia's house, and the two big cedars in the front yard. Now and then, when the trees swayed, he caught a gleam of lamplight.

James was still there with her. Penn swore under his breath. Tilting the cup, he downed the last of the brandy, then poured himself another drink. And then another one.

Dammit, he might as well resign and go to farming himself for all the good he was doing here! Maybe he could make a trade with the Garner brothers—their farm for his station.

The more he drank, the more depressed he became, and the more depressed he became, the more he drank. For two cents, he would jettison his blasted rule book, write his letter of resignation, strip off his uniform, and start rowing toward the mainland.

It had all begun with that blasted woman, Hannah Ballinger! Mrs. Ballinger, relict of the late Edward Ballinger.

Ha! Relict of the devil, more likely!

Well, the devil and Hannah could both go to blazes for all he cared. It was her fault—every last bit of it! Adam and the Drucker girl, starting a baby, for God's sake!

And James, going all soft in the head over a woman who had played them all for fools from the first day she had stepped off the boat, with her big gray eyes and her yellow silk scarf, and her damned violets!

Oh, yes, she had them wrapped around her little finger, she did. Poor Mal and Josie thought the sun rose and set by her hands.

Well, not him! Not Captain Pennington Carstairs Warfield. He wasn't born yesterday, to be taken in by some smooth-skinned little witch with her soft city voice and her soft city manners, and her soft city smile. She hadn't fooled him, not for a minute, by damn!

Penn drained the bottle into his thick white mug and downed it in one gulp, wiping a hand across his mouth. He swore, the sound of his voice echoing in the vast, empty room, and he swore again. After five months his crew was nearly back up to full strength, and what did he have to show for it?

Nothing. Not a damned soul to know or care that he was tired, that he was discouraged, that he was lonesome as a whore at a church circle meeting and mad as hell, thinking of James and Hannah over in the village. Wondering what they were . . .

What they . . .

The cup fell to the floor and rolled harmlessly under the chair. Penn's head fell forward on his chest, his long, muscular legs sprawled gracelessly out before him. After a while a snore issued from his throat. Then a soft oath—a name—and another snore.

That was the way they found him. James first. He had stayed later than he'd expected when Hannah's chimney began to send smoke into the house. Without a ladder, he hadn't been able to go up on the roof and check out the matter from that end, so they had decided to allow the stove to cool down, and naturally, he had waited in order to assure Hannah that there was no danger of fire.

Adam got back just before dark. The twins and

the two new hands were just riding in off first patrol, and after introducing himself to the Garner brothers, James drew Josiah aside. "I want you to go for Hannah," he said quietly. "Tell her Penn's sick and needs her."

"Sick? It ain't nothing catching, is it? Wouldn't want Sara M'rella to come down with nothing."

"No danger. He's just jug bit, is all."

"*Penn?* He ain't never drunk more'n—"

"Yeah, well, this time he did. Now go! Tell her to take your horse, and you stay with the baby." He eyed the two new men, who were standing just out of earshot, looking wary, curious, and exhausted, having set out from the mainland before daylight with scarce a moment to rest since.

James saw Josiah on his way, sent Malachi to stand tower watch until he and Adam could set out, and ordered the two new men to bed.

"Breakfast is at four. Whichever one of you cooks best takes the duty, the other one can take the fourth watch."

James had tried to lever his brother's dead weight out of the chair and onto the bed, but hearing the patrol ride in, he'd left him where he was. A few stiff muscles would be the least of the poor devil's worries a few hours from now, and James had a patrol to ride.

Still, it was puzzling. In all his born days, James couldn't recall a single time when his brother had dived deep enough into the bottle to suffer the aftermath, not even after Margaret had left him. Not even when the *Canarais* had run aground and Penn had lost a boat full of survivors—most of them women and children—when the ship's boiler had exploded before he could pull away in the lifeboat.

He had lost two crewmen as well, but Penn himself had been blown clear by the blast. James had always suspected that his own survival had made the loss even harder to bear. As number-one surfman at that time, Penn had been in charge of the operation, due to the keeper's illness. His had been the authority, his the decision to take out the boat one more time. He had been warned by the other crew on the scene, but he'd gone out anyway. The seas were mountainous, but there was a smoother area in the lea of the foundering hull, and he'd thought he could make it through and back safely. He hadn't counted on the boiler's blowing.

He had taken a chance and lost—lost two good men, as well as nine passengers. The fact that he'd been burned down his entire left side and still bore scars to this day didn't make it any easier to bear, but then nothing ever did. For three days after the *Canarais* had gone down, Penn hadn't spoke a single word.

But neither had he drunk himself insensible. Whatever had got to him this time—and James had a very good idea what it was—it would either work itself out or burrow deeper. Time alone would tell.

"Sick? Is he feverish? I knew that shoulder of his was giving him trouble," Hannah exclaimed. She had noticed how Penn had favored his shoulder ever since he'd got back from chasing down the horses, but when she'd offered to tend it for him, he'd glared at her as if she'd threatened him with a hot poker.

"I ain't real sure, but I think you'd better come take a look, Hannah. Penn ain't never been sick a day in his life."

"Oh, my mercy," she murmured, scurrying around to gather up what she might need—although the station was far better equipped to deal with illness and injury than she was. "Sara Mirella's been fed and changed. Likely she'll sleep until I get back, but if she rouses, just diddle her on your knee and sing to her. She likes birdcalls if you can whistle. The sound seems to fascinate her."

She only prayed she would be in time. And that Penn wouldn't be seriously ill. And that he hadn't allowed the wound on his shoulder to fester until it had poisoned his entire system. She had offered to look after it and he'd nearly bit her head off. Stubborn man! As if showing a bit of bare skin in a woman's presence would compromise him beyond redemption.

With Josiah's help, she climbed aboard the stiff wood and leather saddle and grabbed the reins tightly with both hands. Skirts about her knees and modesty out the window, she clucked and jiggled her hips backward and forward in an effort to prod the shaggy beast into motion. Finally, Josiah whacked the mare on the rump and they set off at a shambling trot.

Hannah had been on a pony exactly three times in her entire life, none of them as an adult. This pony was considerably taller than the Shetland their neighbor had owned, and she didn't trust her one little bit. "I do hope you know where we're going, my dear horse," she panted, "for I certainly don't know how to tell you!"

* * *

Spirits. The room fair reeked of the stuff! Disapproval bristling in every inch of her five-foot-four-inch frame, Hannah proceeded to throw open the window and collect the evidence of a night of debauchery, which included an empty bottle, a mug with a broken handle, and . . .

A silk stocking?

The thing was dangling from Penn's limp hand, trailing on the floor. No wonder she could find only the one when she had packed her belongings to move. But what on earth was Penn doing with it? Not that she had much use for foolish luxuries like silk stockings, but it had been a part of her trousseau and she'd kept it, ladders and all, for sentimental reasons.

She snatched it away and stuffed it into her pocket, sentiment forgotten. "All right then, Captain Rules-and-Regulations," she muttered, "let's get you settled."

He was not feverish—at least his brow wasn't overly warm. But he was sprawled awkwardly in his chair, his neck bent in a way that could hardly be restful. Every time she went to shift him, he swatted at her as if she were a troublesome fly.

"Go 'way," he growled.

"Gladly, as soon as I can reassure your brothers that you're in no danger of expiring."

"Meddlesome female . . . tongue clatterin' away like luffin' jib in a full gale. Go 'way!"

Oh, she was tempted! Tempted to give him a shove that would send him sailing right across the room! Unfortunately, she thought too much of his poor, put-upon brothers to show up their tin god for what he was. They thought he was *ill*?

So be it. She had a remedy that would cure what ailed him in short order. The cook had often made it up for Thomas, and on occasion for Jarnelle. The punishing dose was designed to drive out the devils, if one managed to survive the exorcism.

A few moments later, Hannah returned with the dose she had prepared. Fortunately, she'd found a full bottle of syrup of ipecac in the medicine chest, and improvised the other ingredients from the kitchen.

The first challenge was getting him to swallow the stuff. "Penn, you're going to have to sit up," she said calmly.

"Dammit, go 'way," he repeated without opening his eyes. Really, he looked dreadful. If she hadn't known better, she would have thought that he was indeed quite ill.

"I've mixed up a potion that will soon have you feeling better. We'll deal with your headache after we've got rid of the poison." Placing the cup on the desk, she grasped an arm and tugged.

"Goddammit, woman, leave me be! Go flap your gums some'res else." He muttered something about a deceitful, managing witch, and Hannah flinched from the words as though he'd struck her.

In vino veritas. Was that truly what he thought of her?

Ignoring her own hurt, she plopped the pail she'd brought along in his lap, grabbed him by the hair and shoved his head backward, then held the cup to his mouth until he was forced either to swallow or strangle.

It occurred to her even as she waited with malicious anticipation for the medicine to do its rough work that he could easily have thrown her to the floor, for he was a powerfully built man.

But he hadn't. Oddly enough, it never occurred to her to be frightened of his far greater strength, and Hannah, of all women, had cause to fear a man's strength.

For a moment, neither of them moved. Then Penn groaned and lifted stricken eyes to hers. The next moment he was casting up his accounts, clutching the enameled pail as though it were a lifeline.

"There now, you'll feel better in a little while," she declared cheerfully.

The pail she set on the stoop for someone else to deal with. Briskly, she filled a basin with cold water, took a cloth from the shelf, and marched back to the keeper's room. "Now, we'll tackle that head of yours. I have no doubt it feels big as a pumpkin by now."

"You still here?" he jeered, one eye closed, the other focused accusingly on her as she leaned down to position her shoulder under his arm.

"All right, altogether now—up we go! The sooner I get you settled, the sooner you'll be rid of me," she said smartly. "It's not as if I'd nothing better to do, you know." She shoved, he lurched, and she grabbed his other shoulder in an effort to keep him from tumbling forward.

Penn swore long and loud. "Damn it, woman, are you trying to kill me?"

"I'm sure you don't need my help with that task, you seem to be doing a fine job of it all by yourself.

Now when I lift the next time, try to get your feet under you, all right?"

He grumbled, but managed to stand swaying while Hannah supported his near two hundred pounds of solid muscle, bone, and sinew. If there was an ounce of fat on his massive frame, she decided, it was between his ears. "Now, onto the bed. No, don't try to bend over," she warned when he sagged forward, "I'll deal with your boots."

Somehow, working at odds with each other, Penn ended up lying on the bed, the covers having been folded down to the foot beforehand, with Hannah, her hands on her hips, panting over him.

"You don't have to look so blasted smug," he snarled, wincing with every word.

"Head hurt?" She smiled sweetly.

"No, dammit!" He grabbed the top of his head with one hand, his left shoulder with the other, and Hannah's smile faded. Come to think of it, that left shoulder of his had felt distinctly warm when she'd been jigging him into position.

"Let's get those clothes off and then we'll see to something for your head. I doubt you could keep anything down right now."

At that, both Penn's eyes came open. He stared up at her, awestruck. "You lay one hand on my clothes, madam, and you'll regret it, I'm warning you. Me and my head can survive without your confounded meddling!"

"I've seen your big feet before, Captain Warfield. And for your information, I've seen more of you than your feet!"

"Yes, well, you've seen all of my hide you're going to see. I ain't no blasted peep show!"

"I assure you, I've no interest in your hide, as you call it," Hannah said primly, although she was sorely tempted to laugh. She thought she had come to know Penn Warfield rather well, but never would she have credited him with offended modesty. "Now, would you like to sit up, lean forward, and remove your own boots, or will you accept my assistance?"

Penn closed his eyes and sighed, pain etched in every line of his weathered face. More pain, it occurred to Hannah, than might be accounted for by a throbbing head and an abused stomach.

"You do it," he mumbled finally. And at her smug look, he said sullenly, "Dammit, a man can change his mind, can't he?"

"Yes, indeed. And we'll both pray that your new one works better than the old one did."

The baleful look he sent her made her relent, and she said, "Penn, let me open your shirt and examine your shoulder. Please?" She touched his forehead, brushing his unruly hair off his brow. "Please?"

"Leastwise I know why you're a widow at such an early age," he grumbled. "Bullied the poor devil to death, didn't you?"

It was the whiskey talking, Hannah told herself. It was still in his system, even though it was no longer in his belly. Poison couldn't be gotten rid of so easily. But the fight had gone out of him. His skin was ashen and glistening with sweat. There were shadows under his eyes, and the hollows under his sharply chiseled cheekbones were more pronounced than ever, as were the lines that bracketed his wide, firm mouth. The small, diagonal scar on his chin that, according to James, had come from a flying hoof, stood out in bold relief.

"Poor dear, I shouldn't gloat," she whispered as she unbuttoned the remaining few buttons of his shirt and began to ease it off his shoulder. It was impossible to lay it open all the way, for while he offered no resistance, neither did he offer any help.

Hannah frowned. She laid a hand over the red swelling that surrounded the small, fairly deep cut on the curve of his shoulder, but she hadn't needed the evidence of her palm to tell her that it was badly fevered. "Oh, my mercy, is this why you drank so much? You were trying to run from the pain?"

He opened his eyes to look at her, then closed them again. Hannah could have told him that one couldn't run from pain. It followed like a shadow— the brighter the sun, the darker it loomed.

"If I could only go back and do things differently," she whispered as she wrung out the cloth and laid it over the angry wound. She had made her choice in a moment of panic. It hadn't seemed so wrong at the time.

Penn opened his eyes again at the soft words, wondering if he'd heard her correctly. Wondering what she would have done differently. Wondering . . .

God, he felt wretched! What was she doing here, anyhow? She'd left, hadn't she? James had taken her away and the Garners had arrived, and his damned shoulder, where that damned stallion had kicked him when he was down, was fixing to go putrid on him. Hell of a lot of good he'd be with one arm!

"Hannah—use the carbolic acid. Should've done it myself . . ."

Darkness threatened to smother him. He fought it at first, but when a soft, cool hand pressed against his throbbing forehead, he closed his eyes and surrendered.

Chapter 14

HANNAH had tied the mare's reins to the flagpole with a length of halyard. The men didn't do it that way, but she knew that unless she wanted to walk home, she'd better make certain the animal stayed put. "I'm sorry, my dear, but I just don't trust you," she murmured as she untied the neat bow. It took her four tries to climb up on top of the contrary creature, and even then she could only pray that the mare could see better in the darkness than she herself could.

Home again, she looped the reins over the gatepost and dashed inside. "Did Sara wake up?"

"Never let out a peep. How's Penn?"

"Sleeping off most of what ailed him, but Josie, his shoulder is feverish. Evidently he hurt it rounding up the horses, and it didn't get the proper attention. Now it's inflamed. I cleaned it and used the powders, but someone will need to look at it again in the morning. Penn wanted me to use carbolic acid."

"Gawd, he never! That stuff ain't used for nothing but animal bites."

She nodded. Washing the horse smell from her hands, she hurried to the cradle and gazed down at her sleeping daughter to assure herself that she was all right. "I didn't, of course, but if it isn't better by tomorrow, you're to send for me at once. I might have to lance it. Josie—the skin on his shoulder—what happened to it?"

Briefly, the young man told her of the *Canarais* incident and the burn scars, most of which had faded over the years, while Hannah gripped the back of her rocking chair, a stricken look in her eyes. He promised to come for her in the cart if the patient was not quickly on the mend. "Less'n he gets cross-eyed drunk, though, there won't be no use. Penn ain't one for lettin' folks do for him long's he's on his feet."

As weary as she was, Hannah had to laugh at that. "Perhaps I should have tied him to the bed while I had the chance."

Josiah grinned, his eyes dancing in the lamplight. "I wouldn't want to be nowheres around when he come to. Did you hear we got two new hands? Penn, he drilled them poor devils till they was fit to drop an' then sent 'em inside to commence to cookin' supper. Luke's biscuits ain't near as good as your'n," he said hopefully. But when Hannah failed to offer to return to the station and take over the cooking again, he only shrugged. "Reck'n now you're all settled in nice an' cozy, you don't want to do nothing much but sleep of a morning and play with the baby."

Hannah was smiling as she showed him out the door, but the smile faded quickly. *Was* she really finally settled?

As settled as a body could be, perhaps, living in a borrowed house with a few borrowed furnishings and no possible way to earn a living for herself and her daughter. They would hardly starve. She had never gardened before—the church had always sent a man around to do the parsonage grounds once a week, and at Jarnelle's, she had been far too busy inside the house.

But she could learn. There were fish practically outside her door, and friends within call. There was always mending to be done for the men of Paragon station. It was hardly fitting for the keeper to darn stockings and turn collars, no matter how deft with a needle he professed himself to be.

Best of all, she was finally free of the paralyzing fear that had dogged her every step for so long that she'd thought she would never again smile, let alone laugh.

Her last thought before she got up off her knees and crawled into bed, however, was not of Thomas, but of Penn. Penn, the lonely, wounded hero, who covered his own vulnerability with a crust a mile thick.

The following day dawned bright as an Easter egg. Hannah spent the morning outside, bracing up fallen fence posts and redirecting the rose runners while Sara Mirella lay on a blanket on the porch. By noon she had rolled her sleeves up past her elbows and was heartily wishing she dared tie up her skirts and allow the light breeze to flow under her petticoats. If her mind occasionally strayed in the direction of the station, she quickly looked around for another chore. There was a surprising degree of satisfaction to be found in sheer physical exertion.

The sky began hazing over early in the afternoon,

and dusk came early, bringing with it fresh gusts of cool wind. With thunder rumbling sullenly in the distance, Hannah was torn between wishing for rain so that she could replenish her supply of fresh water, and praying it wouldn't storm. She'd had a deep-seated fear of electrical storms ever since, as a child, she'd seen a man killed by lightning when he'd taken shelter under a tree during a Sunday school picnic.

Yet the strange sense of expectancy in the air was irresistible. Lingering in the doorway, she watched as the wind flattened the pale beach grass and played in the branches of the cedars. Sara Mirella, sated and content for the moment, slept in her arms, her warmth a small hedge against loneliness.

Not that she was lonely. There was companionship less than a mile away, and she had no doubt that she would be welcomed back for a visit anytime she chose to go.

But already two strangers had moved in, filling her place. It wouldn't be quite the same now.

She was turning to go inside to the snug, lamplit security when she saw him. Darkness had just swallowed up the last streak of light in the sky, but even so, there was no mistaking that rangy build, the broad shoulders, and long, powerful limbs, nor the arrogant tilt of his head.

Warily, she watched as Penn slid off his horse and dropped the reins. "Is something wrong at the station? Is it your shoulder? Do you need me?"

Seeing her in the doorway, her sleeves rolled up against the stifling heat, the top three buttons at the neck of her gown open, Penn was caught off guard by the aching sense of need that shot through him. She reminded him of a skittish doe.

However none of his thoughts broke through the harsh discipline of his face. "I've come to apologize," he said stiffly.

"Apologize?"

"For calling you a meddlesome, managing, deceitful witch. Leastwise that's about as near as I can recall. I may have set a word wrong, but I reck'n that's the gist of it." Halting at the edge of the porch, his features in shadow until a flash of lightning illuminated the familiar crags and valleys, Penn waited tensely for her response.

"You forgot the part about my clattering tongue," Hannah said solemnly. "The way you phrased it, comparing it with a luffing jib in a gale was really rather poetic. I think. What on earth is a luffing jib?"

Ignoring the question, Penn said aggrievedly, "I seem to recall that you made a remark about my mind that weren't awful kind." Why the devil was he even here? The woman had removed herself from his keeping. Nothing in the book said he had to come after her, yet it had ridden his back all day, this need to tell her—this confounded urge to see her, to hear her voice, even if only to swap insults.

Hell, he didn't know why he was there, and that was the God's honest truth. He was still fuzzy on the details of what had happened last night, but he had a powerful memory of seeing her bending over him—had he been in bed then? He couldn't remember getting himself there. But he could remember her face bent over his, so close he could see the tiny slivers of gold in the gray of her eyes.

He had a miserable recollection of clutching a pail in his arms and wondering why anyone would set off a flare in his shoulder.

He remembered feeling like hell warmed over, and he clearly remembered the touch of her hand on his body. Soft, cool, soothing even while it hurt like the very devil. He didn't have the least notion of how she'd got there, much less why, but he had a feeling he hadn't shown to his best advantage.

One thing he remembered all too clearly, though, was the sound of his own voice calling her meddlesome and managing and deceitful. And while there might be considerable truth in the words, he regretted speaking them.

A gust of wind, harder than the rest, hurled rain across the porch, and Hannah stepped back. "I reckon you'd better come on inside. You can't very well go home until this passes over." She *reckoned*? Mercy, she had never "reckoned" in her life until she'd run afoul of the Warfield tribe. They even affected her manner of speech!

"I'm not like to melt from a little rain."

"Of course not. And you're immune to lightning, I suppose."

The rain was pelting against his back, plastering his shirt against his muscular body. Penn told himself that as long as he was here, he might as well see if her roof still leaked. The twins weren't exactly famous for their carpentry skills, and James . . .

James, he thought bitterly, had far more on his mind than seeing her quarters all squared away Bristol fashion.

Hannah led the way inside. "Take the chair," she offered, praying it would bear his weight.

But Penn wasn't of a mind to settle. He paced from room to room, examining windows, a tour that took all of three minutes, considering there were only three rooms and a total of four windows.

"Roof leaks in the front room. Fetch me a pot and I'll see to it."

Wordlessly, Hannah laid the baby in her cradle and brought him her only pot. "I hope it clears before morning, for I'll need it then."

Penn's frown deepened as he took the dented, but brightly polished utensil from her hand and moved away. Dammit, she still smelled of violets! Forcing himself to think in more practical terms, he said, "I'll send one of the boys over with a supply of kitchen equipment."

"You'll do no such," said Hannah, crossing her arms over her bosom. "I have sufficient, thank you."

Penn glared at her. They were on opposite sides of the empty room, but as the room was barely ten feet square, it was entirely too close.

Penn recalled the day she had arrived on the island. He had stood no closer to her than this, yet even then he'd been aware of a potent attraction. He'd been drawn to everything about the woman, from her pale, smooth skin—so soft he'd been tempted to reach out and touch her—to her large gray eyes, so clear a man could drown in the depths and never see the danger. He'd been aware even then of her strength and her vulnerability. The way she'd had of bracing herself against the wind and confronting them all with her chin up, and she a woman alone, plainly out of her element.

Since then he had come to know her laughter, her kindness and—

And dammit, she was doing it to him again! The woman really *was* a witch!

"I, uh—like I said, I just rode over to apologize. I'm right sorry if I offended you, Hannah. I'd better get on back now, but I'll send one of the boys over tomorrow with—"

"You'll do nothing of the kind, Penn Warfield, and if you've half a brain inside that thick skull of yours, you'll stay in this house until the storm passes over. You shouldn't be out at all, with that shoulder of yours."

Penn shook his head in wonderment. She was doing it to him again. "Madam, I've been out in storms that would curl the hair on a snake's belly. What's more, there's nothing wrong with my shoulder. And I'm sure as hell not afraid of a little rain!"

He was afraid, all right, but not of the rain. Not of the thunder that rattled the few panes of glass left in the windows. Not even of the lightning that repeatedly stabbed the darkness. What plumb pure scared the caulking right out of his seams was all the crazy notions she was putting into his head. Lately, he'd had feelings and urgings and hungers that no decent man would even *think* about in the presence of a lady.

In the act of making his escape, Penn was halted by a sharp cry from the next room. "Sara Mirella? Hannah, was that the baby?"

But Hannah was already gone. "Ants!" she cried.

"Ants?" He was right behind her. When she bent over the cradle, he bent over her. Sliding the lamp closer on the table, he reached around her to remove the thin blanket that covered the howling infant.

"Do you see any?" Hannah cried anxiously. "Oh, God, where are they?"

A crack of thunder threatened to lift the roof right off the house, and Sara Mirella screamed even louder. Hannah lifted her up, carefully examining the tender skin under her tiny garments for a sign of bites. She had learned just that day that a variety of small creatures considered her house their home.

Penn huddled protectively over both females, ready to do battle on their behalf with whatever predator threatened. Hannah's hair, which smelled faintly of sunshine, faintly of violets, tickled his face. He lifted a hand to brush it away and the hand lingered on her head. It seemed natural.

"There, now," Hannah soothed. 'I don't see any ants—I couldn't find any in her bedding. She couldn't be hungry again so soon, I just fed her and she dropped off to sleep sweet as you please."

Penn, acutely aware of the woman, ran his fingers through the wispy reddish hair on the infant's scalp. He looked behind her ears and checked the creases of her fat neck while Hannah was making a second thorough examination of her clothing.

"Do you think the thunder could have frightened her?" Hannah asked anxiously. "Was there a blast just before she cried out?"

"Reck'n it's possible." The truth was, he hadn't been aware of anything except the woman. Thinking of what he wanted to say to her and what he wanted to do to her—no, *with* her, not *to* her. There was a difference. Wondering how he was ever going to get himself out of this crazy fix he'd blundered into with the all best intentions in the world.

"There now, precious, don't carry on so," Hannah crooned, pretending not to notice that she was standing in the circle of Penn's arms, her head practically leaning against his chest.

"Did you look at her pins?" he asked. Reaching the least bit further around her, he cupped the infant's kicking feet in one large hand, the action bringing Hannah completely against his body. Penn closed his eyes in an agony of ecstasy, knowing he had to get out of there before he shamed himself.

But before his conscience could force him into action, Sara Mirella noisily broke wind.

There was a momentary silence. Hannah's face turned fiery red and she clutched her daughter protectively. Penn began to chuckle. "Leastwise, I reck'n we know what was causing all the ruckus."

Passing wind was not something one discussed in polite company, but Hannah could not deny her relief. "I suppose we do."

"As Mal would say, that was a real gut-ripper." He chuckled some more, and Hannah was alarmingly aware of every inch of contact between their two bodies.

She attempted to move away. "She'll likely sleep now. I suppose I'd better put her down."

Thunder rumbled off in the distance. The storm was passing over, yet the air felt none the less charged. Carefully, Penn took the baby from Hannah's arms and told her to smooth the bedding, which she did, and then she watched as he laid the tiny burden in the homemade cradle. Her eyes suddenly blurred. Her throat ached. She felt for her handkerchief and then remembered that she'd forgotten to put one in her pocket when she'd dressed after her skimpy bath.

"Hannah," Penn said gruffly. Straightening up again, he was standing too close. When she went to step back, his arm barred the way. "Hannah, I've been thinking . . ."

Eyes shining too brightly, she made the mistake of looking up, and all rational thought fled. His face was so close, so dear, so familiar. It was as if her whole life had been leading up to this moment. She lifted her face imperceptibly, and her eyelids drifted down.

Penn groaned. "Ah, Hannah," he whispered, meeting her halfway. What followed was as inevitable as the turning of the tides, an instinctive act of passion between two people who had been alone for too long.

Hannah had been kissed before by only one man. Edward's kisses had been sweet. As for what followed after they were wed—the marriage act—it had been pleasant, even pleasurable after the first few days. She never thought of Thomas's hateful act of violence in the same light, for to do so would have defiled what had once been between her and her husband.

But this throbbing pressure in her loins—this melting of her limbs—this was neither sweet nor pleasant nor violent. It was compulsive. It was shattering! Every sense she possessed came throbbingly alive as she accepted the tentative thrust of a man's tongue for the first time in her life.

His hands were in her hair, and then sliding down her back to hold her more tightly to him, shaping her waist and then moving around to her front to rest just beneath her breasts.

And she ached to be touched there, oh, she did!

But instead, he put her from him. Swaying, she would have fallen had not he steadied her with his hands on her arms. "God, Hannah, I'm so sorry," he whispered hoarsely.

Sorry? Still reeling from the effects of his kisses, still enveloped in the taste and the scent of him, in the feel of his powerfully aroused body moving against hers, Hannah could only shake her head. "The storm," she murmured. Gesturing aimlessly, she tried to pretend that what had happened was due to some rare atmospheric phenomenon, but she knew better.

Penn knew better, too, but until he was completely in control of the situation again, he was not about to argue. "Storm. Electricity. Makes folks do strange things."

They were both breathing hard. Hannah stared down at the tips of her worn black shoes. Penn stared at the top of her head. Outside, the storm drifted out over the ocean. A light drizzle lagged behind, and now and then lightning glowed behind the clouds, but the thunder that followed long afterward was more felt than heard.

Inside the small cottage, the storm still raged. Hannah was the first to recover.

"Your saddle will be wet. I'd better give you something to dry it off with."

"Didn't use one. Peg don't mind the rain."

They were standing several feet apart, Hannah's hands clasped before her, Penn's curled into fists at his side. He looked almost angry.

With her? Was he now going to accuse her of being a wanton as well as a meddlesome witch? Her chin lifted and she gave him a cool, shuttered look. "You'd best have one of the boys change the dressing on your shoulder before you go to bed," she said, just as calmly as if her stomach weren't clenched in knots.

"Yes, I—well, I'd better be going. New hands and all—storm'll be well out over the sea by now. I'd best be . . ."

"Yes," Hannah agreed. "I expect you'd better."

If Hannah thought things would be different between them, she was disappointed. Or perhaps reassured. Before she had quite finished her breakfast the next morning, Adam came to tell her that Captain Dozier's *Hamlet* had been sighted out in the channel.

"I'm on my way up to fetch Oleeta," he said, grinning broadly.

"Her father has agreed, then?"

"He come around right smart once he run out of cuss words. Signed for her, but he won't come to the marryin'. Says him and Chester's got better things to do."

"I'm sorry, Adam, I know Oleeta would have wanted her family there. Am I invited?"

"Why, yes'm, you'n the baby is all part of the doin's. We're gonna have us some music afterwards, and Luke, he's bakin' a cake."

He was still smiling broadly, sun glinting off his square, white teeth and his tumbled golden curls. Hannah couldn't help but smile back. "So we're going to have a real celebration. I'm so glad, Adam. It will be wonderful to have neighbors."

"I'll still be spending more time at the station than here, but 'Leeta, she'll keep you company. Be nice to sleep in a real bed instead of—" Breaking off, he flushed bright red and muttered something about James coming for her later in the cart.

Hannah welcomed the excuse to return to the station, even as she tried to think of some excuse to stay away. The thought of seeing Penn again after last night had her dithering so that she dropped her coffee cup twice before she got it rinsed and dried. Fortunately, it was the station's thick white crockery and not her mother's moss rose sprigged china, which was still packed away in the freight office in Raleigh waiting for her to send for it.

However, by the time James came for her in the cart, she was, to all appearances, at least, nicely composed. She had dressed Sara Mirella in the white lawn gown she had made for her, trimmed with the lace she had removed from the best of her old nightgowns. Her own gown was somewhat shiny in the seat and elbows, but she had sponged it with vinegar and aired it in the sunshine all day. She had brushed her hair until it stood out around her head, then gathered it back into a neat bundle and anchored it with a dozen pins before tilting her best straw hat over her left eye.

Last of all, she pinned a tiny gold fob that had belonged to her father at the high neck of her gray gown and touched the buttons she had moved once more, proud of her trim new waistline. With no looking glass, she couldn't judge the results, which was perhaps just as well, though if James's expression was anything to go by, she must have done something right.

"All set to launch our young'un? We thought we'd get through the christening first, in case she gets fidgity. Adam and Oleeta, they've waited this long. Reck'n a few more minutes won't matter."

"I understand one of the new hands is baking a cake for the occasion," Hannah said as she took her place beside him on the hard plank seat.

"Yep. Luke, he bakes and Silas, he fiddles. Reck'n we'll have us some dancing to go with the launching and splicing."

A long-forgotten streak of sentimentality stirred to life and Hannah pictured a young couple on their way to church hand in hand, to see their baby christened. Perhaps by the time Oleeta's baby arrived, there would be a church in the village. At the very least, one of the houses could be set aside for the circuit preacher to hold the occasional meeting.

James clucked lazily in an effort to chivvy the plodding old cart horse along, and Sara Mirella gnawed contentedly on her fist while Hannah, swaying with the movement of the cart, continued to muse. Mercy! A christening and a wedding, with dancing and party food afterward. How things had changed since her arrival!

Not that she would dance. She had never learned how. For all her father had loved music, he had frowned on dancing. Not forbidden it, precisely, but made his disapproval known. Still, no one could possibly disapprove if she tapped her foot and clapped her hands while the others danced.

"Adam's fixing up Mr. Isaiah's place right nice,"

James said laconically as they pulled into the station grounds. "Reck'n you'll enjoy having neighbors."

"I look forward to it," she replied just as the twins hurried out to take the baby and unhitch the cart.

James handed Hannah down, his hands lingering on her waist as he gazed searchingly into her eyes. "Penn, he didn't say much when he come home last night."

Hannah swallowed hard, feeling as gauche as a young girl. "Yes, I—that is—well, he never does, does he?"

James chuckled, and the brief thread of tension was broken. All the same, she had the feeling that a question had been asked and answered. The trouble was, she hadn't the least notion of what it was.

The Garner brother who cooked had evidently got hold of some vanilla. The station, which appeared all but overrun with strangers, smelled strongly of vinegar, lye soap, and vanilla. Everything—floors, windows, and furnishings—had been scrubbed right down to the bare bones, and someone—Josiah, she later learned—had gathered armsful of wildflowers and some that were not wild at all, but had come from a garden in Little Kinnakeet.

Captain Dozier was there, and the elderly man with the gray beard was introduced as the Reverend Ottoway Milbanks. Then Oleeta drew her into the keeper's room for a hurried consultation.

"I done put my hair up in rags, but Adam, he don't like it much. Says it makes me look like one o' them girls at Rosabelle's."

Hannah didn't know whether to laugh, cry, or swat the boy. "I'm sure he meant that as a compliment, Oleeta. I've never seen the—uh, girls at Rosabelle's, but I'm sure they must be awfully pretty, or else they wouldn't be—well, that is to say, I'm sure they must be pretty."

"Then why don't he like my curls?" the younger girl cried plaintively. She had obviously dressed in her very best outfit for the occasion. It differed from the others only in that it was slightly less faded. Hannah was sick with dismay that she hadn't thought to do something about a dress for the child. She could have contrived some way to get past that prickly pride of hers, surely!

"He fell in love with you when you wore your hair in braids. Men, I'm afraid, don't care for change. Here, let me see what I can do . . ." She removed the yellow silk scarf she had tucked into her breast pocket so that only a corner of it showed, brushed the straight, dark brown hair back and tied it with the square of buttercup yellow. "There. See if you can see yourself in Penn's shaving mirror. Yellow looks wonderful on your dark hair, and the ends wave just enough. Adam will love it."

From outside the room came the sound of laughter, of harmonicas, of Sara Mirella's chortling the way she did when one of the twins tickled her under her chin. And, unless she was very much mistaken, the sounds of a fiddle tuning up.

"Goodness, is that really a fiddle I hear?" she asked in an attempt to distract the poor bride, who was about to break her neck trying to see the back of her head in the tiny speckled mirror hung high on the wall.

"Adam says one o' the new hands fiddles. Reads an' writes, too. I never learnt to read nor write, but I'm aimin' to one o' these days."

"Perhaps we can work at it together when Adam's busy here at the station. It will be nice to be able to read stories to our children when they're old enough, won't it?"

"Hannah?" Penn called through the door. "If you're ready, we're all standing by. Sweetpea, she's gettin' a mite restless, though."

And so it proceeded. First the christening. Sara Mirella Matthews Ballinger, daughter of Edward and Hannah Ballinger. Hannah closed her eyes and prayed the good Lord would forgive her the lie, for she could hardly see what purpose the truth would serve now.

When the call came for the godfather to stand up, five men stepped forward, all clad in somber uniforms, their hair scrupulously wet down and combed, boots gleaming with rare brilliance.

The preacher scratched his jaw beneath his beard. "*All* of you?"

"All of us," Penn replied. There was no arguing with the authority in his voice. The poor Reverend Milbanks didn't even try.

And then Oleeta shoved her way between Penn and Adam and glared at the minister. "Me, too! I aim to be one o' whatever this young'un needs, so you might's well take my name down while you're a-takin' names!"

Sara Mirella, by now hungry again and no longer willing to be put off by the attention she'd been receiving, made known her own demands. The service proceeded hurriedly over the loud cries of the discontented infant, and then, while Hannah hurried to the keeper's room to feed and change her newly christened daughter, the company in the common room had another taste of the homemade wine someone had kindly supplied—the same person who had provided the floral arrangements, as it turned out—and two harmonicas and one fiddle began rehearsing the wedding march.

Here comes the bride, Hannah thought, her untidy emotions threatening to get out of hand as she remembered walking up the aisle in her father's church to those same familiar strains. She could almost feel the fine broadcloth of Edward's sleeve as she tucked her hand in the warm crease of his elbow, her chin wobbling as tears of happiness streaked down her cheeks.

She had never given a thought to how it would feel to hear the same music, the same words. Which was odd, considering that she had come here with the express purpose of marrying again. Marrying, in fact, the very same bridegroom who was preparing this very minute to marry another woman.

Lifting the baby over her shoulder, Hannah began the serious task of getting up any air bubbles.

"Almost ready?" James called through the door.

"Almost ready," she called back. She smiled, and if the smile was dimmed by a few tears, who was to know? Her father used to tell her to count her blessings, and Hannah had learned over the years that when large blessings were scarce on the ground, one made do with small ones.

Chapter 15

AT the last minute, Oleeta grabbed Hannah's hand and said desperately, "Stand up wi' me, Hannah. Adam, he's got a whole slew o' kinfolk, but I ain't got nobody but you an' Sara M'relly."

Proudly, babe in arms, Hannah took her place beside the sixteen-year-old bride in the faded calico and the schoolboy's thick boots, her heavy straight hair, now bent on the ends, tied back with a scrap of buttercup silk. There was something so terribly young and vulnerable about the child, Hannah thought—never mind that she was carrying a child of her own under that single patched petticoat—that she began to sob.

Remembering her own wedding, a whole lifetime ago—remembering her own complete happiness and the loving support of her parents and friends as she'd stood proudly beside her handsome young bridegroom while her father presided, she sniffled and gulped, and then smiled through her tears as she felt Oleeta patting her arm.

"There now," the bride whispered, "don't you go an' pucker up on me, or I'll start bawlin', too, and I kin beller loud enough to bust rock."

Hannah palmed her cheeks and tried valiantly to

make her chin cease wobbling. This was a day for rejoicing. The union these children had made was finally going to be blessed, her own precious daughter had just been christened, and against all odds, she had found a home for them both where they could safely begin a new life.

Count your blessings, Hannah Ballinger, she told herself as her eyes brimmed and overflowed once more.

She wept, but she also danced. There was no way she could refuse. Watching Adam and Oleeta, neither of whom knew the first thing about dancing so far as Hannah could tell, galloping up and down the room—laughing herself silly at the sight of Mal and Josie prancing about to the fiddler's tunes, she was no match for James's persuasiveness, even if her eyes did seek out Penn over his shoulder.

"I promise you, your poor feet will suffer," she warned as he pulled her to her feet.

James deftly removed the baby from her arms and laid her in a makeshift cradle, giving her a knotted handkerchief to play with. Then he led Hannah out onto the floor and placed one of his large, thick-soled boots beside one of her own high-buttoned shoes. " 'Pears to me, ma'am, one of mine would make about three of yours. Reck'n I'll survive."

James was a good enough dancer so that Hannah felt almost graceful as she was swept away in a dizzying series of spins, her feet scarcely touching the floor. By now Adam and Oleeta were simply swaying together, holding hands and whispering in the corner, and the twins had given up cavorting like a pair of monkeys and gone back to making music.

At least she thought it was music. Mal was playing something that sounded like "Deck the Halls" in competition with Josie, who was attempting "Turkey in the Straw," while the fiddle continued to saw out the first few bars of the wedding march. Not that anyone was in any mood to complain. Except perhaps for Penn. Poker-faced, he leaned against the far wall, arms crossed over his chest as he watched the dancers. Fully two hours into the festivities, he had yet to speak the first word directly to Hannah. For which, she tried to convince herself as the normally dour James led her out into another rollicking measure, she was grateful.

"Is this supposed to be a waltz or a polka? Oops—sorry," she gasped as she tripped over her partner's foot again. "I did warn you." Biting her lip, she glanced over her shoulder to find Penn's icy glare boring a hole in her back. He'd been scowling at her ever since she'd climbed down out of the cart, and she wondered helplessly what she had done to offend him now.

"Is Penn's shoulder still bothering him?" she asked just as James conducted them through a set of improvised steps that carried them to the far end of the room. "I never did hear how it happened. Did he get kicked?"

"Stallion kicked him when he was down. Later on, I might've hi— That is, I think he might've fell on it. Coulda busted it open again. Not that he'd let on if his whole arm was a-fixin' to turn blue and fall off."

"I don't suppose he would. He didn't want this match, did he?"

"Adam and Oleeta? Everybody knows Warfields don't marry Druckers."

"Well, those two just did," Hannah declared breathlessly, grabbing James's shoulders to keep from being spun off her feet. "If you ask me, it's past time someone taught his high and mightiness that the entire world doesn't run according to his blessed rules and regulations, and I'm sorry if that sounds unkind, but it's the un—the unsomething-or-other truth!" She blinked rapidly several times in succession. "I think I mean unvarnished. James, do you suppose the wine has gone to my head?"

Laughing, James tucked her head under his chin. His eyes met Penn's briefly, and an unmistakable challenge passed between them.

"Never mind, sweetling, I'll take care of you."

"No more wine for me! Will he accept her, do you think?"

"Who?"

"Penn and Oleeta? I can't stand it if he's going to be rude to her on her wedding day."

James sighed. *Penn again. Always Penn.* "Well, I don't reck'n he'll add much joy to the honeymoon. If I was them two, I think I'd settle for the shed to-night."

Honeymoons. Oh, mercy, she was going to start blubbering again. Edward had taken her to a lovely inn in the mountains for three whole days. She'd been so embarrassed when she'd realized that everyone there had known they were newly married. Which meant that everyone there had known precisely what they did each night when they closed their bedroom door.

"James, they need a place to be alone," she whispered urgently.

"Reck'n Adam, he could pitch him a tent in the old graveyard."

"That's absurd! What about one of the other houses?"

"Most is too far gone. Old Isaiah's is the best of the lot, but it's infested with fleas. Raccoon moved in over the winter."

"There's my house . . ." Hannah smothered a twinge of jealousy at the thought of anyone's sleeping in her bed, gazing out at her fig tree, her rosebush—sitting on her blue bench in the morning with her first cup of coffee, basking in the sunshine that streamed through one of the few intact windows in the house.

And then she thought of the young couple, head over heels in love, aching to be alone together, surrounded by half a dozen men, including two strangers. "I could . . ."

"You could do what, wait out on the front porch?" James's wiry strength guided them along the east wall, and before she quite realized what he intended, James halted in front of the glowering Penn. "Hannah here, she's fixing to offer Adam the use of her house for a spell."

Penn's square jaw thrust out like a cowcatcher on the Norfolk and Southern. Hannah, determined not to allow him to disconcert her, refused to look away from the cool derision in his eyes.

"Seems to me," continued James, "seeing as how we got strangers living here now, you might want to let her and Sara use your room again for a few days. Barring that, I reck'n we could put up the curtain again."

Hannah was rapidly losing her enthusiasm for the project. "I didn't mean—that is, I hadn't actually—"

Something flared in Penn's eyes, but was swiftly damped down. And then Captain Dozier from the freighter *Hamlet*, who, along with his mate, had been invited to attend the celebration, approached, hat in his hamlike hand. "Miz Ballinger, you're looking right hearty, ma'am. Glad to see they're a-taking care of you."

Hannah smiled at him distractedly. She could hardly have looked worse than the poor seasick, frightened, pregnant wretch whose rubbery limbs had barely been able to negotiate the gangplank back in January. "Thank you, Captain. You're looking—ah—well, too."

"That there's a fine young'un over yonder in the basket."

She made a polite response, her mind still on the fix she seemed to have got herself into. How could she allow anyone to live in her house before she'd even got the feel of it herself? Still worse, how could she deliberately place herself under Penn's dominion again? She'd had enough of trying to deal with a man who was as changeable as the weather, cold and forbidding one moment, gentle and caring the next.

The old sea captain took himself off to refill his glass, and Hannah turned to James. "About Adam and Oleeta, James, perhaps they don't even want—"

"I believe they're playing my favorite song,"

James declared, swinging her right out from under Penn's nose as the fiddle launched into a lively rendition of "Skip to My Lou, My Darling."

They danced until Hannah was gasping for breath and then headed for the table to quench their thirst with glasses of the sweet wine. Hannah helped herself to another slice of cake as an excuse to rest and catch her breath.

But then Malachi bowed before her and said, "You don't want to dance wi' James no more, Hannah. He sweats like a boar-hog when he gets hot."

James cuffed him and missed, Hannah giggled, and Malachi, holding her stiffly at arm's length, led her out in a wild romp that sent her skirts swirling up about her knees.

"Are we trying to outrun a whirlwind? Who taught you to dance?" she teased as the musicians eased into another barely recognizable melody.

"Penn. He taught me and Josie how to treat a lady when we turned sixteen. Course, we already knew most of it. Perdita, she's this girl at—"

"I know who Perdita is, Malachi," Hannah said repressively, torn between amusement and disapproval.

And then he was off again, spinning, galloping, and telling her about Perdita's penchant for taffy and red garters and singing in the bathtub.

All told, Hannah thought she performed quite well, considering that she had never danced more than a few steps before, and that only with a girlfriend. And that the music sounded more like fox in the henhouse than "Turkey in the Straw." Likely she would have done even better had she not been so aware that Penn's gaze still followed her every step. She almost wished he would ask her to dance so that she could tell him a thing or two.

No, she didn't! Two glasses of wine—or was it three?—had completely unmanned her.

Unwomaned her?

Oh, my mercy, she thought, she *was* in a bad way! Nor could she blame it entirely on the wine. What had happened when Penn had come to apologize had been no more than a fluke—an aberration due entirely to the excessive amounts of electrical currents in the air. Penn had said so himself, hadn't he? Or had she only imagined it?

Perhaps she had imagined the entire episode, she thought a little wildly as, face flushed and chest heaving, she was led off the floor to the row of chairs lined up against the wall.

Josiah appeared at her side. "I'll fetch you a glass of wine to cool you down," he offered.

"No more wine, please! Water will be perfect," she pleaded, and the twins went off wrangling over which one would fetch her a drink.

They had scarcely left before Penn and Captain Dozier appeared before her. Hannah glanced up, wondering why she should suddenly feel as if the tidy new life she had fashioned for herself was about to come unraveled.

"Miz Ballinger, ma'am? The gentleman asking your whereabouts some time back—did he find you all right?"

"The . . . what?"

"This gentleman that was asking about you over across the sound, I just wondered if he ever caught up with you."

"Oh, no," Hannah whispered, her stricken face losing every vestige of color.

"Freight agent in Elizabeth City give him your direction. He remembered you right off, on account of we don't get many passengers for Paragon no more."

Thomas! It could only be Thomas. Dear Lord, how had he traced her? Days before she'd left, she had deliberately mentioned her cousin who lived up near the Tennessee border, just so that once she was gone, he would think that's where she had run to.

How could he possibly have guessed her whereabouts? She had never once mentioned the Outer Banks, had hardly even known it existed until she'd seen Penn's advertisement.

"Miz Ballinger? Ma'am?"

"Hannah? Are you all right?"

Leaning over, Penn grabbed her wrists and began chaffing her hands, which had suddenly grown icy cold. With wide and oddly unfocused eyes, she watched as his broad shoulders blocked out the light like a pair of giant sheltering wings.

Sheltering wings? Like a bird of prey, more like!

"Too much wine," said James.

"Too much gallivanting," Penn snapped. He took the glass of water Malachi had brought and pressed it into her hand.

"It's all that vaniller extract Luke used in the cake," Josiah opined. "I told him he was usin' too much. Duck eggs ain't fishy tastin' when they're fresh-laid, an' the lard weren't all that rancid."

Suddenly, Hannah giggled. If there was an edge of hysteria in the sound, she prayed no one else would notice it. Penn scowled, making her laugh all the harder.

"Madam, it's time you were setting out for home." He lifted her by her arm, and she discovered much to her amusement that the hinges of her knees no longer worked properly.

"I do believe that last glass of wine has done me a disservice," she observed just before she burst into tears.

James insisted on driving her home, for once overriding Penn's objections. "I'll be bringing her back directly. Tell Adam to give us time to pack a bag and then him and Oleeta can ride on over."

"I don't see no cause for all this switching about," Penn grumbled.

"You remember how riled you was when you and Margaret got married, and me'n Adam threw sand at your window and rosined your doorknob? And Mal got sick in the night from drinking Nate's beer and threw up all over Margaret's new coat?"

"Godamighty. Go on, then! But get on back here, I've wasted too much time on foolishness, as it is."

It was nearly four o'clock, time for the first watch to go out, although the day was clear and there were more than four hours of light left in the sky. "Twins out, Silas up," Penn commanded, meaning the twins would patrol the beach while Silas Garner stood tower watch.

A tower watch alone would have sufficed until dusk, but James knew better than to argue. He'd had twenty-eight years to study his brother's moods, and right now, Penn was like a cocked pistol with a hair trigger. It wouldn't take much to set him off.

James waited until they were out of range of the station and then he turned to Hannah, who had remained silent throughout.

"You want to tell me about it?" he asked.

"No thank you. I mean, it wouldn't do any good. I mean, there's nothing to tell."

"Mmmhmm." He clucked Aristotle into a marginally faster gait and tried again. "There's times when sharing troubles makes 'em look considerable smaller. You take Penn now—he's never been one to share, but Adam and me, we used to talk of a night when the others had gone to bed. Adam, he knows he won't ever rise above number one, on account of he's never been much of a hand with paperwork. It's a good living, but he don't get paid year-round. Still, I reck'n he'll manage, leastwise until the babies start coming. Makes a difference, don't it? Havin' a family dependent on you? Who's following you, Hannah? Kinfolk? An old beau? A bill collector?"

"A bill collector!" she protested with a shrill of brittle laughter. "Mercy me, it must be all these fine silk gowns I had made, and the jewelry—oh, and my mink-trimmed cape, of course!" Her cape had once had a collar of gray coney, which she had removed when it had begun to fade and show bald spots.

James pulled the cart up beside the fence and dropped the reins. Aristotle sniffed the rosebush in search of a succulent morsel. "Hannah, things might not seem so bad if you had a husband to share your burdens. I'd be some honored if you would have me—marry me, that is."

Hannah caught her breath in a gasp. *Dear Lord,*

don't let me start blubbering again! "James, you're the dearest friend I have in all the world. Sometimes I almost think you can read my thoughts. Mercy, but that's embarrassing!" She laughed again, a weak effort, but better than weeping. And then, without knowing quite how it came about, she found herself pouring out her woes on James's accommodating shoulders.

Not everything, of course. If she'd had any idea of accepting his offer of marriage, she would have had to tell him about Sara—about Thomas and what had happened that hot August night—but as she never planned to marry again, there was no real need for him to know the entire sordid tale.

"I—I suppose Thomas thought I owed him something, as he'd taken us in when we had nowhere else to go, with Edward para—that is, so ill for so long after the accident. Jarnelle is unable to bear children, and Thomas had hoped—that is, he just assumed we—that I would stay on in Raleigh in this—this accommodation he'd had built over the coach house."

"You didn't want that?"

Hannah shuddered. "No," she whispered. "I couldn't."

"It took considerable courage to come out here alone to marry a man you'd never met." James watched her closely. He hadn't been mistaken. She was frightened. There was something she wasn't telling him, but he couldn't very well force it from her. "All the same, if you'd stayed, Sara Mirella would have had family to see to her welfare."

"She has me! She has five godfathers and a godmother. I don't know what more a baby could need."

"Yes, well . . . if you should ever change your mind, I'd be right proud to offer myself as stepfather, too. I'd never be able to take the place of her real father, but leastwise, neither you nor she would ever know need so long as I'm able to draw breath."

Hannah covered his hand with hers. She would have given all she possessed, which admittedly wasn't much at that moment, to be able to lay her burdens on James's capable shoulders, but in all good conscience, she couldn't do it.

If Oleeta were to be believed, Penn would be against the match, and not for the world would she widen the rift she suspected she had already caused between the two brothers.

As for her own feelings for Penn . . .

"James, if you'll keep Sara for me, I'll go in and pack a bag and change the linens. I wish I had time to do more, not that there's much I could do."

On the way back to the station, they passed the newly wedded pair astride Adam's mare. Oleeta clutched Adam's waist and grinned shyly while Adam's cheeks turned as red as a yaupon berry. "Lord 'a mercy, you'd think by now those two would be old hands at honeymooning," James murmured. He'd insisted on holding Sara on his lap with one hand, the reins with the other, while Hannah clutched her assorted parcels.

"I think it's sweet."

"And I think this young lady is scuppers awash again. Remind me to throw a tarp over my lap before I agree to tote her next time."

"Agree! You're the one who insisted," Hannah crowed, and the mood was suddenly lighter. Nothing more was said of James's proposal of marriage.

That night while Hannah slept in the familiar keeper's room, James and Penn stood on the shore gazing out over a placid sea. "You find out what's eating on her?" Penn asked.

"Some. Not all." Stoically, James had buried his own disappointment. He had known before he'd asked what her answer would be. Despite the fact that she had come out here to marry a stranger, and would have married him had circumstances not redirected the course of events, things were different now. No man could be around Penn and Hannah long without being aware of the powerful undercurrents flowing between them. Her eyes followed him like a compass needle followed magnetic north. Just as his eyes followed her.

James wasn't inescapably in love—not yet. But the longer he was near her, the trickier it would become to navigate around all the hidden hazards. The way she had of humming under her breath while she was working about the station. The way she had of swishing her skirts when she was irritated—usually at Penn. The way her eyes sparkled with hidden lights when she was angry—always with Penn.

God, he would have laughed if it didn't hurt so damn bad, watching the way those two struck sparks off one another. That is, when they weren't all cozied up together in Penn's room.

Nights when he'd come in from watch, hearing the murmur of their voices from the keeper's room, knowing Penn was in there with her, redoing the paperwork he'd already done during the day just as an excuse to be near her—he'd known. A blind man would've known, but not that pair.

If he'd thought it would have done him any good, he would have pressed harder, but it was too late. It had been too late since the day Hannah had stepped off the boat, with a brave little smile on her face, a terrified look in her eyes, and that silly little scrap of yellow silk tucked into her collar.

Ah, hell, if he couldn't have her for a wife, he might as well have her for a sister. Leastwise he would know she and the baby were cared for.

A shooting star streaked across the black velvet sky. Both men watched. Neither commented. "I asked her to marry me," James said when the silence threatened to go on too long. He waited for the fireworks.

It didn't take long. "You *what?*" Penn roared.

"Well, hell—Adam, he's battened down for the long haul now, but that don't mean Hannah has to do without."

"Dammit, Jay, I told you—"

"And I'm telling you, Penn. That woman needs help. She's scared half out of her mind that her brother-in-law is going to show up and take the baby."

Penn took fully ten seconds to review in his mind what James had told him of Hannah's story. "Like hell he will," he drawled fiercely.

James shrugged. "That's what I figgered. So I asked her to marry me, only she wouldn't say yes right off. Probably needs some time to think about it, but me, I'll feel considerable easier once I know she's got a husband to stand betwixt her and trouble. Warfields is responsible for bringing her out here, so the way I see it, Warfields is responsible for seeing no harm don't come to her."

"If Hannah needs a husband, then I'll damn well see she gets one, but it won't be you, little brother," Penn declared. "I'm the one that mailed out that advertisement. I'm the one that picked her letter over them other women that wrote. And I'm not in the habit of turning away from my duty."

James watched him stride back toward the station, where even now, Hannah was sleeping in his bed. If there was a certain bleakness in his narrow face, there was no one around to see it and wonder.

Penn wasn't the only Warfield who had sworn to do his duty, no matter what the cost.

Chapter 16

BY the time three days had passed, Hannah was chaffing to get back to her home. It was not that she begrudged Adam and Oleeta the privacy they needed just now—nor even that life at the station had changed with the addition of two new men, though it had. It was Penn. If Hannah had thought him difficult before, it was nothing to the way he acted now.

He always seemed to be watching her, although that was nothing new. Whenever she was in the keeper's room, he found some excuse to use his desk. When she was hanging the baby's wash on the line, he was usually somewhere on the grounds, drilling or checking his weather instruments.

For another thing, he was excessively polite, and perhaps that was what bothered her most, because she sensed that underneath that surface politeness there was wariness, anger, and something even more disturbing. She didn't know what, much less why, and it bothered her enormously.

Even when he wasn't with her, Hannah couldn't stop thinking about him, which was purely maddening! It weren't as if she had nothing more on her mind.

She had been there three days, certainly time enough for Adam and Oleeta to conduct a suitable honeymoon, when she dashed into the keeper's room one morning to find a clean bib. Penn was standing at the window staring out, in his hand a handkerchief edged in bobbin lace that she recognized as one of her own.

He turned when she came in the door, and for a moment his eyes were unguarded. *He looks so careworn—so tired.* In that instant before the shutters came down again, Hannah glimpsed in him all the pain, the sadness, and loneliness he usually kept hidden away behind a stoic facade. It was gone so quickly she thought she must have imagined it—yet she knew she had not.

Stubborn, *stubborn* man! "Would you kindly tell me what is bothering you?" she demanded. Her skirts swished around her ankles as she tapped an impatient foot on the gritty floor.

"Begging your pardon, madam, there's nothing bothering me."

"No?" Challenge glinted from her eyes, in the tilt of her firm dimpled chin. There was challenge in every line of her body, had she but known it. "Then perhaps you'll be so kind as to tell me why you're constantly spying on me? I'm beginning to feel like a bug under a microscope!"

"You feel like you're being watched? Is there any particular reason why someone would want to spy on you, Hannah?"

Her eyes widened. "No! Certainly not! I only meant—"

"James told me you were worried for fear your

brother-in-law might want to lay claim to Sara Mirella."

"He had no right!"

"She's his niece, his blood kin. A man has a duty to see that his kinfolk don't go needy."

"No, I meant James had no right to repeat a confidence," she said, flustered, frightened. She bit her lip and looked away. "Sara Mirella isn't needy, she has me. We have a home. And even if there were a problem, it's mine, not yours, Penn."

"Everything at Paragon is my responsibility."

"Oh—oh, poo on your responsibility! Thomas is my problem—not that I'm admitting he *is* a problem, mind you, but if he comes looking for Sara Mirella, then I'll simply hide in one of the other houses until he goes away."

"Then what James said is true—you're afraid he might try to claim her."

Over five years of growing despair, Hannah had built up a thick defensive wall, but it was not impregnable. First there had been Edward. Thomas had known just how to use threats against his own brother to keep Hannah in line.

Now there was Sara Mirella, even though she rather thought he would not be so interested in a daughter as he would have been in a son. Even so, Sara could be used against her. Thomas took pleasure in manipulating anyone he deemed weaker than himself. Hannah had often thought it had something to do with the way Jarnelle treated him, as if he were a mongrel on a leash.

Penn stepped away from the window. Morning light limned his rugged features, making him look older than his thirty-one years. "Hannah, I've something to say, and I'd be obliged if you'd hear me out." Something about his bearing caught her attention, and her instinctive protest died on her tongue. "I know you don't think much of me. God knows I'm not a handsome man, nor an easy one. I don't have a comfortable way with women, like some, but I am the man who brought you out here, so if you and Sara Mirella are in some kind of trouble, then it's my responsibility to—"

"But it's not, Penn! It's nothing to do with—"

He held up a hand, palm out, and Hannah stared, mesmerized at the scars, the calluses. This was the hand that had delivered her baby. This was the hand that had held her so tenderly the night she had woken up in the middle of a nightmare. It struck her that he sounded almost humble, which shocked her into momentary stillness.

"A woman alone is no match for a determined man, Hannah. I want you to know that I'll always stand between you and any man who threatens you and yours. That'd only be right and proper. The way I see it, though, there's an easier way to steer clear of trouble from that quarter."

"You mean the law?"

His mouth hardened into a grim line. "The law would most likely come down on the side of an uncle if it means choosing between him and a widow with no support. 'Less'n he was an out-and-out scoundrel, she'd not have much of a chance with the law. Even if he was, more'n likely."

"But that's wrong! I'm her mother! That's just plain sinful!"

"I'm not saying it's right, Hannah, I'm just saying that's the way of it. Unless—"

"Unless I go on running and hiding until Sara is old enough to—"

"Or unless a man offers you the support and protection of his name."

"But that's just—"

"Crazy? Wrongheaded? I'll not deny it, but it's the way the world works, Hannah."

Suddenly, all the fight seemed to drain right out through the soles of her shoes. She sat down heavily, and if the bed hadn't been handy, she would have collapsed on the floor. Penn moved closer, his dark brows knitted in worry, but he didn't attempt to touch her.

Hannah shook her head slowly from side to side. "I can't believe this is happening," she whispered. "I was so sure he could never find me here."

"That's why you answered my advertisement in the paper, I reck'n. You were looking for a safe harbor."

Wordless, she nodded, and Penn nodded, too. He'd known there had to be some reason why a handsome woman like Hannah Ballinger—even one carrying a child—would offer to marry sight unseen a man in a place like Paragon.

Under the circumstances, he had no choice but to do what had to be done. Clearing his throat, he laced his hands behind his back, glanced once at the ceiling, once at the tips of his big, salt-rimed boots, and cleared his throat again. "Madam. Mrs. Ballinger—that is, Hannah? I'd take it right kindly if you would do me the signal honor of becoming my wife."

* * *

Once more under her own roof, Hannah listened to the sounds of construction coming from the house down the road. The Garner brothers, it seemed, were better at carpentry than they were at seamanship, and as long as the weather held fair and no ships were sighted in distress, the work on Adam and Oleeta's house progressed rapidly.

If she had expected to be courted, she would have been sorely disappointed, but of course, she had expected no such. Penn had explained his position quite clearly, although no more than she had already learned from his brothers. Far less, in fact.

"I was married once before, but she died," he'd said stiffly. "I hadn't thought to marry again, but I'll do my best to provide for you and Sara Mirella. You'll not know fear nor need again so long as I'm here to provide."

He didn't mention love. Hannah had known love, and it was nothing at all like what she felt for Penn Warfield. What she'd felt for Edward had been tender and sweet and gentle. There was nothing at all gentle about what she felt each time she clashed with the hard-bitten keeper of Paragon Shoals. He had only to touch her and she felt as though she were coming down with a fever of the blood. He had only to offer her one of his smiles, as rare as wild roses in January, for her to melt right down to the bones.

He had neither smiled nor touched her, and even so, she had said yes so quickly that for days afterward, she blushed, remembering.

Penn had offered her the protection of his name. He was, after all, a man who saw his duty and carried it out to the best of his ability, and she was, quite simply, one more responsibility that had landed squarely on his overburdened shoulders.

Duty. Responsibility! Was this God's notion of a joke?

As days passed, waiting for Captain Dozier to bring the preacher back to Paragon, Hannah wondered how she could go through with it.

And then wondered how could she not.

Where would they live? At the station, or at her house?

They would probably go on as before. Penn had as good as told her he didn't want to marry her, but would do so only to protect her and Sara Mirella from any threat Thomas might present.

What if she never heard from Thomas again? Would Penn despise her for trapping him into an unnecessary marriage? Should she confess everything beforehand and have him despise her even more?

But if he was to marry her, he had a right to know, didn't he?

Still, if she was no more than a duty, what purpose could it possibly serve?

It would serve her honor, that's what! She had been brought up to believe that honor demanded truthfulness at all times, not merely when it was comfortable.

Sighing, Hannah wondered why it was that some questions produced no answers, only more questions.

In contrast to the brilliant sunlight outside, her small rooms with the boarded-up windows seemed darker than ever. Hannah would have ripped off the boards to allow the light and air to flow through, but with sunshine and breezes would come mosquitoes and those pesky green-headed biting flies!

Dare she ask Penn to order enough panes to replace all the missing ones? How could she ask him anything when she never saw him?

And that blessed stove! The minute she fired it up hot enough for biscuits, smoke started leaking from the chimney into the attic, and by the time the biscuits were done, the whole house reeked of wood smoke.

And then there were the mice. Heaven knows, they had a prior claim, but still, she resented having to share her scant provisions with the pesky creatures.

Still and all, it was her home. And the rosebush was looking more beautiful each day. Pausing, broom in hand, she pictured a young bride walking down the aisle of a church dressed all in white, her arms filled with a bouquet of her very own roses.

"Oh, my mercy," she muttered, sweeping the ever-present sand out the door. As if she were a young bride again. As if there was even a church in this forsaken place!

Besides, if she was going to marry at all, she'd best get on with it, roses or not. Lately she'd found herself scanning the horizon out over the sound several times a day, searching for a sail that might mean Thomas was coming after her.

What if Thomas and the Reverend Milbanks should arrive on the same boat? What then?

Slapping the old slat bonnet she had washed and

mended on her head, Hannah grabbed Sara Mirella and headed for Oleeta and Adam's house. She was in sore need of distraction.

Oleeta, who had just finished painting the window trim lavender, dropped her brush in a can of kerosene. "Thought you'd be busy gussyin' up one o' them pretty frocks o' yourn to get married in."

Hannah saw the shy longing in the young girl's eyes. She knew for a fact that Oleeta owned only a few scraps of clothing, and although Adam had brought her a bolt of calico in her favorite color, purple, she didn't know the first thing about dressmaking, having worn her mother's hand-me-downs all her life.

"Do you know, I've been putting off going through my summer things for weeks, because I get so tired of seeing the same dresses year after year. Do you suppose you might find time to help me figure out how to remake some of them so they'll look fresh and new?"

Hannah was no stranger to pride, but there had to be a way of getting around it. Oleeta had one thing any woman would give all the gowns in the world to possess—a husband who adored her.

For the next few hours, Oleeta exclaimed over every faded and threadbare muslin, lawn, and calico Hannah dragged out of her trunk, even those with medicine stains and those with the seams stretched from Hannah's increasing girth during her pregnancy. There had been no money to buy a new wardrobe, and she'd been forced to make do.

When Oleeta asked about Edward, Hannah described the early days of their courtship. "Edward had a fine tenor voice. He used to play the organ in our parlor, and we'd sing while Mama and Papa kept time clapping hands. Sometimes I played, and Edward sang a duet with Papa—sometimes we all sang and sang until our throats hurt."

Oleeta's plain face grew wistful. "You must've loved him some kind of fierce."

Fierce? That was hardly the word to describe the way she had felt about the gentle man she had married so long ago it seemed another lifetime.

"Yes, I loved him very much," Hannah admitted quietly, but it was not Edward's face that flickered in her imagination, but Penn's. I did love him, she insisted silently. Truly, I did.

"Was it the influenza that took him? That's what took my maw."

Hannah explained about the accident, leaving out the fact that Edward had been paralyzed from the waist down and near comatose for the last eleven months of his life. Oleeta might not have had the benefit of much schooling, but she had a quick, intelligent mind.

They laughed together, and Hannah felt her heart expand painfully as she watched the younger girl prance proudly back and forth, carefully holding up the skirts of a ruffled Swiss muslin with an overskirt and a bloused waist. Pink with small red-sprigged roses, it had been one of her favorite dresses, although now it seemed far too young for a matron with a child who was about to be married for a second time.

"I'm so glad it fits you. Pink always makes my skin look sallow, but with your darker coloring, it looks lovely. Thank you for taking it off my hands, Oleeta. My conscience would've made me wear it and I'd have looked as if I were coming down with a liver ailment."

"I'll set with Sara M'rellie to make up for it," the younger woman vowed, and Hannah nodded acceptance of the bargain. "I reck'n you're going to wear that white frock to get married in. It's kinda plain, but it's right pretty, too."

And Hannah reckoned she was, against every rule of propriety. Penn probably wouldn't notice if she stood beside him wearing a flour sack!

And so it went, the waiting. Waiting for the preacher, waiting for disaster to descend—wondering which would come first, and trying hard not to dwell on either event. Hannah had learned long ago not to borrow tomorrow's trouble, for today usually held more than enough.

But the days held laughter, too. And a surprising amount of joy. The two women sewed and watched Oleeta's house take shape. They played with Sara Mirella and gardened to the accompaniment of a chorus of sea gulls, fish crows, and kingfishers.

The days were busy and happy enough, but once night fell, Hannah would often stand in her doorway and gaze out across the island to the station, wondering what Penn was doing, and why he never seemed to have time for her.

Not that she expected him to come courting, but a polite visit now and then to keep her apprised of the situation wouldn't have come amiss.

It was when she glanced over at the lamplight glowing from the window of Adam and Oleeta's house—they no longer referred to it as Old Isaiah's place—that the loneliness threatened to overcome

her. Knowing that Adam and Oleeta were there together, laughing, sharing, loving one another in
that big ugly bed they had padded with blankets
until Oleeta could save up enough feathers to stuff
a ticking.

Knowing that in all likelihood, the only thing in
her life that would change after her own marriage
was her name.

Sighing, Hannah closed her door and went inside, to where Sara Mirella slept peacefully in her
homemade cradle. It was selfish of her to want
more than Penn had offered. After all, she'd known
love once, which was perhaps more than many
women ever knew. She wasn't fool enough to believe that all marriages were made in heaven. More
than a few had been made in that other place, and
at least for a little while she had known the gentle
intimacy that could exist between a man and a
woman who respected and cared for each other.

But selfish or not, Hannah wanted Penn to love
her. If he could learn to care only a little, she might
stand a chance of thawing that frozen core of his,
of making him forget the woman who had broken
his heart, making him learn all over again to laugh
and dance and forget his precious rule book for
just a little while.

And that, she told herself, was about as likely as
seeing pigs fly.

James came by to see her the next morning. "I'm
off to Norfolk," he said. "Now that we're near
about up to full strength and the storm season's all
but over, I thought I'd take me a leave of absence,

so if there's something I can bring you from the city, Hannah, you've only to make out a list."

"Is the boat in?"

"Not yet. I'll ride Mollie north and catch us a boat ride across the inlet. I've friends on the other side, up the beach a ways."

"Oh. Well, then, I wish you a pleasant voyage."

"Sure you don't want me to bring you something? There's some right fine stories in Norfolk."

But stores required money, and what little Hannah had left must be hoarded against the future. "I thank you, James, but I can't think of a thing I really need."

"Books?" he asked, and she shook her head. "Dishes? I'd offer to bring you back a pretty dress to marry in, but I'm afraid I won't make it back in time." He smiled with his lips, if not his eyes.

"Dishes," Hannah exclaimed, forcing a bright smile. "Do you know, I left a crate of dishes in the freight office in Raleigh, waiting to be shipped out once I—" Once she'd learned whether or not the man who had ordered her by mail would keep her when he found out about the baby.

"Then I'll send word for it to be shipped down to Elizabeth City by rail and have 'em set it aboard the next boat headed this way."

The freight costs would likely take most of her few funds, but they were her mother's dishes, and with them she had packed photographs of Edward and both her parents. Things that had saddened her so that she had packed them away long ago.

"Hannah? Are you all right, love?"

Love?

Before she could collect herself, he clamped both

hands on her shoulders, kissed her soundly on the mouth, and then swore softly under his breath.

Hannah's jaw dropped. With his thumb, James gently lifted it, closing her mouth. "There, I've been wantin' to do that for a long time, and I reck'n by the time I see you again, it'll be too late."

With tears in her eyes, Hannah watched him stride across the yard and spring lightly up onto his chestnut mare. He waved gaily, as though he hadn't a care in the world, which was not at all like James, even in the best of times, and she waved back.

"Oh, my mercy," she whispered.

Penn came that night just after dark. Earlier, Hannah had nursed Sara, brought up her wind, changed her into a dry gown and napkin, and settled her for the night. Then she had bathed in water that had been sitting out on the back stoop in the sun all day. It was pleasantly warm, and she used one of her precious bars of violet-scented soap. She had given half her small store to Oleeta as a wedding gift, and one would have thought she'd offered the girl a king's ransom in precious gems.

She was almost ready for bed when she heard footsteps crossing her front porch. Thinking perhaps it was one of the twins, she snatched up a wrapper and twisted her hair, which she had been brushing, into a coil over her shoulder.

"Who is— Penn?" Mercy, she hadn't seen him since the day he offered to marry her! "What's wrong? Is someone sick?"

He stood awkwardly, framed in her doorway,

twisting his black hat in his hands. "It come to me that you might want James instead of me, for I reck'n you know how he feels about you. God knows, he's been mooning around long enough. So if you do," he said stonily, "I'll send word to hold off on the preacher until James gets back."

He watched her closely through eyes that were like glimpses of autumn sky in his tanned, rugged face. And just as unreadable.

Hannah's foot began to tap. She crossed her arms over her chest. "Are you backing out? Is that it? You've lost your courage?"

Penn's eyes widened. "Well, hell no, madam! And you've no call to go insulting me when I only come to do you a favor!"

"A favor? You call offering me your protection and then withdrawing it a *favor*?"

His brows lowered, his jaw hardened, and he leaned forward until his face was three inches from her own. "If you were a man, madam, I'd have your lights and liver for that!"

"You could try," offered Hannah coolly. A lot more coolly than she was feeling. Drat the wretched man, if he made her cry she would do more than have his lights and liver! She would—she would geld him!

"He come here earlier today, didn't he? What did he tell you?"

"If you're referring to James, he came to tell me goodbye and to offer to do any errands I might need. Not that it's any of your—"

"Dammit, it's *my* duty to see to your needs, not James's!"

"He offered. You didn't."

"Well he can damned well un-offer! Whatever he fetches for you, he can take straight back! If you need anything, you come to me, is that clear?"

"That's perfectly clear," she replied, anger and something even more powerful driving her to seek danger in a way that was totally foreign to her nature. "Do I have to give back his good-bye kiss, as well?"

Why not lie down on a train track? Why not wave a red flag at a raging bull?

"I reck'n I can do that job, too," he said, and catching her by the shoulders, he hauled her ruthlessly against his body and forced her head back against his arm.

Hannah had been kissed many times before, but never in anger. Penn's kiss was hard—painfully hard, and utterly without mercy. Yet it generated not anger in kind, but a fierce kind of exultation that she was at a complete loss to understand.

Heat sang in her veins like a chorus of archangels, until she nearly lost consciousness. And then, imperceptibly, the kiss began to gentle, even as the salt-sweet taste of Penn's mouth became laced with a musky, raw passion. Hannah understood it not with her mind, but with a primitive part of her being that seemed to rise like a Phoenix from the ashes of the past.

She clung to his shoulders, barely able to keep from collapsing, while Penn's hand moved hotly on her back, sliding the thin layers of fabric over her sensitive skin. He nibbled her lower lip, and then drew her tongue into his mouth and suckled it while white-hot fire blazed up in all the secret parts of her body.

Then, suddenly he thrust her from him, staring down at her with eyes gone dark with passion. Hannah, barely able to stand, saw the flutter of his damp white shirt as it echoed the beat of his pounding heart, the swell of his struggling lungs. She started to speak without the least notion of what to say.

"I apologize, madam." Penn spoke first, his voice barely recognizable.

Hannah's heart faltered. He apologized? For the single most memorable, most moving experience of her life, he *apologized*? "I accept," she said stiffly. "Now, if you'll be so kind as to close the door on your way out, I'll bid you good night."

For one long moment, they stared at one another. Two people trapped in a set of circumstances neither had sought. Two people at sea without a notion of how to reach a tranquil harbor.

Chapter 17

THREE days passed before the *Hamlet* warped alongside Paragon Shoals landing. Three days during which Hannah and Penn studiously avoided each other after he had stormed out the door while she stared after him, the notion of any civilized arrangement between them exploding around her like Fourth of July fireworks.

On Wednesday, late in the day, he arrived on her doorstep, his bearing militant. His face might have been carved from granite for all the expression she was able to read. "Word come from the signal office in Hatteras. Boat'll be in by dinnertime. Cap'n Dozier, he won't want to waste time, for he'll have to turn tail and tote the preacher back down the banks, so I'd be much obliged if you'd be ready, madam." He glanced around at her modest quarters. "Reck'n you'll be wanting to get the deed done here." It was a statement, not a question, which was probably what prompted Hannah to tell him she would prefer to be married at the station.

Mercy, she didn't even recognize the contrary creature she was becoming!

Penn nodded once. "I'll have the hands give the place a good turning out," he said, just as if he didn't keep the entire station scrubbed to a fare-thee-well. "Will you be wanting cake and music and all that folderol, same as Oleeta?"

"Heavens, no," Hannah said airily, her heart splintering inside her. "It won't be *that* kind of marriage, so why should it be that kind of wedding?"

If she'd thought his eyes looked chilly before, they turned positively glacial at that. "You're right, madam. We're only wanting to tie the knot all legal-like. No cause for a celebration."

Hannah's lips tightened and she managed to add an additional half inch to her stature with the tilt of her head. "I'm sure we can get it over with in time to send the captain and his passenger on their way south again with all due haste."

"I'll send one of the hands over with the cart in an hour."

"Don't bother. I can walk." She racheted her chin up another notch, daring him to argue.

"It's near onto a mile, it's hot, and Sara Mirella's too heavy a burden."

"My child is not a burden, thank you very much, sir." Oh, Lord, they were back to sir and madam again, she thought woefully. Why did the man insist on taunting her at every turn?

But there was nothing taunting in the way he looked at her as she stood beside him later that morning, wearing her white muslin with the pin-tucks in the bodice, and her best white kid shoes. She had forgotten, unfortunately, that they were half a size too small.

In an attitude of further defiance, she had worn her best *pont du Paris* shawl, and when Oleeta handed her a bouquet of fleabane, Saint-John's-wort, and wild pinks, tied with a band of honey-suckle, she had almost cried off. This was a mockery!

But against all reason as the Reverend Milbanks began to speak, Hannah found her heart warring with her head, hope pitted against despair.

"Do you, Pennington Carstairs Warfield, take this woman—?"

"I do," he said firmly.

"Do you, Hannah Elizabeth Matthews Ballinger, take this man—?"

"I do," she whispered. *Oh, please God, I do!*

Solemnly, they exchanged promises to love, cherish, honor, and obey, and Hannah pasted a bright smile on her pale face. She knew very well which one would do all the loving. The same one who would be expected to obey.

So be it. She had buttered her bread, as one of her father's old parishioners used to say—now she could lie in it.

There was no cake, but there was scuppernong wine for toasts. There were no tears, for after weeping half the night, Hannah had cried herself out. If she'd needed an incentive to go through with marrying a man who considered her part convenience, part duty, she had found it in the calming hour she'd spent nursing her daughter just after dawn.

Congratulations rang out, rousing the sleeping infant, who let her displeasure be known. "Come here, sweetpea, let Uncle Josie take you."

"Peabrain, she don't want to go to you, it's this here necktie of mine she's lookin' at!"

"It ain't no different from mine, fartface."

All hands not on duty had turned out in full-dress uniform, boots done up with stove-blacking, which served quite well until it came into contact with sand. Penn was even wearing a vest, despite the weather. Hannah had never seen him look so handsome. Nor quite so grim.

The moment she could escape, she hurried to the keeper's room, signaling Oleeta to follow. "I'm afraid this gown wasn't made for nursing," she said, turning her back so that the younger woman could unfasten the tiny covered buttons.

"Reck'n not many weddin' gowns is made fer sucklin' a babe." She grinned with the dry humor Hannah had come to appreciate. "Penn, he likes it right smart, anyways. I thought he was goin' to swaller his back teeth when you walked into the station this mornin'." Adam and Oleeta had collected her in the cart, Oleeta looking proud as punch in the rose-sprigged Swiss muslin.

"My, but Paragon Shoals is turning into a veritable fashion center," Hannah teased. "Go on back and enjoy the celebration, 'Leeta. See that the men don't drink too many toasts."

"Reck'n Penn, he'll see to that," the younger woman said dryly.

Hannah reckoned so, too. From the next room, she heard the telephone ring two longs and a short. Paragon's signal. The call, as far as she could make out through the door Oleeta had left ajar, was from Chicamacomico station concerning a missing schooner out of Barbados. She shifted Sara Mirella to her other breast and rearranged the shawl to protect her modesty, even though the two of them were alone.

Alone with Penn's bed, Penn's desk, Penn's shaving things, his bookshelf, overflowing with books on adventure and books on proceedure, and books of regulations.

His blessed, everlasting regulations!

Before she was quite finished, another call came in concerning a shipment of Coston flares Penn had ordered to replace a box of defective ones. Hannah heard firm footsteps come to the door and stop, then turn away.

And then march back again. Penn rapped on the door frame. "Hannah, I need to get to my desk. Are you about done?"

"I'll only be a minute more. Would you please send—"

The door swung open and Penn stepped inside. Hannah did her best to cover herself decently with the lacy shawl.

"I'm right sorry, ma'am," he apologized, standing stock-still in the doorway. "The shipping manifest . . ."

"I'm sorry to be such a bother. I'll be out of your way in a few minutes."

"You're not in my way," Penn said quickly, averting his eyes from the sight of the woman seated in his chair, sunlight streaming in through the window on her silky light brown hair, her flushed cheeks, and the pale blue-white of her breast visible through the flimsy shawl she clutched around her.

Jesus, it wasn't decent for a man to feel this way about a nursing woman, even if she was his wife!

His wife. Mrs. Pennington Carstairs Warfield. Hannah Warfield.

He cleared his throat and pretended an interest in the pens lined up with mathematical precision beside his letter box, the manifest seemingly forgotten.

"Did you need something from your desk?"

"My desk?" He stared at her as if the word was foreign to him. "Oh—my desk! Yes, ma'am, and when Sara's taken her fill, I'd be obliged if you'd look over something I worked up." He toyed with the slip of paper he had pulled from the box, and Hannah, suddenly remembering another slip of paper she had seen there, began to shake her head.

"Oh, no. That's not necessary. Please—not today, at least."

"Today's as good as any other day," he said gruffly.

"Oh, but surely there's no hurry?"

"I reck'n if you're feeling peckish, we could eat dinner first and then go over it together."

Hannah glanced at the brass-cased Seth Thomas on the wall just as it chimed three bells. Ten o'clock. Time for luncheon, only here it was called dinner.

"Me, I didn't have much of an appetite this morning," Penn admitted, and it occurred to Hannah that she hadn't, either. Food was a long way down on her list of priorities at the moment, but there was no point in making things any more difficult. Hadn't she promised to obey not an hour before?

Fighting a storm of conflicting emotions, she turned and placed the baby on the center of the bed, then rearranged her clothing as best she could without help. She fastened the top button and the three lower ones, but those in the middle defeated her.

"Here, let me help do you up," Penn said gruffly, coming to stand behind her.

"If you'll ask Oleeta to step in here for a moment, she can—"

"Oleeta and Adam have gone home. She said to tell you she'll keep the baby for a spell."

"Why on earth should I want her to do that?" Hannah wondered aloud, and then her face turned the color of the wild beach pinks. She felt Penn's warm knuckles brush against the skin of her back above her chemise. Heard him mutter something about "—pesky little devils," and braced herself against the spell of his nearness. Above the sound of the surf and the sound of murmuring male voices from the next room, she was profoundly aware of the sound of his breathing. It was growing harsher each moment.

As was her own. The touch of his hands on her back was like acid on her naked flesh. When he flattened his palms on her shoulders, she nearly strangled. "Oh, my mercy, aren't you done yet?" she cried. "Just do up every other one, and I'll cover up with my shawl."

"Ma'am, I hate to disoblige you, but that shawl wouldn't cover a gnat's a—stern end. Be still, I'm nearly 'bout finished. These here up at the neck, they're the hardest to see. Your hair—"

Her hair had been brushed exactly one hundred strokes, coiled and skewered firmly on top of her head, for all the good it had done. In the salty, humid heat, all the new growth that had come in since she'd given birth insisted on curling like corkscrews around her face and down on her nape.

Closing her eyes, Hannah prayed for patience. And for strength. And for the decency to be grateful to this man who had married her out of a sense of duty instead of leaving her to fend for herself against the threat of losing her daughter.

His hands lifted and she felt their absence acutely. "There, you're battened down all right an' tight, madam." Taking a deep breath, Penn stepped back, and Hannah glanced over her shoulder. The poor man couldn't have looked any more hot and bothered if he'd just finished running five miles through deep sand on the hottest day of the year.

She managed to murmur her thanks, and then she waited for the inevitable. He was going to show her his will, the one she had already seen, and she was going to cry and disgrace herself. She didn't want to think of wills and all they implied, not on her wedding day, yet she couldn't very well say so without revealing that she had already read his private papers.

Penn withdrew the sheet of paper and shook open the single fold. "This here is a set of rules, ma'am. I thought it might make things easier for—"

Hannah's jaw dropped. "A set of *what*?"

"Rules?" Penn repeated, his voice oddly unsure. If eyes could be said to plead, his did, only Hannah was in no mood to be wheedled. "It come to me during the fourth watch that you might be needing—"

"Give me that. I'll tell you what I need, sir," she

said and held out a hand. He placed in it a single sheet with the numbered lines all neatly written out in his small, angular handwriting. Without so much as a downward glance, she ripped the page in two and then tore the two strips in half. "Do you know what you can do with your wonderful rules?" She smiled with glittery sweetness. "You can make a paper boat with them and—*sail it to China!*"

Snatching up the baby, she was out the door before Penn could recover, halfway across the yard before he caught up with her. He spun her around, blue eyes blazed into gray ones, and the blue ones fell first.

"Ahh, hell," he muttered. Turning away, he went in search of Malachi. By the time he found him, Hannah, clutching Sara Mirella to her breast, was halfway to the village, her militant stride churning up dust as she followed the rutted track. "Take the cart," Penn ordered tiredly. "Drag her aboard if you have to, but see that she don't pop a gusset before she gets home."

"Ain't this here supposed to be your honeymoon?" Malachi asked, suspiciously guileless.

A single terse word expressed Penn's opinion of honeymoons, women, and impertinent younger brothers.

In the heat of the afternoon, Hannah borrowed Oleeta's hoe and chopped weeds. She spaded up another section of rich ground out beyond the fig tree, and then spread the oyster shells Josiah had brought her over the acid loam. By late afternoon, she was wet to the skin, itching from insect bites and heaven knows what else, but at least she had worked through her wretched temper.

Penn chopped wood. It had been years since he had chopped wood—that was a chore usually left to the lowliest surfman, but today he needed something more strenuous than a keeper's duties normally provided.

Wife. Witch, was more like it! Dammit, he'd never thought to get himself chained to any woman again, much less one who didn't even pretend to want him! She'd needed a husband, right enough, but not him. Not a man who was too rough, too ugly, and too damned set in his ways to accommodate himself to any woman. He'd had it on the best of authority that he was lower than turtle bait when it came to treating a woman the way she was meant to be treated.

They'd gone a few rounds, him and Margaret. She'd been young, but feisty, and not behindhand in letting him know his shortcomings. The bedding had been good—leastwise, it had on the rare times when he wasn't too tired, and when the boys went to sleep before he did, and when Margaret wasn't ailing with something or in a temper.

All told, the women at Rosabelle's served well enough. It was a right long ways to go for what a man needed from a woman, but it was a sight better than doing without.

Dammit, a married man shouldn't *have* to do without! What would Hannah say if he turned up on her doorstep come bedtime and asked her to do her wifely duty by him?

Leastwise, she didn't have much furniture to throw at his head.

Penn wiped the sweat off his brow. A slow grin spread over his face as he enjoyed the sensation of hot sun beating down on his battle-scarred body. When it came to temper, his first wife couldn't hold a candle to his second one. Margaret had been a slow burner, sulking and smoldering like a damp fuse and then going off all of a sudden when a man least expected it.

Hannah wasn't one to dampen her powder. When something set her off, she blew, clean, clear, and right out in the open. A man could respect that in a woman. Leastwise, he didn't have to creep around for days, wondering what the devil he had done wrong now.

It was nearly dark. The first watch had set out at dusk, the coffeepot had been refilled and set to boil, and the journals posted to date. Lacking a gully washer, Penn swam until he'd washed himself clean of the day's labors, then heated water and stropped his razor.

Three-quarters of a mile away, Hannah sat on the back stoop in a light wrapper and dried her hair while she watched the last bands of color fade from the western sky. In this humidity, her hair needed washing nearly every day, which would have purely horrified Jarnelle, who believed twice a year sufficient.

Inside the house, Sara Mirella slept soundly. She was sleeping through the night lately, which was a blessing. Hannah only wished she could do as well, but it was neither the heat nor the humidity that kept her awake far into the night.

The whicker of a horse sounded loud in the evening stillness. Adam? She'd thought he'd ridden over just after suppertime. Penn had been surprisingly decent about allowing him to spend time at home when he wasn't drilling or on duty, which was a blessing for Oleeta. The child sorely missed her own family. Her brother, especially.

Footsteps crossed her front porch. She knew by now that if there'd been trouble at the station, someone would have rung the bell to summon help. Adam had resurrected the tarnished brass bells, relics of the days when help could be called out from the village in times of trouble, and mounted one in the cupola, the other on a tree between the two houses.

"Hannah?"

Penn? Suddenly, Hannah felt cold. She was wearing only her old faded peach muslin wrapper over her thinnest nightgown in deference to the heavy heat. Her feet were bare. Heavens, she hadn't gone barefooted since she was a child. She was falling into all sorts of shabby habits lately!

He came through the house. When he stepped out onto the back stoop, Hannah was standing, her wrapper tied securely and her toes hidden under her skirts, she sincerely hoped. "Did you wish to see me?" she asked coolly.

"I come to say good night to Sara Mirella." He twisted his hat in his hand. His collar was buttoned to the top and he had obviously just shaved, because she could smell the faint scent of his shaving soap, but he had left off his coat, vest, and the black necktie he wore on official occasions.

"I'm sorry, she's asleep."

"Oh." He looked at the fig tree silhouett

against the silvery waters of the Pamlico Sound. The oyster shells she had scattered earlier gleamed palely in the near darkness. "You, um—I reck'n you sent off for seeds and all. Mal said he offered to clear you a patch."

"I did it myself. I find I rather enjoy gardening."

Stiltedly, they discussed the crops that thrived in the sandy soil and those that did better in the sour black woods dirt near the creek. He mentioned the likelihood that the salt tide would kill it all out before the season ended, and Hannah shrugged. If there was one lesson she had learned and learned well, it was that one must do today what could be done today and not waste time worrying about what tomorrow might bring.

"I brought you some molasses," he said, and reached up abruptly to unfasten the top button of his shirt. "I set it on the table."

"Thank you." She waited. Against all reason, her voice came out all breathy and hoarse, as if she were suffering a congestion of the lungs. "Goodness, it's been warm today hasn't it?"

"Hannah," Penn blurted suddenly, "Dammit, you're my wife!"

She closed her eyes momentarily. "Yes. Did I remember to thank you? No? Then thank you, Penn. And for the molasses, too."

A single stride took him to the edge of the small space and he stood staring out at the raw new clearing she had dug up just that day. His feet were braced apart, fists planted firmly on his taut hips, and Hannah waited without daring to breathe. Was he angry again? Had he come with another set of rules?

As if reading her mind, he said, "One of the vows we exchanged this morning had to do with my duty as a husband and yours as a wife."

Duty. God, she had never hated a word so **much** in her entire life! "I'm aware of that," she said stiffly.

"Well—well, what I'm trying to say is that a man has certain needs."

A woman has needs, too, you stubborn jackass!

When she remained silent, he turned, his face unreadable in the darkness. "Well?"

"Well what? What do you want me to say?"

Penn rubbed the back of his neck. He hadn't meant to yell at her. He'd come here with half a gallon of the best New Orleans molasses that he'd sent for special from Stowe's store down at Hatteras just to sweeten her up. He had planned what he was going to say all the way across the island, only to have the words swept right out of his mind when he'd seen her in that flimsy pink thing with her hair all down her back, and her eyes sparkling at him like chunks of clear gray quartz.

"The thing is, madam, the preacher didn't say nothing about cleaving to the women at Rosabelle's. He made me swear on my honor that I'd cleave particularlike to you."

"Rosabelle's? *Rosabelle's?*"

"We're married now. I don't reck'n a married man's got no business visiting sporting houses, not when he's got a woman at home."

Hannah's ears burned. Her cheeks burned. As she felt the powerful spell of the man she had married only that morning—the man at whom she had taken one look on the wharf all those long months ago and recognized as someone special in her life—she began to burn in other places, as well. "You're asking me to *invite you to my bed*?"

"Is it too soon? I mean the baby and all—are you, uh—mended?"

With a wild urge to laugh, Hannah assured him that she was mended. And then she waited. If he thought she was going to lead the way, he was very much mistaken. He was the one who had lived his life by a set of iron-bound rules, not she. It was all she could do to stay one step ahead of disaster. On the other hand . . .

"Well, then—?"

Brushing past him, Hannah shook her head. "It seems we both said more than was wise, but I'll not quibble other than to say that you'd probably do better to stick to Rosabelle's. I'm not very good at this sort of thing. I expect I've forgot what little I ever knew."

Neither of them spoke another word as he followed her into the bedroom. While Hannah turned down the bed, Penn set the cradle in the next room. A single lamp burned on the upturned crate beside the bed, and they confronted each other, both embarrassed—one increasingly frightened—both determined to get through this awkward phase of their new relationship and move forward.

"Would you like me to blow out the lamp?" he asked.

"Yes, please. I—no." Hannah shook her head firmly. She needed to see the face of the man who would ravish her. Penn wouldn't hurt her. Whatever else he was, he was not cruel, like Thomas. But he was not her gentle, patient Edward, either.

Penn unbuttoned his shirt. Sitting on the foot of her bed, he removed his boots and stockings. "Hannah, there's something I'd better warn you about before you see it. There was this fire a few years ago—that is, if you're offended by scars, then you might want me to blow out the lamp before I go any further."

She almost reached out to him, but the last thing he wanted from her now was her pity. That much she did know. "Would you be more comfortable in the dark?"

"I'm not the one that has to look at me. You can close your eyes if you're of a mind to, but I'd be obliged if you'd leave the light." His eyes moved over her in a way that was unmistakable. She knew the look of sexual hunger in a man's eyes, but with Penn it was different. With Penn, oddly enough, she didn't want to run and hide.

She removed her wrapper, hanging it on one of the hooks Mal had fashioned for her. Her naked toes curled against the wooden floor, scrubbed smooth as satin.

Penn unbuckled his wide leather belt, never once removing his eyes from hers. She unbuttoned the high neck of her thin cotton nightgown, wondering if he would want her to remove it entirely. With Edward, it had always been dark, with a lot of fumbling and the task swiftly accomplished. Edward had never expected her to disrobe.

"Do you want me to—?" she whispered. "My gown?"

"Yes, please," he said, his voice deeper, rougher than usual.

*Then help me! Kiss me! Don't just stand there star-
ing at me as though I were a bird in a cage!*

As if he'd read her thoughts, Penn closed the distance between them. With an inarticulate sound,
he buried his face in her hair, then clasped her face
between his hands and lifted it. When his mouth
came down on hers, she was ready. More than
ready, she was melting, aching, trembling with the
most terrifying feeling she had ever experienced.

Dear God, she had known the best and the worst
of what could happen between a man and a
woman, but neither had been anything at all like
this!

Somehow they found themselves in bed together,
with Penn's drawers and her nightgown in a tangle
around their ankles. When he had kissed her until
they were both wild with a different kind of hunger,
he buried his face in her breasts.

She groaned, and he whispered hoarsely, "Did I
hurt you? I never want to hurt you, Hannah. Tell
me what to do! Tell me how to hold you! I'm not
very good at this, either," he said, with a bark of
bitter laughter that tore at her heart.

"You aren't hurting me, Penn. I've never—it's just
that I—ahhh . . ." She sighed as she felt his hand
on her belly. When he took one of her distended
nipples in his mouth and began to suckle, she
thought she would die from it. How odd that pain
and pleasure could be so close. How odd that the
suckling of a babe could be so soothing, the suckling of a man so arousing.

He was fiercely, almost frighteningly aroused.
She could feel him throbbing against her hip, hard,
hot, and satiny smooth, yet somehow, she wasn't

frightened, either at the size of him nor his massive strength. When she felt one of his fingers slip through the thicket into her dampness, she whimpered, unable to keep still.

"Shhhh. Easy now, easy, love . . . this will make it better for you," he whispered.

Hannah's eyes widened. She stared at the circles of yellow lamplight cast on the ceiling as her breath came quicker and harsher. "Oh, my mercy—what are you doing to me?" she gasped. Her hips surged uncontrollably. Edward had never—this wasn't possible! Once, she had felt the faintest shadow of what she was feeling now, and it had been pleasant. She had enjoyed it and looked forward to repeating it, but never had she experienced anything of this magnitude!

"Ahhh, Penn, I can't—"

"Shhh . . . yes, you can. It's like riding a wave, Hannah. Just let the power take you, go with it—let yourself fly free!"

And she did, because she was helpless to resist. Higher than she had ever dreamed possible, swifter than lightning—sweeter than the hope of heaven. And while the shimmering bands of pleasure still pulsated around her, Penn moved between her trembling thighs, entering her with a single thrust.

He lowered himself onto her breasts for one brief moment and she felt his hot breath against her damp skin, felt the fierce thunder of his heart mingle with the dying thunder of her own.

He moved inside her. She was too limp to hold him, too limp to help him. And then, to her astonishment, it began all over again. The sweet, rising tide of passion, as irresistible as the wildest storm surge. Instinctively, she wrapped her legs around his lean, hard body, lifting to his rapid, powerful thrusts, until they were both hurled headlong onto the shore, cast up more dead than alive.

Hannah recovered first. Her head on his sweaty shoulder, one of his legs over her hips, she stared at him in awe. The lamplight, dimmed now by the sooty chimney, cast shadows on the scarred skin down his side, and she touched him there, running her palms lightly over a surface that resembled rumpled tan satin.

There was a scar on his chin, and one on his shoulder, and she thought now, dear God, the chances he's taken! The times he could have been killed! What if I lost him now? How could I ever bear it?

Tenderly, she brushed the dark hair off his forehead, admiring the noble height of his brow, the level line of his dark brows—the thrust of his twice-broken nose and the strength of his jaw. She was glad he didn't wear a mustache, as so many men did. His mouth was too beautiful to be hidden by a bush. Wide, firm, curved only when he allowed the curves to show, but sweet and soft when he slept.

Reaching over to the table, she tilted the chimney and blew out the lamp. That night, she slept more soundly than she had slept in a long, long time. Hours later, with the sun just beginning to peep over the windowsill, she opened her eyes, stretched her limbs, and smiled drowsily. Turning, she said, "Good morn . . ."

He was gone. Not so much as a dent in his side of the bolster. The sheet on that side of the bed was smooth and cool, and there was not a single sign that anyone had slept there besides herself.

Perhaps no one had, she thought with a flurry of mild panic. She was certainly no stranger to dreams.

But there was no way she could have dreamed what had happened a few hours ago, she told herself. It had been outside the boundaries of her meager experience.

As she sat up and swung her legs off the bed, echoes of pleasure gave way to an unaccustomed stiffness. She tried to convince herself it was from all the gardening she had done the day before, but she was sore in places that had nothing to do with gardening.

And if she needed more proof, there on the floor beside her bed was one of the bone buttons she recognized as having come off a man's drawers. The wedding had been no dream, nor had the wedding night.

As for the marriage . . . well, they would just have to wait and see.

Chapter 18

HANNAH kept to her own side of the island. If the station had caught on fire, she told herself angrily, she would not have deigned to go close enough to smell the smoke! The morning after her wedding day she spent with Oleeta, talking of babies, gardening, and families.

Oleeta missed her own. She spoke often of her younger brother, Chester, rarely of her mother, who had died many years ago, and never of her father. But Hannah could see the lingering sadness in her dark eyes, even though she pretended not to care that her own family had not bothered to attend her wedding.

That afternoon Hannah washed bed linens and baby things, thinking longingly of the rotary paddle washer she had learned to use after Jarnelle had decided that she was cheaper than an outside laundress. Taking on the household laundry in addition to all her other duties had been difficult, but she had learned. Nor had she ever complained.

Nor was she complaining now, but she did find herself thinking occasionally of the many conveniences to be found in the city. Especially, at this moment, that blessed rotary washing machine!

Hannah bailed out the boiler, emptying the water on her garden. Ironically, surrounded by water as they were, fresh water was another luxury she had come to appreciate. There were no wells. James had told her that at times they went for months without rain and all the cisterns would go dry, while at other times it rained incessantly and all the cisterns filled to overflowing, but then a high tide would wash over the island, contaminating all the fresh water with salt.

As she had not yet managed to get a clothesline put up, she draped the wet sheets on the fig tree, her drawers and corset covers over the rail on the back stoop, and the baby's napkins and tiny gowns along the few bare sections of picket fence. Eyeing her day's work, Hannah thought again of all the things she had once taken for granted. Luxuries or not, she wouldn't trade a single moment of her new life for all the grief, fear, and intimidation she'd left behind.

Meanwhile, Sara Mirella discovered her feet, and managed to occupy herself happily by trying to get her toes into her mouth while Hannah hung the wash. Tempted to rush right over to show Oleeta her precocious daughter's new talent, Hannah reminded herself that Adam was home for supper, and Oleeta would have other things on her mind. James would have appreciated it, but James was still in Norfolk. At that Rosabelle place, most likely.

Men! Even the twins were full of plans to get back to Rosabelle's, to visit Perdita and some little twit who could cross one eye and not the other.

Not that Hannah thought for one moment that

unilateral eye-crossing was the woman's only attraction.

As for Penn, she supposed he wouldn't be needing Rosabelle's establishment anymore. Having offered her the protection of his name, he obviously expected in return the use of her body to relieve his natural urges.

Hannah slammed the tub down over a stob so hard it dented the bottom, then flung the wash stick at the fig tree, breaking off a brittle branch.

"Oh, damn and blast," she cried. She was hot, tired, dirty—she had a meal to cook on a balky stove, unless she felt like adding starvation to her list of miseries—and all she could think of was that maddening man! The island was too small to hold the both of them!

But by dusk, she was feeling more complaisant. Sara Mirella had wrought her usual soothing spell. Hannah had eaten the baked fish and potatoes Adam had brought over on his way back to the station, tidied her house and her person, and now she sat on the back stoop in the rocking chair she had dragged outside, watching the sun sink beneath the coral-stained waters of the Pamlico while Sara Mirella suckled contentedly, making drowsy little noises and kneading her swollen breasts with tiny fists.

Hannah sighed. What more could any woman wish for?

"Don't ask," she muttered under her breath.

Penn came just after dark. The baby asleep, Hannah had moved her chair to the front porch. To take advantage, she told herself, of the brisk breeze, *not* to gaze across at the station. The wind had swung around to the northeast earlier in the day, offering a nice relief from the unseasonable heat.

"Good evening," he said as soon as he gained the porch. "It's turned off some cooler." He held something behind his back. His hat?

"Yes, it has. Is everything going well at the station?" She continued to rock, both feet patting the floor on the forward roll.

"Tol'able, thank you, ma'am. The Garners is quick learners and hard workers. Makes a difference."

"I'm sure it does," she agreed, wondering what he wanted, why he had come, and why her voice should sound so much like the wheezy high-C on her father's old parlor organ.

Suddenly, he thrust out a bouquet of limp boneset and morning glories that had twisted shut. "Happened to see these here flowers today— thought they might brighten up the place. They, um—look a mite wilted, but I reck'n they'll freshen up some if you put 'em in a jar of water."

Which led to finding something to put them in, which led to offering Penn a glass of cold tea made from the yaupon Oleeta had showed her how to pick, chop, parch, and brew.

Which led directly to a dead end.

Penn drained his glass of the green, sweetened tea while Hannah stared at the working muscles of his tanned throat. He'd unfastened the top two buttons on his shirt. Now he unfastened the next one down. He raked his fingers through his hair, leaving it every whichaway, and asked about Sara Mirella.

"Sara? Oh. Oh, Penn, guess what! She's learned a new trick," Hannah said eagerly. Eyes sparkling with pride, she told him about her daughter's unerring aim from foot to mouth, and how she had actually laughed aloud today. "Honestly, Penn, she learns something new every day. And she's grown so much she doesn't even look like the same baby."

"Lord be thanked for that," he said feelingly. "I didn't want to hurt your feelings, Hannah, but she weren't what you'd call real pretty, leastwise, not right off."

Hannah smiled ruefully, knowing he spoke no more than the truth. "But I thought she was, you know. I thought she was the most beautiful baby ever born, even if she was supposed to have been a boy. Would you like me to wake her so you can play with her?"

"No! I mean, don't go to no trouble on my account. I didn't come to see Sara Mirella. That is, I did—I mean, I wanted to be sure she was faring all right, but mostly I came to see you, Hannah."

Hannah's heart suddenly lodged somewhere near the base of her throat, making it impossible for her to breath properly. "I—you did?"

"Adam, he goes home every night, don't he?"

Hannah nodded. Why were they wasting time talking about Adam?

"The rules say a man's allowed off one day a week betwixt sunup and sundown, but the way I figger it, once storm season's done with, the rules have got some slack to 'em. Adam, he drills of a day and stands his share of the watches, but it don't do no harm, the way I see it, for a man and his wife to, uh . . . spend time together."

Ahhh . . . so now she knew where he was headed. Knew now why he had come. It was there in his eyes, in the strained look around his mouth—in that wonderful, pitiful bouquet of wilted wildflowers he had brought her.

"Would you like to go to bed, Penn?" she asked softly, feeling, for once in her life, in command of her own fate.

The big, brave hero who had risked his own life countless times to rescue others, stared down at the toes of his boots. "Please, ma'am, if you don't mind too much. I near about couldn't sit a horse coming over here for thinking about last night." Embarrassed, he laughed, and Hannah laughed with him, and suddenly, everything was all right.

More than all right. It took only a single touch for the melting and the aching and the throbbing to begin all over again. By the time they reached the bedroom, Hannah was burning with need. By the time Penn removed her gown and undergarments—she had left off her corset in deference to the heat—neither of them could wait another moment. He tore off his own clothing, flinging it aside, and stood before her, proudly, rampantly male.

And then he lowered her onto the bed. "Oh, my sweet soul, I needed this!" he groaned, sinking into her eager body with a single thrust. For a moment, he let her feel his full weight, burying his face in her throat to inhale the warm, womanly, violet-touched scent of her.

Hannah was ready for him. She had never been more ready in her life. The thought of denying them what they both wanted was beyond all reason, and if there were to be regrets, she could deal with them tomorrow.

She would probably have a lifetime of tomorrows to come to terms with Penn's constricted idea of marriage, but for this moment at least, he was hers.

Penn's breathing sounded as harsh as tearing canvas in the small, silent room. Hannah held him as he began to move inside her, slowly at first, then faster, and then roughly, unevenly, as if he had lost control of his own body. Just before he shuddered, groaned, and collapsed over her, she felt her own climax begin. It soared high, wild and hot as a sunstorm as she felt his seed scorch her womb.

He took her twice more during the night, once slowly, with exquisite tenderness, and once more with an urgency that couldn't be denied.

When Hannah awoke, he was gone, the bed beside her neatly spread. She cried for a few minutes, swore awkwardly, and then, noting the squared corners of the top sheet he had tucked in so carefully on his side of the bed, she began to laugh. Dear Lord, how could a woman love such a man?

How could she not?

Penn lay awake in his bed back at the station and stared at the ceiling. He had plumb evermore lost his mind. Adrift in uncharted waters, he'd been driven so far from all that was safe, secure, and familiar that he was damn near scared to go to sleep for fear of where he'd fetch up!

It weren't as if he'd never had a woman before. Hell, he'd had dozens of women! He'd been married to one for near on two years. Since then he had lain with most of the girls at Rosabelle's at one time or another. But not once, not even with Margaret, had he ever been in danger of forgetting all about duty and regulations and responsibility—of turning his back on the only way of life he knew.

She was a city woman, his wife was, used to things he'd be hard-pressed to provide, even though the government paid him a respectable salary. As there was nothing to spend it on closer than a day's ride away, he had long been in the habit of mailing it off to a bank on the mainland.

From little things Hannah had let drop, he thought she was used to servants, although he'd never once known her to complain nor shirk a chore. How much would a maid cost? Or a housekeeper? He remembered thinking the first time he had taken her hand that day down at the landing that it was the hand of a lady, for all it was callused and rough. Her clothes were far finer than any he'd seen on any of the island women. Not as colorful as those the women at Rosabelle's wore, nor near as fancy. They sure as shooting didn't hug her body the way Rosabelle's girls' did, tight up around their corseted waists, squeezing out bosoms and bottoms lush enough to float a whaleboat.

All the same, there was something about the way his Hannah dressed—about the way she spoke and the way she carried herself—that set her head and shoulders above any female he had ever laid eyes on, let alone laid hands on.

Yet for all he'd married her, she might as well be on top of one of those mountain ranges he used to dream of exploring. Oh, she was his to bed. They had both made certain vows, and Hannah was a woman of her word. If he knew nothing else about her, he did know that much. They had both re-peated words about loving and cherishing, but they both knew why she had married him. Someone had threatened her. Her late husband's brother, ac-cording to James. She had run away, and now the bastard was sniffing her trail again, wanting to lay claim to his brother's child.

"Over my dead body," Penn muttered. They were his now, Hannah and her baby, and if there was one thing he knew, it was how to take care of his own.

Lying awake, Penn was listening to the howling of the wind and the pounding of the surf, mentally gauging the weather, when he heard a whinny, a thud, and a voice. Instantly, he was alert.

The twins? They were riding in early. Estimating the lapse of time since he'd heard the clock in the common room strike six bells, he figured it was a good three-quarters of an hour short of changeover time.

He was considering getting up to stir the fire for coffee when suddenly the door burst open and James appeared there, bearded, dirty, and haggard. "What are you doing over here, you crazy fool? Where's Hannah?"

Penn came to his feet in a single motion. "What the hell are *you* doing, barging into my room?"

"Where is she? Godamighty, don't tell me you let him take her!"

"If it's my wife you're talking about, she's where she belongs, in her own bed, not that it's any of your business!" They both knew why James had left the island so hurriedly. Penn's conscience wasn't any too easy on that score, but for better or worse, the deed was done now. "I'd advise you, little brother, to—"

James didn't wait for Penn's advice. He lunged, catching Penn high on the right cheek and knocking him against the far wall. Penn bounced back, shook his head like a stunned bull, and swung. Heavier and far more powerful, he didn't even try to pull his punches this time. Three blows and it was all over. Penn hauled his younger brother up off the floor, ducked his shoulder under the dead weight, and staggered across to the sleeping room, dumping the limp form onto a canvas cot. Swaying slightly, he removed James's boots, loosened his belt, and tossed a sheet over him to ward off any mosquitoes drawn by the smell of blood and sweat.

Two beds over, one of the Garners snored loudly, undisturbed by the ruckus. Penn slapped the big bare foot protruding from under the sheet. "Last watch goes out in half an hour, number six. Hit the deck!"

"Unngh . . . uff . . ."

Behind him, James roused. "Damned if you ain't the blindest jackass in captivity," he muttered thickly. "Don't deserve a woman like Hannah. Ah, Jesus, Penn, you broke my nose!"

"Good. Teach you to meddle into my business."

"Yeah, well, you'd damn well better take care of her, because if you don't, I will. If that bastard Ballinger ever lays a hand on her, I'll track him down to hell and back and geld him up to his stinking armpits!"

"I take care of what's mine," Penn said in a tone that was all the more deadly for its very softness.

"Like you did Margaret?"

The sound of Penn's fist striking the door frame brought Luke Garner to his feet. When Penn left the sleeping room, the Hyde County surfman was stumbling around in the darkness in search of his boots. "Comin', I'm comin', dammit—hitch up th' mule fer me, I'm comin'!"

It lacked a good half hour until full daylight when the bell on the tower began to clang. All hands froze, staring at the trapdoor to the roof, and then Silas, who stood tower watch, poked his head in the opening.

"Flare just went up! I seen it plain as day, it was redder'n hell on fire!"

James stumbled into the common room, wide awake, unmarked save for a swollen nose.

Penn nearly tripped over Luke, who had been gulping down a mug of cold coffee, ready to relieve the watch.

"Location, dammit! North or south, offshore or on?"

"North and onshore, far's I could tell!"

"Keep a close watch, man! Report everything you see!" Swinging about, he shouted, "James, open up the boathouse!"

"On my way!"

"Garner, go with him, lead out the horses and start hitching up." Tugging on his britches with one hand, he grabbed the telephone to alert Little Kinnakeet station to cover the Paragon patrol and stand by to send help if needed. Chicamacomico, to the north, would have seen the signal, and would already be gearing up to go to the scene. Penn, his left cheek bruised and split, his right knuckles swollen, could only hope Adam hadn't been rutting so hard he hadn't heard the bell. Hoped, too, that the boy had managed to get a few hours of sleep. Off-season storms could be tricky as the devil. Unpredictable. If there was more than one ship in trouble, they'd be needing all hands from all three stations.

There was only the one. The three-masted schooner *Mattie Curtis* had come out of Philadelphia on Saturday late in the day, bound for Savannah. The captain had been feeling poorly. He put it down to some oyster stew he had eaten the night before. They lost time when the towboat ran into trouble near Reedy Island in the Delaware River, but by late on Monday they were standing south with an easterly wind off Fenwick Island Lightship. The captain was shaky, but on his feet again when the first officer came down with a bad case of the scours.

During the night the wind fell off some. A green helmsman, also suffering from having patronized a certain waterfront dining establishment, ignored the schooner's increasingly sluggish response. Due to the rain, no one removed the hatch covers to examine the cargo holds, which were filled with anthracite coal bound for Savannah and points south and west.

Off Cape Henry, they ran into fog. When the wind picked up enough to blow the fog away, they made good time. But the rain continued and the wind pushed them steadily shoreward, and with the weather so thick, it was impossible to be certain of their true position.

Not until almost four days after leaving port did the full gravity of their situation become known. A seaman reported breakers over the stern just as another reported the aft hold awash. Captain Hathaway quickly ordered the staysail to be taken in and both bower anchors let go, and for the next few hours they managed to hold position with the mainsail and trysail set to head them into the wind.

But not even the eighty fathom of chain let out on each anchor could hold the doomed ship against the enormous seas. They dragged ever closer to the breakers. The mainsail halyards were let go, the sail run down, and one man was lost when he was washed from the shrouds by the seas that now swamped the decks.

They struck just offshore some mile and a quarter north of Paragon Shoals just before daybreak on the second day of June in the year 1899, due to the weather, an improperly loaded cargo that had shifted in the rolling seas and sprung the seams of the log-bottomed hull, and a pot of oyster stew that had been held over a day too long in a cheap waterfront restaurant.

The crews of two stations were on hand in less than an hour after she went aground, but conditions by that time were all but hopeless. Seas were already washing over the beach, making the launching of a boat impossible. One boat carriage was overturned on the flooding beach, the team tangled in the harness. It took both crews to right her and sort out the frightened horses.

Josiah, glasses trained on the foundering ship, yelled, "Jesus, Penn, there's a woman aboard!"

The moment the vessel was within range, Penn was ready, his Lyle gun loaded with a six-ounce powder charge and a No. 7 shot line. His first shot fell short. The line parted on the second try. Already the ship was beginning to break up.

Swiftly, silently, the men went about the business they had devoted their lives to. A second faking box was quickly set into place, the gun loaded and made ready as Penn tried to gauge the wind and find a lull. The rain had cleared, but the wind, if anything, had picked up, blowing spume so thick it was possible to see only sporadically.

James wiped the salt spray from his eyes in time to see the mainmast go, carrying with it some poor devil who had the misfortune to be caught in the ratlines. And then several figures could be seen diving over the sides.

Penn signaled Midgett, the keeper from Chicamacomico. "We'll take to the corks!" he cried over the sound of the howling wind. "They're going over!"

It was quickly decided that three men from each station would don the bulky cork jackets. Carrying forty-five yards of shot line apiece, they waded out into the wild surf to meet the survivors, while their mates hung onto the line from shore, feeding it out as they went. When a broken hatch cover grazed his thigh, Penn didn't even feel it, his eyes on the nearest body clinging to a floating water cask. Several times he barely avoiding being crushed by floating wreckage, but eventually he reached his destination. Catching the half-drowned woman by the hair, he pried her grip loose from the cask, grasped her under the arms and turned toward the distant shore.

And so it was that eventually, five of the seven-man crew of the *Mattie Curtis*, as well as the single passenger, a widow by the name of Matilda Gump, were placed in the service carts for the journey to Paragon Shoals Lifesaving Station.

Oleeta and Hannah were on hand to receive them, with freshly boiled coffee, stimulants, heated sandbags, and dry clothes from the Women's National Relief barrel, as well as whatever food they could lay hands on. Hannah had been wakened by the clanging bell, and then Oleeta had come for her, telling her what it portended.

She was hurrying past the row of cots that had been set up along one wall when someone grabbed at her skirt, and she looked down at the gray face of the middle-aged woman who was dressed in a man's flannel nightshirt, her thin hair in a braid over her shoulder. "Mrs. Warfield, the captain—did he say anything about his papers?"

Mrs. Warfield? Mercy, the woman was speaking to her! "I'm afraid I haven't spoken to him, Mrs. . . . ah, Gump." The captain of the schooner had been closeted with Penn in the keeper's room ever since they'd arrived, both of them still wet and needing attention, to Hannah's way of thinking. Penn's face alone bore a number of visible injuries. Both his left cheek and his right hand, particularly the knuckles, looked dreadful!

"He put my husband's Bible in his waterproof case for safekeeping. Please, would you ask him—?"

Hannah knew there was much to be discussed between the two men while the details were still fresh. Eventually, an officer from the Revenue-Cutter Service would conduct an investigation into the circumstances of the wreck, but Penn had his reports to write up and Captain Hathaway no doubt had his own.

Hannah didn't need to give the matter a second thought. This poor woman's Bible was every bit as important as any number of official reports. "I'll speak to him now, Mrs. Gump. You'd best lie down and try to get some rest."

The gray-haired woman looked nervously at the room full of men, some wearing dry uniforms, some dry underwear—whatever could be found in the relief barrel that would fit. "I can't lie down here," she whispered. "Isn't there another place? Perhaps someone from the village—"

"Yes, of course," said Hannah. "You can go home with me, but first you wait right here while I see about your Bible. My father was a minister. I know what a comfort the Word can be in times of trial."

Aside from his obvious injuries, Penn's shirt was torn in two places, and there was a stain that looked suspiciously like blood on the leg of his trousers. He looked shockingly pale, the lines bracketing his stern mouth etched deeper than ever. She wanted nothing so much as to hold him in her arms until the rest of the world faded away.

"Yes? What is it, Hannah? Do you need something?"

Tearing her gaze away from Penn, she said, "Captain Hathaway, your pardon, but Mrs. Gump is asking about a Bible. I believe it was in with your papers?"

The waterproof packet was lying open on Penn's desk. Shoved to one side was the book in question, somewhat faded and scarred, but evidently none the worse for the ordeal.

"Yes, yes—poor woman. You'd have thought it was the crown jewels, the way she pleaded with me to keep the thing safe. Timid as a mouse, scared of water, scared of trains. Husband's a missionary. Dead now. Caught one of those heathen diseases and popped off just when she'd finally screwed up her nerve to go join him." Being both overwrought and a northerner, he spoke so rapidly Hannah had trouble following his discourse. "On her way now to live with her sister, I believe. There's another name for your list, Captain Warfield. Have to get the woman's direction and notify her that her sister survived, else she'll likely think the worst when she hears the news. There'll be reports in the papers by the end of the week. Yes, yes—must notify the sister. God, I hate writing these letters!"

By the time Hannah made arrangements for Matilda Gump to move across the island until the survivors could be transported to the mainland, she was beginning to have second thoughts. The woman was wound up tighter than an eight-day clock, and showed no signs of running down!

"I'm sure I don't know what I would have done if you hadn't offered, Mrs. Warfield, for I could never have closed my eyes in a house with so many men. Not but what they haven't been . . . Oh, my, I still can't believe it! But I tell you truly, I can hardly wait to have a nice cup of hot tea, for I—"

It would be yaupon, not China, Hannah thought as she closed her ears to the constant commentary. Nor was the woman going to be pleased when she saw the meager accommodations. Hannah had already decided to offer her the only bed in the house and set up a cot in the front room for Sara Mirella and herself.

"Well, as for tea, we'll certainly see what can be done. You're most welcome to share with my daughter and me, although our home is rather small ... and not completely furnished just yet. But Captain Warfield will be far too busy at the station for the next few days to come home, so we'll make out just fine."

While the poor woman rattled on about her late husband's preferences in just about everything from tea to tooth powders, Josiah drove them home in the cart, along with a cot, some bedding, and a slab of bacon, promising to bring more supplies as soon as things settled down at the station.

Hannah, thinking of all the provisions she had accepted so far, and how little she'd been able to do in return, didn't argue. She would come to terms with her pride when she had the time to spare.

Only once did she manage to see Penn. Headed over to Oleeta's for a moment's respite two days later, she saw him riding Pegasus across the barren stretch and waited until he reined up beside her.

"Did you need me?" she asked.

"I've not seen you lately." He dismounted and

touched Sara Mirella lingeringly on the cheek. "Do you have everything you need?"

"Yes, thank you. Josie brought bacon and corn-meal, and Mal brought me some tinned milk and cane sugar. He said he traded a sack of beans for it down at Kinnakeet station. Did you know about it? It's probably against the rules—government rations, and all. But Mrs. Gump says she can't drink tea without milk and sugar—she has a nervous stomach. She says she can barely tolerate my heathen brew, but she can't drink coffee at all, and as we don't have chocolate . . ." Hannah smiled and shrugged expressively.

"Talks a mite, does she?"

"A mite," Hannah conceded, feeling a glow spread inside her at the sight of his large rough hand stroking the soft reddish fuzz on Sara's pink scalp. The bruise on his cheek was fading, the small cuts on his swollen knuckles healing quite nicely. Sun, salt water, and a healthy constitution were a potent healing force, which was fortunate, for as Hannah was coming to realize, lifesaving was an extremely hazardous business.

"Cap'n Hathaway says she could talk the hind legs off'n a jackrabbit. Boat's due in sometime tomorrow to collect the lot of 'em, but I was worried you might miss having city folk for company once she left."

Hannah chuckled. Still watching the way Penn's hand caressed her daughter, she missed the look in his eyes at the soft, husky sound. "I don't suppose city folk are all that different from anyone else. Perhaps we're not as quiet as island folk," she teased gently.

Hannah wanted his hand on her own head. She resented the woman who had moved in and proceeded to complain about everything in the house, after pushing Hannah's things aside to make room for her own few possessions. Resented the lack of privacy and resented her own feelings of guilt for her lack of Christian charity.

"Boys have been collecting stuff off'n the beach," Penn said. He didn't mention the body of the third mate, whose remains had washed ashore later the day of the storm and were buried out behind the station on a rise of land that held yet another victim of yet another shipwreck. He'd only just finished writing the letter to the boy's family, which was why he'd needed to get away.

Needed to see Hannah, if he were honest with himself. To see her, to hear her voice—to touch her warmth for just a moment. It was a weakness he could ill afford, one that he was going to have to overcome. At least, as long as she didn't know about it, she couldn't use it against him.

Oleeta came often, fascinated with the woman who had lived in two different northern cities and taught school until she was married to the Reverend Gump. "We're going to have us a school here to Paregon soon's we get big enough. Penn, he says we kin have a church an' a school and ever'thing soon's he finds wives fer James and the twins."

Hannah held her breath for fear Matilda Gump would offer to stay on and organize their school.

Instead, the woman sat stiffly in Hannah's rocking chair, holding a thick china cup of yaupon tea, her little finger crooked just so. "James. That's your brother, I believe?"

"No'm, my brother's named Chester."

"Are you sure his name is not James? I never forget a name. It's a gift that comes of teaching school and helping the Reverend Gump manage his congregation before he was called to go to the jungles of Brazil."

Hannah and Oleeta looked at each other. Had the woman suffered more than a fright and a thorough wetting? She had seemed so meek when they had first brought her into the station, but once she'd got her second wind, she had commenced to talk and hardly paused since then for breath. Matilda Gump had opinions on everything and offered them freely.

"I only got one brother, ma'am, and he's called Chester after my grandpaw that walked funny ever since he was bit on the behind by a hog."

"My soul! Well, if you say his name is Chester, then Chester it must be. All the same—a *hog*, did you say? My word! All the same, I could have sworn I heard him called James. Naturally, I saw the favor right away. You've both the same eyes, the same coloring, the same set of bones. I must say it's a blessing that your nose is some smaller than his. It must be a burden to go through life knowing your nose looks like a potato. Not that the boy didn't seem pleasant enough, for I've never been one to criticize what a body can't help."

Oleeta made a strangled sound in her throat, but Hannah only looked thoughtful.

Could it be? Was it possible? And if it was . . .

Oh, my mercy, Hannah thought, no wonder Penn always said Warfields didn't marry Druckers!

Chapter 19

IT was early in the day when the survivors of the *Mattie Curtis* gathered at the landing to board the shallow draft schooner that would carry them, along with the few of their possessions that had been recovered, to the mainland. Hannah, for one, would be glad to see the last of them, for her houseguest, Mrs. Lorimer Q. Gump, widow of the late Reverend Gump, had not stopped talking long enough to draw breath since she'd first set foot on Hannah's front porch.

Now she stood off to one side, Hannah's second best gown hanging from her sparse frame, and Hannah's best hat with the three curled feathers jammed down over her thin gray topknot. Hannah could hardly allow the poor woman to travel all the way to Savannah with no more then the ruined dress she had come ashore in, which was now all she possessed, and there had been nothing suitable in the relief barrel.

At the foot of the gangplank, Penn conferred with Captain Hathaway while the others settled themselves on board. Hannah waved a last farewell and had already turned to go when Matilda Gump let out a wail that could be heard all the way out to the reef.

"My Bible! Oh, my stars, my poor Lorimer's Bible!"

"Gawd, what now?" Hathaway muttered.

"Oh, for mercy's sake," Hannah whispered.

"What is it? Where is it? For God's sake, someone fetch the woman her confounded Bible!" Penn glared at the small assembly that consisted of Hannah, Oleeta, who was holding Sara Mirella, and Silas Garner, who had driven the others over in the cart.

"Stop the ship!" screeched the agitated widow. The *Hamlet* was still fast to the wharf. "Mrs. Warfield, you left Lorimer's Bible in my room!"

"In *my* room," amended Hannah under her breath. "On the shelf, I expect," she added as Penn leapt on Pegasus's back and wheeled his mount toward the village. "*Anything*," she thought she heard him mutter, "to ram a cork in that infernal crock of wind!"

A scant two minutes later, Penn slid off Pegasus's bare back, dropped the reins to the ground, and leapt onto the porch. Would he never see the last of that meddling woman? As a rule, he tolerated company right well, often even welcomed it, despite the tragic circumstances. A big, half-empty station and a deserted village could get a mite lonesome.

But, dammit, he hadn't been near his wife's bed in *three whole days*! He'd come damn near to busting his britches, just thinking about what he was missing! Another day and he would have dragged her off into the nearest yaupon thicket.

"Shelf. Hannah's room, on the shelf," he muttered aloud as he strode through the door and glanced around for a shelf.

It was there on the far wall, a newly erected plank some two feet long. It held a candle and two Bibles, both well worn. He carried both over to the window and opened the cover of the first to check the nameplate.

It was the wrong one. "Hannah Elizabeth Matthews," he read. "Born the twelfth day of September in the year of our Lord, 1875. m. Edward Homer Ballinger, August 14, 1893." Just as he went to close the cover and replace the book on the shelf, his attention was captured by another date. The date of Edward Ballinger's death. He read it again, mistrusting his own eyes.

Godamighty, she had come out here to marry a stranger before her first husband was even cold in the ground!

Penn had all day to wait before confronting his wife. There was the wreck commissioner to be dealt with. Then there was a call from Captain Hooper at Little Kinnakeet concerning the telephone pole that had been undermined yet again in the recent overwash, and James kept nagging at him about Hannah's smoking chimney. "Dammit, Penn, if you won't let me fix the thing, then fix it yourself!"

Raking the younger man with a chilly look, Penn ordered him out on patrol, never mind that the sky was cloudless and the sea, while it was still churned up dirty, was calm enough. He sent Luke Garner with the necessary materials to patch the chimney, warning him not to make a pest of himself and not to linger over the job, and then he set about ordering the rest of his command. Now that they had the place to themselves again, there was bedding to wash, food stores to replenish, and drilling to be done.

Before the day was half over, his crew was wishing him to Jericho.

Dammit, she should have told him! He was a reasonable man—he would have understood. Leastwise, he would have given it his best shot. But she hadn't even trusted him enough to give him a chance!

He had naturally figured the man must have died soon after planting his seed, and as her time drew near, she had panicked. There was nothing wrong in a widow's marrying after nine months, although a year was more common. Still, under the circumstances, he would have readily understood, if she'd only seen fit to confide in him.

The trouble was, the more he thought about Hannah, the more he remembered Margaret. Not to mention his own mother, who had managed to have a sizable family even though her husband was at sea far more than he was at home, sometimes for two and three years at a stretch.

It hadn't occurred to Penn to wonder about it at the time. At that age, a boy had more important things on his mind than arithmetic. But as the years went by and he'd heard whispers—whispers that always cut off short as soon as he came near— he'd added two and two and come up with a sum he hadn't wanted to believe.

Soon after that he'd begun to look at the men living in the village and wonder. Was this the one?

What about that one? Isaiah Burrus, a second
cousin of his father's, had provided Mirella
Warfield and her sons with fish, fowl, and collards
from his garden for as long as Penn could remember while Car Warfield was busy hauling logwood
from Honduras and rum from the Indies. Was he
the one?

Penn remembered staring so long and hard at
red-bearded Old Isaiah after the twins were born
that the poor man had asked him one day if his
eyes were failing him.

After a while, it had ceased to matter. One by
one, the villagers had drifted away, some going no
farther than their own front yard to join husbands
and wives, parents and children in the family
burial ground. By then Penn had been too busy trying to put food in the bellies of his own family to
worry overmuch about whether the younger
Warfields were his brothers or his cousins, or some
unseemly combination of the two. They wore his
father's name. His mother had borne them all. That
made them his brothers.

And then there had been Margaret. His beautiful,
unfaithful Margaret, who had wanted more than he
could give her. His name, his labors, and the passion of his body had not been enough for Margaret.
She'd told him once that he was too big and too
dull and he'd never even learned how to laugh,
much less dance.

All of which was true. He couldn't dance—at
least not well enough to actually *do* it. He *was* dull.
Nor had he found much to laugh about over the
years.

He had foolishly dared to think that Hannah

might be grateful enough for his protection to over-look his shortcomings. It had never occurred to him that she might have shortcomings of her own.

It was dark by the time Penn set out for the vil-lage. This time, he didn't bother to bathe and shave and splash on a palmful of Adam's bay rum. He didn't even bother to change into his clean shirt. He went as he was, coatless, hatless—sweat, dirt, and all—a fever seething in his soul even as another kind of fever simmered in his blood.

Hannah had spent the day turning out her bed-room, airing it out and then swatting the mosqui-toes before they could search out Sara Mirella's tender flesh. She had picked flowers—the wild beach pinks, star of Bethlehem, and blue-eyed grass—and made bouquets for all three rooms, and taken time to parch a batch of fresh green yaupon shoots for tea. Oleeta told her that the wild native tea was meant to be cured in hogsheads, using heated ballast stones, but lacking hogshead or stones, Hannah had found that a hot stovetop served well enough.

If it happened that she had also taken time to bathe, using a sliver of her precious violet-scented soap, and to wash her hair again, leaving it loose to dry, it was hardly surprising.

And if now and then she happened to glance across at the pale silhouette of the station rising from the salt haze that hung persistently over the surf, then that was hardly surprising, either.

Penn rapped on the door frame and let himself in just as Hannah finished giving Sara Mirella her supper. Startled, she drew her shirtwaist around her and hastily did up the buttons. "Is everything all right? Did you need me for something?"

Her heart was jumping like a sackful of grass-hoppers.

Ignoring the warm, enticing scent of her, the sight of her unbound hair and her softly flushed cheeks, Penn studied the small, cracked fireplace, in which a jar of flowers bloomed incongruously. "When did your husband pass away, Hannah?"

It was the last thing on earth she expected. He sounded almost accusing. "Edward? Come sit out on the porch and we'll talk. I made fresh tea."

"I'll not bother you for refreshments, madam."

Madam. Oh, Lord, not again!

Avoiding her eyes, Penn repeated the date that had burned into his mind when he'd read it that morning. "Did you even wait to see the poor man decently laid to rest before you set out to snare yourself another husband?"

Hannah stiffened. "Snare! I wasn't the one who advertised for a spouse!"

It might have been shock he saw on her face. Or bewilderment. Penn chose to read it as guilt. "Was Ballinger your first husband? Or have you got hus-bands stashed away like cordwood? Some women aren't satisfied with only one man." His mother hadn't been. Nor had his wife.

"Penn, you knew I was widowed," Hannah rea-soned. "I explained all that when I agreed to marry you."

But Penn was too angry and too hurt to be rea-sonable. "How long did you plan on staying here, Hannah? Until you threw Ballinger off your scent? It must've surprised you when Dozier said he was asking after you. Not many men would think to look out here on the Banks."

Something inside him—a small whisper he was determined to ignore—reminded him of all the times he had seen her with the twins, teasing and tender. Of all the times he had admired her quiet efficiency as she cared for the survivors they brought into the station. He remembered too well the quiet comfort of her undemanding companionship, the glow on her face as she suckled her baby. James loved her, and for all Penn knew, Hannah loved him right back.

Anger and despair warred within him. Goddammit, the woman had stolen his self-respect! No matter how dull a man was, there were some lessons he shouldn't have to learn more than once.

Slowly, Hannah sank down onto the blue bench. If he had driven a stake right through her heart, he couldn't have hurt her more. She hadn't expected him to love her, not right away—maybe never—but she had never expected this. "Penn, I—"

"Don't bother to lie, Hannah. I know when Ballinger died. I know when your letter to me was written, for I looked at the date again to make certain I hadn't mistook it. Five days, Hannah! Godamighty, you didn't even wait for the flowers to wilt on his grave!"

"I couldn't! You don't understand, Penn, I had no—"

"No choice? There's always choices, madam. You had a roof over your head, didn't you? Food on the table? Your husband's brother had taken you into his home. He would hardly throw you out when you were carrying his brother's baby. You had family to look after you, Hannah, but instead, you chose to run off and find yourself another man before you'd even decently mourned the father of your own child."

Hannah surged to her feet, gray eyes stormy. "Stop it! Let me tell you—"

"If you've anything to say for yourself, I'm willing to give you a fair hearing, but I warn you, madam, I'll not tolerate lies."

Her lips clamped shut, small rounded chin taking on a firmness that bordered on aggressiveness as pride rose once more to the occasion. "And if I refuse to explain myself to you, Captain Warfield? You'll do what? Turn me out of my house? Drive me off your island? Bundle me aboard the next boat? I didn't ask you to marry me, you big, blind jackass, that was *your* idea! Well, either you take me on faith, or you don't take me at all, for I refuse to beg!"

Penn's eyes burned with cold blue fire. "In that case, madam, I'll not take you at all."

Both stiff with anger, they glared at one another. The muscles of his chest seemed to swell even as she watched, threatening the seams of his sweat-stained shirt. Face burning, she dropped her gaze, and it fell on his narrow loins, on the masculine bulge of his crotch, and swiftly she squinched her eyes shut, but not before the image was burned into her consciousness. The image of an unforgiving face atop an aroused body, pride in every inch of his bearing.

He had no patent on pride, the wretched man! What had he to be so proud of? His sweet, gentle disposition? His handsome face? That unruly crop of hair that looked as if it had last been cut with the dull edge of a hatchet? The scars and bruises he collected like a sugar bowl collects flies, unfortunately, only added to his raffish attraction.

Hannah told herself she *didn't* love him, not the least bit, she didn't! What sane woman would love a proud hulk of a man who daily dared the devil and bore the scars to prove it?

"Well?" he prompted. "I'm waiting to hear what you've got to say for yourself."

"Then hear it, you shall," she said sweetly. "Listen closely." She leaned forward, her eyes sparkling like wet agates. "Shut the gate behind you on your way out—then turn left and go straight to the devil. I've no doubt you're on comfortable terms."

A muscle twitched in his jaw. "That I'll not deny, madam."

Hannah whirled about before he could read the pain in her eyes. *You shed one single tear, Hannah Ballinger, and I'll never forgive you!*

Staring bleakly at his wife's rigid back, Penn fought against the desire to sweep her up into his arms and carry her off to bed. No matter what kind of ruins she had left behind her, she was his wedded wife, and he wanted her. Against all reason, he had never wanted a woman more.

And therein lay the danger. "If you need anything, madam, you may send word by Adam."

"Thank you." She would shrivel up and die first!

Penn hesitated. Something flared briefly in his eyes and was as swiftly gone. "You're welcome. Just see that you take good care of Sara Mirella."

"I don't need you to tell me my duty, sir."

"Ah, hell," he said softly. Struggling with an emotion he couldn't begin to understand, much less express, Penn clenched his fists against the need to touch her one last time and stalked out into the hot, humid evening.

Once upon a time, when she was a child, Hannah had watched a puppet show and been completely convinced that the marionettes were small living creatures. Even though the strings were quite visible and the puppeteers came out after the show and took their bows, she was never completely convinced that some spirit didn't inhabit the assemblage of wood, paint, rag, and string.

She had learned to her sorrow five years ago that it was quite possible for a body to go through the motions of daily life without being wholly alive. Strings were manipulated by need. The need to care for a husband who couldn't care for himself. The need to protect an unborn child. And later, the need to care for that child and to secure some kind of a future for them both.

Now, her heart one vast, empty ache, there was still the need to eat and to wash and to plant and to smile. And at times such as this, when Oleeta came to visit, to talk and smile some more.

"You fixin' to come down with somethin'? Ain't got enough fire in ye to spark a lightnin' bug."

"It's the heat."

"How many petticoats you wearin'?"

"Just one," Hannah admitted. She had never in her life worn less than two, and those over a corset, a corset cover, drawers, and a camisole.

"Reck'n if the good Lord hadda wanted folks to cover up, He'd've borned 'em all wi' fur 'n' feathers." Oleeta herself wore one of her thin cotton dresses. What she wore under it was her own secret. Hers and Adam's.

"Are you over the morning sickness?" asked Hannah, determined to change the subject.

"Ain't heaved in near onto a week. What comes next?"

"Nothing, if you're fortunate. Later on, when you're larger, you might suffer a bit of indigestion, but if you watch what you eat in the evenings, that shouldn't be a problem." There were other things, but Oleeta would soon discover those for herself. At least she wouldn't suffer the indignity of not being able to button her own shoes, for she seldom wore them. Her small dusty feet were as brown as acorns.

"I come to tell ye I'm going down to Kinnakeet. Adam, he's got to ride down to fetch somethin' from the store, and he told me I could buy somethin', too. He gimme a whole dollar. I thought I'd buy me some cloth so I can git started makin' things fer the baby."

"Oh, that will be wonderful," Hannah exclaimed with the nearest thing she'd shown to animation since Penn had left her the day before. "We'll both sew. Sara's outgrowing her gowns already, which means your baby already has a start on her layette."

A dozen times that afternoon, Hannah glanced out the window. Not that she expected to see anyone. It was, she had to admit, lonely in the village with no one there but herself and the baby. Usually she saw Oleeta a dozen times a day, out hanging the wash, or weeding the garden, or shoving out in the flat-bottomed boat to the net Adam had set just offshore, that provided both houses with fish for the table.

She had just washed her supper dishes and stepped out onto the back porch to empty the dish-water on her fig tree when she thought she heard something crashing through the brush up the road a way.

A dog? She had never seen a dog in the village, although occasionally she'd spotted a bushy-tailed cat stalking the shoreside in search of a meal.

Mercy, was that a scream?

Probably just a sea gull. They made a dreadful racket feeding out over the sound.

"Leee-eet! Help meee!"

Dear God, it *was* a scream! Coming from the far end of the village—but there was nothing there except for a roofless ruin of a house and a few gravestones on the high ground.

Hannah didn't hesitate. Glancing once at the cra-dle to be sure Sara Mirella was safe and sound— she was asleep, as luck would have it—she grabbed the lid-lifter off the stove and, closing the door qui-etly behind her, lit out at a run. Someone—a child, from the sound of the voice—was in dire trouble!

"I'm coming! Where are you?" she screamed.

"Watch out, he's madder'n a hornet!" the shrill voice returned.

"Where are you?" she repeated breathlessly. Blackberry brambles clawed at her skirt and her exposed arms. Snakes, she thought—she'd seen two just that morning in the backyard. Dear Lord, what good was a lid-lifter against snakes? A stick would have been better—a hoe better still, only she didn't have one yet.

"Up on the ridge—I clumb a stone," the child yelled.

Iclumbastone?

And then everything happened at once. She caught sight of a small brown figure perched up on top of a leaning tombstone just as the underbrush erupted behind her. Spinning around, she caught one glimpse, which was more than enough to send her flying toward the child. Beady black eyes, a pair of filthy tusks that had curled back until they were grotesquely misshapen, and a stench that nearly rocked her off her feet.

Just before she could grab the child and race for the nearest tree, the blast of a shotgun split the air. The beast kept coming, snorting through the blood that gushed from his awful maw. The child clutched the tombstone, his eyes round as marbles as death rushed to devour him. And then suddenly, the beast keeled over, kicked once, and was still.

After a moment, the boy slid cautiously to the ground. He stepped closer, his eyes riveted to the bloody carcass, as Hannah sank gently toward the earth, having fainted for the first time in her entire life.

"Is 'e good'n dead?" the boy whispered reverently. "Holy mackeral, look at the size o' them tooshes!"

"Hannah—Godamighty, I didn't hit you, did I? Hannah, wake up!" James burst onto the scene, threw down his shotgun and knelt beside the unconscious woman. "It's all over, sweetheart, wake up now."

"Betcha he'll go nigh onto five hunnert pounds! You gonna keep his tooshes? I seen a man mount 'em on a board and hang it on his wall oncet. Kep' 'em right there over the dinner table, leastwise till his wife, she—"

Hannah opened her eyes and stared up into James's familiar face, dark with concern. "Hannah, what the devil did you think you were doing?"

He sounded cross. He looked worried. He stank like an abbatoir.

No, it was the monster that stank. James smelled the way he usually did, of sweat, horse, and brown soap. Presently, with a touch of tar and gunpowder.

"What happened?" she asked weakly. She was lying in the sand, and it was hot, and there was sand-spurs all around her. Evidently, she had landed in a bed of the pesky things. "Remind me next time I faint to choose a better place."

Swearing softly with relief, James lifted her carefully and turned toward the boy, who was bending over the wild boar with every evidence of relish. "Come along, boy."

"I got my knife. Wanna start in on 'im now?"

"He can wait a spell. First we'd better—"

"Can't wait too long. Rot in this weather. Least-wise, hadn't we oughtta gut him? His bowels is all—"

Hannah moaned and closed her eyes again, more than a little nauseated from the close call and the awful stench.

"Later. You can tote my gun for me, boy. Now run on ahead and fetch your sister, tell her she's needed at Hannah's place."

"Sister? Is that Chester?" Hannah murmured

weakly, trying to lift her head from James's shoulder.

"Reck'n so. Sure looks just like her."

Indeed he did, Hannah agreed silently. And he looked even more like James. "Oleeta will be glad to see him—only she's not home just now."

"Kinnakeet?" James asked.

She nodded, wishing he wouldn't jostle her quite so much. Something, probably a sandspur, was digging into her body with every brush of her skirt as he hurried down the path.

"Shoulda known. Adam rode down, an' them two are tightern'n ticks on a coon dog."

At that same moment, a solitary figure was riding hell-bent across the barren stretch between station and village. The small boar-hunting party reached Hannah's house just as Penn slid to the ground beside the front gate. Hannah's eyes flickered open, but one look at Penn's glowering face and she shut them again, wishing she could sink back into comfortable oblivion. *Oh, please not now, Lord. One disaster at a time is all I can deal with.*

"What the blue bloody blazes do you think you're doing with my wife?" Penn roared. Two strides and he was beside them. Glaring at James, he shoved his arms under Hannah's limp form and snatched her away, and Hannah yelped as the sandspur dug into the tender flesh just above her shoe top and stayed there.

"Don't be a fool, big brother, what does it look like I'm doing?"

The boy nudged James's elbow. "Is this here Leeta's house?"

"Who's he?" Penn demanded, his arms crushing Hannah against his sweaty chest.

"Who does he look like?" James, his aquiline nose only faintly misshapen by now, glared at him.

"Oh, my mercy, can't you two open your mouths without shouting?" Hannah protested weakly.

Ignoring her, Penn said, "Looks to me like one o' your by-blows!"

James's dark eyes glinted angrily in his narrow face. Chester, his own dark eyes moving from one to the other with avid curiosity, tugged on Penn's shirt and said, "He kilt the boar. Shot 'im deader'n a doornail. Ol' boar's tooshes curled all the way 'round his ears." He turned to James, all boyish eagerness. "Did you see them chompers o' his'n, mister? Reck'n he'd 'a eat us both if you hadn't come along an' shot 'im dead. Her," he nodded dismissively at Hannah, "she couldn't even 'a clumb a tree in them shoes she's a-wearin'. Come a-runnin', though. Reck'n she's got gumption, even if she ain't got no more brains than a piss ant. Went at 'im with a rusty ol' lid-lifter."

James rumpled the boy's hair, which was stiff with salt and gritty with sand.

"Don't underestimate Miz Hannah, son. Reck'n she was fixing to ram the thing in his mouth and jam his jaws apart when he opened up to swaller you." To Penn he said, "I'll take the boy over to Adam's place. Him and Leet'll be along directly. You'd better see to your wife." James stressed the word, and a laden look passed between the two men. "The boy weren't stretching the truth, Penn. She come that close to being hog fodder. If I hadn't been out chasing that damned new stallion of Mal's and took along my gun on account o' snakes . . ."

He shrugged expressively. Collaring the skinny tanned boy, he shoved him toward the path, leaving Penn holding Hannah and staring down at her, all the emotions he had tried so hard to root out of his soul there for her to see.

Only Hannah wasn't looking. Hot, sandy, still trembling from coming within a whisker of being killed by a wild boar, she had closed her eyes to better appreciate the warm security of being held in her husband's arms. It wouldn't last. It never did. But while it lasted, she meant to enjoy every sweet moment to the fullest.

One day at a time, her father used to say. One step at a time.

The baby was crying. Hannah didn't think she'd been crying long, for in truth, the whole incident couldn't have taken more than twenty minutes, and she'd been sleeping when Hannah had left her.

"I'd better see to her," she murmured as soon as Penn had carried her into the house.

"See to yourself first. I'll take care of Sara M'rella."

Hannah didn't wait for a second invitation. Turning her back, she lifted her skirt and found the sandspur that had buried itself in her skin right through her cotton stocking, and pried it loose. There were several more clinging to her skirt and petticoat, which she also removed, and then she hurried to the kitchen to fill a basin with water. With the breath of that filthy, awful beast still fresh in her memory, she had never felt so dirty in her life!

Well, yes, she had. Once.

"Need a hand?"

Penn appeared in the doorway, a dry and momentarily contented Sara in his arms. His look was guarded, neither cold nor warm. Which was more than she had dared expect, considering the way they had last parted. Hannah had removed her dress and tossed it out the back door to be washed. Penn stared at her delicate body in the thin white undergarments. Her face and forearms already showed the effects of gardening without a bonnet, with her sleeves turned back. Even with the scratches on her arms from the briars she had brushed through, he found the sight of her far too arousing. Against the pale gold of her lightly tanned face, her eyes seemed larger and clearer than ever, the pale swell of her breasts above the rounded neckline of her chemise even more intimate by contrast.

Rooted to the spot, he told himself to leave while he still possessed the will. The very last thing he needed was to see her like this, when the mere thought of her, fully clothed, was enough to bring him to his knees.

But someone needed to tend her scratches before they became inflamed, he told himself. He would force himself to think of her as a survivor, someone temporarily in his care.

He swallowed hard. "Hannah, those scratches—"

"Would you hand me my hairbrush from the bedroom? I need to brush the sand out of my hair."

"I'll brush it for you," Penn said gruffly. The words were out before he could stop himself, and he swore silently. He hadn't come here for this. He had come here to—

God knows why he'd come here. He'd been headed for the surf to swim the flies off Pegasus when he'd heard the shot. Knowing James had gone after that fretsome stallion Mal was trying to tame, knowing the cottonmouths were in rut and would as soon charge a man as move out of his way, he'd ridden over to investigate.

And then he'd seen them coming out of bushes, Hannah lying there limp as a sack of meal in James's arms—

He had known then that no matter what she'd done, he couldn't bear to lose her. He might never claim more than her body—she might never want more from him than his name—but he refused to give her up.

Chapter 20

PENN touched her hair. A few grains of sand fell to the floor. A bit of grass was caught in one of her hairpins—she had lost most of them when she'd fallen—and he plucked it carefully away, hairpin and all, and slid it into his pocket without even being aware of it. Dimly, he recognized the fact that he was in a bad way, foundering without a hope in hell of rescue.

Sometime during the long hours of the night he had reached the conclusion that nothing essential had changed. He had told himself that he could still live his life the way he had always lived it, quite apart from the woman. With the help of a large dose of medicinal brandy, he had argued the matter all out in his head until it made perfect sense. Hannah was a duty, like any other duty, requiring his regular, but not his constant, attention. She was no more than another journal to be posted. Another weather instrument to be read and recorded. One more drill to perform.

She was a duty, he assured himself—no more, no less.

And that, God help him, was the biggest lie he had told since he'd sworn to Miss Marthenia that the wind had blown all the figs off her tree, and him caught red-handed in her backyard with his jaws poked out like a blacksnake in a hen's nest.

The truth was, he had taken one look at Hannah when she'd stepped off the boat, with that silly scrap of yellow tucked around her neck and a damn-your-soul tilt to her chin, never mind she was green around the gills and so weak she could hardly stand against the wind. He had wanted her for his own, even then. When he had realized she was swollen with another man's child, he had wanted her still.

And now he had her, only it wasn't enough. He wanted her to want him back, and there was the very devil of it!

He had honestly thought he could do it. Marry her, support her—he had already sent off a mail order for a pair of gold-rimmed reading glasses. He would give her the protection of his name. Aye, and sleep with her now and again when the urge came on him, and then leave her be. He'd thought it sounded like a reasonable arrangement.

Penn wasn't a man given to admitting his weaknesses. When he discovered one, he rooted it out before it could take hold. The trouble was, Hannah was a weakness that refused to be dislodged.

"Lean over," he said gruffly. "I'll brush the sand out, and then we'll see to the scratches on your arms."

"You don't have to do this," Hannah protested, but she was already tilting her head back. Hands braced on the back of her rocking chair, she waited. At the first tentative touch of the brush, she suspected she'd made a mistake. For nearly twenty years she'd been brushing her own hair. It would never have occurred to Edward to offer to do something so intimate, not even before he'd become incapacitated.

Oh, my mercy, she must have jarred her brain loose when she'd fainted! If he'd offered to use the brush on her backside, it might have been safer. He had certainly been furious enough. "Penn, why were you so angry? Was it because of Chester?"

"The boy?" Slowly, steadily, he stroked. Warm air drifted in through the window, bringing with it the soft whisper of the surf and the bickering of a flock of birds feeding under the cedar trees. Nearby, Sara Mirella murmured peacefully as she explored her naked toes. "No cause to be riled up at the boy. You're the one went charging off like a rogue flare, leaving your daughter all alone."

That wasn't exactly what she'd meant. However . . . "Sara Mirella was sleeping peacefully, and I did shut the door. What would you have me do when I hear a child screaming for help? Ignore it?"

"Ring the bell. That's what it's for."

Hannah winced as the brush hit a tangle. "I didn't think. If it had been Sara, would you have wanted me to ring the bell and wait for help, not even knowing if anyone had heard it?"

Patiently, Penn unsnarled the knot and then brushed out the length of hair lying across his callused palm. He couldn't bear to think of Sara in danger. Nor could he bear to think of Hannah charging off through the underbrush after a wild boar. If anything had happened to her—!

"Penn, is there some family relationship between the Druckers and the Warfields?" He stiffened, but before he could deny it, she continued. "Because Mrs. Gump noticed right off the way James and Oleeta look so much alike. And they do, you know. She thought they were brother and sister."

Slowly, the color drained from Penn's face, leaving it gray, the lines even more harshly etched than usual. "God, no," he whispered.

"And Chester—"

But he was gone. Without even saying goodbye, he dropped the brush and left, crossing the room to the door in three strides.

Hannah stared after him for a long time before she bent over and collected her hairbrush. After a while, she resumed brushing, a thoughtful look on her face. She'd been right, then. But surely Penn, at least, would have known. Wouldn't he?

The house Adam had chosen for his bride was in better physical condition than Hannah's, though it lacked certain amenities. There were no rosebushes, no trees in the yard—nothing to break the barren stretch of wild grass but three gravestones and a freshly turned garden patch.

"Adam back yet?" Penn asked quietly when James appeared at the door.

"Not yet. Me'n the boy was having a cup of coffee. You want some?"

"I want to talk. Come out here, will you, Jay? This don't concern the boy."

James set his cup on a windowsill and the two men strolled out into the front yard. Turning their backs to the house, they stared out across the narrow strand to the station. "I reck'n maybe it does. You got it all figured out by now?" James asked after a while.

"About Ma and Drucker? You think there's anything to it?"

"I'd lay odds on it. Funny, we didn't think to look to the no'th'ard. Just because Ma was from Kinnakeet, we didn't look no farther than here and there."

"I didn't know you even looked," Penn said dryly, and James shot him a speaking glance.

"I looked. I might've been born on the wrong side of the blanket, brother, but I weren't born yesterday."

Both men sighed heavily. Both men hooked an elbow in one palm and stroked their jaws thoughtfully. After a while, James ventured an opinion. "Adam, he's in the clear. Pa's eyes an' Pa's hair. Pa's bow legs, too." Then he added a reverent, "Thank God. Be one sweet mess if he was Drucker's spawn, too, wouldn't it?"

"Don't even think about it," Penn said, adding a string of softly voiced oaths. "What about the twins?"

James shrugged. "Have to ask Drucker. They don't look like nobody I know 'ceptin' each other."

"Jesus." Penn closed his eyes in silent supplication.

James nodded. "I'll ride on up to Salvo directly. Reck'n the old bastard'd sooner tell me than you. Leastwise, we know you're Pa's, else you'd've been born better looking. Adam's got his coloring. You got his features. Pa, he was smart, but he weren't exactly known for pretty." He smiled, but it was a wintery effort.

Some time later, Penn watched from the soundside, where he'd gone to be alone with his troublesome thoughts, as James and Chester mounted up and headed north. Chester was up aboard one of the station's half-wild ponies, controlling it as easily as did most of the banker youths, who learned early to ride any horse they could capture.

Adam and Oleeta had returned some time ago, and the five of them had talked for a long time. After that, without going by Hannah's house again, Penn returned to the station, set the watch, and stared down unseeingly at an open journal. He had a lot on his mind. With any luck, once James got back from Salvo, he would have even more.

The whippoorwills were just tuning up for their nightly serenade when Hannah, having fed Sara Mirella and bedded her down, came to stand beside Penn on the front porch. He had ridden over just as she settled down for the evening feeding, and offered to wait outside.

Perversely, she had wanted him inside. With her. He was her husband, after all. "So it's true?" she said now.

"About old man Drucker and Ma?" Penn laughed harshly. "Yeah, I reck'n it's true. James says Drucker admitted it. The old sot might be mean as hard-boiled lye, but so far as I know, he don't lie."

After a while, Hannah said, "I'm sorry, Penn. I know it must have been a blow."

"Tell it to Pa. I'm beginning to see now why he stayed away from home so much."

"She must have been lonely—your mother."

"She had the five of us, dammit!"

"Sometimes children aren't enough."

"You think that makes it all right? You think just because a man's work takes him away from home—just because he can't always give his woman everything he'd like to give her, that makes it all right for her to run off with another man?"

"She didn't actually run off with Drucker, did she?"

He shook his head. "Ma? No. It might've been better if she had. Leastwise, we'd have known, instead of wondering all these years."

He sounded bitter and hurt, but no longer quite so angry. Resigned, she supposed. Resigned to accepting what couldn't be changed. It was a lesson everyone learned sooner or later if they were to survive.

"Perhaps she truly cared for Mr. Drucker," she suggested, wanting to touch his arm—wanting to hold him until his body lost some of that awful stiffness. She wished he would curse, or cry, or do *something* to relieve the tension.

But men like Penn Warfield didn't cry. They might swear, but they wouldn't whine. Edward had whined constantly after a year or so in bed. Nor had she ever blamed him. But Penn was made of sterner stuff. Hannah had an idea he would break before he bent.

Without any inflection at all, he said, "Reck'n she cared as much as any woman can care for a man."

His wife or his mother? How much of the pain he was feeling now, Hannah wondered, was for Margaret and how much of it was for Mirella?

"She would've married him, James said. Drucker don't mind talking when he's got a few drinks into

him. Trouble was, he said she'd already been promised to Pa. Money had changed hands, and it was a
deal so far's Grandpaw was concerned. A woman's
tears don't cut much ice when there's a parcel o'
land involved. Pa had land in Scarborotown
Grandpaw wanted, and Grandpaw had a daughter
Pa wanted."

"That's sad," Hannah murmured, and Penn
laughed, the sound of it nearly tearing the heart
right out of her body.

"In case you were wondering, your name's
Warfield, not Drucker. Me and Adam was Pa's, at
least. Drucker owned up to James, but he didn't
know about the twins. Said Pa'd come home about
the right time."

What could she say? It wasn't the first time
something of that sort had happened, nor would it
be the last. Gossip had it that there were more
cuckoos in more respectable nests than anyone
dreamed, but when one happened to be the cuckoo
in question, it must be painful beyond belief.

"If you don't need me, Hannah, I'll get on back
to the station. Might be I'll find time to ride over
tomorrow."

"Yes . . . that is, no. I mean, of course." She
didn't know *what* she meant!

Oh, yes she did, too, only she wasn't about to
beg.

Tomorrow seemed a million years away as Hannah watched her husband ride off, his rangy body
moving as if it were one with the tall roan gelding.
She would have done anything within her power to
ease his pain, because his pain was her own. But

he wouldn't allow her to help him. Men like Penn didn't need anyone else.

Women like herself, she was sorely afraid, did.

It was nearly midnight when Penn knocked on the bedroom window. Hannah, long accustomed to rousing at the lightest sound, was awake instantly. Trouble, she thought, hurrying to the front door.

"Oleeta?" For some reason, that was her first thought. Riding horseback, especially astride, was not the wisest course when one was in the fourth month of pregnancy.

"It's me—Penn." He leapt up onto the porch from the side, and wordlessly, she held the door open for him. "I reck'n it's kind of late. Did I wake you up?"

She could have laughed if she hadn't been so worried. "It's all right, Penn. What's wrong? Is someone sick? Do you need me?"

Someone was sick, all right, Penn thought. Himself. Did he need her? Oh, yes, more than he dared admit, he needed to bury himself in her arms, in her sweet flesh, until he lost sight of all the sorrow and ugliness in the world.

"I shouldn't have come here," he muttered. "I wasn't thinking."

The trouble is, you dear, sweet ox, you've been thinking entirely too much! Hannah led him silently into the bedroom and then lifted Sara's cradle and set it in the next room. "Now," she said firmly. "Take off your boots and sit down. I'll make tea."

"No tea," he said, but he unfastened his boots and parked them neatly side by side under the edge of her bed. For some reason, this brought a lump to Hannah's throat. *They belong there, you great, stubborn oaf! Why can't you see that?*

He hiked one end of the bolster up against the headboard and leaned against it, staring morosely at his big, callused hands.

Unable to sleep, he had stood tower watch with James for the past hour. James had asked how Hannah was taking the news, and Penn had told him it was nothing to do with Hannah.

"You're wrong, Penn. She's family now."

"Dammit, it's got nothing to do with my wife," Penn had repeated, to which James had shrugged and stared out into the darkness, watching the phosphorescent breakers line the shore.

It hadn't made it any easier, knowing that James loved Hannah, too. As for her feelings toward him—toward either of them—Penn was as much in the dark as ever. Margaret had been right about one thing—he knew about as much about women as a rock knew about floating.

The two of them had talked some more about Drucker and about Mirella Warfield. Eventually they would come to terms with the situation. What else could they do? Penn had even laughed when James had burst out with, "But why Drucker? Ma must've been a good-looking woman in her younger days. If she'd wanted a man in her bed, she could have done better than that filthy old buzzard. He smells worse'n that boar hog I shot today, and if he's changed clothes in the past ten years, it don't show."

But then he went on to say, "Funny thing, isn't it? The way a man takes it on himself to make decisions about another person's life, and pretty soon, everything gets all twisted out of shape?"

Like a compass needle reacting to magnetic north, Penn's thoughts veered back to Hannah. "Dammit, she didn't have to answer my letter! I didn't force her to come out here!"

James's look of innocence was visible even in the near darkness. "I was talkin' about Ma's folks. If they hadn't been so all-fired set on having that piece of soundshore property Pa owned to put a fish house on, we might've all been borned Druckers instead of Warfields."

"Jesus, give it a rest, will you? I'm going to bed," Penn had snapped.

He'd left, but he hadn't been able to sleep. After a while, he'd got up, pulled on his pants and boots, and whistled up Pegasus from the paddock. And now, here he was, no closer to any answers than ever, but with the added burden of a big load of guilt riding his back. His grandfather hadn't been the only one so hell-bent on playing God that he'd screwed up the lives of everyone around him.

Hannah opened the window, blew out the lamp, and slipped into bed beside him. Her slight weight barely made a dent in the hard mattress. "You'd best get some sleep," she whispered. "We rise early around here."

Her heart was pounding so hard she was sure he could hear it. Carefully, she tucked her nightgown around her so that if they should accidentally touch in the night, it wouldn't be bare flesh against bare flesh.

In the warm darkness, every sound was magnified. The creak of old wood losing the day's heat.

The croak of a night heron—the splash of a jumping mullet.

The harsh sound of Penn's breathing, and the uneven sound of her own.

"Hannah?" he whispered loudly after an eternity had crept past. "You asleep?"

"No."

"I just wanted you to know I'm sorry for all the trouble I caused you."

"Which trouble is that, Penn?"

"Well, hell . . . bringing you out here, to start with!"

"I came of my own free will."

"Not letting James marry you, then."

"James would have married me if I'd wanted him."

"You didn't want him?"

She hesitated. Quiet summer nights invited confidences. Confidences brought intimacy, and intimacy bred vulnerability. Guardedly, she said, "James is a wonderful man. He deserves someone special."

After a while, Penn said, "So do you, Hannah. All the same, I'm glad it's not James."

Hannah absorbed the wound silently. She had known for weeks that he wanted better for his brother than a penniless widow with a child to support. Why should hearing the words spoken hurt so much?

The rope netting under the mattress protested as Penn shifted his considerable bulk, and Hannah clutched the mattress in an effort to keep from rolling downhill. She felt his warm breath stir her hair against her face, and then felt the tentative touch of his hand on her waist. Two layers of cotton—a sheet and a nightgown—were hardly enough insulation to keep her from bursting into flames.

"Hannah?" His voice was a soft rumble, barely above audible range. "Would you mind very much if I—if we—"

"If it would please you, Penn." *Dear God, yes!*

"I'll try not to keep you from your sleep any longer than it takes to, um . . ." He moved closer, one arm sliding under her as he lifted himself on the other.

"Are you going to take off your clothes?" It seemed to Hannah that there was something almost indecent about making love to a man fully dressed except for his boots. Besides, it would be over almost before it began.

"If you don't mind too much, it'd be more comfortable." He sounded almost embarrassed.

"I don't mind, Penn," she said, and sitting up, she drew her nightgown over her head and tossed it aside.

In the dark light of a half-moon, she watched the large, shadowy figure, elbows out as he unbuttoned his shirt. She heard the clink of a brass belt buckle, and then the slithery sound of cloth against skin, and then he came down beside her again, the heat of his body radiating around him, the virile, musky scent of his maleness causing her to grow damp.

She was lying on her back, and she turned toward him just as he rose up on his knees to mount her. Not yet, she wanted to cry. Kiss me first! Touch me! Make me believe I'm more than just a convenient body, more than just a duty—more than just someone to hold for a few moments in the night and walk away from without looking back.

Rolling down the incline toward his greater weight, she accidentally brushed against that part of him that was most fiercely male. He gasped. She groaned. And then, acting on sheer instinct, she reached out and touched him there.

He was incredibly soft to be so hard—incredibly hard to be so soft. And hot. Oh, my mercy, he was burning, blistering hot!

"Sshhe-eww!" Penn expelled his breath in one long, feeling gasp. "Hannah, I'm not sure I can—"

"Oh, Penn, I'm sorry—it was an accident." She tried to jerk her hands away, but he caught her wrists.

"No! Don't move away—please," he groaned, and covering her hand with his, he moved her palm slowly, stroking, clasping. Hannah thought she would expire. She could taste her own need, her whole body shook with it. She wanted him inside her, but first . . .

She didn't know what. She only knew that if something didn't happen quickly, she was going to die. "Please," she whispered, lowering her head to kiss him in an act so daring she would never again be able to face him in the daylight.

The sibilant sound of his indrawn breath was loud in the stillness. "My sweet soul, woman, what are you trying to do, kill me?"

She withered instantly. "I'm sorry. Please—I didn't mean—"

Tenderly, his massive strength sheathed in clumsy gentleness, Penn gathered her to him, stroking her back, her hair, her face. "Don't go away from me," he begged. "Hannah, would you let me—?"

And she did. And he did.

Twice more during the night he took her. Once fiercely, once with a slow fire that left her hollow and tearful. Penn held her while she cried, and then, somehow, for no reason at all, Hannah found herself telling him about Edward.

"He had such a lovely tenor voice. We used to sing a lot. He loved Mama's corn pudding. And playing croquet. He was good at everything he tried."

"I reck'n he could dance, too. Women like men who can dance."

"My father frowned on dancing. It was mostly the holding, I think. He was afraid it would lead to . . . other things."

Penn chuckled, and the sound reverberated up and down Hannah's spine, touching off small avalanches of feeling. "What about after you were married? I don't reck'n it mattered much where it led then."

"Probably not, but we'd only been married a week when Edward fell from a tree and injured his back."

The darkness was a vacuum that subtly worked its spell, drawing forth years of pent-up pain and frustrations, longings, and lost dreams. Penn pressed her head against his shoulder as she spoke about all the promising new treatments that had come to nothing, and the slow loss of hope. About losing their cottage and the loss of her parents, and having to leave Kernersville and move to Raleigh to live with Edward's only remaining family.

"His parents had died before I ever met him. There was only Thomas and Edward left." A shudder passed through her, and Penn drew the sheet up over their bodies. "I never liked Thomas. I know it's sinful, but I came to hate him so much I could barely stand to be in the same room."

"Wasn't there anywhere else you could go?"

She turned to him, her hands moving over the sleek, taut flesh of his muscular chest. Breathing deeply of his familiar scent, the essence of sun and sea and all things clean and fine and free—so different from the sickly medicinal odor she had lived with for five years, she said, "No. If there had been, I would have gone, but Edward grew increasingly helpless. He required constant care, and what little money we had saved up went to pay his medical bills. After our savings and what little we realized from the sale of our home was gone, we—that is, I—I had to beg for every penny."

He rocked her gently, his face buried in her hair. "God, sweetheart, I'm so sorry. I only wish there was some way I could make up to you for all the suffering."

"At least Edward didn't suffer. For the last two years, he was so heavily sedated, he hardly knew me. Taking care of him was like caring for Sara Mirella, only infinitely sad, because there was no hope, and we both knew it."

What could he say? What could he ever do to make up to her for all the pain and sadness she had suffered? If he could have brought back her Edward whole and sound, he would have.

While Hannah slipped into an exhausted sleep,

Penn lay awake, thinking about the sheer hell her life had been. And her husband, poor devil, hadn't even lived to see his daughter!

His daughter? Penn wondered.

Chapter 21

EYES shadowed from lack of sleep, Hannah struggled to overcome her disappointment at finding Penn gone again when she awoke. Nothing had changed. Why should she be disappointed? As usual, the bed was neatly spread on one side, his end of the bolster plumped and cold. There were no boots under the bed, no sign at all that he had ever been there.

Unexpectedly, she felt a surge of sheer fury. She could have sworn that all the rage had been rung out of her long ago, by necessity. Damn the man for being so stingy with his affections! And damn her for caring!

Gradually, full remembrance of the night returned. Of the lovemaking, which even now had the power to make her face flush—of the confession that was not quite a confession, but near enough. She had as good as told him that Sara Mirella could not possibly be Edward's child.

Warmth leached from her body, leaving her chilled and weak as she wondered what on earth to do now. Where could she go? How could she bear to see the silent condemnation in his eyes?

A dull headache followed her through her morning chores. After nursing Sara Mirella and placing her on a blanket in a sunny corner of the kitchen to play her favorite game of fingers and toes, Hannah wet a cloth in cool water and placed it on her own brow. She wasn't given to headaches. She would allow it a quarter of an hour, no more.

Twenty minutes later, she was in her garden, sleeves rolled back, hair twisted up in its usual coil. The trouble with giving in to one's ailments was that it allowed one entirely too much time to think.

All day she kept busy. Just before suppertime, Josiah came by to bring her some butter bean plants he had liberated from a garden in Kinnakeet. "Someone gave them to you? How wonderful!" In truth, the six-inch seedlings were rather wilted, however if she got them into the ground and watered them well, perhaps a few would survive.

"Reck'n I sorta helped thin 'em out," he admitted, and Hannah knew better than to inquire further.

There was no sign of Penn. She sat out on the front porch until long after dark, swatting mosquitoes and deliberately not gazing at the station, her thoughts scattered and unrewarding. After a while, she gave up and went inside, where she spent a restless night trying to convince herself that no man was worth this amount of misery.

Over the next few days, each of the younger Warfields came by to beg her to do something about Penn, who was about to drive them all to mutiny. "If it ain't one thing, it's another," Malachi wailed. "Can't nothing please him no more! I ain't never seen him like this before, Hannah. My fingers is puckered up so tight from scrubbing and whitewashing ever'thing in sight, they're rougher'n a shark's belly. Won't you please just come talk to him?"

Hannah showed him how to whip a few drops of rainwater into melted beeswax and tallow and rub it into his hands and fingernails, but she refused to go talk to Penn. Later that day, she manipulated a cramp from Josiah's back, brought on by launching the surfboat four times in succession with only three men to help him, but she drew the line at inviting Penn to come take supper with her.

"If something don't sweeten him up right soon, we're gonna lose every hand we got," Adam grumbled when she went over to take a plate of molasses cakes to Oleeta. "Luke says he'd sooner pull stumps the rest of his life than have his ears skint back from listening to Penn's cussing. Can't you do something about him, Hannah?"

"No, sir. That I cannot. If your brother wishes to see me, he knows where I live. I'll not interfere with his business."

Adam sighed. "Seems to me that life *saving* ain't so much what he's about lately as life *ruining*."

But Hannah remained adamant. She had more pride than to go chasing after a man who wanted her for only one purpose, and that rarely enough. Her sole concern was for those poor boys . . . truly it was.

Penn continued to stay away. Fortunately, she found plenty to keep her busy, for not only glass but screen wire had arrived for both houses. Adam saw to his own doors and windows, and one or another of the twins was usually at Hannah's house, framing screens, fitting glass and partaking of her baked fish, biscuits, and boiled wild greens.

When Thomas Ballinger arrived on an unscheduled packet out of Elizabeth City, Malachi was whistling while he nailed together a frame for a screen at the back door. Catching a glimpse of a stranger in a three-piece suit walking up the path, he started around to the front of the house just in time to see Hannah's reaction as she answered the door. And then he lit out for the station.

"He went right in the house without even knocking," he panted some ten minutes later. "When Hannah seen him, she turned white as a turkle egg. Penn, you better get on over there, fast, something's bad wrong. First thing he did was tell her he'd come for his son. Reck'n he got her mixed up wi' some other woman, huh? Penn?"

"She let him in the house?"

"I just told you, he didn't ask. He slammed the door back on the hinges and shoved right past her, and Penn, I'm telling you, she looked real scared. Last I seen she was pokered up stiff enough to slip through a knothole!"

Penn didn't wait to hear more. Whistling a distinctive three-note call, he mounted the roan on the fly, not bothering with a bridle, much less a saddle, and was halfway across to the village by the time Malachi finished describing Hannah's visitor. Before the dust even settled, he was at Hannah's front door.

The bastard—and Penn had a pretty good notion of who he was—was still there. Two raised voices could be heard quite clearly. One was Hannah's. One was male, with a distinctly city accent.

Penn took half a second to subdue the rage that threatened to overcome him. If he was going to kill the bastard, he wouldn't do it in Hannah's house, where it might upset her and the baby. Taking a deep breath, he forked his hair back with unsteady fingers and reached for the door.

And then his hand fell back to his side. What if she didn't need him? What if she didn't even want him there? All he really knew about her was that she'd been married before and her husband hadn't fathered her child, and that some man, probably her brother-in-law, had been asking about her on the mainland.

Still, Mal had said she looked scared, and Hannah didn't scare easy. If this was Ballinger, and if he so much as looked crossways at her, the bastard was going to regret the day he'd been born.

Penn shoved open the new screened door in time to hear a nasal male voice saying, "Married? With Edward dead little more than six months? Don't bother to lie to me, girlie. I know what you came out here for, but you can't tell me any man in his right mind would have you once he saw the shape you were in. Now hurry and get him, the boat's waiting. Jarnelle has agreed to take the boy and raise him as our own, and I'll see you don't suffer. There's still that place I had built above the—"

"Thomas! Didn't you even hear what I said? I'm married! I have a new husband now! He's at his station, not half a mile away, and all I have to do is ring a bell and he'll be here before you can reach the front gate."

"A likely story," the man sneered. "You must take me for a fool."

"Thomas, I'm warning you, if you don't leave me alone, I'll—I'll—"

"You'll what? Stupid woman, you couldn't even run away without leaving a trail a blind man could follow. If you think I'm going to leave my son out here in this godforsaken place, you're—"

"You don't have a son, Thomas. I—I—"

"Shut up, woman! Just stop lying and go get him!"

"H-how did you find me?"

"Are you really so stupid it never occurred to you that when I saw you'd cut something out of the paper, I wouldn't make it my business to find out what it was?"

"But you'd already read the paper, I made sure of that! Please, Thomas, just go away and leave me alone."

"I'm not leaving here without my son."

"I keep telling you, I didn't have a boy. I—I lost the baby!" she lied frantically. "No! Please don't—!"

For a large man, Penn could move with the stealth and speed of a panther. Ballinger's right palm was mere inches away from Hannah's face when Penn caught him by the back of the neck and jerked him off the floor.

A strangled sound emerged from the smaller man's throat as his face turned a mottled shade of red. The toes of his neatly polished shoes dangled impotently as Penn held him aloft and glared into his bulging eyes. "Mister, my wife asked you politely to leave. Now I'm telling you. If you ever set foot in the same county with my wife or my daughter, you're buzzard bait."

"B-but—but-but-but—!"

"The only reason I don't throw you overboard right now is that I eat the fish out of these waters, and there's some things that are so foul, even the crabs won't clean 'em up." His teeth were bared in a parody of a smile that made Hannah's blood run cold. "Tell you what I'm going to do, Ballinger—I'm going to give you a head start. For the sake of my wife's first husband. But I'm warning you, if you're not off this island before I change my mind—if I ever set eyes on you again—if you ever so much as whisper my wife's name, I'm going to hunt you down like a rabid dog. And when I find you—and make no mistake about it, I'll find you—then I'm going to geld you with a rusty fork and nail you to the nearest tree by your ugly little pecker so the buzzards'll have something to look down on." The smile widened, and Hannah shivered. "Is that clear?" Penn whispered. And when the suspended man could only gabble in fear, Penn shoved his face closer and repeated, *"Is—that—clear?"*

James and Adam, alerted by Malachi, were waiting outside when the front door opened and a stranger in a brown three-piece suit with a stricken look on his face came sailing off the porch. "Stow him aboard the packet, head first in the forward compartment, where he'll puke all over his nice shiny boots as soon as they pass outside the lea of the island." Then, without a backward look, he turned away.

Sara Mirella had slept through the entire event. When Penn got back inside, Hannah was holding her tightly, her own face totally devoid of color save for the stark shadows around her enormous eyes. Penn rubbed his hands down the sides of his trousers, as if to rid them of filth. It took a great effort to damp down the rage that still seethed inside him, but Hannah didn't need his anger.

For a long time, he simply stared at them, mother and child. His wife and the child he had delivered with his own two hands.

"He won't bother you again," he said quietly.

To his knowledge, Hannah had not shed a single tear during the entire event. Too much pride, he thought. Looking at her now, in her worn blue dress, her thick coil of hair slipping its mooring, and her soft, full lips trying so damned hard not to tremble, he thought, God, she's a warrior of a woman.

At the sight of the tears now threatening to overflow, he muttered gruffly, "Reck'n we'd better talk. Will she go back to sleep?"

"If I put her on her stomach, she will. Penn, how did you—?"

But he shook his head. "Settle her down first," he said. It had taken him three days in hell to come to terms with the fact that no matter who had fathered her child—no matter what kind of life she had led in the past, he could no more stop loving her than he could walk on water. He knew the essential Hannah—she was the woman he loved more than he loved life itself. No matter what she'd done before, it didn't matter to him, but he had a feeling she needed to get it off her mind before the healing could begin.

"Did Malachi ask you to come?" she asked after she had put the drowsy baby down.

"He didn't have to ask. He told me you were in trouble."

"Thomas is my brother-in-law," Hannah admitted, staring intently at a torn fingernail. "I suppose you guessed as much."

"He's Sara's father."

She shuddered. "Yes. Would you like to know what happened?"

"Not unless you want to tell me." If she had ever loved the bastard, he didn't want to know it.

Hannah closed the door so as not to disturb the sleeping child. Returning, she seated herself carefully, brushing a wrinkle from her skirt. "You know that Edward couldn't have fathered a child. I should have explained before, only—well, it's an ugly story. I've almost made myself believe that she really is Edward's, and that what happened—never actually happened."

Penn drew up the bench and sat down. Now that the moment of truth was at hand, he found he didn't want to hear it, but he sensed that she needed to tell him. "I can wait, Hannah. Maybe tomorrow . . ."

"No, please. If you don't mind, I'd like to get it over with," she said, and then plunged ahead. Eyes on her twisting hands, she proceeded to outline the bleak and hopeless life she had led for nearly five years with her wealthy in-laws.

Penn, no stranger to the vagaries of human nature at its best and at its worst, filled in the sketchy outline, painting a picture of threat and intimidation. Penniless, she'd been anchored there by an invalid husband and a total lack of resources. Worked like a slave, no doubt, and used in a way that made him regret his leniency. He should have taken care of the sneaking little bastard while he'd had the chance.

"Jarnell could never keep maids—not the young ones, at least. Thomas was— Well, anyway, once I took over most of the housework, she didn't bother to hire anyone else. At least I felt as if I was earning our keep. If only Thomas—"

Here it came, Penn thought. Teeth clenched tightly to keep him from breaking in and making her stop, he heard her hesitant tale of living under the constant threat of a rutting bastard and his cold-blooded wife, held hostage by a man who was barely alive.

In a quiet voice, Hannah told about having to lock the bathroom door, and then her own bedroom—about how the keys had disappeared, and finally, about the night Thomas had come to her room drunk and forced himself on her before she could grab the scissors from her sewing basket.

Penn, his eyes glacial and his fists knotting and unknotting at his sides, heard her out in silence. Never had he felt more like tearing another man limb from limb with his bare hands.

Never had he felt so totally helpless.

"Edward never knew," she whispered. "Thank God for that much, at least. And Penn, I know it wasn't fair—it was truly dishonest, answering your letter and then allowing you to believe that Sara— that my baby was— Well, I know I can never make it up to you, but I just didn't know what else to do. I had nowhere else to turn."

"Hush! Oh, sweetheart, hush now!" Kneeling before her, Penn gathered her into his arms and rocked her from side to side. Hannah had got through her confession dry-eyed, but in his arms, she quickly came apart.

And so did Penn. Somehow, she was on his lap on the floor, her cheek pressed tightly to his, her tears mingling with his. The first words of love were uttered then, although afterward, neither of them would ever be able to say who had spoken first. It didn't matter.

"It was that yellow scarf—and the smell of violets." Penn's hard hands trailed the sensitive skin of her throat, and he kissed the underside of her trembling chin.

Hannah gasped and shut her eyes. "I knew right away you were the one. I didn't even see the others," she admitted, tilting her face to meet his kiss.

Long moments later, she whispered, "And mercy, Penn, I was so scared—if you'd let me, I would've probably worn my cape until the middle of August, at least."

He chuckled, and the sound set off a series of tremors in the most intimate parts of her body. "I've never been so scared in my life as I was when our baby came sliding out right into my hands. And Hannah—if we ever have another baby, I want to be there."

"*If* we ever have another baby? What happened to all your fancy plans to repopulate the entire village?" Hannah teased.

"Yeah, well . . . I reck'n maybe it's time we Warfields backed off and let nature take its course."

Hannah, her hands sliding under his shirt to caress his scarred and muscular shoulders, grinned impudently. "Truly? Starting now?"

Laughing aloud, Penn captured her hands before they could get into any more mischief. "Starting now," he growled playfully. And then he grew serious. "Hannah, I'm not very good with words. Reck'n I'm not good with a lot of things. But if it matters—if you ever wonder about it—don't."

"Don't what, Penn?" Searching his face, she found a mixture of doubt and pride, humility and strength . . . and something else that made her heart constrict painfully. "Don't love you? It's much too late for that, my dearest keeper." For an instant, his eyes dimmed. And then his face filled with such radience that she knew. Beyond the last doubt, she knew. "You love me, don't you?" she whispered.

Penn swallowed hard. "Yeah. I do. I'm not real good at talking about it—"

"Yet," she amended, and he grinned.

"Yet. But I reck'n I can learn. I reck'n when a man gets so full of something that feels this good, he can't hardly keep it inside. It just kind of spills all over the place."

"I'm sure your rule books covers the situation," Hannah teased.

"A busy man don't have all that much time for studying rule books."

"You're just going to let nature take its course?"

He nodded, his hands doing rather spectacular things to her body, and then he stood and swung her up in his arms. "If it's all the same to you, though, Mrs. Warfield, I'd as lief nature took its course in the bedroom. The kitchen's all right for some things, but when a man's got serious loving on his mind, he needs a lot of leeway."

Seated at the scarred oak desk in the keeper's room, Malachi chewed on the nib of his pen as he scanned the letter he was composing. *Two yong wimen, pritty and does cooking, likes to swim and ride horses.* "Josie, what was that there word James said meant sweet-natured?"

"Biddable?"

"Yeah, that was it! How d'you spell it?"

"Bee, eye, dee . . . Oh, hell, let's just go find our own!"

DANGEROUS DESIRE

ANNOUNCING THE
TOPAZ FREQUENT
READERS CLUB
COMMEMORATING TOPAZ'S
1 YEAR ANNIVERSARY!

THE MORE YOU BUY, THE MORE YOU GET
Redeem coupons found here and in the back of all new Topaz titles for FREE Topaz gifts:

Send in:

 2 coupons for a free TOPAZ novel (choose from the list below);
- ☐ THE KISSING BANDIT, Margaret Brownley
- ☐ BY LOVE UNVEILED, Deborah Martin
- ☐ TOUCH THE DAWN, Chelley Kitzmiller
- ☐ WILD EMBRACE, Cassie Edwards

 4 coupons for an "I Love the Topaz Man" on-board sign

 6 coupons for a TOPAZ compact mirror

 8 coupons for a Topaz Man T-shirt

Just fill out this certificate and send with original sales receipts to:
TOPAZ FREQUENT READERS CLUB-1ST ANNIVERSARY
Penguin USA • Mass Market Promotion; Dept. H.U.G.
375 Hudson St., NY, NY 10014

Name_____

Address_____

City_____State_____Zip_____
Offer expires 1/31 1995

This certificate must accompany your request. No duplicates accepted. Void where prohibited taxed or restricted. Allow 4-6 weeks for receipt of merchandise. Offer good only in U.S., its territories, and Canada.